LEAVE
NO
TRACE

LEAVE NO TRACE

A National Parks Thriller

A. J. LANDAU

MINOTAUR BOOKS
NEW YORK

First published in the United States by Minotaur Books, an imprint of St. Martin's Publishing Group

www.minotaurbooks.com

Design by Meryl Sussman Levavi

Library of Congress Cataloging-in-Publication Data

Names: Landau, A. J., author.
Title: Leave no trace: a national parks thriller / A. J. Landau.
Description: First edition. | New York: Minotaur Books, 2024. | Series:
    Michael Walker; 1
Identifiers: LCCN 2023045084 | ISBN 9781250877338 (hardcover) |
    ISBN 9781250877345 (ebook)
Subjects: LCGFT: Thrillers (Fiction) | Novels.
Classification: LCC PS3612.A547494 L43 2024 | DDC 813/.6—dc23/
    eng/20231023
LC record available at https://lccn.loc.gov/2023045084

Our books may be purchased in bulk for promotional, educational, or business use. Please contact your local bookseller or the Macmillan Corporate and Premium Sales Department at 1-800-221-7945, extension 5442, or by email at MacmillanSpecialMarkets@macmillan.com.

First Edition: 2024

10 9 8 7 6 5 4 3 2 1

To the exceptional individuals who make up the National Park Service, your dedication and commitment to ensure that the history and preservation of the over four hundred parks, monuments, and historic sites do not vanish from the earth are appreciated more than words can express.

There is nothing so American as our national parks.

—Franklin Delano Roosevelt

THE STATUE OF LIBERTY

Designated as a national monument of
the United States on October 15, 1924.

"Dad, you need to see this," Danny Logan said to his father.

Josh Logan's eyes were glued to an incoming email on his cell phone in the shadow of the Statue of Liberty.

"Dad!"

Josh Logan finally looked up from his screen. "What?"

Danny pointed out toward Upper New York Bay beyond Liberty Island. "Something's wrong."

His father's eyes started to cheat back toward his cell phone.

"Dad, look!" Danny said, still pointing. "Look!"

Josh Logan finally turned his gaze in the direction his fifteen-year-old son was motioning toward. "It's a boat, kid."

Danny gestured toward the water again. "Park Police use an M2–37 catamaran or Jet Skis now, but that's the old M1–44 they don't use anymore."

"So?"

"So what's it doing here? I know my boats, Dad."

His father's lip curled upward. "What I know is that we came here to see the Statue of Liberty, not for more boat talk."

Danny looked back at the M1–44 that was stationary in the harbor. "Okay," he said grudgingly.

"I got those VIP tickets to visit the crown," his father said, checking his watch. "We'd best get moving."

Danny looked over at his mother wiping chocolate off his nine-year-old sister's face. His father collected his mother and sister, and Danny trailed the three of them into the neat line of tourists heading inside the pedestal, constructed within the star-shaped remains of Fort Wood, on which the

Statue of Liberty stood. Danny knew the pedestal was all that remained of the actual fort, which had been regarrisoned just in time for the Civil War. The rest of the buildings had stayed in place until the wake of World War II, when their crumbling structures were torn down to make way for the modern facilities comprising what was now known as Statue of Liberty National Monument, one of the crown jewels of the National Park System that was better known for more expansive attractions like Yellowstone.

"I'm going to take some pictures," Danny said. "Save me a spot."

Before his father could argue the point, he jetted away from the line inching toward the entrance to the pedestal. Danny looped slightly around, stopping on the grass halfway between the Fort Wood pedestal and the raised shoreline.

He fixed his gaze on the craft maybe a few hundred feet offshore, a football field away. He zoomed in his iPhone as far as it would go, and pressed the record button. The uniformed Park Police officers drew so close he thought he might be able to reach out through the lens and touch them.

One of the uniformed men on the boat seemed to be recording him as he was recording them, with an identical iPhone 15 Pro Max. There were three other park policemen on the deck, standing stiffly and staring straight ahead with eyes that didn't seem to blink. Something about them, the whole scene, left Danny unsettled, especially one of the men, who looked tall enough to almost reach up and touch the sky. One of the other Park Police officers should have been at the boat's helm, yet all four were watching the island.

Danny felt his heart skip a beat. "Dad," he called, forgetting that his father was holding his place in line to enter the crown with their VIP tickets.

He swung around just as his family reached the front of the line, where a pair of uniformed park rangers were posted on either side of the entrance to the pedestal. All of a sudden, he wanted very much to be with them instead of out here, recording these park policemen manning the wrong boat.

That's when something blew Danny off his feet. His ears popped an instant before the world went silent. He had the sensation he was flying, conscious of something seeming to rattle around in his head. He tried to breathe but there was no air, as if it had been sucked out of his lungs, sucked out of the world.

Flashes erupted before him, everything starting to fade to black. His last waking thought before a pervasive numbness enveloped him was skidding to a stop atop a varying level of ground that should have been flat. His vision and consciousness fluttered amid the landscape that had cushioned his fall.

A landscape of bodies.

PART ONE

———✦———

National parks are the best idea we ever had.
Absolutely American, absolutely democratic,
they reflect us at our best rather than our worst.

—WALLACE STEGNER

———✦———

CHAPTER 1

FRONT ROYAL, VIRGINIA

Near Shenandoah National Park, which was designated
on December 26, 1935.

His cell phone ringing jarred Michael Walker awake, drenched in sweat
as always. He fumbled for it on his bedroom night table, and saw **ANGELA
PIERCE** lighting up in the caller ID. He cleared his throat and, for some
reason, made sure he was decent before sitting up to take the call.

"Morning, boss," he greeted.

"It's afternoon, Michael," said Angela, special agent in charge of the
Atlantic field office of the National Park Service's police and investigatory
unit, located in Great Smoky Mountains National Park.

"It's my day off."

"Not anymore. Turn on your television."

Michael fumbled for the remote, just as he'd fumbled for his phone.
"What's going on?"

"Just turn it on."

‡‡‡

It didn't matter what television station Michael tuned to; they were all the
same, without exception. All with overhead or long-distance camera shots
of wreckage, carnage, and a dark, shifting cloud that could only be a debris field dominating the scene on Liberty Island. It took Michael several
moments to fully realize that the Statue of Liberty had toppled over backward atop the rubble that had once formed the landmark's base, glimpses
through the cloud revealing that the last remnants of Fort Wood were
gone, too.

Oh my God . . .

The sight was incomprehensible, his mind having difficulty processing the shock that made him feel as if he were still asleep. He remembered a similar feeling back in 2001, when he was just a kid, the Twin Towers first burning and then collapsing downward behind a thick curtain of smoke and kicked-up debris. Somehow, it was worse with the statue, almost like the country itself had fallen.

"Terrorists?" Michael heard himself ask.

"Too early to tell, but what else could it have been?"

Angela Pierce had been the youngest woman, and first African American woman, to become a Special Agent in Charge with the National Park Service's Investigative Services Branch (ISB). And she had championed Michael's efforts to return to the Park Service after an incident on Mount Rainier cost him his left foot three and a half years ago.

Surgery saved his foot, at least temporarily. When a combination of time and physical therapy failed to restore his mobility or forestall an endless series of infections, Michael opted for amputation in order to be fitted with a state-of-the-art prosthetic that would restore a far greater measure of his mobility and independence. Because his knee and much of his ankle had been spared damage, he learned to walk without a limp and found in recertifying to become an Investigative Services Branch special agent that he could do almost everything he could before, just not quite as well or as fast.

The prosthetic had restored a surprising degree of form and function, but not enough for him to handle the rigors of patrolling a park. That explained why he had chosen to become what was essentially a detective, working both in and out of uniform to investigate crimes that took place within the grounds of any property the National Park Service operated. The training had proven rigorous for even a fully nondisabled man. Michael neither was granted nor sought any quarter. If he couldn't cut it anymore, so be it. The thought of a desk job was more than enough to motivate him through those arduous months.

"Michael," he heard Angela's voice blare, "are you listening to me?"

"I was watching the scene. God-awful."

"And then some. I need you at Dulles in an hour. A chopper will be waiting to get you to the site."

"ISB doesn't have anyone detailed to New York's Joint Terrorism Task Force?"

"I'm the proxy right now, which makes you my proxy on-site."

That Joint Terrorism Task Force, though under the auspices of the FBI, would assume jurisdiction. But the National Park Service would maintain a seat at the table, which Michael would be occupying.

"I'll call you as soon as I'm on-site," Michael said.

He turned up the volume on the television so he could hear the latest updates from the scene while showering. He imagined the death toll would stretch well into the hundreds, the number of wounded into the thousands, especially since it was summer—peak season for all the sites maintained by the Park Service.

Michael flipped through the channels as he dressed and fitted his prosthetic foot into place over the bone, shaved and shaped into a stump to accommodate it. He checked the time. The Park Services chopper was already waiting for him at Dulles. He was going to be late. But some things couldn't be rushed, like fitting his prosthetic in place and going through the everyday ritual of getting used to the feeling of walking with a fake foot.

Michael finished dressing to the background sounds of news reports coming from the scene.

"Do we have any reason to fear that more attacks are coming?" an in-studio anchor asked a terrorism expert.

Yes, we do, Michael thought.

CHAPTER 2

THE STATUE OF LIBERTY

Dedicated from the French to the United States on
October 28, 1886.

I dreamed this last night. . . .

Gina Delgado, assistant special agent in charge of the FBI's New York
field office, ducked under the rotor churn of the helicopter that had just
landed on Flagpole Plaza, diagonally across from the Statue of Liberty's information center. The night before, Delgado had barely slept, her slumber
roiled by nightmares she couldn't recall until now.

Her grandmother had been *psíquica,* Spanish for psychic. Gina got
used to her *abuela* saying matter-of-fact things about what was to come.
Like the time she had told Gina the results of a soccer game Gina was going to play in or, more seriously, the time she had refused to let Gina get
into a friend's car and later that day the car had crashed, sending all the
girls inside to the hospital.

"You're going to do something no woman has ever done," the old
woman had said the day Gina graduated from high school, hugging her
tight.

And now she was the youngest FBI ASAC in the country, the only
Latina, and one of the few women who'd reached that level in the bureau.

In the immediate aftermath of the attack on the Statue of Liberty, officers from the United States Park Police on-site had responded just as
they'd been trained to do. They divided their duties between tending to the
wounded, controlling the living, and securing the area. The latter meant
clearing Flagpole Plaza for use as a makeshift helipad for emergency responders and officials to land, including Gina's chopper.

Less than five minutes after the FBI received the call at its New York
field office, in the Jacob K. Javits Federal Building on Federal Plaza, an

agent was driving Gina and two other ranking special agents from the office toward the Downtown Manhattan Heliport, where a bureau chopper was already warming. Ten minutes later they had landed here on Flagpole Plaza, where Gina would be taking control of the response and ensuing investigation. Her mentor and current boss, Special Agent in Charge Rod Rust, would have been cast in that role if he weren't out on medical leave. In addition to stepping in for him to run the office, Gina had taken Rust's place on New York's primary Joint Terrorism Task Force team, which worked both international and domestic terrorism cases and leads. Law enforcement partners, mostly culled from the ranks of NYPD detectives, handled the task force's day-to-day rigors, but for a major attack like this, it was all hands on deck.

The sight from the air had confirmed her worst suspicions, the overview of the scene covering the eight acres of Liberty Island providing a viewpoint very different from that of the jumpy cell phone video the news networks were showing. The Fort Wood pedestal on which the statue rested had been the percussion point, ground zero. The fact that virtually none of the pedestal remained intact provided a keen notion as to the type of explosives used and, if she was right, suggested that a very sophisticated enemy was behind this, with access to cutting-edge ordnance. There was also the debris field to consider, which, from the air, looked completely symmetrical to her.

That debris field extended onto virtually the entire clay-colored Flagpole Plaza, sparing only the area of the flagpole itself, near which she'd landed on a makeshift helipad. Within the blast radius, the carnage was horrifying, the very worst centered in the area where the pedestal had been reduced to rubble. The bodies she was able to glean strewn within the rubble were too plentiful to count, not even accounting for those currently entombed. But the survivors, many covered in dust and grime mixing with the blood painting their exposed skins, made for almost as devastating a sight.

How many of the injured had come here with someone who was currently among the missing, a kinder way of saying "buried under the rubble" or "downed somewhere within the blast cone"? From the air, Gina could see that the park police were using their paramedic skills, making the best of limited first-aid supplies from the Liberty Island first-aid station. Gina also spotted a number of civilians, caked in concrete dust, pitching in.

That was the thing about tragedy; it brought out the best in people, breaking down all barriers in favor of the intensity of the moment.

It was the kind of scene that she'd been trained to respond to and that nonetheless sucked the breath out of her. To combat that, Gina trained her initial focus not on the carnage but on the spread and relative containment of the explosion itself, focusing on the forensics it would be her first task to assemble. And her initial assessment was that the party behind the attack was at the very least as experienced with setting explosives as she was and that significant access to the site would have been required to plant whatever had toppled one of America's most enduring symbols.

Gina stopped halfway between Flagpole Plaza and the information center, kicking at the debris before her as she looked toward one of the senior field agents who'd accompanied her here.

"Hey, Paradise," Gina said to John Milton, who shared the name of the author who'd penned *Paradise Lost,* "find me someone who can advise on any work crews with access to the pedestal over the past six months. Likely for an extended period of time."

Milton made a note on an old-fashioned memo pad.

"Forensics teams are just behind us," the second senior agent, Dan O'Leary, reported, bureau-issue iPhone held high.

"Meet them when they land," Gina said, as the chopper that had shuttled them here lifted off to make room for the next to land. "And find the ranking Park Police officer on scene. Let him know the cavalry has arrived."

‡‡‡

From there, Gina embarked on her own recon of the site. In addition to tending to the hundreds who'd been wounded, some seriously, the biggest challenge was the need to evacuate Liberty Island. As near as she could tell, it would take no less than fifteen jam-packed ferry trips to get the job done, maybe more. That meant that an untold number of the survivors, currently being gathered in the open space near the cafeteria and spilling out onto the pier, would be stranded here for hours. She knew herding them together in that location must be standard procedure and protocol for such an emergency and would have to rely on the Park Police to maintain control until a literal boatload of reinforcements from New York City police and fire, not to mention the National Guard, arrived in one of those ferryboats. Once they'd been off-loaded, the initial lot of survivors would be shepherded on, as many as the boat could carry taken back to the Battery Park terminal, where more first responders would already be waiting to board.

She started at the outer perimeter of the debris field of rubble strewn from the obliterated Fort Wood pedestal. She felt detached from the scene around her, as bodies of the dead and injured continued to be lifted from the debris by volunteers and Park Police officers covered in concrete dust, grime, and blood. Not surprisingly, the largest chunks of rubble were gathered closer to the origins of the blast, thinning out farther in the field, explaining how the Park Police had managed to clear Flagpole Plaza for chopper landings so quickly; it was 250 yards from where the pedestal had been standing. And the closer she drew to the blast center, the more it was bodies being pulled from the rubble instead of wounded.

"ASAC Delgado, do you copy?" Gina heard in her earpiece.

"Copy," she said toward the cordless mic clipped to her flak jacket that she preferred to the standard earpiece, which was more subject to interference.

"ISB is on scene and requesting to see you," the voice said.

"Tell him or her I'm busy."

"It's a him, and I already did, Chief, and he reminded me ISB has jurisdiction until told otherwise."

"Then tell him otherwise."

"I tried that, too. He's not budging until he gets word from his own superior."

Gina felt her expression crimp into a scowl. "All right, tell him to meet me at the base of the statue," she said, having drawn even with that. "He can't miss it."

><

CHAPTER 3

LIBERTY ISLAND

Originally Bedloe's Island and renamed by the United
States Congress in 1956.

---

*"Assistant Special Agent in Charge Delgado is waiting for you by the base,
sir."*

The FBI special agent hadn't said whether Delgado was a man or a
woman, but Michael knew it was a her as soon as he spotted a woman walking about the thickest rubble on her own, processing the scene in her mind
ahead of the forensics teams that were just setting up shop.

Delgado was all of five feet nine inches tall, firmly built, and looked
plenty athletic, although the extra bulk layered around her upper body
was due more to the flak jacket she was wearing beneath her windbreaker with FBI stenciled across the back than hoisting heavy weights.
Her complexion was a bit pale, and her neatly coiffed short hair was
coated in the concrete dust still sifting through the air on the ever-present
breeze.

He approached the ASAC of the New York field office of the FBI, lifting
the ISB badge dangling from his chest.

"Special Agent Michael Walker, Investigative Services Branch."

"Gina Delgado, Special Agent Walker," she said, extending a hand encased in an evidence glove. "Call me Gina. I'm running lead right now for
the Joint Terrorism Task Force."

Michael took her hand and realized he'd forgotten to bring his own
evidence gloves along. "Michael."

She smirked tightly. "Nice uniform, by the way."

"Not required, but I wanted to be easy to identify."

"Sure, because ISB has jurisdiction for the next five minutes or so, once
Washington gets things sorted out."

"If it's the same Washington I'm thinking of, it'll probably be more than five minutes."

"A formality, anyway. The Joint Terrorism Task Force has already assumed command and control."

"If you say so. But even then, I'll remain on as liaison to the JTTF, standing in for my boss, so you better get used to me."

Delgado looked down, and seemed to be studying his prosthetic foot. "How'd you lose it?"

"Good catch. You must know your way around prosthetics, Gina."

"I know my way around war. Unfortunately, one often leads to the other."

"This was the result of what the Park Service calls an 'incident,'" Michael said, finally answering her question. "I took three bullets in the foot and lower ankle."

Gina's eyes widened in recognition. "I remember hearing about that. Mount Rainier, right? Another ranger was killed in the shoot-out, a woman."

Michael nodded stiffly. "That's right."

"I didn't know ISB agents were prone to getting in shoot-outs."

Michael glanced down at his foot. "I became an ISB agent afterwards."

"Oh. What were you before?"

"A law enforcement park ranger."

"I didn't know law enforcement park rangers were prone—"

"I get the idea," Michael interrupted. "I'm sure you got into more than your share of shoot-outs in combat."

"Who said I saw combat?"

Michael returned her smirk. "You said you knew your way around war."

"War and combat are two different things." Delgado stifled a cough. "I should have worn a surgical mask."

"The smell?"

"All the concrete dust kicked up into the air. Plays hell with the lungs. You don't realize until it's too late, when you can't stop coughing."

Michael joined her gaze at the toppled Statue of Liberty. The crown had dented upon impact, carving a divot the size of a car door into it, but the statue was otherwise intact. Even in such a condition, it was massive and impressive, a testament to the enduring spirit of the country.

"Any ideas about what could have done this?" Michael wondered.

"You mean who."

"No, I mean the kind of explosives they used."

"You know anything about explosives, Michael?"

"Only what the aftermath looks like when they go off."

Delgado walked into a thicker section of the debris field. Michael followed, the uneven terrain testing the limits of his prosthetic. He watched Delgado sift through the rubble at their feet and come away with a jagged chunk of concrete that had been part of the pedestal.

"See how the scoring pattern runs all the way through?" she asked him. "If this were a typical explosion, triggered from beneath the pedestal, the scoring would be much more evident on the lower part and concentrated in that single section."

Michael took the chunk from her extended grasp but didn't inspect it. "And what does that tell you?"

"Something I'm not ready to share."

"I'm still in charge. Technically."

"In that case, I'll share something else: Three hundred."

"The death count?"

Delgado nodded. "Roughly, as of now. Triple it for a more accurate number. Still want to be in charge?"

"Until I'm told otherwise."

"In that case, I can tell you, given the nature of the blast, whoever did this had to be someone with significant access to the grounds. I've got an agent compiling a list of all the work crews on-site over the past six months."

"Plenty of construction was done in the months while the statue was closed because of the pandemic, including a new exhibit inside what used to be the pedestal and finishing the museum that's now serving as the triage center."

"I didn't know the full extent of the renovations."

"I had a longer helicopter ride than you did to get up on things."

"Washington?"

Michael nodded. "Out of Dulles. But I'm based in Virginia at Shenandoah National Park."

Delgado nodded. "Nothing much there to prepare you for something like this."

"Nothing much anywhere to prepare anyone for something like this, Gina."

Before Delgado could respond, a voice blared over the wireless microphone clipped to her flak jacket.

"ASAC Delgado, do you copy?"

She tilted her head to better speak into the mic. "I copy."

"Need you in the command center ASAP, Chief."

"What have we got?"

"It's better you hear it for yourself."

CHAPTER 4

LIBERTY ISLAND

Listed on the National Register of Historic Places
in 1966.

Michael didn't wait to be invited to accompany Delgado to the command center; instead, he assumed he was welcome and tagged along. She voiced no objection, sparing him the need to remind her that, technically anyway, he was still the one in charge here.

But he'd had nothing to do with rapidly converting the information center into a makeshift command center bustling with activity. Anything movable inside the center had been shoved aside. Folding tables had been brought in and computers set atop them. Numerous whiteboards had been placed on easels at varying distances. Some of the whiteboards already had writing scrawled across them, and several operational computers had FBI personnel poised at them, with windbreakers stowed across the backs of their chairs to expose flak jackets that must have been a mandatory part of their wardrobe. The nearby structure that held Park Police headquarters was far too small and cramped to accommodate even this much.

An agent spotted Delgado and strode over, his approach slowed when he spotted Michael.

"This is Michael Walker, from the NPS's Investigative Services Bureau," Delgado said by way of introduction.

"Branch," Michael corrected.

The agent gave Michael a taut look before returning his attention to Delgado. "Can I speak to you for a sec, Chief?"

Delgado nodded. "Sure."

The agent led her into an area farther back in the converted information center, cluttered with spindles holding various brochures, including maps and suggested walking tours for Liberty Island, along with full-color pamphlets detailing its fabled history. Michael could tell their brief conversation was a bit tense, the agent seeming to be making a point Delgado didn't necessarily agree with.

He didn't accompany her back to Michael.

"Special Agent O'Leary raises a good point going forward on this," she began. "What's your security clearance, Michael?"

"My boss has one as an 1811-series law enforcement official."

"I was asking about you. Your boss's clearance isn't transferable."

It had been an oversight on Angela Pierce's part, understandable given the circumstances.

"I don't have one," Michael admitted.

Delgado shrugged. "Once things settle down, we can work on something provisional. In the meantime, we're going to be discussing sensitive information that goes to the heart of the nation's defenses."

"I get the point, but the National Park Service is still running the show here."

"Not anymore," she told him. "The secretary of homeland security just *officially* gave the Joint Terrorism Task Force organizational and investigative jurisdiction, but I'll keep you in the loop."

"I still won't have a security clearance."

"I meant on any matters not requiring one."

Michael's gaze flitted to a door in the back of the information center, currently being guarded by another agent wearing a black FBI windbreaker. "You've got my number, ASAC Delgado. Just call or text, if you need me."

A harried-looking man wearing an FBI windbreaker over his flak jacket approached Delgado and eased her aside, speaking briefly.

She nodded and slid back toward Michael. "I need you to take charge of the grounds with the Park Police. CNN is reporting threats of another attack on Liberty Island."

CHAPTER 5

LIBERTY ISLAND

Although the island is in New Jersey waters,
New York State has territorial jurisdiction.

FBI and Park Police personnel had converted a storage room in the back of the information center into an interview room. They'd jammed the portable shelves against each other to create enough space for a table and a couple of chairs, providing a modicum of privacy in a chaotic scene that defied it.

When Gina entered, Tom Fenton, a National Park Service grounds and maintenance supervisor assigned to Liberty Island, sat behind the table wearing a uniform identical to Michael Walker's but without a ranger badge, just a name tag. A laptop rested before him, its screen dark. She noticed he was wearing glasses with a tinted lens on the right and a clear lens on the left.

"Macular degeneration," Fenton explained. "Before you know it, I'll be wearing two tinted lenses, if I'm lucky enough to be able to see at all."

"I'm sorry. And I didn't mean to stare, Ranger Fenton."

"I'm not technically a ranger, Agent, so it's just 'Mister.'"

In the civilian world, Fenton might be called the island's general manager, responsible for all aspects of the site's operations including grounds maintenance. That made him the man charged with overseeing any and all construction projects. In that respect, the agent who'd summoned her here had explained, Fenton had information pertinent to the current investigation, specifically with regard to the Fort Wood pedestal.

"Nice to meet you," Gina said, taking the chair directly across from him, while her two senior special agents, O'Leary and Milton, squeezed into seats on either side of her, both readying memo pads, since FBI agents were prohibited from recording interviews.

"I was checking leakage issues in the museum when it happened," Fenton said, understandably shaken and jittery.

Gina nodded, then got right to the point. "You supervised the reconstruction of the statue's pedestal over the past several months, is that correct?"

"It is. The deterioration of the concrete had reached the level where the entire structure was compromised. We had no choice but to shut access to the statue down for two months to complete the necessary repairs, though Liberty Island remained open."

"And what did these repairs entail, Mr. Fenton?"

"Concrete inevitably degrades over time, and the job turned out to be a much more extensive project than we thought. The original plan was to reinforce and secure the Fort Wood pedestal and the statue's base with mesh, over which we'd apply several layers of concrete. This happened when Liberty Island was closed during the pandemic. The problem we encountered was the structural integrity of the pedestal had been severely compromised by water seepage into the concrete itself because the boreholes hadn't been graded properly. That meant the water just stood there inside the concrete until it weakened the surrounding layers. That resulted in internal cracking. And you know what they say about the damage you can't see."

Gina didn't respond, coaxed Fenton on instead.

"So the project needed to be expanded to allow for filling in the old drainage lines and drilling new ones—a challenging task to say the least when dealing with a structure of this age, not to mention the size, scope, and volume. And we couldn't get it done before the island reopened in July of 2020, even though Lady Liberty herself remained closed. Anyway, to complete the work on the pedestal, we finally had to shut down again for eight weeks this past spring."

Two hours ago, the reconstructed pedestal had been blasted into rubble, the tons of concrete and granite fragmenting into deadly projectiles. Gina kept her features flat, showing no reaction to where Fenton seemed to be going with this in keeping with her own theory about how the blast had been rigged.

"These new drainage lines, Mr. Fenton," she asked, "do you have the operational plans, the schematics?"

Fenton tapped his laptop and the screen sprang to life. "Right here, along with the security footage of the work crews filling and drilling."

Gina exchanged glances with the agents on either side of her.

"We'd like to see this security footage, Mr. Fenton."

CHAPTER 6

LIBERTY ISLAND

A lawsuit in 1987 unsuccessfully tried to give
Liberty Island back to New Jersey.

The thousands awaiting transport off the island had been gathered in the open stretch of space between the cafeteria and the Park Police headquarters building, the snarl of bodies extending out onto the pier all the way to the loading platform. Michael could tell from the agitation and attempt by many to push forward closer to the pier that word of a threatened second attack on Liberty Island was already filtering through the crowd. More people than not had their phones out, likely tuned to CNN or another news station, to get the latest updates on what might be coming.

He could see a smattering of Park Police officers filtering through the crowd, hoping to retain the relative calm that was being threatened. As if to reinforce that thought, a convoy of four Park Police helicopters, with gunmen poised in the open doors, flew directly overhead, circling and drawing thousands of eyes upward. So, too, both the Park Police patrol boat and personnel patrolling the harbor on Jet Skis redoubled their efforts to keep all pleasure craft drawn to the aftermath of the tragedy a quarter mile back. Even with the naked eye, he could see that the uniformed officers on board the patrol boat were wearing body armor and wielding assault rifles. Farther off on the waters of Upper New York Bay, he spotted a trio of Coast Guard crash boats racing toward the scene to reinforce the makeshift barrier.

With that, he called Angela Pierce.

"I was just going to call you," she greeted. "Sorry you had to hear the news from somebody else."

"Which news, the fact that the FBI's taken over or that we're facing the threat of a second attack?"

"The FBI and Joint Terrorism Task Force being assigned jurisdiction was inevitable, and we can hope this threat is bullshit."

Michael looked about through the clouds of concrete dust swirling thicker the closer he drew to the remains of the pedestal. "Not a lot of hope here, from what I can see. What's my security clearance, by the way?"

"You don't have one."

"That's what I thought. Can you contact the National Guard and NYPD and ask them to repurpose their men already on-site closer to the pier?"

"I was worried about what might happen, once word got out about a potential second attack."

"It's out, and from what I saw things could get bad in a hurry."

"On it, Michael. Just hold down the fort as best you can."

After finishing the call with Angela Pierce, Michael walked about the scene rounding up as many National Guardsmen and NYPD officers as he could, not wanting to squander the minutes required for official orders to be passed down. The strain of traversing the uneven terrain was testing Michael's prosthetic limb to its limits. He could climb hills or stairs, often barely noticing the difference between his titanium foot and the flesh-and-blood one it had replaced. He could even approximate running, although there were other, more specialized models manufactured with such taxing activities in mind. But Michael wasn't sure there was any prosthetic that could handle the rigors of a debris field like this.

His training had taught him that when it came to investigations, sometimes the most casual observations produced the most dramatic results. So in walking the scene amid more of the injured and dead still being extracted from the rubble, Michael processed everything he saw as if it were a clue. The sights and smells were bad enough, but the sounds were even worse. The cries, sobs, the moans, groans, and shrieks of pain filling the air in the absence of words, other than orders being barked and the occasional scream from some indistinguishable figure pushing aside rubble with their hands.

"I've got one, I've got a survivor!"

Makeshift stretchers had been erected out of canvas tarpaulins, the island's meager medical supplies being pushed to the limit even as helicopters continued to arrive with fresh ones, along with both medical professionals and additional EMTs to tend to the multitude of wounded. The rescuers labored amid the wafting clouds of concrete dust that swirled about like miniature tornadoes, whipped up by the stiff breeze. An estimated fifteen thousand tourists had been on Liberty Island when the explosion ignited, and Michael avoided trying to figure how many of those had been killed or seriously wounded.

Stomach clenched tight, Michael resumed his survey of the scene. He slid past the twenty-six-thousand-square-foot museum, completed in 2019, which had been converted into a triage unit where desperate attempts to save lives and treat the wounded were visible through glass the blast had cracked into spiderweb patterns, but not shattered. All the floor space was now tasked as a treatment center, with the exception of the statue's original crown and torch, which remained on display inside. The whole scene was visible through the cracks marring the floor-to-ceiling windows. The doctors and nurses who'd choppered in had come in their scrubs covered by light jackets, dragging as much equipment and as many supplies as they could manage to carry with them.

Michael moved on, circling round the part of the island he hadn't covered yet in search of more personnel to repurpose to the area of the pier, but there weren't many. Park Police and supplemental law enforcement personnel continued to search the wreckage and the farthest reaches of the debris field for more of the dead and wounded. Because transport capacity was so limited, the dead were first left as they were and then covered with a supply of tarpaulins sliced into strips for lack of body bags. The first K9 units would be arriving shortly to sniff out any of the living or dead visual inspection had missed. Michael watched the first ferry, now packed to the gills with survivors, streaming away from the dock over by Café Plaza.

He tried to maintain some level of detachment from the scene, in order to view it with an investigative eye, but that lasted only in between the cries of the victims, mixed with potential rescuers yelling out for help when they unearthed another survivor beneath the rubble. The air felt thick, leaving him with the sensation that he had to push his way through it for reasons that had nothing to do with his prosthetic foot.

"Excuse me . . ."

Michael heard the young, scratchy male voice and swung to find himself looking slightly down on a boy with a mop of hair hanging over his brow almost to his glazed eyes, concrete dust covering every inch of his clothes and skin like a blanket. His face was flecked with blood.

"Have you seen my parents?"

CHAPTER 7

LIBERTY ISLAND

New Jersey provides Liberty Island's utility services,
such as sewage and electricity.

The security footage on Tom Fenton's laptop was dull, monotonous, and redundant, offering a wide view of construction work being performed on the Fort Wood pedestal and statue base from a variety of angles. The footage would have to be scrutinized by experts with all those pictured plugged into the most sophisticated and technically advanced facial-recognition software on the planet.

"Did you run background checks on all the men and women who the contractors hired?" Gina asked Fenton.

"Of course. The results are all on my computer, too. Obviously, nothing raised any flags, or I'd already have told you."

"Go back to the work log you clicked on before I asked you to bring up the video. I want to see the duration of each facet of the job and which crews were last on the scene prior to the statue's reopening."

Gina watched Fenton tap away on his keyboard, the screen changing from video picture to text. He turned the screen toward her, so Gina could study the results.

"We worked seven days a week, double shifts the last five weeks of the process, to make sure the renovations were completed before our scheduled reopening."

"July 4, right? Two weeks ago."

Fenton nodded. "We thought a grand reopening on the Fourth was just what the doctor ordered," Fenton said, not bothering to disguise the irony in his voice. "Same thing we did after 9/11."

Gina spotted something near the end of the work log and made sure the agents on either side of her saw it, too.

"Seven-day work weeks for those five weeks prior to reopening," Gina confirmed.

"Yes."

"No exceptions."

"None. Believe me, I was on-site for virtually all of it."

"Even Tuesday, July second?"

"Of course."

Gina turned the screen back toward him, so she could indicate to Fenton what had grabbed her attention on the work logs. "Then why is there no security footage from that day?"

CHAPTER 8

LIBERTY ISLAND

When the area was settled, this island was known for its
extensive oyster beds.

"When did you last see them?" Michael asked the boy, who'd suddenly appeared alongside him.

"What?"

"I was asking about your parents," Michael said louder, realizing the boy's eardrums had likely been damaged as a result of his proximity to the blast.

"I can't find them," the boy said, his dazed voice cracking. "Maybe they left without me."

The boy was staring straight at the carnage and destruction before him without seeming to notice it. Michael always had trouble judging kids' ages, but he had this kid pegged as fifteen for sure. His dark hair was lightened by an even coating of light-toned concrete dust that also dotted his face in the spots he hadn't wiped clean. His skin was blanched with blood blotches and bruises, enough for Michael to glean he'd likely been standing close to the Fort Wood star-shaped pedestal when the explosion had gone off. It was a miracle he had survived. And the fact that he couldn't "find" his parents suggested that the same could not be said for them. Michael's uniform explained why the kid must have approached him.

"You came here with your family," Michael said, consciously raising his voice so the kid could hear him.

The boy nodded in stiff fashion, as if he'd forgotten how to manage the gesture. "My parents and little sister."

"What's your name, son?"

The kid stared straight ahead, not seeming to blink, either not hearing Michael or having slipped off into a daze. He was clearly in shock. Michael's training as a law enforcement ranger had included emergency medical training that would make any EMT proud. Michael knew he should bring the boy straight to the triage center, but couldn't bear the thought of simply handing him over to the growing cadre of medical workers without the time or energy to comfort a kid who might very well have lost his family here today.

"Have you seen my parents?" the boy persisted. "I can't find them. We were on a boat, a big boat. My sister got seasick. She puked."

"When was the last time you saw her?"

"I don't remember."

"Can you tell me your name?"

"There was another boat," the boy said in the same dazed tone, which sounded like he was making the words up as he went along.

"Are you carrying a wallet?"

"I . . . don't know."

"Check your pockets."

The kid did, came out only with an iPhone, its screen cracked into a spiderweb pattern.

Michael extended his hand. "My name's Michael."

"Danny," the kid said, taking it.

"Nice to meet you, Danny. Can you tell me about your parents?"

"I can't find them."

"When did you last see them?"

"Before I saw the boat."

"The ferry?"

Danny shook his head. "The Park Police boat. Out there," he added, pointing to the area of Upper New York Bay directly facing the Statue of Liberty, a popular place for pleasure craft. "Except it wasn't."

"Wasn't what?"

"A Park Police boat. Old model. An M1–44 instead of an M2–37."

Michael nodded, impressed. "You know your boats."

"I love boats. I know everything about boats."

"Tell me about this boat that you saw," Michael said to the boy, feeling something scratching at this spine.

Another nod. "Watching."

"You were watching the boat," Michael assumed.

"They were watching."

"Who?"

"From the boat." The boy counted out with his fingers. "One, two, three, four."

"Men or women?"

"Watching."

"Where were you standing?" Michael asked the kid.

"Watching."

"I get that. They were watching from a boat out in the bay."

"Not just watching," Danny told him. "Filming."

Michael's gaze turned involuntarily toward Upper New York Bay, better known as New York Harbor. It could be that the Park Police had added a second patrol boat over the busy summer months, but, if so, where was it now? If this boy, Danny, was right about what he saw, then surely the older craft would be on station this very moment. The fact that it wasn't made Michael wonder about the four men Danny had spotted on the boat's deck. If they hadn't been park policemen, then who were they?

The fact that they were filming the scene strongly suggested they knew what was coming and had acquired an outdated Park Police boat model to blend into the scene. Michael spotted the newer model patrolling the harbor now, keeping all approaching boat traffic back, with the help of Jet Skis manned by Park Police personnel. Those Coast Guard crash boats were now settling into position as well.

"You're sure they were filming?" he asked the boy.

"Because of the way one of them was holding his phone. Same way I hold mine when I'm filming." The boy stopped, then started again. "I watched them filming the statue," Danny said, holding his big iPhone with the cracked screen up for Michael to see. "And then I started filming them."

‣━◦━‣

CHAPTER 9

LIBERTY ISLAND

The statue's torch was structurally damaged from the
Black Tom explosion on July 30, 1916.

Gina watched Tom Fenton finish checking his computer for the missing day's footage, coming up empty at every turn.

"I don't know what to say, Agent," he said, sounding somewhat confused.

"Is the footage backed up somewhere?"

Fenton nodded. "To the Cloud. I checked. It's not there either. I must have somehow . . ."

His voice tailed off and Gina didn't push him to continue.

"I'm sorry, Agent."

"It's not your fault, Mr. Fenton."

"But I must have—"

"You didn't erase the footage. It disappeared because somebody wanted it to disappear."

Fenton's mouth dropped as he processed the import of those words, which further magnified the scope of what had happened here. The attack had been months, if not years, in the planning. That suggested any number of possibilities and realities to Gina, one of which rose above all the others:

Whoever was behind the attack on the Statue of Liberty wasn't finished yet.

"You said you were here on July 2," Gina said to Tom Fenton, after a pause that seemed longer than it really was.

"Yes," he replied, his voice cracking, clearly unsettled by the missing security footage from both his laptop and the Cloud. "But I wasn't with the work crew. I was in my office, on Zoom and the phone, prepping for the reopening."

"Do you recall what work the crew in question was performing that day?"

"General cleanup and finish work on the pedestal and base."

"And this finish work . . ."

"Applying coats of sealant on the concrete."

That got Gina thinking. "Requiring what kind of equipment? Industrial-strength sprayers, I'm guessing."

Fenton nodded stiffly. "And hoses, too, to power-wash the concrete ahead of sealing it. They brought their own generators to power both. I remember now that I took a walk over there just to check on things, and it was loud as hell. Deafening."

"Did you get a look at the workmen?"

"A look, yes, but I wouldn't be able to identify any of them." Fenton waved a hand in front of his face. "They wore masks and face coverings. A few had respirators on, a fairly common practice when working with sealant."

"Do you have the name of the contractor or subcontractor who'd be able to tell us the identities of everyone who was a part of that crew?"

"I do. Let me just see here . . ."

Fenton went back to his laptop, taking a minute or so to find the material.

"I'll write it down for you. Can I borrow a pen and some paper?"

Special Agent Milton eased his pen and memo pad to Fenton, who proceeded to jot down the information.

"I included the phone number, too."

"Thanks," Gina told him. "Saves me the trouble of looking it up. And we'll need to keep your laptop, so if you could also write down your password . . ."

Fenton did so without protest. He handed the memo pad to Gina with a shaky hand instead of giving it back to Milton. She noticed that his face had paled and his lips were trembling so much it looked like someone had stuck a jackhammer in his mouth.

"I, I, I . . ."

"It's all right, Mr. Fenton," Gina said, when he continued to stammer. "This wasn't your fault. No way, nohow. But I have another question for you. This work crew that seal-coated the pedestal, which ferry stop did they use?"

"Battery Park City Terminal," Fenton replied, referring to the station at the southern tip of Manhattan. "Required for security screening of whatever equipment and tools they were carrying, even their coolers and lunch boxes. We took every precaution imaginable; at least, we thought we had. At the terminal, everyone boarding the ferry for Liberty Island has to pass through two layers of security. And that's just to buy their tickets for the trip over and to gain access to the statue."

"And you mentioned background checks were conducted on all the workers."

Fenton nodded. "Once the contractors supplied us with the names, absolutely."

"So, theoretically, whatever workmen were here on July 2, the day we have no video footage for, must have passed a background check."

"They wouldn't have been allowed on the ferry otherwise. Park Police provided backup security personnel and every person assigned to a work crew was required to check in."

Gina watched Fenton breathing rapidly, unable to settle himself down.

"We spent the whole of July 3 going over every inch of the island with bomb-sniffing dogs," he told her, shaking his head. "We doubled up on crews to inspect every square inch of every building. I need you to tell me, I need somebody to tell me, how they got the bomb in place."

"I will, Mr. Fenton, as soon as I figure that out myself," Gina lied, since she believed she already had.

‡‡‡

Gina closed the door behind Tom Fenton, leaving her alone in the converted storage room with Special Agents John Milton and Dan O'Leary. All three of them were standing, still processing the revelations gleaned from the interview with grounds supervisor Tom Fenton and wondering the same thing:

What was on the missing footage from July 2? Or, more importantly, *who*?

Gina looked toward Milton. "Paradise, I need you at the Battery Park City Ferry Terminal."

He was jotting down notes on his old-fashioned memo pad. "To pick up those check-in logs, right, see what workmen were here on the island July 2 . . ."

"Along with the security footage, so we can see what they look like. We can match up the check-in times with the time stamps." Gina looked toward

O'Leary. "You work on assembling a list of every contractor involved in the renovation and every worker who manned one of their crews, off-site fabricators as well as on-site personnel."

O'Leary made some notes on his matching memo pad. "Got it."

Gina looked at both of them. "Then let's go figure out who planted the explosives."

CHAPTER 10

⊢•⊙•⊣

LIBERTY ISLAND

Used as a quarantine station for incoming ships in the
mid-1700s.

Michael took the kid's phone from his grasp. It wouldn't turn on, but he held on to it anyway. His heart had notched up several beats. He could hear his own breathing through the eerie quiet and stillness that had settled over the scene, as if everyone dared not utter a word.

"And then I started filming them."

"I tried to call my parents," Danny said. "They didn't answer."

"Do you remember where you were standing when you noticed the boat?"

"Four men. Filming."

"Yes."

Danny's gaze moved stiffly about. "It's not there anymore. Boom! I remember the boom. It was loud. Hurt my ears. I was flying."

"And then?"

"What?"

"And then?" Michael repeated, louder so Danny could hear him.

"I called my parents but they didn't answer." The boy scratched at the thick layer of concrete dust plastered to his hair. It didn't budge. "Before you found me."

Michael held up the phone for Danny to see. "Can I borrow your phone, Danny?"

Just because he couldn't turn it on didn't mean the contents were lost, including whatever Danny had managed to film of the men in the boat before the blast came.

"Sure," the kid said. "Can you call my parents?"

‡‡‡

Michael steered the boy toward the museum, the island's newest facility, where the triage unit had been set up behind cracked plate-glass windows. He found himself shielding Danny protectively as they walked. If the kid had seen the men on the boat, it could very well mean they had seen him, too. That made Danny an eyewitness, potentially the only one. They couldn't know if he'd survived, but anyone meticulous enough to stage an attack of this magnitude wasn't about to take any chances, which meant the kid wasn't safe. Not now, not here, not anywhere until whoever was behind the attack was caught.

"Danny?"

The life had faded from his eyes again. Michael took a closer look at the even coating of concrete dust riding the boy's hair and ran his hand through it to clear the top layer off.

He flashed the phone before Danny, as they reached the clutter of the wounded and injured waiting to enter the triage center in the Liberty Museum.

"Can you tell me your password?" Michael asked him.

‡‡‡

Thanks to the additional emergency medical technicians and the group of doctors who'd just landed, a separate triage center for those whose injuries could wait a bit for treatment had been set up outside the museum. Michael flashed his badge and cut the line with Danny in tow, entering the museum to the pungent scent of alcohol mixing with the coppery undercurrent of blood. There were moans and occasional cries of pain. The recovery area was roped off to the side and consisted of air mattresses stored on-site for emergencies.

For some reason, the scene evoked phantom pain in his prosthetic foot, as he made straight for a park policeman standing watch, and flashed the badge dangling from his neck with a hand still laid on the dazed Danny's shoulder.

"Michael Walker, ISB. I need you to take charge of this boy."

"Come again?" the park policeman said.

"He's a material witness to what transpired here today, and he needs to be under guard at all times, including during transport to the hospital."

"Where are his parents?"

Michael eased Danny slightly aside. "I don't know where his parents are," he said, softly enough to keep the boy from hearing. "I was going to check to see if they'd been logged in here."

"That much I can help you with. But I don't take orders from you, Officer."

"It's Special Agent," Michael corrected.

"You want an escort and protection for this kid, you better climb higher up the totem pole, Special Agent."

Michael nodded. "Stay right there."

"Hey, no problem. This is my post."

Michael moved back against the glass, keeping Danny in view as he hit Angela Pierce's private number. The call went through to voicemail.

"Michael Walker, boss. I'm calling from the site and I need to speak with you stat. It's an emergency."

He ended the call and waited, expecting the callback to come inside of a minute. Actually, it was thirty seconds.

"What's going on, Michael?" Angela said, by way of greeting.

"More than I can recap at this point."

"Everything I've seen looks god-awful."

"Worse than awful. Pictures can't do it justice. And speaking of justice, I may have an eyewitness who can identify the bombers," Michael told her, exaggerating the facts a bit.

"The FBI's running the show, Michael. This needs to go through them."

"It will, but they're already stretched to the limit personnel-wise. And, correct me if I'm wrong, but we're still in charge of the grounds, right? I just brought the kid, our witness, into triage."

"Kid?"

"No trace of his parents."

Dead air filled the line.

"What do you need?" Pierce asked him.

"Authorization to keep a park policeman on him at all times."

"Under guard, in other words."

"Protected here and at whatever hospital he ends up at."

"Can you stay with the kid until I make some calls to secure the detail?"

Michael hadn't taken his eyes off Danny, whose attention seemed rooted on the crown. "For sure."

"Keep your phone close, Michael. I'll call the director. This shouldn't take long."

"Thanks, Angela."

"And Michael? For God's sake, be careful."

He thought of the hundreds of dead who could have used that warning a few hours ago. "Will do."

‡‡‡

Angela Pierce called him back ten minutes later. "What's your exact location?"

"Just inside the museum, which has been turned into a triage center for the wounded," Michael said, Danny back by his side.

"You're sure about this, Michael? The kid's an actual eyewitness?"

Michael felt the outline of the boy's phone through his pocket. "Yes, I'm sure."

"The FBI needs to be in the know on this," Pierce told him. "I assume you've met whoever's running the show from their end."

"I have. ASAC from their New York field office and a part of the JTTF."

"Gina Delgado?"

"Know her?"

"Only by reputation. She's good, Michael."

"What about arranging protection for this kid?"

"On-site and should be approaching you any moment to take over. Anything else?"

"Yes. Reach out to Park Police command up here and find out where their patrol boat was at the time of the explosion."

"It wasn't on station?"

"There was a patrol boat on station but, according to my eyewitness, it was the wrong model, an M1–44 instead of an M2–37."

"We haven't used the M1–44s in years."

"Somebody was in one today, boss. The kid claims he filmed them."

"You mean there's a recording of whoever might have done this?"

"Yes, but I haven't viewed it yet and the kid's phone is damaged, so who knows if the footage is still there."

A pause followed, long enough to make Michael think the call had been dropped. "Angela?" he said.

"Still here. That's a lot to process. Let me call Park Police command. In the meantime, you need to update Delgado, or one of her subordinates, about all of this."

The call finished, Michael looked back at Danny, trying for a reassuring smile that didn't come.

"You find my parents?" the boy asked him, his voice flat and strained.

"Not yet."

Danny looked around him, as if seeing the museum turned triage center for the first time. "Everybody in here's hurt. What happened?"

"There was an accident."

"Bad?"

"Pretty bad, yes."

"Is that why my head hurts?"

"Hey, ISB," Michael heard a voice call to him.

He turned to see the park policeman he'd approached originally stopping just before the two of them. "What can I do for you?"

"Apparently, it's what I can do for you. I just got assigned to babysit your boy there," he said, not sounding happy about it.

Michael checked his name tag, which read BELLSTOCK. "What's your first name?"

"Frank."

"I'm Michael and I have every reason to believe this boy could be in serious danger."

Frank looked toward Danny for a moment. "Can you tell me why?"

"Sorry, no."

Frank stole another glance Danny's way. "You already said he was a material witness."

"And that's all I'm going to say, other than his parents and sister, well . . ."

Bellstock nodded. "I get the idea. You give me their names, I can see if they've been checked into triage."

"A man, a woman, and a young girl." His gaze bore into Bellstock's. "I think they were either inside or up close and personal to the pedestal when it blew. What the kid saw, what drew him away, is what makes him a material witness. I want you to glue yourself to that boy and get him checked out here. Then get him on the first med flight you can."

Frank nodded. "Why Park Police? Why not the FBI? This is their gig now."

"They can use all the help they can get, so I made the call," Michael said, sticking his hand into his jacket pocket. "If the kid asks for his phone, tell him I've got it." He eased Danny's phone out and showed it to Bellstock. "It won't turn on."

"Let me see that."

Michael handed the phone to him and watched Bellstock press a button on the right and left, instead of just the right, the familiar Apple icon appearing dimly through the cracks in the glass.

"Voilà," Bellstock said, handing the phone back to him. "It was already on, but the sensor must have broken. Just hold your thumb on the screen to make it light up."

"It doesn't work like the iPhone 8 I've still got," Michael said lamely, taking it.

"You should upgrade."

Phone in hand, Michael moved aside, brushing against a uniformed ranger wearing glasses that had one tinted lens and one clear one who'd been standing just behind him. His name tag read FENTON.

"Sorry," he apologized, but Fenton had already moved on.

Michael swiped up on the now lit up, cracked screen and plugged in the password Danny had given him: the year he was born, followed by his age when he got the latest iPhone model as a fifteenth-birthday present.

The iPhone's home screen lit up beneath the cracks, the biggest lines in the spiderweb pattern disguising the icons under them. The camera icon was just above the cracks in a still-whole portion of screen. Michael touched it and watched a still shot of the Upper New York Bay waters beyond Liberty Island take shape, the beginning of the footage Danny had shot before the explosion.

With a Park Police patrol boat centered in the frame.

CHAPTER 11

LIBERTY ISLAND

Adolphe Philipse and Henry Lane purchased the island
for five shillings in 1732.

Gina found the supervisor of the first of the FBI's evidence response teams to arrive on Liberty Island working the blast site from the statue out, the woman rendered almost unrecognizable by the dust and grime her work had kicked up.

"Milligan," she greeted.

"Chief Delgado, I heard you were running things."

Linda Milligan, just past fifty and a recent grandmother, had been a member of the evidence response team since her second child had been born, almost thirty years ago.

"What should I be looking for?" Milligan asked, deferring to Delgado's experience with explosives.

"Conductive filament, likely one point seven five millimeters in diameter."

"Standard."

"But effective."

"What's our working theory, Chief?"

"Too early to elaborate. But if my initial assessment proves correct, there should be traces of carbon, at the very least, running through the congestions of rubble closest to the base."

"Also standard."

"Because it's effective and easy to work with."

"How much depth we talking about?"

"The entire pedestal."

"Wait," Milligan started, but then stopped.

"Go on."

"We're not talking about an ordinary bomb here, are we, Chief?"

Delgado frowned, the sights, sounds, and smells of the day starting to take their toll on her. "Nothing's ordinary here, nothing at all."

"I'm guessing they brought dogs in here to sweep the place before the grand reopening."

"And every day since, including this morning."

"So whatever explosive was used is undetectable to canines."

Gina nodded once. "Look for traces of the microprocessors they must have used to detonate the explosives."

"'Microprocessors' plural?"

Delgado nodded. "There should be traces of between four and six of them."

Her phone rang and she moved aside to take a call from John Milton. "Delgado."

"It's Tom Fenton, Agent. And I have some new information to share with you."

Gina squeezed her phone tighter. "Something else about that construction crew, Mr. Fenton?"

"No, about an ISB agent who's on-site. I overheard something that you should know. . . ."

‡‡‡

His call with Gina Delgado complete, Tom Fenton pressed out another number from memory, not saved to his contacts.

"Yes?" a man answered in a voice accompanied by a hollow echo, before any ring sounded.

"There's a witness," Fenton told him.

CHAPTER 12

LIBERTY ISLAND

A massive stone fort was constructed on the island in
1807, and was renamed Fort Wood in honor of
an American Army engineer who died in the siege of
Fort Erie on the Canadian front of the War of 1812.

Michael moved around to the back of the Liberty Island museum turned triage center and stood in the shadows to better see the screen of Danny's phone. He hit the play icon but couldn't tell right away whether the footage Danny had filmed was rolling or not. The kid had zoomed in on the boat in a way that captured most of it beneath the spiderweb series of cracks in the scene.

Michael tried to enlarge it by pinching the screen, but the damage to the glass kept him from succeeding. He couldn't see much, hardly anything really. Even that, though, was enough to tell him that there were indeed four shapes standing on the boat's deck and one of them was holding something that might well be an iPhone at their eye. The boy filming them as they were filming the statue.

Get this phone in the hands of ISB's tech department and, he felt certain, they'd be able to salvage the footage. But what did he think he was doing here? He should have already turned the phone over to Gina Delgado and the FBI and Joint Terrorism Task Force, who were running the show in which he was a mere bit player.

Still holding Danny's phone, Michael was struck by something that should have occurred to him before. It took several upward swipes to bring the home screen back, at which point he touched the email icon. He found what he was looking for right there in the boy's email address, making him feel even more stupid for the oversight.

Michael pocketed Danny's phone and pulled out his own in its place, calling park policeman Frank Bellstock.

"How's the kid?" he asked, when Bellstock answered.

"Getting checked out now. I jumped the line after what you said about him, material witness and all."

"I've got a last name for you. It's Logan."

"You in the area?"

"Just outside."

"I'll meet you at the entrance."

‡‡‡

Park policeman Frank Bellstock was waiting just inside the glass doors when Michael entered.

"This way," he said, and Michael tried to shut out as many smells as he could and ignore the ones he couldn't as he trailed Bellstock through the moans, mutters, and sobs of the wounded waiting either to be seen, to receive further treatment, or to be evacuated off the island to an area hospital.

They entered the museum director's office along in the building's far rear just off an alcove. This, too, had been reoriented toward a desperate purpose, the furniture shoved out of the way to make room for a half dozen whiteboards mounted on easels being manned by park policemen either bloodied, bandaged, or both. Two other uniformed officers sat unbloodied behind laptop computers entering data that must have been connected to the whiteboards, which contained names in three different colors: red, green, and black.

"Red denotes accounted for, both wounded and otherwise. Green means still missing, and black means deceased," Bellstock explained.

The growing number of names in black was chilling, too many to count. And Michael knew the process well enough to know that these were only the ones who'd been positively identified.

"Fourth board along the row, tenth name down."

The process absurdly reminded Michael of searching for a number on a bingo card before the next one is called. The tenth name on the fourth board was scrawled in black: **JOSH LOGAN.**

"Shit" was all Michael could say.

"Yeah."

"What about his wife and daughter?"

"You got names for them?"

"Not besides Logan."

"Hope they show up in red or green, then, but I wouldn't count on it. Josh Logan's body was pulled out of the center of the rubble. He must have just entered the pedestal when it blew. I don't need to draw you a picture, if his wife and daughter were there, too."

"No, you don't," Michael said.

"So how'd the kid survive?" Frank Bellstock asked him.

"Beats me," Michael lied. "You stay with him until I called?"

"Those were my orders."

"And?"

"Concussion for sure. As for the other cognitive symptoms, shock's a very real possibility but so is a TBI."

"Traumatic brain injury . . ."

"Depending on how close he was to the pedestal when it blew, there could be significant swelling of his brain and maybe bleeding, too. Need a CT scan to determine that, along with the extent of damage to his eardrums. All told, it's a miracle he survived this. Hell," Bellstock added, "it's a miracle *anybody* survived this."

"When's Danny being airlifted to a trauma center?"

"He's on the top of the list."

"Thanks, Frank," Michael said, genuinely meaning it.

"Hey, you hear what I just said about his condition? Don't thank me. Kid got moved to the top because the doctors consider his condition to be critical."

Michael felt himself nodding. "Call me when you get there and settled in. My boss will have a Park Police detail relieve you as soon as she can."

"Tell her not to rush, Mike," Bellstock told him. "The longer I can stay away from here, the better."

Michael's cell phone rang and he stepped aside to answer it, UNKNOWN displayed in the caller ID.

"Michael Walker," he greeted.

"Ranger Walker, this is Park Police dispatch. I've got that information you requested on where our patrol boat was at the time of the explosion. . . ."

CHAPTER 13

LOWER MANHATTAN

Castle Clinton in Battery Park was designated
as a national monument on August 12, 1946.

Blocks of rooms had been reserved across several hotels closest to the Battery Park City Ferry Terminal for first responders who'd be returning to Liberty Island after grabbing a few hours of sleep, since the threat of an imminent second attack turned out not to be credible. Michael had been booked into a Hampton Inn just a quarter-mile from the terminal. He could feel how tired he was in the elevator, leaning up against the cab wall and actually feeling his eyes close involuntarily. His room was located near the end of the hall on the fifth floor, and Michael realized he should have asked for one closer to the elevator.

His overtaxed leg felt like it was on fire. State-of-the-art prosthetic or not, there was only so much stress any leg attached to a fake foot could take. He might not walk with a limp, or look any the worse for wear, but living with a prosthetic meant living with limitations and a whole new set of rules.

His room was simple and functional, boasting plenty of TV channels he didn't plan on watching and a shower with good pressure. He couldn't resist tuning the TV to CNN with the volume muted so he could watch the ongoing scene at Liberty Island under the spill of the big construction lights. The way the light array had been set up reminded him of a sporting event, all shining down on the center of the action near the toppled Statue of Liberty. He wondered how long it might be before Lady Liberty resumed her watch over New York Harbor.

Once settled, he carefully washed his prosthetic, fittings, and liner with a damp cloth. He'd neglected to pack his cleanser in the go bag he'd taken with him and ended up using a bit of the liquid body soap from one of those small hotel bottles. He then wiped everything clean with a wash-cloth and dried the entire prosthetic with a bath towel.

He had slipped off into a nap any number of times with his prosthetic still in place, but believed in the orthodoxy of never wearing it while sleep-ing, given the strain it placed on muscles and joints. Better to give his leg a much-needed rest while in bed and hope he remembered he still only had one foot upon climbing out of bed in the morning.

It was amazing the grime the prosthetic had picked up through the long hours on Liberty Island. The washcloths he used were stained with dirt and grit, which had somehow worked its way inside the liner, as well, regardless of the snug fit of the limb.

Even now, the whole experience of the day that had bled into the night-time scene playing on CNN felt surreal, the product of a dream and not re-ality. Michael lay on his back on the bed, too tired to take off his clothes. He knew he needed a shower as much as his prosthetic had needed a cleaning, but couldn't lift himself from the bed to hop his way into the bathroom. It was amazing how good he'd gotten at hopping around, Olympic level really.

He had just grasped his phone to check for any new emails when it lit up with a number he recognized as Frank Bellstock's.

"How's the kid doing, Frank?" he greeted.

"We're at New York-Presbyterian downtown."

Michael swallowed hard. "Any diagnosis?"

"He does have a concussion but the CT scan showed no skull fracture. Best of all, there's no bleeding on the brain."

"What about his hearing?"

"Partial rupture of both eardrums it'll take surgery to repair."

"Does he remember anything about his family?"

"That's the other thing I wanted to tell you. I just got word they pulled a woman and girl from the rubble who've been identified as his mother and sister."

Michael felt his stomach sink. He'd been fully expecting this, but Bell-stock's words hammered home the fact that Danny Logan was now an orphan.

"A shitty day for a whole lot of people, Walker."

"Thanks for following up, Frank."

Michael hung up and looked back toward the TV, at the whole process continuing under the spray of the big construction lights that turned the night to near daylight brilliance, with those incessant swirls of dirt and debris looking like swarms of insects in the spill of the LED bulbs.

A steady, relentless knocking fell on the room's door. Michael hopped to the door gingerly. He braced his hand against the wall as he threw back the lock, and eased the door open without checking the peephole to find Gina Delgado standing before him, two of her agents standing on either side of her.

"Something you want to tell me, Michael?"

CHAPTER 14

LOWER MANHATTAN

Battery Park was named for the artillery batteries
installed to protect the settlement in the late
seventeenth century.

The agents remained in the hallway as Michael closed the door behind him and Delgado.

"I'm sorry," he said, hopping over to the night table where Danny Logan's phone with the cracked screen sat next to his phone.

Her eyes fell on the television instead. "Can you turn that off?"

"Remote's right there."

Delgado clicked the TV off and watched Michael hop toward her with Danny Logan's phone in hand.

"What were you thinking, Michael?"

"I wasn't, at least not clearly." He studied Delgado briefly, didn't see much anger or resentment in her expression. "Why bother coming yourself just to dress me down?"

"Because, truth be told, in your shoes I would have done the same thing. I also wanted to thank you for rallying the forces for crowd control when we were this close to a riot."

"Is that why I'm not under arrest?"

Delgado's expression didn't change. "When were you going to tell me about the kid, a potential eyewitness?"

"You're getting ahead of yourself, Gina."

"That's ASAC Delgado."

"We're not on a first-name basis anymore?"

"I only do that with colleagues I can trust."

"The kid was speaking gibberish. He was in shock, didn't even really comprehend where he was or what had happened. He's at NewYork-

Presbyterian downtown with some significant injuries, under the protection of a Park Police detail."

"And prior to that, he was being guarded by a park policeman you got assigned to that task. We were already shorthanded on the island. What gave you the authority to take someone off their post?"

"I thought we were working together, ASAC Delgado."

"We were, until you decided not to provide some vital information." She paused, gaze dipping from the kid's phone to Michael's exposed stump. "I spoke to your boss."

"Then you know she had nothing to do with this. She gave me an order and I disregarded it. I'm sorry for behaving like an asshole. So are you going to arrest me, send me to the principal's office, make me go to bed without my dinner?"

Delgado's stare bored into him. "I know what happened on Mount Rainier, Michael, the details you left out about that shoot-out, what you called an 'incident.'"

"Angela Pierce told you that, too?" Michael asked, through the lump that had formed in his throat at mention of Rainier.

She shook her head. "I Googled you."

"I don't want your pity, ASAC Delgado."

"Gina. And you lost your wife that day, so you could use some."

Michael tried not to react.

"The fact is if you hadn't responded the way you had today," Delgado resumed, "we might have missed out on Danny Logan, and his phone, altogether."

"How'd you know I had it?"

Delgado ignored his question. "Have you looked at the footage? Is there anything we can use?"

Michael held up Danny's iPhone Pro Max, enclosed in the top-of-the-line Otterbox case. "Not much to see through a broken screen."

"One of the bureau's digital forensic labs is located in the city. They can make sense of anything."

Michael had worked cases several times in conjunction with one of the FBI's regional computer forensics labs, in large part since the Park Service had cut back on such services in favor of the strategic partnership now in place. He watched as Delgado unslung a laptop case from her shoulder Michael hadn't noticed before.

"But why not see what we can see, before sending the phone over to them? And I've got something to show you, too, in the spirit of cooperation."

‡‡‡

Michael sat in a chair at the room's small table set by the window. The combination heater and air-conditioning unit hummed in the background; hard to tell which kind of air it was blowing. Once the laptop fired up, he watched Delgado work the keyboard and click the mouse.

"Let's say for the moment I'm respecting your boss's security clearance. But what I tell you still can't leave this room, okay?"

"Got it."

With that, Delgado tilted the laptop so they could regard the screen together.

"Abridged version, Michael: The security tapes of Liberty Island were blank for July 2 because somebody didn't want anyone to see or be able to identify the work crew on-site that day. The same crew also took every precaution imaginable at the Battery Park City terminal. But they missed a single hidden camera on board the ferry itself."

She worked the mouse and clicked on an unnamed icon on her screen. A picture of five men appeared, but only two were facing the camera. One was taller and broader than the others by a wide margin, his frame wide enough to block the features of the three men standing in his shadow, and sporting close-cropped hair worn the way a cop or soldier would wear it. The fifth man was visible only from the side. They were all lugging toolboxes that had been searched methodically by security and were dressed in work clothes that didn't match.

"Okay, who are they?" Michael asked.

"According to the work logs for the day, subcontractors for the concrete company that rebuilt the Fort Wood pedestal coming to apply the final two coats of sealant."

"What's the company say?"

"We finally managed to reach the right parties an hour ago. They confirmed the job and the workers' names. We emailed the visuals but those parties don't know what the men look like, so we're waiting for them to check and confirm one way or another."

"If this work crew was legit, why make the security footage from the island disappear?"

"I don't know, Michael. I always tell my people they've got to be patient, but it's not working on myself right now."

Michael looked at the screen. "Is there enough on the security footage for facial recognition?"

"I haven't gotten that far yet." Delgado held his gaze, looking vulnerable for the first time. "I feel sick. I may not ever eat again."

Michael eased Danny Logan's iPhone Pro Max across the table. "Maybe this will help you get your appetite back."

‡‡‡

Michael had never been a techie, so Delgado stringing a cord to connect the phone to her laptop and working the keyboard like a maestro impressed him no end. She started rolling the footage Danny had shot without announcement, Michael unaware she'd gotten that far in the process until it began unspooling on the fifteen-inch screen.

They watched in real time first, both leaning closer to the screen when Danny's camera zoomed in, revealing a clearer picture of the men on the deck. Neither of them spoke, their breathing restrained and shallow. Michael knew Delgado was thinking the same thing he was, that this was happening in the last moments before the blast and that the men on this boat had very likely been the ones who'd triggered it.

They let the footage play out in that initial viewing. Michael saw the same thing Danny must have, one of the men on the deck of the supposed Park Police patrol boat filming with a big cell phone, camera aimed straight at the Statue of Liberty. The sound of the blast screeched through the computer's speakers, then grew muffled, almost like powerful winds blowing into the speaker. The angle changed and Michael realized that for a brief time Danny had continued to film while launched airborne by the blast overpressure. It was indeed a miracle he had survived, Michael thought, as the frame spun and settled before the screen went black.

"I called the Park Police about the boat," he said.

"Why?"

"Because according to the kid they don't use that model anymore, an M1–44 instead of an M2–37."

"How would he know something like that?"

"Apparently, he knows his boats. His phone is filled with pictures of them."

"And what did the Park Police tell you?"

"That there was a single patrol boat on station, and that it was an M2–37. At the time of the blast, it had just reached the ferry terminal in Battery Park to respond to a disturbance."

"You check that out, too?"

Michael nodded. "There was no disturbance. It was a false report. The kid was right. The M1–44 had no business being there."

Delgado seemed to weigh that for a moment. Michael could see the pieces coming together in her mind.

"Let's take another look, Michael."

‡‡‡

For their next viewing, Delgado enlarged and refocused the footage, made it as big as she could without sacrificing all notion of clarity. And that was enough to confirm that the man standing in the center of the deck was indeed holding a similarly big iPhone up in line with his face.

"Stop," Michael said. "Run it again. The man, the biggest one, farthest to the right, has something in his hand."

Delgado rewound the footage, zoomed in a bit more, and spot-shadowed the hand in question, holding something with his thumb across the top.

"The detonator," she said.

"Can you spot-shadow his face?"

"Sure."

The resulting product was too blurry for the naked eye to make much out of other than a high and tight military haircut.

"Look familiar?"

"Holy shit," said Gina.

She spot-shadowed the face of the massive figure on the ferry, who had what looked like the same haircut. Then she dragged it over the face of the big man on the boat holding what could be a detonator.

MATCH, the screen flashed over and over again.

PART TWO

The national park idea has been nurtured by each succeeding generation of Americans. Today, across our land, the National Park System represents America at its best. Each park contributes to a deeper understanding of the history of the United States and our way of life; of the natural processes which have given form to our land, and to the enrichment of the environment in which we live.

—George B. Hartzog, Jr.,
National Park Service director 1964–1972

CHAPTER 15

BATTERY PARK

Warrie Price established the Battery Conservancy
in 1994.

"Now, let's see if we can match the face to a name," Gina Delgado said.

Michael could see the flashing red MATCH reflected in the reading glasses Delgado must have donned without him noticing. They made her look more scholarly, he thought, while less intense and focused at the same time.

He watched her fingers dance across the keyboard, tilting the screen away from Michael so he wouldn't be able to see its contents.

"Sorry, the site I'm accessing is classified."

"I'm getting used to that," Michael said.

"And you should call your boss. You've got some explaining to do."

‡‡‡

Michael hopped to the bathroom and closed the door behind him. He lowered the lid of the toilet and sat down and was easing the cell phone from his pocket when it vibrated with an incoming call. ANGELA PIERCE lit up in the caller ID.

"Hey, boss," Michael greeted.

"You want to tell me what you were thinking?" Pierce snapped.

"I guess I wasn't."

"Ignoring my instructions and holding back information from the FBI? No, you weren't. And by requesting park policemen to guard this boy, you involved the Park Service."

"I'm sorry you had to hear about it from the FBI."

"I didn't."

Michael felt as if a cold draft had hit him. "Secretary of the Interior Turlidge's office?"

Angela didn't bother confirming the assumption. "Sorry if I sound pissed, learning that one of my agents went rogue that way."

"You have every right to be pissed."

"But you don't have the right to be this stupid, Michael. You know Ethan Turlidge still blames you for his daughter's death, and wanted you drummed out of the Park Service. He's been waiting for a reason to have you suspended or fired for cause. He's not just out to destroy your career, he wants to humiliate you, ruin you, and you served up the means to do that for him on a silver platter."

"The man's got a dartboard with my face on it, Angela. He doesn't need any more reason to come after me."

"But you gave him one, all the same, Michael."

"The boy's an eyewitness. And there's strong reason to believe he recorded the men behind the bombing. I couldn't risk him getting lost in the shuffle. I made a judgment call and hung you out to dry in the process. I'm sorry."

Silence greeted his response. He could feel Angela thinking on the other end of the line.

"You weren't there," Michael resumed. "No matter how many agents the FBI was able to bring in, they were still stretched thin."

"Sorry still doesn't cut it," Angela said tersely.

Michael felt the phone vibrate with another incoming call. "That's Turlidge on the other line, Angela," he said, recognizing the 202 number.

Michael ended his call with Angela Pierce, but decided not to take Ethan Turlidge's, letting it go to voicemail and hoping his former father-in-law didn't leave a message.

"Walker," Delgado called to him, "we've got something."

—•———•—

CHAPTER 16

BATTERY PARK

Native Americans and Dutch settlers called the spot
Capske Hook, a term meaning "rocky ledge."

"We got a name for the big guy we isolated on Danny Logan's video," Delgado reported, once Michael had rejoined her at the table. "Abel Rathman."

"I'm guessing there's more."

"There is. According to this, Abel Rathman is dead."

Michael waited for her to continue.

"Two years ago," Delgado continued, "in a helicopter accident."

"Rathman was army?"

"Nice guess, Walker."

"Who else rides helicopters?"

Delgado nodded, conceding his point. "It was a training accident," she continued. "Fort Bragg—well, Fort Liberty today."

"I'm guessing Rathman was Special Forces, then."

"The specifics of his service require me to pierce an extra layer of security, but it's a reasonable assumption." Delgado took off her glasses. "You mind if I change the subject?"

"Go ahead."

"Your father-in-law is Ethan Turlidge."

Michael had been expecting that. "Former father-in-law. He's hated my guts even before my wife Allie was killed at Rainier. Blamed me for turning her against him. All I did was open her eyes up to the fact that he only pretended to be an environmentalist. She confronted him and they didn't speak for the last year of Allie's life. He didn't even come to our wedding, ASAC Delgado."

"It's Gina."

"Does that mean you forgive me?"

"No, but I couldn't have spared an agent to guard your boy, even if I wanted to. So long as you're confident the Park Police have this, I'm good."

Michael stopped just short of smiling, something he hadn't done all day. "You okay with me visiting the kid in the morning to see if he remembers anything else?"

"Just file a complete report with me on your conversation, and call me immediately if something comes up I should know." Delgado rose, one of her knees cracking. "I need to get back to the site."

She started for the door, but turned back when she was almost there.

"About Ethan Turlidge . . . There's something you should know, Michael."

Before Delgado could continue, her phone rang.

"Delgado," she answered. "Yes, hold on." She looked at Michael. "Sorry, I need to take this."

Michael watched Delgado exit and close the door behind her, wondering what she'd been about to tell him about his former father-in-law.

CHAPTER 17

ASHFORD, WASHINGTON

In 1988, the Washington Park Wilderness Act
designated specific lands in Mount Rainier National
Park as Mount Rainier Wilderness and as a component
of the National Wilderness Preservation System.

Jeremiah walked about the land where he'd been born and raised. As a boy and a young man, he thought he'd be spending the rest of his life on this bucolic patch that bordered the Gifford Pinchot National Forest. As far back as 1988, it had been technically part of the town of Ashford. That's when the government had seized it, leading to the day that had changed his life forever.

Nestled amid a grove of evergreen trees with the Cascade Mountains standing protectively in the background, the ten acres were among a dozen properties the government had taken as part of the Washington Park Wilderness Act and assigned as a part of Mount Rainier National Park. The other eleven owners had left grudgingly under scant protest. Jeremiah and his family had not.

He walked to the former site of the shingled farmhouse his grandfather and great-grandfather had built with their own hands. It was long gone now, razed as if to wipe out any trace of the generations that had lived here. For years afterward, the farmhouse's footprint was visible as a sunken outline in the soft ground that had dried and browned, as if it had died the same day as his father. At some point, that same ground sparked new growth of grass and brush that hid all traces of the home that had once stood there. Memory of it had been as fleeting as that of the blood spilled on the site. Forgotten now. Forgotten forever.

But not by Jeremiah.

He heard footsteps approaching and knew who it was without turning.

"How'd you find me, General?" he said to Archibald Terrell.

"You didn't answer your phone. The only time you don't answer your phone is when your past draws you here, Ferris."

Jeremiah bristled at being addressed by the name he had, for all intents and purposes, shed, finally turning to face a man who looked distinctly uncomfortable not wearing a military uniform.

"Sorry," said Terrell. "I know you don't like me calling you that."

"Because Ferris Hobbs is the man I used to be. Jeremiah is the man I am now."

"People don't change, my friend. Only the world does, by our own making."

"That's what drew me here today," Jeremiah told him. "What we're doing. What's coming."

Terrell was small in stature, his soft features and complexion belying the brutal battlefield nature that had earned him the nickname "General Terror." He never looked any different, from his neatly coiffed hair to the stiff bent of his spine. His fingernails bothered Jeremiah the most, always clean and neatly trimmed, in stark contrast to his own, which were forever riddled with a layer of grime beneath them.

"Your father died here," Terrell said, taking a single step closer.

"He didn't die, General, he was murdered." Jeremiah turned back around, imagining the farmhouse as it had been that day in 1988. "It happened right here, in this very spot. My family refused to vacate the land like our neighbors, defied the court orders, and fired warning shots over the heads of the first federal marshals sent to evict us. The next day, they came back in force." Jeremiah made a half circle with his hand through the air, directing Terrell's gaze to the tree line. "They staged there, a hundred of them maybe. Shut down the road, so we couldn't get any supplies in. Shut off our water and septic system, killed our power. But we were prepared, we were ready."

Terrell's gaze beckoned him on.

"After three weeks, negotiations allowed my mother, brother, sister, and uncles to leave without fear of arrest. My father wanted me to go with them, but I refused. I expected to die that day, General. Maybe part of me wanted to die."

Jeremiah led Terrell around to where the side of the house had been.

"The sniper's bullet cracked through a window right here and grazed me in the shoulder. An accident, what was later called a misfire. My father grabbed the M16 he'd smuggled home from Vietnam and burst out onto the porch, firing into the tree line. He didn't hit anybody, but a dozen bullets found him. I watched him fall, watched him die. Saw the light fade from his eyes. You know the worst thing about all that?"

Terrell didn't respond.

"I froze. I should have picked up his rifle and resumed shooting. But I just stood there, watching the pool of blood widen beneath my father."

"It took some time, some years," Terrell told him, "but you finally picked that rifle up. That's what all this is about, a second chance for both you and the country."

"You come all the way out here to reassure me?"

Terrell drew up alongside him. "You didn't tell me the latest shipment out of West Virginia had been delayed."

"There was no need to. A few of my trucks needed repairs. All that weight means the suspension systems require reinforcement. Just like the country, General."

That seemed to mollify Terrell, who nodded with a smile.

"The convoy will be on the road later today," Jeremiah continued.

Terrell nodded again, the breeze unable to lift a hair from his still helmet of a scalp. "You remember when you first approached me three years ago?"

"I do."

"You told me your name was Jeremiah, after the prophet. 'I will turn their mourning into joy and will comfort them and give them joy for their sorrow,' you said when I asked you what you wanted to talk to me about."

"That's right. From the book of Jeremiah. 'Should you not fear me? Should you not tremble in my presence?' That's what you said back to me. You know your Bible, General."

"I told you that day I was fighting a holy war."

"I took the name Jeremiah, because I'd become a different man. I'd already buried the one I used to be six months before, after the funeral."

"Remember the first question you asked me?"

"'How many men have you killed?'" Jeremiah said.

"You remember my answer?"

"'Thousands from a distance. A handful up close and personal.' I asked because I wanted to know if you were serious about waging this holy war of yours."

"Well," Terrell started, "we're about to kill a lot more than thousands, so I guess your question has been answered."

"I still wish I'd picked up that rifle, General," Jeremiah listened to himself say, as if someone else were speaking. "In that moment, I wanted to kill those men at the tree line more than anything else in the world. There weren't enough bullets to do that, but it didn't matter because I didn't try."

"Second chances, just like I told you. They killed your father and took your land, and now we're going to take this country back from them. Because of what your trucks are hauling west."

"I guess I can't shoot them all, can I?"

Terrell's expression flirted with a smile that threatened its marble-like finish. "Not unless you happen to have ten million bullets handy."

CHAPTER 18

‖‐‖‐◦‐◦‐‖‐‖

LIBERTY ISLAND

Native Americans began to inhabit the island
in AD 994.

"Morning, Chief," greeted Milligan from the evidence response team, working in the wreckage at the very same spot where Gina Delgado had left her
the night before.

"Please tell me you took a break after I left."

"Did you?"

Gina let her question hang in the air. Milligan's blue overalls and matching jacket marked ERT were now colored gray from all the concrete dust
swirling about. She was literally knee-deep in the refuse of the blast. The
sun had come up, lending the scene an almost surreal stillness. So quiet
and calm, she could hear the wings of a bird flapping overhead. The devas-
tation was even more striking without the clouds of residue that had hung
over the site yesterday. Gina had hoped that daylight would have eased the
eeriness of viewing it under the spray of LED construction lights piercing
the clouds of concrete dust. Instead, the day's first light and clear air made
the sight of the toppled statue in the field of residue inside the blast cone
even more horrifying than when she'd first arrived yesterday. The cushion
of shock was gone and the adrenaline that had fueled those initial hours
depleted. A sense of duty, coupled with the awesome responsibility she was
tasked with, had propelled her through the previous day. Now, though, Gina's head had cleared with the air, bringing home the reality of what lay
before her.

"Chief?" Milligan prodded.

Gina snapped alert again.

"I thought you were somewhere else."

"Anywhere is better than here," Gina said, trying to clear the hoarseness of fatigue from her voice. "Any new revelations since I left?"

"Just about all the bodies have been pulled from the rubble. Over seven hundred at last count, spread equally across the debris field."

Gina's eyes widened. The number hadn't surprised her; it was something else.

"That was my thought, too," Milligan said.

Gina watched Milligan sift through the rubble at their feet and came away with a jagged chunk of concrete that had been part of the pedestal. "See how the scoring pattern runs all the way through? If this were TNT triggered from beneath the pedestal, the scoring would be much more evident on the lower part and concentrated in that single section. And, now that I've been able to inspect the scene, I'm convinced we're looking at a blast that didn't blow upward as much as outward. I know from what you said yesterday that it doesn't surprise you."

Gina remained silent.

"And you were right about the conductive filament being carbon-based. You even nailed the size: one point seven five millimeters in diameter."

"Standard, as I mentioned."

"I've also found trace evidence of either five or six microprocessors that could have acted as triggers for the detonating mechanism, also like you suggested. But there was something else you didn't tell me."

Milligan stopped there, as if waiting for Gina to comment and then resuming only when she didn't.

"You know what did this, don't you, Chief?"

"Yes," Gina conceded, "because I've worked with it myself." She hesitated, then decided to share the specifics with Milligan. "Astrolite. Ring any bells?"

"Soft ones, Chief. Astrolite is still used in commercial and civil blasting applications, but has largely been superseded by cheaper and safer compounds."

"True enough, but it's extremely durable for a liquid explosive, retaining its potency even when sitting atop the ground or absorbed into soil for days at a time after dispersal."

Milligan nodded, seeming to weigh Gina's words, not looking satisfied. "That doesn't sound like the Astrolite I'm familiar with."

"Because there are three advanced versions of the explosive never made available for commercial use, two of which I worked with in Iraq that were developed strictly for the military. The most recent addition was Astrolite X, notable in large part for leaving no trace behind."

Milligan gazed about the debris field around them. "Except, as a liquid, it would have sat atop the concrete of the statue's pedestal instead of penetrating it."

"Astrolite X is extremely malleable," Gina told her.

"Meaning . . ."

"What happens when you inject air into cream?"

"Whipped cream."

"Picture doing the same with liquid Astrolite."

Gina watched Milligan do just that. "You're talking about some kind of foam."

"Based on the debris field, where was the blast centered?"

"We already covered that, Chief. The blast was utterly symmetrical."

"Meaning all parts of the pedestal blew at the same time. It's the only explanation for the radius of the blast and spread of the debris field."

Milligan asked, "But Astrolite in foam form wouldn't have soaked into the concrete, either. What am I missing?"

"The fact that the pedestal was recently refinished. The crew could have blown the Astrolite foam into the gaps, cracks, and fissures, filling up all of the air pockets that form naturally in all concrete structures."

"So they used this Astrolite X," Milligan said, her voice suddenly sounding distant.

"Or the next level, next generation. Throw in the fact that it was undetectable to the bomb-sniffing dogs walked about the grounds."

"In other words, something we haven't seen before, Chief."

"Something *nobody's* ever seen before."

"You have."

Gina's phone buzzed with an incoming call, and she recognized Special Agent John Milton's number.

"I'm in the field, Paradise," she greeted.

"I'm in the command center. How soon can you get here?"

"On my way now," Gina said, already walking toward the building. "What's up?"

"More information about Abel Rathman you need to hear ASAP, Chief."

CHAPTER 19

NEW YORK-PRESBYTERIAN
LOWER MANHATTAN HOSPITAL

The original New York-Presbyterian Hospital was
founded in 1771 as New York Hospital.

Michael saw the park policeman assigned to guard Danny Logan just opening the door to the boy's room as he approached.

"Hey," Michael called.

The call seemed to startle the man. He turned from the door and regarded the uniform before Michael himself. Michael had donned a fresh one before heading to the hospital and wondered how many washings it would take to get the residue and smell out of the one he'd worn yesterday, though no amount could wipe out the haunting memories.

The park policeman's name tag identified him as BUCKLAND. He was about Michael's height, but built like a linebacker, which meant that going through him to get to the kid would be a tall order.

"Special Agent Michael Walker, ISB," he said, extending a hand.

Buckland took it in a grasp that felt like steel. "Nice to meet you, Agent."

"How is he?" Michael asked.

"I was about to check. Just came on duty. Everything he's been through, it's just terrible. I heard he watched his parents and sister get killed."

"He was right there when the pedestal blew. He probably doesn't remember anything he saw."

"How come no effort has been made to locate his relatives?"

"Standard procedure with an eyewitness who may be in danger. Do nothing to draw any attention to his presence initially."

"You think he's in danger, Agent?"

"That's why you're here," Michael told him.

NewYork-Presbyterian Lower Manhattan Hospital wasn't only the closest major trauma center to Liberty Island, it was also the best equipped to handle the massive influx of patients from such a catastrophe.

"How bad is the kid hurt?" Buckland asked him.

"I checked with the attending. His internal injuries, miraculously, are minimal and his skull is intact, though he suffered a moderate concussion. A number of cuts, lacerations, and bruises, some hearing loss in his right ear and loss of ninety percent in his left. Too early to predict how much he'll regain after surgery. All told, it's much better than it could have been, physically anyway."

Michael looked toward the hospital room door, which wasn't quite closed all the way. "I thought I'd check on him. Hopefully, he remembers me from yesterday."

"I'm sure he wishes he could forget," Buckland offered.

‡‡‡

"I remember you," Danny greeted, as Michael closed the door behind him. "You're a cop or something."

"Something. I'm an investigator with the Park Service, something called the Investigative Services Branch."

"You need to speak louder. My hearing's all messed up, especially on the left side."

"I said that I'm an investigator—"

"Not that loud. And I already heard that part."

Michael moved closer to the bed, angling himself to the boy's right. The back of the bed had been raised all the way, so Danny was sitting straight up, staring at a wall-mounted flat-screen television that wasn't turned on. The cuts on his face had been bandaged, and a thicker gauze wrap covered the whole of his left ear. His hair hung over his face in uncombed clumps, but it was the first time Michael had seen his face without a thick layer of blood-smeared concrete dust coating it. His eyes were wide, both fearful and uncertain.

"You helped me yesterday," the boy said. "You were nice."

"Comes with the job, Danny."

The boy's eyes widened at the mention of his name. "I don't remember your name."

"Michael."

"My parents are dead," Danny said matter-of-factly, as if still trapped in the haze of shock.

"I know."

"My sister, too. Did I tell you about the men in the boat?"

"Yes."

"Do you think they did it, killed my parents and sister?"

"That's a strong possibility, yes."

"I can't find my phone. I remember taking a video of the boat."

"I've got your phone."

"Did it help?"

Michael nodded. "A lot, I think."

"What happens now?"

"I catch the people who did this."

Danny looked down at his lap, then up again. "What's going to happen to me?"

"Who can I call for you?" Michael said, aware he'd be breaching protocol by doing that. "Any relatives in the area?"

"I'm pretty close to my aunt and uncle. They've got kids same age as me and my sister. They live in Florida."

"Do you remember their phone number?"

Danny shook his head. "It's on my phone. You can check."

"What are their names?"

The boy included the names of his cousins as well, and Michael wrote them all down. As soon as he was done here, he'd call Gina Delgado to see if she or her tech people could find them among the kid's contacts. It was a call he did not look forward to making, but was prepared to make nonetheless because Danny needed family now, even if that meant skirting the rules.

"I don't want to live in Florida," Danny said, as Michael returned the notebook to his pocket. "Why is there a guy guarding me?"

"He's there to protect you."

"Because of what I filmed, those men in the boat?"

Michael nodded.

"Do you have a family, Michael?"

"I had a wife."

"What happened?"

"She died."

"Oh," Danny said, seeming to look at Michael differently. "You miss her, right?"

Michael nodded.

The boy's eyes welled with tears. "I miss my parents. I even miss my sister." He leaned further forward, shedding some of his bedcovers. "And you have to find the people who did it, the men in that boat."

Michael had muted his phone but felt it vibrating in his pocket and took it out, recognizing Gina Delgado's number. "I need to take this," he said to Danny, moving to the boy's left side, so he wouldn't be able to overhear Michael's side of the conversation as clearly. "How's your morning going, ASAC Delgado?"

"Where are you, Walker?"

"NewYork-Presbyterian downtown," Michael said, leaving it there.

"I'm at the site. I've got some new information you need to hear about Abel Rathman and that helicopter crash. . . ."

CHAPTER 20

LIBERTY ISLAND

Archibald Kennedy purchased the island and
established a summer retreat in 1746.

Gina had entered Liberty Island's information center, now the JTTF's command center, twenty minutes earlier. It was less frantic but more crowded than yesterday, thanks to the arrival of White House liaisons, high-ranking Homeland Security officers, and equally high-ranking NYPD officers from the force's Special Operations Bureau. She also noted the presence of civilians wearing lanyards dangling from their necks identifying them as from either the mayor's office or the governor's office.

Priorities on the Liberty Island investigation were evolving. Work was now focused on removing the debris. The damage to Lady Liberty herself was limited to dents, divots, and blast scoring. The statue had already been deemed structurally intact. Some repairs could be effected in its current condition, but the decision had already been made to raise the statue back up in its damaged state as a testament to and symbol of the country's resiliency. Let the world, and the perpetrators, see that Lady Liberty could be knocked down, but not out. The same thinking figured into the decision not to shutter any of the other national parks and memorials, even the smaller ones, a feat that would require even more personnel than securing them.

Gina couldn't have agreed more. As such, her responsibilities upon returning to the site would include oversight of the massive construction machines, starting with front loaders and dump trucks, that had arrived on the island this morning to begin lifting and hauling the rubble away. Instead of being discarded, it would be stored in a secure location in case further forensic inspection was required.

She recalled how anything inside the information center that could be moved had been shoved aside to make room. Today much of it had been removed altogether to create more floor and table space. Seemed like everyone who'd shown up from all the departments represented had brought a laptop along and felt entitled to claim some table space for themselves. Gina was grateful for the fact that she wasn't the one who needed to deal with all that commotion.

On her way to the back room where she'd interviewed Tom Fenton the day before, she noticed that the spindles holding informational literature had been removed as well. She entered the converted storage room to find Special Agent John Milton alone at his laptop at the folding table. He never looked up from the screen or keyboard as he dragged the room's second chair over closer to him.

"You need to get a good look at this, Chief."

Gina sat down. "What am I looking at, Paradise?"

Milton clicked his mouse on an icon at the bottom of the screen. "That helicopter crash that killed Abel Rathman and eleven other members of the Special Forces." He looked at her for the first time since she'd entered. "Our Hostage Rescue Team trains with Delta, so I know the territory at least a bit."

That surprised Gina. "I didn't know you were HRT."

"That's because I was eighty-sixed after getting selected. Asthma."

"That sucks."

"Tell me about it." Milton turned his attention back to the screen. "The chopper was on a training exercise, those twelve Special Forces operatives inside including Rathman, when it got caught in thick fog and slammed into the Great Smoky Mountains. You're looking at the wreckage."

Gina shifted her chair to get a better view. "Not much left. Couldn't have been much left of the bodies either."

"There wasn't, virtually nothing. The chopper exploded on impact, scattering chunks of the fuselage, and remnants of the bodies, for a quarter mile."

"Okay, so if Abel Rathman died in the crash, how did he show up as part of a work crew rebuilding the pedestal and then on that boat yesterday?"

"Glad you asked, Chief." Milton worked his mouse again, and a picture of Rathman in uniform appeared on screen right next to the computer-enhanced shot of the big man captured on the boat in Danny Logan's video. "What happens to bodies subjected to that kind of trauma and ensuing fire?"

"Is this a quiz?"

"Humor me."

"Well, for starters whatever skin wasn't burned away entirely would be charred, clothing and jewelry fused to the remaining flesh and bone, sometimes melted."

"Pull your chair closer again," Milton said. "This is what you really need to see."

Milton worked his mouse again, the entire screen taken up by three pictures of human remains salvaged from the scene, as Gina shifted her chair sideways again.

"Notice anything, Chief?"

"What's left of the uniforms isn't fused to what's left of the bodies." She looked from the screen to Milton. "How can that be?"

"Only one explanation: The bodies inside the chopper were already dead when it crashed."

‡‡‡

"Assume they'd been drained of blood," Milton continued. "Assume they'd been stored in the cooler of a mortuary, morgue, or hospital. You'd still get some fusing, but absent any blood, and with the temperature of the bodies around freezing, nowhere near the amount you'd get with living tissue."

"So these twelve special operators were never on board the chopper that crashed; they were only *supposed* to have been on board."

"Notice anything else?"

Gina tightened her gaze on the three pictures again.

"You won't find it there, Chief."

She looked toward Milton instead. "So what am I missing?"

"How many victims did the crash claim in total?"

"Twelve, Paradise."

Milton nodded, smiling tightly. "There you go."

"Meaning there was no pilot," Gina realized.

"Because whoever set the thing didn't want to sacrifice one of their own men, Chief. They must have been flying the chopper on remote."

CHAPTER 21

NEWYORK-PRESBYTERIAN
LOWER MANHATTAN HOSPITAL

The original New York Hospital had opened an asylum,
adjacent to the hospital, in 1808, but moved to more
tranquil surroundings, overlooking the Hudson River,
at Broadway and 116th Street.

"Is this a test, Gina?" Michael asked Delgado from Danny Logan's bedside. "Because if it is, my forensic training covered the fact that clothing doesn't fuse to dead bodies the way it does to living ones."

"Which means when that chopper crashed, there were twelve dead bodies on board instead of Rathman and the other Special Forces troops. What's missing, Walker?"

"Holy shit," Michael said, a chill spreading through him.

"That's what I said."

"What happened to the pilot?"

"I said that, too. Because there was no pilot. Somebody must've been flying that chopper on remote." She hesitated to let her point sink in. "If army personnel from Bragg hadn't kept the wreckage to themselves, there would've been evidence of that," Delgado continued. "Suffice it to say that whoever was behind faking that helicopter crash slipped up there."

"You have the names of the other troops supposedly killed in the crash?" Michael asked her.

"They were all Special Forces, maybe not quite as seasoned as Rathman, but close. We're cross-referencing their backgrounds for any other possible connections besides Fort Bragg: missions, postings, commanding officers, deployments—everything. It's slow going because so much of their work was top secret to the point that the army won't even acknowledge it."

"At least we can safely assume three of them were on that M1–44 boat with Rathman in the harbor yesterday, leaving eight unaccounted for."

"Who says it's only eight? I've got one of my agents scouring army logs for other accidental deaths that fit a similar pattern. Not an easy task, given that such records aren't accessible to anyone outside of JSOC. That's the Joint Special Operations Command."

"I know what it is. Just like I know we should now be able to get pictures of the other eleven operatives."

"Working on that as we speak and expect to have their photos and redacted bios in minutes. Once I've got them, I'll cross-check the pictures with what we were able to lift off the security camera on that ferryboat. We might get lucky there, but there isn't much to go from those shots besides the one captured of Rathman. I'll also place all twelve of them on the intelligence wire with a Black Flag designation."

"What's that mean?"

"That's right, I forgot about your lack of a proper security clearance."

"Don't rub it in."

"Black Flag is our highest-priority suspect list, normally reserved for suspected terrorists on the level of Bin Laden. And it includes not just airport TSA stations and ticket counters, but also tens of thousands of security cameras and priority alerts sent to every law enforcement entity across the country."

Silence settled between them on the line.

"What the hell's going on here, Gina?" Michael said, breaking it.

"Whatever it is, we wouldn't know a thing about it if it wasn't for you finding Danny Logan and the video he shot. Maybe I should let your former father-in-law know about that."

Michael let her comment go. "How did you learn about the kid being an eyewitness to the attack, that I was holding back on you?"

"From the ground supervisor, man named Tom Fenton."

"I bumped into him in the triage center," Michael recalled.

"That must be how he overheard you talking about Danny Logan with a park policeman inside the museum turned triage center. Why?"

"Because what if whoever's behind all this, and that chopper crash, knows about Danny, too?"

More silence greeted Michael's question, going on so long he began to fear the call had failed.

"Gina?"

"Sit tight, Walker. I've got a hostage rescue team standing by in the city, ready to deploy as soon as I give the word. Just in case."

"Just in case may have happened."

"I can have them there by chopper in fifteen minutes, twenty tops. They can land on the roof pad used for medevacs. Can you hold the fort until then?"

"They'll have to go through a park policeman as strong as King Kong, too. We should be able to . . ."

"Michael, are you there? Is something wrong?"

"Probably not. It's just that, well, King Kong's uniform doesn't fit him."

"Too small?"

"Too big. Could be whoever obtained it for him wanted to make sure it *wasn't* too small."

‡‡‡

Michael had his phone back at his ear, Angela Pierce's number already ringing.

"You need to return Secretary Turlidge's calls, Michael," she greeted. "He's going ballistic."

"Sure, I will. But I need you to do something for me first. I'm at New York-Presbyterian in downtown Manhattan with Danny Logan, who's being guarded by a park policeman I've never met before named Buckland. Can you text me a picture?"

"Sure, but there's no need. I made the assignment myself, because she's one of our best."

"She?" Michael managed.

A knock fell on the door, before it eased open to reveal the man wearing Buckland's name tag. "Everything okay in here?"

CHAPTER 22

▸·••·◦·••·◂

NEW YORK-PRESBYTERIAN
LOWER MANHATTAN HOSPITAL

**In 1940 the original location, then known as
New York Hospital, was the site of the first successful
catheterization of the human heart.**

"Sure," Michael said, his voice cracking, phone with the line still live held by his side. "Fine."

He stole a glance at Danny, unsure what the kid might have figured out from his demeanor, even though he'd only heard one side of the conversation through a bandaged left ear. The boy's expression was empty, same as it had been when Michael had entered the room. No change.

"I got this, if you want to get going, Agent," the man who wasn't Buckland told him.

"Thanks. Just wrapping up here."

Michael left it there and hardened his gaze as much as he could. The man dressed as a park policeman looked at him strangely for a moment, then smiled.

"Whatever you say, boss. You need me, I'll be right outside the door."

Michael managed a nod and waited for the man to close the door behind him before jerking the phone back to his ear.

"Was that," Angela started over the phone, then left her thought hanging.

"Yes," Michael said, lowering his voice. "You need to send a detail over to the real Buckland's home. If he's got her name tag . . ."

"Yeah, I figured that out for myself."

"The imposter's big. It's not Buckland's uniform he's wearing. He was ready for this. That means word of Buckland's assignment came from the inside, Angela. Something else you should know. The supposedly dead guy on that boat yesterday was Special Forces."

"Shit."

"It gets worse. He supposedly died in a helicopter crash, along with eleven other operators."

"So if he's still alive . . ."

"My point exactly."

Silence fell over the line, Michael's gaze fixed on the door. He pulled his jacket back to free his gun.

"How you want to play this, Michael?"

"We're on the sixth floor, so that rules out the window."

"I'm being serious."

"So was I."

"Hospital security?"

"One step above rent-a-cops. If the fake Buckland is one of those special operators from the helicopter, they won't even make it out of the elevator."

"I could make the call," Angela said, groping, "say we've learned of a threat to the boy's life and that we're moving him."

"This guy would see through that like window glass. I'm calling Delgado. She mentioned they've got a hostage rescue team on standby in the city."

"And how do you think your guy would react to them storming the hall?"

"Not well, Angela. The window is looking better and better as an option."

"How much time you figure we've got?"

"I don't know. Not a lot. Stay by your phone. I'll call you back after I'm off with Delgado, see if the FBI has any ideas."

"What the hell?" Danny said from his bed, his eyes as fearful and uncertain as they'd been yesterday, as Michael ended the call and pressed Delgado's number.

Delgado's phone was ringing. Michael held up a hand to signal Danny to be quiet. "Me again," he greeted when she answered.

"We just got off the phone five minutes ago."

"When I said what if whoever's behind all this, and that chopper crash, knows about Danny, too."

"Not your exact words, but close enough."

"I think they killed the park policeman who was supposed to be guarding the kid."

Even with his hearing compromised, Michael knew, Danny could hear what he was saying. But he had no choice. Not a good idea right now to talk from inside the closet or bathroom.

"So the guy you found guarding the kid, another of our dearly departed Special Forces troops?"

"I think you're getting the picture."

"Keep painting."

"The grounds manager, Tom Fenton, who knew about the kid, Gina. The grounds manager would have been responsible for supervising all construction crews."

"That's why I brought him in yesterday. He helped point us in the right direction, toward the construction crew Rathman was a part of. That's how we got that picture from the ferry ride."

"Maybe this Tom Fenton didn't know the ferry had cameras. Even if he did, the guy must've figured that information wouldn't lead anywhere."

"If it hadn't been for Danny Logan, it never would have."

"But now it has, and the kid's a loose end."

"I can scramble the HRT to get you and the boy out."

Michael replayed what he'd just said to Angela Pierce in his mind. "I'm not sure I've got the fifteen minutes you said it would take."

"If you can get to the roof, I can get a chopper there in ten."

"I'm not even sure I can get out of the room right now."

The door started to crack inward.

Michael went for his gun.

⊢•◦•⊣

CHAPTER 23

LIBERTY ISLAND

Bedloe's Island was a military outpost for 130 years.

"Michael!" Gina yelled into her phone, at the sound of some kind of commotion. "Michael, talk to me! What's happening?"

"False alarm. And I think I know how to get the kid out of here without a gunfight."

"How?"

"No time to explain. I'll call you back."

"Michael—"

Her home screen returned, the call ended.

Gina jogged her phone to the numbers Tom Fenton had provided yesterday and tried them both.

"Tom Fenton isn't answering his phone, home or cell," she told John Milton, lowering her phone to the table. "Send a detail to his house."

"This the same guy we had in here yesterday, the site manager or something?"

"That's the guy."

"Where's he live?"

"Queens."

"Locals could get there faster."

"We need to keep this in the family, Paradise. No outsiders." Gina rose, fixing her gaze on Milton. "I want to be on the phone with him as soon as they arrive."

"You going back into the field, boss?"

"I'm taking the chopper to New York-Presbyterian. Have the hostage rescue team meet me there."

CHAPTER 24

NEW YORK-PRESBYTERIAN
LOWER MANHATTAN HOSPITAL

The hospital cared for more than three thousand
American soldiers who were wounded while fighting in
the Revolutionary War.

"Sorry," Michael said, when the tray the nurse was holding rattled to the floor.

He closed the door behind her, careful not to look toward the man wearing Buckland's name tag seated just outside.

The nurse, whose name tag identified her as JEN COS, leaned over to retrieve the contents of the tray. She looked to be in her late thirties, with her hair pulled up in a bun. Fear and uncertainty swam in her eyes, which were fixed on Michael's pistol.

"Sorry," he said again, lowering it while raising his free hand in a calming gesture.

"I just came to draw some blood," Cos told him, collecting a syringe, tubing, and vials from the floor. "I'll need to replace all this and come back."

"No," Michael said, louder than he'd meant to.

His tone startled her again and she dropped the tray again, scattering the syringe and vials for a second time.

He flashed the badge that dangled from his neck. "I'm Special Agent Michael Walker with the ISB."

"ISB?"

He got that a lot when working cases off the grounds of the National Park System. "Investigative Services Branch of the Park Service." He paused to let that sink in. "You know what happened at the Statue of Liberty yesterday, Jen."

"Of course."

"Are you aware that this boy was an eyewitness and is currently in the protective custody of the Park Police?"

She looked toward Danny, who gestured in a half wave, half salute.

"I just came to draw blood. Can I go get a new tray now?"

"I need you to do something else for me," Michael told her.

‡‡‡

Alarms began to chime from the machines placed around Danny Logan's hospital bed. Mere seconds passed before a grouping of doctors and nurses, one pushing a crash cart, streamed down the hall straight for Danny's room.

Michael yanked open the door to find the fake Buckland, a Special Forces operative almost for sure, already on his feet.

"What happened?" he asked, clearly unsettled by the oncoming doctors and nurses.

"The kid coded," Michael said. "The nurse was drawing blood and all of a sudden he stopped breathing."

The bigger man trailed Michael into the room. The whole time Michael clung to the hope that the fact that the code team wasn't applying chest compressions, only feeding the boy oxygen from a portable tank, wouldn't betray the ruse.

He also could only hope that the fake Buckland didn't notice Danny flash a thumbs-up sign with a hand dangling off the bedcovers.

"Let's move him!" one of the doctors ordered.

And in the next instant a pair of orderlies who had accompanied the code team into the room were speeding Danny's bed down the hall, surrounded by medical personnel and trailed by Michael and fake Buckland all the way to the elevator. Michael felt his phone buzz with an incoming text from Delgado and acknowledged it without breaking pace:

CHOPPERING IN NOW. HRT EN ROUTE

He normally hated texting, which had driven his wife Allie crazy, but it certainly came in handy sometimes. Michael counted his blessings that fake Buckland was positioned in a manner that kept him from seeing the text. The next part of Michael's plan was the most precarious and could go wrong in a heartbeat. Only seconds more to consider that move, with the service elevator coming up fast. The doors opened just as the code team reached it, and Michael watched Danny's bed being wheeled inside, shrouded by doctors and nurses.

It creaked, squeaked, and left scratch marks on the hallway floor, thanks to a stuck wheel.

Michael and fake Buckland, bringing up the rear, had started to enter the cab together when Michael twisted into the bigger man and slammed a shoulder into him. It was like hitting a brick wall, but on an angle that sent fake Buckland sideways far enough for Michael to lunge all the way inside the cab ahead of him as the doors were closing. He thought he heard pounding on the steel as the door sealed all the way.

"We need to get to the roof!" Michael said, gun in hand now.

The code team exchanged nervous glances.

"This elevator doesn't go there," Nurse Cos told him.

Michael thought fast. "Then take me as low as it goes."

"The basement," she said.

The lobby was out, because Michael had no idea whether fake Buckland had backup in place there or not. The basement was the next best option, either to escape through or to wait in for Delgado and the hostage rescue team to arrive.

"The basement it is," Michael instructed, reaching for his phone while watching one of the orderlies press a button marked *B*.

‡‡‡

The pictures of the twelve deceased Special Forces personnel out of Fort Bragg, supposedly killed when their chopper crashed into the Great Smoky Mountains, had just come in when Gina's phone rang. She answered it before the first ring was complete.

"I'm landing now, Michael," she said, hoping he could hear her over the sounds of the chopper.

"Plan B, Gina. Couldn't reach the roof. The basement was the next best thing."

"What about the imposter?"

"He didn't make it into the elevator," Michael said, leaving it there.

"I just got the pictures. I'm texting you the sheet now. Tell me if anyone besides Abel Rathman looks familiar."

Gina hit send, counting fifteen seconds in her mind as the helicopter descended for the hospital's landing pad.

"He's here, all right," Michael said. "Fourth picture down, named Grun-wald."

Gina regarded the picture in question. Grunwald had a head the size of an anvil.

"Anything on the real Buckland yet?"

"NYPD was responding. I haven't heard anything. They might report to your boss first. This is kind of unprecedented."

"We know what they're going to find."

"Sadly."

"How far out is your hostage rescue team?" she heard Michael ask through her headset.

"Five minutes."

"An eternity."

The chopper settled onto the landing pad.

‡‡‡

Michael felt the elevator grind to a halt at the basement level, settling with a light thud. The doors slid open.

"You just saved a life, just not the way you're used to," Michael told the code team that had followed his instructions upstairs to the letter, after being initially befuddled by the ruse. "I'll take things from here."

NEW YORK-PRESBYTERIAN
LOWER MANHATTAN HOSPITAL

New York Hospital, which would later become
New York-Presbyterian, was founded by a royal charter
from King George III of England in 1771.

The orderlies helped him wheel Danny's bed out of the elevator cab, reluctant to retreat until Michael cast them a nod. The door closed behind them, leaving him alone with Danny at what looked like the center of a vast hallway.

"Looks like something out of a horror movie," the boy said.

Michael found that appropriate enough, given that a monster was giving chase. "Can you walk?"

"A little unsteady, like yesterday. Don't think I can run, though."

"Hopefully you won't have to."

"When am I going to get my phone back? It's got, like, my whole life on it." Danny looked down, as if studying his lap. "What's left of it anyway."

"Since the screen's broken, why don't I see if we can get the contents transferred onto a brand-new one?"

The boy perked up. "That'll do."

"Now let me help you get out of that bed. . . ."

Danny laid his arm over Michael's shoulder. Michael first maneuvered the boy to the right so his feet dangled off the bed, then eased him to a standing position, and held firm until the boy found his footing.

"I don't have shoes," he said, looking down at his bare feet.

Michael looked back toward the elevator, then tried to find an exit sign, to no avail.

"We need to move," he told Danny, helping him with his first few steps.

The boy moved stiffly and tentatively at first, as if not trusting his own legs, but quickly found an awkward rhythm along the slick and shiny tile floor. The mechanical subbasement was neither as cluttered nor as noisy as older versions with which Michael was more familiar. Gone were the hissing and rattling of pipes, the clanking of exhaust baffles dumping out heat sucked from the vents. Instead, white PVC piping ran in labyrinthine fashion up the walls and along the ceiling, pulsing with life and dripping moisture onto the shiny finished flooring. Huge machines Michael took for heat pumps and air exchangers colored royal blue climbed the walls, humming softly and rumbling slightly louder when kicked up into the next gear. Exhaust fans with huge metal blades spun at various intervals to prevent the air from stagnating or overheating, and space-age turbines hummed, routing power through the complex.

Michael led Danny along the darkest path he could find to better conceal them, off of the walkway that sliced down the center of the subbasement and past various heavy fire-retardant security doors behind which were housed the hospital's various HVAC controls. It might not have been as cluttered down here as he'd expected, but there was still more than enough noise emanating from the slew of machines to drown out any approaching footsteps.

He rotated his focus between what lay ahead of them and what was behind, since the rear made for the most likely origin of any attack. Sure enough, Michael had just turned back to the front when shots echoed from the rear, puncturing the PVC piping overhead and pouring steam everywhere.

Michael tucked Danny behind him and fired off a succession of his own shots toward a figure that looked ephemeral in the steam, more phantom than man. Michael emptied the last of his SIG Sauer's magazine toward the shape, which responded by firing off a dozen shots in a fashion rapid enough to make it seem as if he were firing on full auto.

Michael dragged a whimpering Danny with him to the floor to avoid the fire, pulling the boy across the smooth surface toward cover, as he tried to track fake Buckland through the gushing steam. Fresh magazine jammed home, he readied himself to open fire as soon as the bigger man came into view again.

But the boot holding his prosthetic foot got lodged in the gap between one of the big turbines' housing and the floor. That left him squarely exposed, like a target on a shooting range, providing only a small modicum of cover for Danny. The boy was sobbing now, the trauma no doubt triggering a flashback to his experience on Liberty Island yesterday. Reliving that pain all over again.

Michael thought he glimpsed the soldier rushing toward them, then thought it had been a trick of his eyes trying to peer through the steam. The man's shape was there, and then it wasn't, reappearing somewhere else with a swiftness of motion that defied reason. Almost like this man could "will" himself from one spot to another, action and thought one and the same. With the steam serving as cover, the soldier was closing on Michael's snared form, there until he wasn't while drawing near enough to make sure his next shots didn't miss.

Michael fought to jiggle his jammed boot free, but couldn't rotate his prosthetic foot enough to manage the task. He needed to find a way to neutralize fake Buckland, at least flush him out within the steam, while not exposing Danny to fire. Gina Delgado would have landed by now and the FBI's Hostage Rescue Team would be only minutes away now.

If he could hold out for those minutes . . .

A shadow danced in the steam, silhouetted by it briefly. Gone as quickly as it had appeared, only to reappear closer to him. Baiting Michael to aim erroneously, at which point the man would stage his attack.

Michael covered Danny's good ear with one hand and fired with the other. Erroneously on purpose, with the SIG's barrel tilted upward, toward the traffic jam of PVC piping forming the base of a network that ran through ductwork all the way through the building.

Ten shots, the resulting muzzle flashes carving through the mist, just as the bullets cut through the heavy plastic to send a torrent of steaming oil lubricant spraying downward.

Michael glimpsed the soldier's shadowy shape freeze briefly, then jerk about in the manner of some crazed dance. He heard grunts, gasps, groans, and pictured the oil soaking the soldier's pilfered Park Police uniform. A retching sound followed, evidence that at least some of the oil had made it into his mouth, followed by a series of high-pitched screams.

Michael thought he caught two glowing eyes glaring at him from behind a dark mask of dripping oil, and fired off remaining rounds. As the mist began to dissipate, though, he could see no fallen body, the soldier having vanished with a black viscous trail of footprints through the hospital's subbasement left in his wake.

Danny was sobbing now, eyes squeezed closed and hands clamped over his ears, as if to shut out the world.

"It's okay," Michael soothed. "He's gone."

Even as he kept an eye peeled in the direction the soldier had lumbered off.

NEW YORK-PRESBYTERIAN
LOWER MANHATTAN HOSPITAL

In 1804, New York Hospital attending physician
Dr. David Hosack accompanied Alexander Hamilton
to his fatal duel with Aaron Burr.

Pistol aimed that way, Michael kept Danny Logan protectively in his shadow, until multiple footsteps pounded their way from the elevator.

Gina Delgado led the way, stopping short when she spotted Michael through the dissipating, superheated mist. She lowered her Glock, watching Michael point toward the other end of the hall, the direction in which fake Buckland had fled.

"Go!" Delgado signaled the hostage rescue team commandos, decked out all in black and clad in body armor.

She stooped alongside Michael. "I'm sorry," she said. "I should have had the bureau take over the detail."

Michael could feel Danny shivering alongside him. A quick glance the boy's way revealed him to be pale with shock.

"We need to get him back upstairs, Gina."

"Your foot's stuck."

"Need some help there."

"It's really wedged in," Gina said, when her initial efforts at freeing Michael's prosthetic foot failed.

She continued easing it gently from side to side, until the boot holding the prosthetic came free. "Can you walk?"

"I'm fine," Michael said, standing up and putting weight on the foot to make sure it hadn't suffered any damage.

They helped Danny up together, the boy's arms dangling by his sides as if he'd forgotten how to use them. Four members of the hostage rescue team rushed back their way to join the operators flanking them protec-tively.

"Nothing," a man, whose features were obscured by his helmet and blackout visor, reported. "Just a door that didn't seal shut all the way and a trail of oil leading outside. I left two men there, just in case." The visor turned toward Michael. "Nice work."

Delgado's phone beeped, and Michael watched her check the screen. "We just got a hit on another of those dead soldiers."

"Where?"

She looked up at him, as if she couldn't believe what she'd just read. "Philadelphia, Michael. Independence Hall."

CHAPTER 27

LAKE VIEW CEMETERY, SEATTLE

**Actors Bruce Lee, Brandon Lee, and John Saxon
are among the interred.**

Jeremiah watched a convoy of his trucks roll through the gates of the sup-posedly shuttered truck depot across the country in West Virginia. The Wi-Fi he'd had installed inside the family mausoleum worked surprisingly well. He did his best thinking within these walls erected by his great-grandfather, inspired by the remains of the family members who'd pre-ceded him to the heavens, particularly the most recent two, the remains of which lay in urns occupying the mantel he'd placed his folding chair beneath. Everyone in his family had been cremated, starting with his great-grandfather, who had died literally the day he had completed the structure, not living to see the theft of the land he had cleared himself, settled, and made a home from.

All the pictures in the grid before Jeremiah were clear and crisp, al-lowing him to follow the loading process every step of the way. Since they were motion-activated, his laptop screen automatically shifted from one grid to the next all the way to the fifty-five-gallon drums and much larger, grayish-silver dry casks that had already been prepped for loading.

He'd learned that this former truck depot was about to be cleared and leveled for construction of a theme park or something, accounting for the site's abandonment and making it perfect to suit his needs as a way station.

The drums were reinforced versions of the standard fifty-five-gallon variety, repainted white because anything colored white attracted the least attention. The silvery dry casks, on the other hand, were massive cylindri-cal housing structures that stretched to thirty feet high and twelve feet in diameter. In contrast to the canisters, which were loaded into the backs of his custom-rigged eighteen-wheelers, the casks needed to be hauled on flatbeds or trailers. Today's convoy featured an equal mix of those, with shell housings for either yacht hulls or prefabricated housing already in place. The casks would otherwise attract too much attention in transit, if carted in the open, even considering that the trek to their final destination would be made exclusively on back roads. The route had already been checked to ensure the integrity of every mapped mile, a precaution further reinforced by a vehicle scouting the road ahead in case any structural surprises were encountered along the way. Hills and slick roads were to be avoided whenever possible. That was the first priority in mapping out a route, along with consideration of the detailed weather forecast, since it would take upward of a full day to reach the convoy's final destination from here.

His laptop screen switched to the actual loading area of the depot, where a bevy of workers worked an armada of forklifts and front loaders with tires as tall as he was. It looked like a battle scene with construction vehicles instead of tanks and self-propelled artillery. Jeremiah rotated among the available views of the loading process itself, impressed no end by the majestic order to it. Every move looked practiced and rehearsed, as if this were all routine when, in fact, it was anything but. This was the twelfth trip from the former truck depot to the convoy's ultimate destination.

It was also the last one.

"O Lord," he said out loud, as a giant front loader with a fork attachment effortlessly lifted one of the multiton casks and slid it inside the husk of iron built to look like the hull of a yacht, "avenge me against my persecutors."

Jeremiah 15:15.

‡‡‡

West Virginia

Camouflaged to mix with the brush atop a hillside overlooking the shuttered truck depot, Lantry moved his binoculars from left to right and back again. He had greeted the arrival of the trucks with relief, after residing atop this hill for two days in expectation of the convoy's arrival, something he'd learned from those he was serving.

Lantry was a member of the Lakota Sioux Nation. At the age of eighteen, he was still considered a boy, because he'd yet to perform a feat that made him worthy of entering manhood, even though great things were expected of him because of his uncle who had practically raised him.

His uncle was a great man and a legendary warrior who had fought in Vietnam as part of something called the Phoenix Project. Now he was dedicating his life to helping to complete the memorial to the even more legendary Crazy Horse, a massive likeness of him atop a horse carved into the side of a mountain in the Black Hills of South Dakota. It was a task that would never be finished in his uncle's lifetime, but represented one warrior paying tribute to another. Having turned seventy recently, his uncle still disappeared for stretches at a time, returning without explanation and bearing the marks and bruises he might have brought back from the jungle with him decades before.

Lantry would never be the kind of man his uncle was, but if he managed this assignment well, he would cross the formal threshold of manhood and be a source of pride for his people instead of scorn. He eased a satellite phone from his jacket pocket and thought of his uncle spending hours at a time with hammer and chisel in hand while perched on a narrow platform dangling from ropes. He switched the phone on and dialed the proper number.

"They're moving," Lantry said to the man who answered. "Send up the drones."

CHAPTER 28

LOWER MANHATTAN, NEW YORK CITY

New York City originated at the southern tip of Manhattan Island in 1624, at a point that now constitutes the present-day Financial District.

The team's safe house was actually an office building for a number of reasons, among them being that the service entrances and heavy traffic in and out would help obscure their presence, in contrast to residential establishments where people were more likely to spot a stranger. Grunwald had called ahead to say he was coming in and was in dire need of medical attention.

Rathman elected not to make a report until he knew the full scope of the man's injuries, and had gotten a more detailed explanation of how he'd failed to take out a bedridden boy. Rathman had served on enough missions with Grunwald to know he could perform the impossible. Apparently, though, the impossible did not extend to eliminating a single juvenile witness.

He heard the soft beeps of someone entering the security code outside the office door. It was modestly, though appropriately, furnished, because to leave it empty was certain to draw attention. That was standard operational procedure for any special-operations missions that required advance surveillance in foreign countries. Rathman had heard of any number of missions going south for even less of an oversight than that, but had experienced nothing of the sort during his tenure of service. That made Grunwald's failure all the more maddening, piled atop the low-probability snag of his team being noticed and then filmed in New York Harbor yesterday.

Rathman had no trouble killing kids; in point of fact, he had no trouble killing anyone at all if it was part of the mission. He saw only the ends, the means rendered moot. He'd killed so often and so many that he was numb to the process. Rathman's flesh-and-blood targets might as well have been cardboard, for the lack of remorse he felt over ending their lives.

The door swung open and Grunwald entered, still dressed in the uniform of the Park Police that was darkened black in the places where the oil had made its mark. But that was nothing compared to his exposed skin. Being doused with the noxious, steaming fluid had blistered his skin and left him with a patchwork of second-degree burns that had turned his face almost scarlet, blanched with nodules that were already leaking pus. The hot oil had also burned off swaths of his hair, exposing a patchwork of swollen, lumpy portions of his scalp. Grunwald was a big man, but Rathman was a head taller and cast his gaze downward to regard his fellow special operator.

Grunwald wore the oil like a second skin, its stench radiating off him, leaving Rathman to breathe through his mouth. One look was enough to tell Rathman the man would need skin grafts and intravenous morphine to stem the pain from his ravaged nerve endings. Rathman had wanted to wait to see the severity of Grunwald's wounds before summoning medical assistance. Now he saw that there was nothing that could be done.

"Where's medical?" Grunwald wondered, collapsing in a fabric chair that would hold that awful smell forever.

"What happened at the hospital?" Rathman asked, instead of responding.

"Some park ranger cop didn't buy my costume."

"A park ranger did this to you?"

"I told you, he was a cop, some kind of detective or something. Now, *where's fucking medical?*"

"En route. But you're going to need a lot more than they're prepared for."

"So get it."

"How about something for the pain?" Rathman asked, extracting a prescription bottle from his jacket pocket and tossing it toward the man in the chair.

"Thanks," Grunwald said, catching the bottle in midair and popping off the top.

"I mean this," Rathman said.

Grunwald looked up to see the silenced semiautomatic pistol in his hand.

Rathman fired twice. Grunwald's hands flopped downward. The pills spilled out of the prescription bottle and rattled across the floor.

"Sorry, my friend," Rathman said out loud.

PART THREE

The establishment of the National Park Service is
justified by considerations of good administration,
of the value of natural beauty as a National asset,
and of the effectiveness of outdoor life and
recreation in the production of good citizenship.

—THEODORE ROOSEVELT

CHAPTER 29

LOWER MANHATTAN, NEW YORK CITY

European settlement of New York began with
the founding of a Dutch fur-trading post in
Lower Manhattan, named Nieuw Amsterdam
(New Amsterdam) in 1626.

"Philadelphia PD SWAT is already on-site clearing the entire area, securing both the perimeter and interior," Gina said, as she and Michael raced toward the roof and the FBI chopper. "An FBI tac team will be joining them in minutes, along with the city's bomb squad, dogs included. If there are any explosives inside or around the building, they'll find them before we arrive."

"They can stage out of the Park Service headquarters beneath the Liberty Bell."

"They'll stage from outside, once the evacuation is complete. Philly has a mobile command center we can base from."

They emerged from the stairwell onto the roof to find the chopper already warming.

"Thanks for letting me tag along," Michael said. "After last night . . ."

"No thanks necessary. I need someone who knows the site inside and out," Gina told him. "I assume that's you, considering Independence Hall is part of the park system."

The helicopter would ferry her and Michael to Penn's Landing Heliport in Philadelphia, a roughly forty-minute flight. The distance between there and Independence Hall was only a mile and could be covered in five minutes with sirens and flashers going.

"No one else joining us?" Michael asked, fitting on the headset lying next to her in the rear seat.

Gina signaled the pilot to take off. "We've got a fuel problem, which means we've got a weight problem. No time to gas up. We need to get a move on."

The hospital staff had gotten Danny settled in a different room, which would now be protected by rotating members of the FBI's Hostage Rescue Team.

"The soldier who got away isn't getting very far, not with the damage done by that oil," Michael suggested. "You need to put out the word to all area hospitals, clinics, and urgent-care centers."

"Already did," Gina responded.

"What about the real Buckland?" he wondered.

Gina's eyes moistened. "NYPD found her dead in her apartment. Broken neck."

"What about the twelve Special Forces troops who supposedly died in that helicopter crash? Have you found any other connections besides Fort Bragg?"

"No, but something's off."

"Meaning . . ."

"In spite of what's at stake here, I haven't been able to access their service files. The army blames a glitch in the system pertaining to the fact that they're listed as deceased."

"It doesn't sound like you're buying that."

"Not for a minute. There's something else going on here. I've got Homeland Security trying to push the right buttons, but so far that's been a dead end, too."

Michael let that settle for a moment. "Should I ask about the latest from Independence Hall?"

"Peak attendance for Independence Hall is right around noon during the summer season," she told him. "We've still got time."

Michael checked his watch. "Not much."

"How long does a minute last, Michael?"

"What?"

"It's a question one of my instructors asked me in Army Ordnance School, and the answer's always the same."

"I'm guessing there weren't a lot of women in your class."

Gina frowned. "You're looking at her."

"And what would I find if I got a look at your file, ASAC Delgado?"

For reasons she couldn't quite grasp herself, she shared something with Michael Walker she almost never did. "That I was deployed to Iraq to help rebuild the country as part of the Army Corps of Engineers. And that's what I was doing when I was transferred to special operations to blow up bridges and roads, instead of building them."

"Interesting choice."

"I didn't make it."

"I was talking about signing up for bomb school. I'm sure you had your reasons."

"And I've never shared them with anyone."

Michael held her gaze long enough to make Gina feel uncomfortable. "How about you make me the first?"

CHAPTER 30

SAN ANTONIO, TEXAS, 1999

The city was originally a Spanish mission
and colonial outpost, dating back to 1718.

Boom!

It was a sound Gina had loved ever since she was a little girl, starting with fireworks. Her father, Rodrigo, did excavation work on big construction jobs, specializing in high-rises. Gina was ten when her mother died of cancer, the middle child between brothers, and she took up much of the rearing for her younger brother, Diego.

To reward her for those efforts, whenever possible her father would bring her to work with him. Gina was never happier than when she was around construction sites, wearing a hard hat stuffed with newspaper so it would fit on her head. The real highlights were the few occasions when she accompanied her father to blast sites. He'd explain the nuts and bolts of everything he did for her, enjoying that as much as Gina enjoyed hearing it.

She'd go home and make her own "pretend" booms and graduated to actual ones when she hit the age of twelve and figured out the best places to buy illegal fireworks for Fourth of July celebrations. Gina stockpiled them, not for the Fourth but the entire year to come. Draining the black powder from the biggest ones and blowing up trash cans, dumpsters, and abandoned cars with the resulting product. She'd hear her father's words in her head as he fished the wire in place and twisted it around the detonator, graduating from fuses to remote detonation thanks to electronic kits she purchased at Radio Shack the way her friends graduated from dolls to boys.

Fashioning her explosives made her feel closer to her father and was the only time she didn't miss her mother. It was just a hobby, her father not only allowing it but eventually providing real det cord for her concoctions when she hit fifteen. That summer she apprenticed with him on a jobsite; union rules kept her from the proximity of the blasts, but hearing them was almost as good. The feel of the world shaking, feeling so small and weak compared to the violent blast her father had just triggered. The sight of the debris cloud kicked up into the air, spreading outward, the final result revealed once it cleared.

She was so consumed with taking care of Diego that Gina barely acknowledged her older brother, Luis, taking up with a vicious, rising San Antonio street gang called Tango Blast. He seemed happy to wear their colors, sometimes not coming home for days at a time.

Until one day when he didn't come at all.

Gina overheard the police telling her father how it had gone down, how he'd been ordered to perform a hit on a rival gang leader and ended up getting shot himself before he even got his gun out. The members of Tango Blast came to his funeral in their colors and boots, standing stiff and still; eyeing her, Gina thought.

It was actually Diego they were looking at, then the same age Luis had been when he joined the gang. The gang came calling, and Diego hid under the porch steps shaking until they left. That night he told Gina he was going to run away to avoid ending up like his older brother.

She told him she'd handle it.

Gina walked right into the gang's headquarters in East San Antonio, located in a building that had once housed a laundromat on a block scheduled to be razed. She pleaded her case to the gang leader, who told her that if she ever came back every member of the gang would have his way with her, him twice. He told her he was cutting her a break this one time out of respect for Luis.

Gina walked out with the certainty that she'd be back.

She knew where her father kept his secret stash of dynamite for off-the-books excavation jobs he did in order to put college money away for his three, now two, kids. She took three sticks from the stash, wired them together in the biggest bomb she'd ever rigged. Then she showed up at the Tango Blast headquarters in the guise of a pizza-delivery girl, and tucked a warming bag packed with the day's real special into a sewer grate right in front of the building.

Gina didn't trigger the blast until the four bangers who were inside the building when she first arrived had left, dragging the grate down and padlocking it before taking their leave. It was six o'clock at night, her father and brother no doubt wondering where she was. Gina felt her heart hammering against her rib cage when she extended the antenna on the detonator, flipped the switch to the on position, and readied her thumb.

Pressing the button was the greatest moment of her life until the next one, when the blast came. Gina felt the wave like a hot brush of wind on a steamy summer day, felt her skin prickle with something that felt like electricity. She heard the explosion a flicker of an instant after she saw the building erupt in that magical debris cloud, close enough to the blast to wear a sheen of it home over her clothes. She should have fled right away, but she couldn't, drinking in the scent of char and the pungent scent of clay she'd added as a stabilizer. The lingering odor from the nitroglycerin was sweet, reminding Gina somehow of cotton candy and popcorn. She'd only intended on damaging the building, but the overpressure resulting from the containment of the blast in such a small space reduced the entire front half of the former laundromat to rubble.

It looked like somebody had taken a chain saw to the building and cut it right down the middle. And if Tango Blast didn't get the message about leaving her brother alone, then she'd come back and do it again with them packed inside.

At least, that's what she told herself, not really thinking clearly. One girl scaring off the most dangerous street gang in the city? It seemed so nonsensical as to be absurd. But she'd gotten away with it, and Tango Blast now had bigger things on their minds than dragging Diego into their ranks.

Then, a few nights later, the doorbell rang, and when her father answered she heard the words that would change her life forever.

"FBI, Mr. Delgado," a voice in the foyer said. "I need to speak to your daughter."

Her father ushered a tall, thin man wearing a suit into their small house's den. The man took a chair directly in front of the couch where Gina was seated. Her father remained standing, hands by his hips, fingers flexing the way they did in the final anxious moments before it was time to trigger a blast.

"I'm Special Agent Roderick Rust," the man greeted, "and I'm in charge of the bureau's National Gang Intelligence Center. Have you ever heard of it?"

Gina shook her head, which suddenly felt heavy.

Rust smiled thinly. "Don't worry, no one has. We're not official yet. Maybe someday, but not yet." He leaned forward in his chair, shrinking the distance between them. "One of the NGIC's primary targets is a gang operating right here in San Antonio that's been spreading across the country. Tango Blast. Have you heard of them?"

Gina managed a nod.

Rust nodded, too. "I know the gang's role in the death of your older brother and I know about their intention to enlist your younger brother in their ranks, too. Would you like to know how I know that, Gina?"

She tried to shake her head, but it wouldn't move.

Rust continued anyway. "We had their East San Antonio headquarters under surveillance, both recording devices and cameras planted where nobody could find them. I don't have to tell you what those cameras picked up last week, do I?"

This time, Gina managed a single shake of her head.

"It took a while for us to ID you from the footage," Rust continued. "It's important for you to know that you're in no danger from Tango Blast, Gina. As we speak, the gang members in question are being rounded up and arrested, a major sweep we had to accelerate on account of your interference in our investigation."

"I'm sorry."

"So am I. We were building an even stronger case, much of which you blew up."

"I'm sorry," Gina repeated, her voice dry and cracking.

"I'm glad you're sorry, Gina. I understand why you did what you did. And the truth is, it wouldn't have been necessary, and your older brother would still be alive, if the bureau had gotten off its collective ass when I sounded the warning three years ago. That's why I'm here, to make that right."

Gina looked toward her father, who stood rigid, his eyes not seeming to blink. His "blast face," she had called it since she was a little girl.

"Are you going to arrest me?" Gina managed to utter.

"No," Rust told her, "I'm going to be your mentor."

CHAPTER 31

PHILADELPHIA

In 1682, Philadelphia became the first city in the
Americas to guarantee religious freedom.

"And now I'm his ASAC," Delgado finished. "He arranged for me to attend the University of Texas at San Antonio on a full ROTC scholarship. From there, I worked toward qualifying to become a combat engineer over the intervening summers by doing hands-on demolition training at Fort Hood, Texas."

"Then came Iraq," Michael picked up, "originally with the Army Corps of Engineers."

"Officially, I never left that post."

Delgado's phone rang, keeping Michael from pressing the matter further. He felt the chopper begin its descent, Penn's Landing Heliport sharpening into focus from a mere speck in the Philadelphia skyline. He noticed that Delgado was wearing a blank expression as she lowered the phone from her ear.

"Tom Fenton is dead, too," she reported. "The team I sent to his house found him shot twice in the head."

‡‡‡

A big black SUV was waiting for them on the tarmac of the heliport, courtesy of the FBI's Philadelphia field office. Michael and Delgado both climbed into the back, and the driver tore off before they'd gotten their doors closed all the way.

They reached the perimeter of the Independence Hall complex in barely five minutes, siren screaming and lights flashing the whole way. The area had already been cleared and the streets closed off in what was clearly a textbook, multijurisdictional response. As their SUV parked in the middle of the shuttered Chestnut Street, adjacent to the hall itself, Michael saw that the area was swimming with uniformed officers, tactical operatives wearing body armor, and plainclothes personnel who'd donned windbreakers instead. He saw FBI, ATF, and even DEA personnel milling about the mobile command center. This had been an all-hands-on-deck call, explaining why any federal law enforcement agency with a presence in the city would be on-site.

Michael stayed close to Delgado, and this time she didn't tell him to back off for want of a proper security clearance. He followed her to a man wearing a flak jacket beneath his FBI-issue windbreaker with a dangling badge that identified him as the SAC, special agent in charge, of the bureau's Philadelphia office.

"We found the bomb," he told her, wiping the sweat from his brow with a handkerchief.

✝✝✝

"I didn't want to put the word out on the radio, because of the news networks listening on our channel," the SAC, whose last name was Wyman, continued. "City bomb squad is assessing right now. They say we're looking at a timing device, but they haven't located the countdown clock yet."

"It could be internal."

"We're jamming all cell phone frequencies to stop them from detonating the bomb that way. We can watch them defuse the mother on the security feed inside."

"No," Delgado ordered, "tell them to stand down and wait for me. Tell them not to breathe until I'm inside."

Wyman looked as if he was about to protest.

"This isn't my first rodeo, SAC Wyman. And my authority with the Joint Terrorism Task Force extends as far as I want to take it. So please tell the men inside to hold in place. Tell them I'm coming in."

✝✝✝

Michael watched Wyman hand Delgado a walkie-talkie.

"With cell phone service shut down, this is our best means to communicate. It's preset to the proper channel," he said, not bothering to offer one to Michael.

Delgado handed it back to him. "Change it. Whoever planted the bomb would know the frequency you've cleared. They could remote-detonate the bomb that way as a backup, with cell service down."

Wyman didn't argue, just accepted the walkie-talkie back and did as Delgado instructed, then brought his own device up to his lips. "All personnel, this is Special Agent in Charge Wyman. Change your channel to sixteen. Repeat, change your channel to sixteen."

Delgado took her walkie-talkie back from him and clipped it to her belt and then turned toward Michael.

"I can take things from here, Special Agent Walker."

"And just when we were becoming a team . . ."

"Last time I checked, the national parks were your specialty, not bombs."

"Last time I checked, Independence Hall is part of the National Park System."

Delgado turned her gaze on the building that had stood since 1753. "Then let me do my job and keep it that way."

CHAPTER 32

INDEPENDENCE HALL, PHILADELPHIA

The Pennsylvania legislature loaned out the famous
Assembly Room for the meetings of the Second
Continental Congress, which is when the Declaration
of Independence was debated and signed.

A Philadelphia PD SWAT team member in full tactical gear opened the majestic entrance to Independence Hall as Gina approached. From the doorway, she could see that the vestibule and stairwell leading upstairs were swimming with the rest of his team.

"I want the building cleared of all but essential personnel," she instructed, leaving no room for discussion in her voice. "That means bomb squad and no one else."

The man regarded the FBI ID dangling from her neck. "You sure about that, ma'am?"

"It's ASAC Delgado and, yes, I'm sure." When the officer still appeared reluctant, Gina resumed, "If that bomb goes off, I want to minimize loss of life. Clear?"

The man nodded, her point driven home. He gestured to the left, toward the majestic door leading into the Assembly Room, where the head of the bomb squad was standing, his features mostly obscured by his tactical helmet and lowered visor.

"Lieutenant Barletta, ASAC Delgado," he greeted, as she approached. "What we're dealing with looks pretty clear-cut."

Gina saw four men in identical gear clustered behind him and a fifth closer to the majestic room's brick fireplace, which she didn't believe was still in working order. Truth be told, she really didn't know this facility well at all, having been inside only once before, as a young girl on a family trip. She followed Barletta inside, remembering the Assembly Hall as being considerably bigger, sprawling on the level of the Senate chamber in the U.S. Capitol Building. Everything appears in much grander scale to a child, a sense carried in memory no matter what she had learned to the contrary in the years since.

"We've got a timing mechanism and what looks to be a standard detonator wired to the kind of plastic explosives I've seen all too often," Barletta explained.

"C-4?"

Barletta nodded. "Mounds of it affixed to the interior of the chimney, connected by standard monofilament wiring and attached to a detonator working off a trio of microprocessors: one for the timer, one for the detonator, and one for the trigger."

"Clear-cut, like you said, Lieutenant," Gina told him, not adding what his evaluation had really conjured in her mind. "Now, how about I take a look?" she added before he could interject anything.

Gina's memory of the room's layout and furnishings, meanwhile, was surprisingly on the mark, although she recalled darker green table coverings than was actually the case. Gina noted that the coverings that drew the most direct sunlight streaming through the windows beneath the like-colored valances had suffered considerably more fading. There weren't as many tables as she remembered, all of them covered with books, quills, and parchment paper that were historically accurate, neatly arranged upon their tops. A glass chandelier, recently refurbished according to the intelligence she'd received while speeding to the scene, hung from the ceiling over the center of the room. The elegant carvings and moldings had all been meticulously restored to their original condition, the room so pristine and historically accurate that the year might as well have been 1776, if not for the electric switches, outlets, and lights. But the chandelier still had candles wedged into its dozen holders, which left Gina picturing someone lighting them before each session in centuries past.

She detected a slight humming that would have been cause for concern, had she not spotted an air exchanger and purifier tucked into the Assembly Room's front corner. It was obtrusive and broke the historical illusion the room otherwise clung to firmly, but such devices were employed in a multitude of government buildings post-COVID-19, especially those sites that attracted large numbers of tourists. She noted a fine mist emanating from the machine's unseen vents—evidence, Gina suspected, of a clogged filter that was pushing microscopic dust particles back into the air instead of trapping them. That would also account for the noise, given that the machine's automated fan would have been running at a higher than normal speed to do a job the clogged filter prevented it from doing.

Gina moved to the chimney right up next to the bomb squad tech who was holding a thermal pole camera. He handed her a big cell phone connected to the camera by Bluetooth and crouched on an awkward angle to thread it back up the chimney. The pole camera had originally been designed to plug directly into a smartphone accessory port and allow users to peer into completely dark areas and find concealed persons by heat signature. The Department of Homeland Security had been responsible for tweaking the tool to allow for a bird's-eye view of a similarly concealed explosive device, to be utilized by first responders not necessarily schooled in bomb detection or defusal.

"Dogs found the bomb," Barletta explained, moving in step with her. "We cleared them out before you got here."

"This the only hit you got?" Gina asked him, recalling that an explosive dogs couldn't detect had been used on Liberty Island.

"One and only that turned up in the sweep," Barletta confirmed. "And we did multiple sweeps with different dogs just to make sure."

Gina checked the phone she was holding. "Nothing yet," she told the tech wielding the thermal pole camera.

"Our first thought was someone scaled down inside the chimney to set the bomb, using the roof to gain access," Barletta explained. "But it turns out the chimney's sealed, just an ornament now."

"A pretty dangerous ornament, all the same, Lieutenant. Wait, stop! There it is," she said, regarding the bomb on the phone screen. Then she turned toward the chimney. "Narrow space, close confines. Only one person here small enough to shimmy inside."

CHAPTER 33

INDEPENDENCE SQUARE, PHILADELPHIA

Independence National Historic Park was established on June 28, 1948.

Michael stood silently in Independence Square, near Walnut Street, amid a gathering of park and armed law enforcement rangers responsible for securing Independence Hall. Tension was thick among all the law enforcement gathered on the scene, but was thickest for those for whom the hall was a part of their everyday lives.

He gazed across the plaza. Had the bomb been located yet? Had Delgado and the Philadelphia PD bomb squad begun work at defusing it?

Michael couldn't stand still any longer, couldn't stomach doing nothing. So he drifted back through the clutter toward the security perimeter that had been set up on the south side of Walnut Street just short of Washington Square. For distraction as much as anything, he scanned the crowd in search of anything awry. His mind conjured the notion of spotting someone clutching a handheld detonator, ready to trigger the blast when either whim or timing dictated.

With all the streets closed off, the area was limited to pedestrian traffic, which allowed Michael to notice a legless man pushing himself along on a skate-wheel platform, heading down the center of Walnut Street through a cluster of spectators who moved aside for him. Since losing his foot, he had paid more attention to the disabled, especially those far less equipped to manage the kind of daily living that everyone else took for granted. The man on the skate-wheel platform, like a large skateboard or small dolly, could have been a war veteran who lost his legs serving in Iraq. Maybe, Michael mused to himself, he had served with Gina Delgado.

That was when he caught a glimpse of blue material peeking out beneath the legless man's shapeless khaki-colored pants, and felt his insides tighten. Michael picked up his pace, drawing closer, trying to get a better look. A sliver opened up in the crowd, and his next glimpse left him all but certain he was looking at a National Park Service royal-blue maintenance uniform beneath the disabled man's raggedy clothes.

Michael was jogging now, closing the gap, fighting against the urge to scream "Stop!" or something comparable. The man on the skate-wheel platform seemed to be picking up his pace, the lone figure heading away from the spectacle instead of toward it. The crowd continued to part to allow him to pass, and Michael quickened his pursuit through the same channel.

He had closed to within ten feet when the figure spun suddenly. The wheels of the skate-wheel platform screeched to halt as the man extended the legs he'd tucked beneath him and a pistol flashed in his hand.

‣•◦•‣

INDEPENDENCE HALL, PHILADELPHIA

In 1816, the city of Philadelphia purchased the entire
block that Independence Hall sits on today in order
to stop a real estate scheme to develop the State
House Yard, which would have included demolishing
Independence Hall.

Gina fit the tactical helmet over her head and tightened the strap, then
tested the built-in LED light, which glowed as bright as a spot. Lieutenant
Barletta had already opened the squad's bomb-defusal case, revealing the
tools of a trade she was extremely well-versed in. The people who knew
how to set and rig explosives were normally the best-skilled at defusing
them; they just seldom got the opportunity to practice that skill. But Gina
had, multiple times in Iraq on all manner of IEDs and suicide vests.

Gina switched on her light. Then she checked the width and depth of
the chimney again, easing herself backward to loosen the straps of her
bomb vest and then peel it off.

"Not a good idea," Barletta cautioned.

"Won't do me any good if it blows, anyway. Get your men out of here.
Just leave one behind to play nursemaid for me," Gina told him, referring
to the tech who places requested tools in the hand of the man or woman
defusing the bomb.

"That would be me," Barletta said, then turned to his men. "The rest of
you make tracks out of here. That's an order."

"And back everybody up beyond Independence Square fast," Gina
added.

"We set the perimeter at Chestnut Street," one of the techs said.

"You know how far glass and brick fragments can fly?" Gina asked them. "I've seen the damage that kind of debris can do to a person when traveling at a thousand miles an hour. Push the perimeter back farther."

Her tone left no room for argument, and Barletta again signaled his men to take their leave.

Gina squeezed her way into the chimney of the hall where the Declaration of Independence and Constitution had been debated and signed, shimmying up until she was facing the bomb. The nagging feeling of something being off here struck her again. She hadn't seen the complete files of the twelve supposedly dead special operators, but it stood to reason all of them would have been too big to manage the squeeze she just had. So how had one of them been able to plant the bomb in such a tight space?

Eyeing the bomb itself, Gina returned to the task at hand. The device looked surprisingly rudimentary. She would have designed a housing, transistor mechanism, and detonator that weren't so plainly obvious. This one had just three simple wires—red, white, and blue—no more complex than the device she had rigged at the Tango Blast headquarters in East San Antonio as a teenager. She didn't figure special operators shopped at Radio Shack, and the chain had long been out of business, anyway.

Maybe she was missing something else. Maybe the device only appeared to be simple and crude to throw her, or anyone else defusing the bomb, off track.

Gina used a tool that looked like something lifted off a dental hygienist's tray to feel around the bomb's housing to see if there was a wire that would trip if she pried it off. Finding none, she tucked the first tool away and eased a shorter one with a thinner head from her pocket. She fit it into the first of four grooves on the housing and popped it free, repeating the process three more times while holding her breath each time.

She steadied herself with a deep breath after that and positioned the fingers of both hands on either side of the housing and pulled it straight toward her face, careful not to contact any internal component of the bomb. The device looked even more rudimentary than she'd anticipated. Its internal clock was no more than a mechanical wheel-like knob that would turn with a click at regular intervals until it lodged in a deeper groove. At the bottom of that groove sat a microprocessor that would then set off a charge to the capacitor acting as a trigger. The resulting electrical signal would ignite the fuse, triggering the blast.

Contemplating the blast itself made Gina realize what had been plaguing her. Planting the bomb inside a confined space secured by brick would contain the blast force and prevent the kind of massive structural damage that resulted when a blast fed off itself as it widened out into a cone. That was what had happened in the open space of Liberty Island when the pedestal had blown. The damage to the Assembly Hall would be severe, yes, but Gina could think of a dozen ways to plant the same amount of plastic explosives to take out much of Independence Hall.

Gina dismissed that thinking for now. "Scissors," she called to Barletta, stretching a hand downward and feeling him slip a pair into her grasp.

She fit a small clip-on device that resembled a hairpin into the next notch the turn wheel was advancing toward. Then she chose the moment it clicked into place, and froze, to cut the red wire, which was the ground, followed by the blue.

If she'd missed anything here, she was about to find out. The final wire, the white one, carried the charge itself. If she'd missed a backup trigger, clipping that wire would set off the explosives, destroying a second national treasure twenty-four hours after the Statue of Liberty had been toppled.

Gina reviewed the mechanics of the bomb again and traced the connections to the C-4 itself, confirming her initial conclusions. Then she checked everything again in reverse, searching for anything she might have missed.

If I set a bomb to go off this way, what would I do to fool the person defusing it?

She ran through a checklist in her head, but none of those elements were present. Gina fit her scissors into place with the small, razor-sharp blades separated. Then she closed her eyes as she squeezed the handle together.

Click.

That was it. The bomb had been defused. She steadied her breathing, gave it yet another once-over to make sure the job was indeed done, and then shimmied back down and started to squeeze out of the chimney through the fireplace.

Barletta helped her to her feet, and took the helmet she'd just removed.

"Nice work, ASAC Delgado. Congratulations," he said, clapping her on the back.

Gina wasn't listening. The Special Forces troops from Fort Bragg, or whoever was behind them, had killed Tom Fenton after he'd given up Danny Logan. Thanks to Fenton, they knew the boy was an eyewitness, knew he'd filmed four operatives on that stolen Park Police boat out in the harbor just before the blast was triggered. That meant they knew they could be IDed, in which case . . .

In which case . . .

They would have known the bureau was on to them, having traced their identities back to that staged helicopter crash in the Great Smoky Mountains. And one of those special operators had been captured on an Independence Hall camera barely two hours ago, while she and Michael Walker were still in New York.

"I don't think so," she told Barletta. "We're missing something."

CHAPTER 35

INDEPENDENCE SQUARE,
PHILADELPHIA

Construction on the building started in 1732.

Michael saw the squarish pistol coming up and around toward him. He was already in motion. Instinct driving him, he'd launched his prosthetic foot forward, and it connected with the man's wrist just as his finger found the trigger.

Bang!

An errant shot fired up and to the right left Michael's ears ringing, the gun separated from the man's grasp as he tried to lurch all the way to a standing position. Michael pounced before he could, pinning the man beneath him. The man's frame felt like banded steel. Michael felt virtually weightless as the man pushed and shoved to free himself, Michael left struggling to maintain the upper hand. No way to draw his own gun and fearing more that the man might find it first.

He must have been one of the dead soldiers, quite possibly the one who'd set the bomb. Then why was he still in the area? Why hadn't he fled already?

Michael's mind raced between thoughts, his consciousness clashing with the instincts driving him. Feeling the man gaining the advantage and with his pistol rendered useless, he found his hands closing on the sides of the skate-wheel platform as a grip like iron started to tighten on his throat. He recorded the fact that the National Park Service maintenance uniform was contained under a baggy pair of grime-riddled pants in the moment he brought the platform down hard on the man's face.

Contents of a jacket pocket or small rucksack scattered around him, clacking to the pavement. Michael brought the platform up again, and was halfway into a third strike when the man's feet slammed into him, propelling him backward with the platform separated from his grasp. He hit the pavement hard, but maintained the presence of mind to finally draw his gun, angling it on the man now scrambling for the pistol the initial impact had stripped from his grasp.

Heavy footsteps pounded everywhere, shouts and screams coming from the law enforcement rangers Michael had just been standing among, the downed man's gun trained on him for a brief moment before shots rang out.

Michael smelled the stench of cordite from the gunfire, saw the thin wisps of gun smoke fluttering in the air. Saw the man's body punctured with holes leaking red, his eyes open and sightless. Saw the objects that had scattered around him when he'd wielded the skate-wheel platform as a weapon.

Candles.

CHAPTER 36

INDEPENDENCE HALL, PHILADELPHIA

The Liberty Bell, with its famous crack, was displayed on the ground floor of the hall from the 1850s until 1976, and is now on display across the street in the Liberty Bell Center.

"The candles!" Gina heard Michael cry out, as he burst into the Assembly Room. "It's the candles!"

He was clutching a handful of them in his grasp, sending her gaze to the chandelier and the like number wedged into the holders there. Same size, same color, same consistency—same everything.

With one crucial exception.

"Plastic explosives," she said more to herself, understanding the presence of one of the special operators in Independence Hall earlier that morning.

Plastic explosives molded into the shape of candles as either a fallback plan or the plan all along. Gina stopped short of considering how Michael had come by them.

She looked toward Barletta. "Too high for the dogs to uncover or recognize."

"Where's the trigger?" Barletta asked. "What's the trigger?"

A shaft of light struck him as he said that.

"Oh my God," she realized. "It's the windows. . . ."

"You mean the glass?" from Michael.

She swung toward him, gaze lifting upward. "No, the light! It hits the candles and—"

"Sunlight as the detonator," Michael interrupted.

"Or the heat it generates." Gina's eyes remained rooted on the chandelier.

"But not enough explosives to blow the whole building." She looked toward Barletta, eyes widening. "Your visor," she said, pointing.

It was still lowered over the lieutenant's face, the plastic smeared with a chalky residue she hadn't noticed before. Barletta pulled the tactical helmet off and inspected the visor.

"What about it?" he asked, not noticing anything awry.

Gina moved toward the air purifier in the room's far front corner. "I should have known as soon as I saw it, should have realized."

"Realized what?" Michael asked, before Barletta had a chance to.

She yanked the machine's plug from the outlet, ridding the room of the annoying din it had been making. "The dust. The machine was rigged to fill the air with it."

"Oh my God," Barletta said, eyes sweeping the room in search of something he couldn't see.

Gina swung toward Michael. "The candles explode, igniting the dust particles that have collected in the air and triggering a blast powerful enough to turn all of Independence Hall to rubble."

"So let's just remove the candles."

Gina ignored him, tracing the sunlight starting to pour through the bank of windows on the building's eastern side, four of them. No drapes, shutters, or blinds to close—just the decorative valances. Michael followed her thinking, as the sunlight crept ever closer to the dangling chandelier.

"They'll be rigged with a trip wire. Take one from its holder and they all blow." She stepped into a swath of sunlight streaming in through the nearest window. "We need to find something to cover the glass, shut out the light."

Barletta gazed through the window, into the sun. "Like what?"

"Anything we can find. I don't know. . . ."

"I do," said Michael.

He rushed to the nearest window and mounted the sill, keeping the weight off his prosthetic foot until he found a delicate balance.

"Walker, what are you doing?"

Michael was feeling about the wall behind the valance. "Trying to find the security grille."

"The *what*?"

"Landmarks like this were fitted with them when the National Park Service was put in charge," he explained, still feeling about beneath a curved metal sheeting behind the top of the valance. "Perforated, lightweight Kevlar that coils upward into the top mount when not in use." He found what he'd been searching for and adjusted his angle to work the release. "And slides downward when needed."

Michael pulled the catch and the Kevlar rolled downward into place over the window, secured by a weighted base at the bottom. He moved on to the next window, while Delgado and Barletta moved to the remaining two.

He checked the angle of the sun, saw its rising angle flirting with the chandelier through all three of the other windows. Understanding the operation of the security grilles better now, Michael located the second one almost immediately and let it uncoil. Barletta had managed to work his into place as well, leaving only Delgado's.

"I can't find the catch!" she called out to Michael.

He thrust himself up next to her on the narrow sill, feeling the housing of his prosthetic nearly give from the sudden weight torque. Wobbly now, he stretched a hand upward to feel for the catch, noting that the sunlight streaming through the window was starting to reflect off the chandelier's curved glass. Inches from the candles themselves, detonation mere moments away.

Michael slipped, about to lose his footing, when Delgado grabbed him.

"Hurry," she implored.

No longer worried about tumbling off the sill with her holding him, Michael stretched his right hand as high as it would go, and was standing on his toes when he found the catch and pulled. The security grille uncoiled downward, covering the whole of the window just as the sun was about to reach the candles rising from the chandelier.

"Good work," Delgado said, still holding on to him.

"Thanks for the assist."

‡‡‡

Delgado deemed it safer to have the entire chandelier removed intact than to risk trying to remove the plastic explosives molded into the shape of candles. Barletta's crew was summoned back to handle that effort, following Gina's instructions every step of the way right until the moment the chandelier was lowered to the floor. She then personally affixed the candles into place with tape from the bomb-defusal kit. An armored vehicle was then backed right up to the entrance of Independence Hall, the chandelier eased into the back by four of Barletta's men.

He climbed into the back with them while they held it steady.

"Thanks, ASAC Delgado."

"Call me Gina, Lou."

Moments later the armored vehicle slid off slowly to triumphant cheers and applause from the bevy of law enforcement personnel still gathered on Independence Square.

"Take a bow," Michael said to Delgado, as she drew her phone from a pocket.

Michael watched her check a text message that must have just come in.

"Not so fast, Walker," she said, still regarding it. "We just got a hit on another of those dozen soldiers: the Gateway Arch in St. Louis."

CHAPTER 37

PHILADELPHIA

Philadelphia is home to the nation's first African
American church, Mother Bethel AME, founded in
1794 by Richard Allen, a former slave.

Before Michael could respond, Gina called Special Agent John Milton.

"Paradise," she said, interrupting his greeting, "who have we got at the Gateway Arch?"

"Pulling it up on my computer. Dan Massori, from the St. Louis field office," Milton resumed, after a brief pause. "I know him. We went through the academy together. He's good."

"He better be: another of the not-so-dead special operators was caught by a security camera there yesterday, disguised as a Park Service maintenance man, just like at Independence Hall. Patch me through to Massori at the site."

While waiting for Paradise to patch her through to Special Agent Dan Massori, Gina asked Michael to fill her in on the broad strokes of the Arch's history. The Arch took its name from St. Louis's role as "the Gateway to the West" during the westward expansion of the country in the nineteenth century. The gleaming archway, now part of Gateway Arch National Park, commemorated the Louisiana Purchase, in 1803, and the subsequent opening of the West to settlers following the Lewis and Clark Expedition, in the early 1800s, which had commenced nearby. The park also included the Old Courthouse, where the enslaved Dred Scott first sued for his freedom in a legal case that would go all the way to the U.S. Supreme Court in the middle of the nineteenth century, amplifying the debate over slavery as the country moved closer to civil war. Access to the complex came via an underground entrance that fed into the belowground visitor center for the ride to the curved Arch's top.

"By the way, how'd you know about those security screens inside Independence Hall?" she asked him, when he was finished.

"Since ISB agents can be sent pretty much anywhere at any time, we have to be familiar with all the sites the Park Service is responsible for," he told her.

"Can you tell me more about the Gateway Arch?"

"What else would you like to know?"

"The kind of logistics someone needs to blow it up."

She watched Michael nod, likely trying to determine where to start. "Well, it's roughly the height of two football fields, six hundred and thirty feet, and the distance between its legs is equal to that. Inside are two tram lines, each of which consists of four cars that can carry up to five seated people at a time. Trams because the curved design took elevators off the table."

"Okay," she said, urging him on.

"The tram ride to the viewing platform at the top of the Arch takes four minutes. Sixteen windows face east and the same number face west, for views of the city, river, and surrounding land. Underground, at the base of the Arch, the Museum of Westward Expansion inside the visitor center features displays showing what life was like in the 1800s as well as exhibits on the construction of the Arch."

"What's it made out of?"

"Stainless-steel outer skin with an inner skin of carbon steel. It's the tallest memorial in the U.S. and the tallest stainless-steel monument in the world."

"No inner core?" Gina asked, thinking of how the pedestal holding the Statue of Liberty had been rigged to blow.

"No, the inner and outer steel skins are joined to form a composite structure. If you're looking for the best places to rig explosives, I'd say the viewing platform at the top or the visitor center at the base that contains the museum."

"How big is the visitor center?"

"Seventy thousand square feet."

"High ceilings?"

"Relatively."

"Lots of oxygen to feed off, then."

Gina considered the potential of that option, along with the viewing platform. Planting the bomb in the museum would cause the most overall damage, the blast percussion following the tram line up along each of the legs. But taking out the viewing platform, rupturing it, could lead to the destruction of the entire interior. The way the Arch was constructed made it a bomber's dream, because there was little venting and plenty of space for the explosive gases to expand and feed off themselves after the initial detonation.

"How many can the viewing platform accommodate at once?" she asked Michael.

"Around a hundred and sixty, although that number gets stretched a bit because of families and school groups, especially this time of year."

Gina felt a chill. "Families and school groups . . ."

Michael nodded grimly. "The insurance company underwriting the project estimated that thirteen people would die during the construction," he added.

"And did they?"

He shook his head. "Plenty of injuries, some of them serious, but no deaths." Michael stopped, then started again. "When the last part at the top of the Arch was brought in position to link the legs, many people predicted that it would collapse. They were wrong, too."

"Well, let's hope we're wrong about it being the third target."

She heard Paradise's voice over her phone's speaker.

"I've got Special Agent Dan Massori on the line from St. Louis, Chief."

- - - - -

CHAPTER 38

GATEWAY ARCH NATIONAL PARK, ST. LOUIS

Dick Bowser, who had dropped out of college so he could enlist during World War II, was given two weeks to build an elevator-style system for the Arch.

"Special Agent Massori," Delgado started, putting her phone on speaker and centering it between her and Michael, "this is Gina Delgado, assistant special agent in charge of the New York field office. I'm running point for the Joint Terrorism Task Force on the investigation into the Statue of Liberty bombing."

"I'd like to say it's nice to be speaking with you," Massori said, sounding young to Michael, "but . . ."

"I have ISB Special Agent Michael Walker here with me."

"Nice to meet you, Agent," Michael chimed in.

"Your law enforcement rangers have been great to work with, sir. They were waiting for me when I arrived this morning and gave me the grand tour."

"Things have changed considerably since then," Delgado told Massori. "We've confirmed ID of a man who is part of a suspect group on the premises on several occasions in the past week, including yesterday morning."

"And when you say 'suspect group,' I take that to mean . . ."

"Persons believed to be connected to both the bombing on Liberty Island yesterday and attempted bombing at Independence Hall in Philadelphia earlier today," Delgado told Massori.

A heavy pause fell over the line.

"There've been no reports issued on that one."

"Because the explosive device was just defused," Delgado said, not bothering to elaborate further. "That's where we're calling you from."

"So the fact that a suspect has been spotted here several times going back a week would have given him ample opportunity to plant explosives."

"That's what we're afraid of, Agent Massori."

"Oh," the agent said suddenly, drawing the word out.

"What?" Michael and Delgado asked him together.

"I reviewed the maintenance logs as soon as I got here this morning, before the Arch opened for business. All sixteen tram cars, eight each on the north and south sides, have undergone routine maintenance during that same time frame."

"Where are you?" Michael said toward the speaker.

"About to climb inside one of the trams to do another check of the viewing platform," Massori said, a nervous edge now clear in his voice. "Not too crowded here for a Sunday. People must be spooked by what happened at the Statue of Liberty yesterday."

They have every right to be, Michael thought, remaining silent.

He watched Delgado raise the phone to her lips, but she left it on speaker so he could continue listening in. "I want to see what you're seeing. I'm ending the call so you can call me back at this number with your video on."

"Roger that."

"But before you call her back," Michael started, "I want you to call the law enforcement park rangers down in the visitor center and tell them to shut it down and begin an orderly evacuation. Is that clear?"

"Yes, orderly evacuation."

"No call for panic. Then have the extra park rangers stationed outside establish a perimeter covering all of the park area. Clear?"

"Yes, clear."

"How many times did the Missouri State Highway Patrol bring their dogs in?" Gina asked him.

"It was city PD actually. Two dogs, four sweeps of the visitor center, viewing platform, and all the tram cars."

"Okay," she said, "make the call to evacuate and secure and call me back with your camera on."

She ended the call. Barely a minute later her phone buzzed with the incoming FaceTime call from Massori. This time she could see his face, a bit off center and absurdly large because he was holding the phone too close. He had olive skin and curly hair, looking to be of Middle Eastern descent.

"Okay," she started. "Where are you?"

He jerked the camera around so that the screen filled with the sleek capsule he'd be riding upward. Those cars ran the tram tracks up and down in a constant loop. Michael knew that the design of the Arch had been complete, and construction about to commence, before the best way of ferrying people from bottom to top and back again had been determined. Elevators were the first and most obvious option, but the arch's sloped construction rendered them infeasible because no one had ever built a curved elevator shaft.

So the designers, led by a man named Dick Bowser, had opted for a different method based on the form and function of a Ferris wheel. The process so fascinated him that Michael had committed Bowser's own words to memory:

"The eight small capsules, used in each of the two Arch trains, are similar to the barrels used in cement mixers. Each train capsule has a five-foot-diameter barrel that is open on the front and closed on the back. The back has a center pivot shaft, and surrounding the open front there is a frame with rollers, so the barrel can rotate within the frame that is supported by wheels running in the channel-shaped tracks."

Michael also knew that the capsules, the tram cars, were powered by a heavy-duty machine with cables, counterweights, and all of the safety features of a modern high-speed passenger elevator.

"I'm entering the car now," Massori reported.

Michael watched the glass doors slide open, Massori's face bulging off the screen as he entered. Those glass doors provided the only view of the sloped shaft through the duration of the ride; there were no windows on the car's sides or rear. Five seats inside, with Massori as the only passenger.

Delgado said, "Okay, get me closer to the seats. Upholstered?"

"No, solid plastic or some kind of composite. They don't detach," Massori told Delgado, lowering his phone to demonstrate.

"Closer," Delgado ordered, "and run your hand across the entire seat. Do you feel anything lumpy, hard, or out of place inside?"

"No, nothing," he reported. "I'll check again."

Michael watched him repeat the process after the car rocked into its four-minute climb up to the viewing platform.

"Nothing, ASAC Delgado."

The capsule was affixed to the tram rail with brackets that allowed it to tilt at a variety of angles through the climb. With Massori as the only passenger, and his occasional narration all that broke the car's silence, Michael noted a constant din, like a clacking and clunking sound, as if the rail needed to be lubricated.

"I'm two minutes from the top," Massori told them both, breathing a bit easier. "Just about the halfway point."

"Aim your camera through the glass doors," Delgado instructed.

Massori obliged, revealing a tube beyond that resembled a curved elevator shaft.

"What now?" he asked, as the capsule continued its climb.

Michael missed the next exchange between Delgado and Massori. He knew that the plastic seats were the only component of the cars and carrier frames that wasn't made of aluminum. The original solid aluminum track had bent under the weight and riding force of the cars, so it had been replaced sometime in the 1980s with a composite material. When that material began to crack and fail well ahead of its anticipated life span, the design shifted back to aluminum, with the center hollowed out to better resist the forces that had bent the original track, thanks to the reduced weight lessening the drag.

"Delgado!" he realized, his insides seizing. "It's the tram line! They're going to blow the tram line!"

‡‡‡

"The dogs would have caught the scent of the explosives when we brought them up the Arch's interior stairs this morning," Massori countered.

Michael moved closer to Delgado, and she angled the phone to include him on camera. "Not if they were planted *inside the aluminum*! The rails that carry the trams are hollow."

"Point the camera outside the glass doors," Delgado said, a nervous edge riding her voice. "Give me a look at the rail."

"I'm not sure if I can get eyeballs on it from this angle," Massori said, pushing his phone up against the glass door. "Let me see if I can get more of a downward—"

A bright flash erupted on Delgado's screen, accompanied by a deafening screech, before the FaceTime window went all black.

"Massori, Massori, can you hear me? Massori, talk to me!"

Delgado swung toward Michael, her eyes plaintive and pleading.

"Massori!" she said again, stare locked with Michael's, the phone trembling in her hand. "Massori!"

He was gone.

CHAPTER 39

BLACK RIVER QUARRY, RENTON, WASHINGTON

Settled on the site of a Duwamish Indian village in
the 1850s and platted in 1876, Renton was named for
William Renton, an industrial pioneer.

Jeremiah was never happier than pounding rock with a sledgehammer, unless he was doing it in the Black River Quarry, currently operated by Stone-
way Rock & Recycling, on the edge of the Black River Riparian Forest.
There was nothing so beautiful and rare these days as unspoiled land, and
the quarry had changed little since his great-grandfather had hammered
away at the granite right here to build the family crypt. The crypt where
Jeremiah spent so much of his time to be close to those he'd lost.

Smashing rock left him contemplating how his great-grandfather had
managed to haul away all that rock by wheelbarrow and horse. There were
no pictures or writings to immortalize the man's efforts. Jeremiah pictured
his great-grandfather lashing a cart to a horse, more likely a pair of horses,
and guiding them all the way to the cemetery thirty miles away. A typhoid
outbreak had claimed the lives of three of his seven children and, instead
of languishing by their bedsides as they lay dying, Silas Hobbs set out to
build a final resting place for them with his own two hands. And now
the remains of Jeremiah's own children had joined those of his great-
grandfather, along with other deceased members of the Hobbs family line,
in the crypt.

In true biblical fashion, his children had fallen as sacrifices to a greater
cause.

*For I spake not unto your fathers, nor commanded them in the day that
I brought them out of the land of Egypt, concerning burnt offerings or sacrifices.*

Jeremiah 7:22.

And as Jeremiah, Ferris Hobbs's burnt offerings that began on Liberty Island were destined to end with an inferno that would consume the corpse of the country he had come to hate. He had come here to pound rock in the wake of learning his efforts had been dealt a crucial setback. Independence Hall should have been rubble now, reduced to a dust-blown pile little different from what remained of the boulder before him, only bigger. The failure stung, destroying the orderly progression of the symphony of destruction he had composed in his mind.

He let his sledgehammer fall and moved to his ringing phone, peeling off one of his gloves to pick it up. He smelled his own sweat, now caked with the rock dust kicked up from the boulder disintegrating before him.

"Congratulations, sir," greeted Rathman over FaceTime. "The general asked that I call you personally to report."

"The Gateway Arch?" Jeremiah asked, still peeling off the second of his work gloves.

"The blast didn't topple it, as we hoped, but I suspect the structural damage may force it to be rebuilt from scratch. No word on the number of casualties yet."

"That doesn't change the fact that we failed at Independence Hall, Rathman," he told the big man pictured on his screen. "I want to know who disrupted our plans."

"I should have that information for you soon, sir. But the general also asked me to inform you about something more pressing."

With that, Rathman aimed the camera toward a spherical metal object about two feet in diameter.

"A drone," Jeremiah recognized, nonetheless.

"It was shot down while hovering over the convoy that left the depot in West Virginia this morning. Someone was following us. The general wanted you to know that we're tracing the drone's origins. Meanwhile, our lead and trail vehicles are on the lookout for more of them, and we will be holding at our forward operating base as soon as the convoy arrives onsite after nightfall. Where there's one . . ."

"I get the point. We need to find out who's flying these drones and, more importantly, how much they know."

"They wouldn't need drones if they knew enough to be anything but a nuisance, sir."

"That may be true, Rathman, but if they have an inkling as to the convoy's ultimate destination . . ."

"We'll find them before they pose any threat. The general told me to assure you of that."

A swirl of wind whipped up the dust from Jeremiah's rock pile and blew it into his face. His eyes felt as if somebody were rubbing sandpaper against the pupils, but Jeremiah spoke through the pain and refused to close them, feeling his eyes fill with tears to wash the dust away.

"We need to stay on schedule, Rathman. No setbacks. That's priority one."

"I understand, sir."

"See that you do." Jeremiah's face flirted with a smile. "A delay wouldn't be fair to the ten million who are about to die."

CHAPTER 40

EN ROUTE TO GATEWAY ARCH
NATIONAL PARK, ST. LOUIS

Welders had to work meticulously to guarantee that
their measurements were accurate. The permissible
margin of error was less than half a millimeter.

An FBI jet was waiting for them at Philadelphia International Airport, priority takeoff and air clearance secured to get them to St. Louis with as little delay as possible. Michael and Gina had exchanged barely a word since rushing here from Independence Hall.

Because there was nothing to say.

This felt different from the Statue of Liberty bombing to Michael. He had watched only the aftermath of that before being detailed to the scene, spared the horrific moments of the blast itself. But he and Delgado had been on the phone with Special Agent Dan Massori when the explosion inside the Arch had been triggered, leaving them to experience it in real time.

Delgado had plugged her dying phone into an outlet next to her seat on the jet as soon as she'd sat down. She'd been on it straight for the minutes leading to takeoff and the first hour they were in the air. Michael knew that the death toll would be nothing on the order of Liberty Island yesterday, especially given that the evacuation provided several crucial minutes to empty the visitor center. In addition to that, somehow the viewing platform had withstood the blast and maintained its integrity despite the severe structural damage the Arch had suffered. Dozens of injuries had been reported up there, but no deaths, while at ground level an unknown number had still been inside the visitor center at the time of the blast. Michael clung to the hope that the bulk of them had survived, which didn't change the fact that another American landmark had been attacked and ravaged.

Michael watched Delgado switch from one line to another, and then combine them, making notes on a pocket-sized pad as she listened. He focused his thinking on the steady hum of the aircraft's powerful engine, until it reminded him too much of the slight rumble he'd heard in the moment before the blast was triggered inside the Gateway Arch. Hoping to distract himself, Michael switched on the flat-screen television mounted on the cabin wall, but ended up tuning in to the aftermath of the carnage before the scene shifted abruptly to a replay of the blast itself, captured from outside the Arch in a cell phone video. The Arch seemed to buckle and sway when the blast sounded. The superheated steel appeared to glow red for a lingering moment before fading out as if controlled by a dimmer switch.

"Turn that off," he heard Delgado order, off her phone now.

Michael complied, about to do so on his own anyway.

"We're going to be in the air for a while," she resumed. "Plenty of time for you to tell me what happened on Mount Rainier. I could use the distraction."

"Now, Gina?"

"Quid pro quo, Walker. I showed you mine. Now you get to show me yours."

CHAPTER 41

⊢•⊕•⊕•⊣

MOUNT RAINIER NATIONAL PARK, THREE AND A HALF YEARS BEFORE

**Walt and Lillian Disney spent their honeymoon at
Mount Rainier in July of 1925.**

"That must be him," Law Enforcement Park Ranger Michael Walker said, handing the binoculars to the smaller figure crouched next to him. "Hidden in that hunter's blind."

His fellow park ranger, and wife, Allison, took the binoculars in her gloved hands and pressed the eyecups against her eyes. The cold breath misting before her face had fogged them up, and Allison swiped a covered fingertip about the glass before raising them back into position and working the focusing wheel.

"Yup," she said, studying the scene three hundred yards away at the foot of the hillside, just short of the natural cover formed of Douglas fir and evergreen brush within which Allison and Michael had concealed themselves. "I make his rifle as a Remington 7600 Pump Action that fires a thirty-ought-six round. That's consistent with the shell casings we've been finding in the areas where poaching is out of control." She lowered the binoculars and grabbed the Nikon from her backpack, glancing toward Michael. "And I'm betting the rounds we've managed to dig out of trees will be a perfect ballistics match."

Poaching was a problem in several national parks, but had been running rampant in Rainier. Allie had been devoting as much on-duty time as she could spare and as much off-duty time as sleep deprivation would allow to find the parties responsible. She'd caught a break a few months back when a photo posted on social media by a visitor to the park caught what looked to be the carcass of a dead animal, likely a bear or mountain lion, covered by a tarp in the rear hold of a white SUV. And a vehicle matching its description had been spotted on park grounds that morning.

"You check the picture I texted you?" she asked him, as if reading his mind.

"What picture?"

"The SUV with the covered animal in the back."

"You know I hate texts, Allie."

"Right. When we got married, I should have made you say 'til text do us part, instead of 'til death.'"

Michael watched Allie fire off a series of pictures. She turned the focus wheel on the telephoto lens and fired off some more in a continuous *clack-clack-clack.*

"You should have worn a flak jacket," Michael told her.

"They're too heavy and smell bad."

He viewed the poacher below, huddled in the blind, as little more than a speck with the naked eye. A drone had pinpointed his location two hours before and he hadn't moved from the natural blind in the interim, no doubt waiting for one of his targeted animals.

A flash of motion drew Michael's gaze toward the trail that followed the tree line. A young couple who might have been Michael and Allie a decade or so back were hiking along the snow-swept trail that sliced through the foothills, the grade steepening the farther it climbed upward out of the forest where the tree line thinned. The pair seemed oblivious to anything but the natural world around them.

Something made Michael grab the binoculars back from Allie and study the scene below—not the hikers so much as the poacher with the Remington hunting rifle slung from his shoulder. Michael saw that the man's hunting goggles were angled so he could follow the couple from the blind. Once the couple had rounded a bend on the trail that grew thicker with snow, Michael spotted the hunter rise and slip southward through the trees.

"He's going to follow them along the trail on the other side of the trees," he said to Allie.

Allie took the binoculars back, following the man until he disappeared into the thick brush inside the tree line. Then she tightened the focus wheel on the young couple traipsing through the snow without a care in the world.

"Looks like he's after different prey today," Allie said, concurring with the judgment Michael had already made.

"Working his way up the food chain," he agreed.

Allie rose stiffly and checked her SIG Sauer P229. "Let's go stop him."

Michael and Allie descended on a sideways angle meant to keep their presence camouflaged by brush, tree, and snow cover. The idea was to circle round and intercept the young couple before the hunter could.

They covered ground fast, aided by Allie's vast knowledge of the park that left them closing ground fast. Their breathing had started to get labored when an icy crunch sounded at a point where the trail intersected with the makeshift path they were plowing toward.

"It's them," Allie said, keeping her voice down for good reason this time.

The crunching grew louder, the bend of the trail narrowing the distance between them and the hunter's targets. Michael drew his pistol and trudged ahead of Allie, picking up his pace through the ten-inch snow pile. His path brought him straight onto the trail, startling the couple even before they caught sight of the gun.

"I'm a park ranger," he announced, gun barrel tilted low.

He unzipped his green parka to reveal his dangling badge and uniform, as Allie drew alongside him, gun drawn as well.

"The two of you need to come with us," she said, between breaths. "You're in trouble."

"We're just out for a hike," the young man said. "We didn't do anything wrong."

"I meant to say danger," Allie corrected. "You're being hunted. We need to move fast."

"There's a ranger station just up the hill," Michael picked up. "You'll be safe there. Just follow us."

Michael took point, gun poking at the air before him. It was hard to shoot with winter gloves donned, and he pulled his right one off with his teeth, then switched the SIG back and pocketed the glove. He felt the numbing cold, fanned by the stiff breeze, in his fingers immediately.

Click.

Michael's first thought was that it was no more than a snow boot crunching a stray stick. Then he swung and saw the black shiny pistol held in the young man's hand, the young woman holding a matching one on Allie.

"Lose the guns," the young man said.

Michael and Allie dropped their pistols into the snow, then watched the young man and woman strip off their wool caps in eerie unison, revealing faces that looked like mirror images.

Not a couple at all, then: They were twins, brother and sister!

The male twin gestured back toward the trail from which Michael and Allie had taken the bait. "This way."

The young man moved and started to backpedal, but hit a depression in the ground, which stripped his balance away. He was listing heavily to regain it in the instant Michael pounced, ducking and launching himself low in a football-style tackle.

His twin spun at the sounds of the commotion, and Michael glimpsed Allie seizing the moment to snatch her gun back from the snowpack.

Boom! Boom! Boom!

The shots rang out as Michael took the male twin down into the cushiony blanket of white, the young man's head thudding against a snow-covered boulder, the hand holding the pistol pinned beneath Michael's leg.

Boom! Boom!

He glimpsed Allie firing from her back on the ground, muted red splotches widening on her green ranger-issue parka. Three of them.

Boom! Boom! Boom!

The three fresh gunshots were muted, distant and close at the same time. Michael felt like he'd been kicked in the ankle and foot, could feel the heat of the pistol partially pinned beneath that very leg.

Before him, downhill a bit, the female twin wobbled, got off two more shots, which both missed, before Allie's next shot impacted her face dead center and spewed red mist into the air.

"Michael!" Allie gasped.

Michael looked down, one glove and one bare hand coated in red. Without realizing, he'd pummeled the male twin's skull into the boulder recessed beneath the snow, and an ink blotch of blood was widening beneath what remained of the back of the male twin's skull. His eyes had rolled back in his head. He wasn't breathing.

Neither was his twin, the young woman lying on her back staring up at the sky.

"Michael . . ."

Allie was lying on her back, too, on an angle slightly pitched down the hill. Michael started to push himself back to his feet to go to her and collapsed, forgetting all about his foot now sheathed in a blanket of numbness.

CHAPTER 42

GATEWAY ARCH NATIONAL PARK, ST. LOUIS

Due to security concerns, the Secret Service has prohibited all presidents from visiting the top of Gateway Arch.

"I managed to get Allie to the nearest ranger station," Michael continued, "then passed out after dressing her wounds as best I could."

Gina looked down toward his prosthetic foot. "Who dressed yours?"

"It doesn't matter. When the search and rescue team got there, Allie was dead. Turned out she'd died back on the mountain, but I could have sworn I could feel her breathing. I wouldn't have stopped anyway, wouldn't have left her out there."

"No trace of that hunter from the blind?"

Michael shook his head. "And the bodies of those twins were gone by the time local law enforcement arrived on the scene. They were able to get DNA from the blood, but it didn't score a match."

"The hunter, you said Allie took pictures of him in that blind."

Michael nodded. "But from that distance, there wasn't enough to make an ID, not even close."

"Still have the pictures?"

Michael nodded. "They're on my phone."

"Text me everything you've got, including those shots your wife texted you lifted from security-cam footage of that white SUV," she told him. "Let me take a run at this."

"You'll be wasting your time, Gina."

"We'll see about that," she said. "I'll do some digging, see what I can come up with."

"Thanks. I appreciate that. I won't get my hopes up, though."

"I find anything, you'll be the first to know."

The jet began its descent for St. Louis International Airport.

‡‡‡

The black SUV that had been waiting for them on the tarmac sped, along with a lead vehicle, through traffic with flashers and sirens rolling. The vehicles streamed across the grassy knolls that formed the Arch complex, skirting the hills that would have wreaked havoc on their suspension systems. The entire area had been cordoned off; east to the Mississippi River, west to South 4th Street, north to Eads Bridge, and south to I-64.

The scene was exactly as Gina had pictured it, swimming with revolving lights and law enforcement vehicles from a mix of agencies that ran the gamut of locals, FBI, ATF, and the state police. As they drew closer, she saw men outfitted in black windbreakers labeled EPA, but had no idea why. Figures were milling about talking into walkie-talkies or cell phones, giving reports and awaiting their next marching orders. A triage area had been set up, fronted by what looked like a mobile medical unit the size of a city bus.

In stark contrast to yesterday on Liberty Island, there weren't a lot of wounded to tend to. The evacuation had left less than thirty inside the visitor center, many of whom were still alive and just needed to be rescued. There were also somewhere around 150 patrons trapped on the viewing platform. She could see the shapes of people looking out from behind the blown-out windows. Besides that, at first glance the outside of the Arch seemed to have suffered no physical damage. But on closer inspection, Gina thought the force of the blast had bent it backward and raised one leg slightly above the other. She wasn't sure whether this was a trick of the eye, kind of an optical illusion springing from the angle from which they were approaching.

Gina would enter the Arch as soon as it was deemed secure via the underground tunnel, in order to form her own assessment of the explosives utilized and relative extent of their effectiveness. In her experience, nothing beat direct inspection, the ability to conjure meaning from the sights and residue of smells left behind. Sometimes some combination of those was enough to tell her what explosives had been used, along with the precise manner of their placement and amount. Preliminary reports indicated that the force of the blast, the rattling percussion inside such a confined space, had utterly ravaged the Arch's interior and brought all the refuse downward, collapsing the visitor center in places and accounting for whatever number of lives had been lost.

Gina climbed out of the SUV as soon as it screeched to a halt, trailed by Michael, and was met almost immediately by a man wearing an FBI-issued jacket with ID dangling from his neck identifying him as Will Jarvis, special agent in charge of the St. Louis field office. He had set up his makeshift command post at the point where visitors entered the monument through the west entrance, which faced Fourth Street and the Old Courthouse.

"ASAC Delgado," he greeted.

"SAC Jarvis," Gina returned, shaking his hand. "And this is Michael Walker from the ISB."

She could tell Michael's attention was elsewhere and prodded him again.

"Michael?"

He snapped alert before returning his gaze to a grouping of park rangers consoling each other over the loss of their brethren who'd bravely stayed behind inside to make sure the visitor center was fully evacuated.

"I want to be with my fellow rangers," Michael told her, adding, "if that's okay with you."

"Sure. Of course," Gina said. She watched him trot off, slightly favoring his prosthetic foot, then returned her attention to Jarvis. "Your people did a good job securing the scene."

"They had it plenty easier than you did on Liberty Island yesterday."

"All things being relative. Fill me in, SAC Jarvis. Tell me something I don't know."

‡‡‡

Jarvis had no information about the Gateway Arch attack that Gina hadn't already seen and reviewed. A portion of the underground tunnel closest to the visitor center entrance had collapsed and was currently being cleared to facilitate entry by first responders. Jarvis reported that he was in direct contact with a St. Louis police officer assigned to the scene and that the officer had reported that a large section of the museum had collapsed as well. It would take quite considerable time and effort to clear the rubble and remove the bodies of whoever had been trapped.

"Any idea of how many?" she asked Jarvis.

"Three park rangers were making a final sweep when the bomb blew, Chief Delgado. Potentially, only them."

Gina heard the hum of helicopters approaching.

"That's how we're going to evacuate the observation deck," Jarvis reported, as the National Guard choppers came into view, "precarious but our only choice. The fire department doesn't have a ladder truck that can reach high enough and we're short on hang gliders."

The noise of the helicopters almost prevented Gina from hearing her phone ring, **ROD RUST** lighting up in the caller ID.

"I need to take this," she told Jarvis. "It's your counterpart from New York."

"Tell Rod I said hi and to take better care of his back."

"Already told him that myself," Gina said, stepping away to answer. "I'm on the ground, boss."

"We've got a problem," Rust told her.

CHAPTER 43

›‹‒‹‒◦‒›‹‒

GATEWAY ARCH NATIONAL PARK, ST. LOUIS

Even though the Gateway Arch was completed on
October 28, 1965, it wasn't until June 10, 1967, that the
Arch was officially inaugurated and the visitor center
was opened to the public. Going to the top wasn't
possible until July 24.

"We're going to search every inch of what's left in there for them," Michael
told the six park rangers who'd survived the blast that had reduced the
visitor center to rubble. They'd led the evacuation, but the uniforms and
skin of several were covered in debris, indicating they'd tried to reenter
the structure but hadn't gotten very far. "I'll man a shovel myself, if that's
what it takes."

"Shovels are for digging graves," one of the men said.

Michael had never met the four men and two women who had gotten
out alive. He knew the Gateway Arch ranger contingent had been increased
yesterday, along with that of every other landmark deemed a potential target, in the wake of the toppling of the Statue of Liberty. But he didn't know
which of these, if any, were regulars as opposed to personnel new to the site.

"I'm sorry," Michael said. "Bad choice of words."

"Is it true?"

"Is what true?"

"That a threat was called in before the Arch blew."

"First I've heard of that."

"Are you one of us or one of them, Agent?" one of the women asked
him.

Michael did something he'd never done before, the heat of the moment
getting to him. He pulled up his pants leg to reveal his prosthetic foot rigged

into a fitting connected to a boot that matched the one on his flesh and blood foot.

"This happened on Mount Rainier. Does that answer your question?"

The woman nodded sheepishly, looking embarrassed.

"Good, and call me Michael. I was the lead at the Statue of Liberty yesterday. We lost some good men and women there, rangers and Park Police."

"We may have lost three good ones here, too," another of the men said, an edge of bitterness creeping into his voice.

Michael took a memo pad from his pocket. "I'd like their names."

"Why?"

"To call their families."

The park rangers gathered around him swallowed hard, virtually in unison.

"They took our phones," the other woman said, "and told us we weren't permitted to contact anyone."

Michael looked toward Gina Delgado across the grassy plaza and wondered if the FBI was responsible for that, some half-baked policy he'd never heard of before.

"Can you call our families, let them know we're okay?" she asked him.

"Just give me the numbers. . . ."

He was jotting down the last one when he saw Delgado waving him over.

"Looks like you're needed over there," another ranger said.

Michael flapped his memo pad. "Whatever it is can wait until I make these calls."

CHAPTER 44

GATEWAY ARCH NATIONAL PARK, ST. LOUIS

Forty blocks were razed to make way for the St. Louis Gateway Arch and its adjacent ninety-one-acre national park, which included dozens of factories and 290 businesses.

"It's this ISB agent you're working with," Rust continued. "Michael Walker."

"He's a good man, boss. He's the one who saved Independence Hall this morning, prevented thousands more casualties, including me."

"So I've heard. But try telling that to the secretary of the interior."

"Who is also Michael's former father-in-law and can't stop blaming him for the death of his daughter."

"Michael?"

"Special Agent Walker."

"He lost a foot, right?"

"And a wife."

"Ethan Turlidge kept reminding me of that. He told me he tried to keep Walker out of the ISB out of concern for his mental stability."

Gina turned her gaze on Michael, who was talking on the phone now, having moved away from the park rangers he must have been consoling. She looked up and saw the National Guard choppers hovering overhead, testing the lines they'd be using to lift those trapped inside the platform to safety.

"I've worked with Walker for twenty-four hours straight," she told Rust, "and I can tell you in all confidence that there's nothing unstable about him."

"Even after that incident at Presbyterian Hospital?"

"What incident? He saved a kid's life."

"There were other ways Walker could have handled it."

"Not in his mind, and the results bore him out. He saved our only eye-witness from a trained killer."

"The same eyewitness he hid from the bureau. The end doesn't justify the means."

Gina didn't bother responding.

"This could reflect badly on you," Rust told her. "Life's too short to let that happen, and careers can be even shorter. You don't want to make ene-mies out of cabinet-level secretaries, and Ethan Turlidge is the kind of guy who will go after anyone who gets in his way."

She saw Michael finally coming toward her.

"Gina?" Rod Rust's voice prompted.

"I'm here," she said, nodding to Michael to acknowledge his approach. "I'll talk to Walker."

"Good, because I've got a message you can deliver to him. . . ."

CHAPTER 45

GATEWAY ARCH NATIONAL PARK, ST. LOUIS

To climb to the top of the Arch by foot, you would have to take 1,076 steps. By comparison, the Washington Monument has 897, and the Willis Tower in Chicago has 2,109.

"Who were you talking to?" Gina asked Michael, after he jogged back over.

"Families of the surviving rangers over there," he said, pointing that way. "They told me someone confiscated their phones."

"What? First I've heard of that."

"It's not bureau policy?"

"To prevent survivors from calling their families? No, why would it be?"

"It's somebody's policy, and if not the bureau, then who gave the order?"

Gina shrugged. "Beats me. That makes no sense."

"So what do you need?" Michael asked her.

"For you to remain calm."

"Don't think I like the sound of that, Gina."

"It's out of my hands."

"I don't like the sound of that either."

"My boss just called, special agent in charge of the New York field office."

"Okay . . ."

"He got an earful from your former father-in-law, criticizing you six ways to Sunday, and questioning your role in the investigation."

Gina could see Michael's face flush with red. "He's the goddamn secretary of the interior. He should know what my role is."

"I believe his point was that you have no role and that your skills could be put to better use elsewhere, along with the rest of the ISB."

"Where?"

"My boss mentioned a park called the Gates of the Arctic. Alaska, right?"

Michael nodded. "A park with no roads or trails, and no sunlight for six months. What's not to love?"

"So quit. Walk away."

"And give Turlidge the satisfaction? Not a chance, Gina."

"You need to call him, Michael, at the very least."

"That sounds like an order."

"That's the way my boss put it to me. You don't want to make things any worse for yourself with Turlidge."

"He's sending me to Alaska in the middle of a crisis. How much worse can it get?"

Gina settled herself with a deep breath. "I want to tell you something that needs to stay between us."

"Okay," Michael said half-heartedly.

"I mean it. It's about Turlidge."

Michael made a sealed-lips motion across his mouth. "This have something to do with what you started to tell me last night in the hotel?"

"It does," Gina said, figuring he deserved to hear what she had to say. "I was running an investigation into your former father-in-law, not long after he became secretary of the interior."

Michael's expression tightened as he waited for her go on.

"He was implicated in the theft of cobalt, lithium, and nickel from the nation's strategic stockpile."

"The primary components of electric car batteries . . ."

"The country's been stockpiling them so we can build the batteries here. We had a source that implicated Turlidge in the plot. Apparently, he was going to sell the stuff to our competition in Europe and Asia."

"You said '*was* running an investigation,'" Michael noted warily.

"Because the investigation was called off."

"By who?"

"I don't know. The order came from on high in D.C., bureau headquarters. At first, I thought it was because everything we had was circumstantial, except for that source. Then the source disappeared and the case was closed."

"At first," Michael repeated.

"I went to my boss with it and he told me to back off, stand down, or something like that."

"Why are you telling me this?"

"Because it felt all wrong. Under the circumstances, I think I'll take another run at it. Shake some trees and see what spills out."

"I thought you were ordered to back off or stand down."

"Right, something like that. But I've got a short memory."

Gina saw Will Jarvis approaching.

"The tunnel has been cleared, ASAC Delgado," he told her, eyeing the open underground entrance to the Arch. "We're about to enter the visitor center."

"I promised those park rangers over there we'd find our people who are unaccounted for," Michael said to both of them, aiming his gaze for the uniformed cluster. "Don't make me a liar."

Jarvis touched his earpiece.

"We've been ordered to stand down," he told Gina, when the brief communication ended.

"By who?"

"Headquarters."

"FBI headquarters?"

"Is there another?" Jarvis asked, failing to manage the smile he tried for.

"Why would they order you to stand down?" Michael wondered.

"No idea," Gina told him. "But we're going to find out soon enough."

CHAPTER 46

GATEWAY ARCH NATIONAL PARK, ST. LOUIS

Fewer than one hundred workers were hired to
construct Gateway Arch instead of the estimated
five thousand needed.

"It's about time you called me back," Ethan Turlidge, Michael's former father-in-law, greeted after Michael had stepped away to make the call he'd promised Delgado. "And congratulations on your transfer to Alaska. I would have preferred Siberia, but there were no postings available. Anyway, I hear the Gates of the Arctic is beautiful this time of year."

Michael continued to walk, needing a quiet place to talk amid all the activity surrounding the Arch. "When are you going to let this go, Ethan?"

"When I get my daughter back, Special Agent Walker."

A heavy silence fell over the line, Michael spared having to respond to that when Turlidge resumed.

"And keep it 'Mr. Secretary,' if you don't mind."

"Allison hated your guts . . . Mr. Secretary," Michael said, before he could stop himself. "You thought I turned her against you, but she made that decision all on her own."

"You're lucky I backed off having you fired," Turlidge shot back, his voice rising.

"You were wrong from the start. You questioned our judgment. You didn't believe the statement I gave about the circumstances surrounding the exchange of gunfire that claimed Allie's life."

"I was then, and am now, merely considering an alternative scenario."

"Right, one where we started shooting first and the two suspects who sought to kidnap us were innocent victims."

"According to your report, they were kids, Walker."

"Midtwenties doesn't make you a kid, Mr. Secretary, and their guns trumped their ages."

Turlidge hesitated. "The matter is still being reviewed."

"It was already reviewed to everyone's satisfaction, except yours."

"Everyone else didn't lose a daughter."

"And your response was to try to ruin her husband."

"You had no business coming back, Special Agent Walker. The Park Service is not a place for someone who can't follow the rules. I warned your boss that you'd screw up again. The only surprise is that it took so long." Turlidge paused to let his point better sink in. "You embarrassed the entire Park Service yesterday by not handing that boy, an eyewitness no less, over to the FBI. Give me a few more weeks and you'll be begging to make your posting in Alaska permanent. Meanwhile, don't forget to send me a postcard."

The call ended there, just as the first of the U.S. Army vehicles rolled on to the scene.

‡‡‡

There were five in all, an open Humvee leading the way trailed by three others with troops manning .50-caliber machine guns in the turrets. The final vehicle was a covered personnel carrier. The convoy stopped on a dime, and soldiers wearing body armor and armed with M4 assault rifles spilled from the insides, fanning out to secure the scene.

Slightly out of breath, Michael made it over to Delgado and Jarvis just as the soldiers from the lead Humvee, led by a colonel with Airborne stripes who'd been seated next to the driver, approached them.

"Who's in charge here?"

"That would be us," Delgado said, before Jarvis had a chance to. "I'm Assistant Special Agent in Charge Gina Delgado of the New York field office, currently attached to the Joint Terrorism Task Force overseeing the investigation, and this is—"

"Doesn't matter, ma'am," he said, cutting her off. He looked toward Michael and cast him a disparaging look after checking his dangling ID badge. "You're not in charge anymore."

"That's ASAC Delgado, Colonel, and on whose authority are you assuming command?"

"The United States of America, ma'am."

"That doesn't answer my question."

"It's all I'm authorized to say, ma'am." Michael watched the man move his eyes from Delgado to Jarvis. "I'm also authorized to order the two of you to pack up shop and have your people evacuate the area. We'll take things from here."

Delgado took a step toward him. "I notice there's no name on your uniform. . . ." She swept her gaze to the soldiers on either side of him. "No names on your men's uniforms either."

"That's right, ma'am."

"I also noticed you didn't say what unit you represented, Colonel," Delgado noted.

The man standing before her tensed, just a bit.

"And you are aware this is U.S. soil, where the military is not permitted to operate under constitutional statute."

The colonel stopped just short of a smirk. "Technically, we're National Guard, ma'am."

"Technically, would your presence have anything to do with that helicopter crash in the Great Smoky Mountains two years ago?" Delgado asked the colonel.

He just looked at her.

"You know," she continued, "the crash that supposedly claimed the lives of twelve members of the Special Forces who weren't really on board?"

The colonel looked away, first back at Jarvis and then at nothing at all.

"They were based at Fort Liberty back when it was still Fort Bragg," Delgado resumed, not bothering to hide the edge in her voice. "Is that where you're posted? I'm sure the National Guard must have had a very good reason to come all this way."

"You have your instructions, ma'am," the colonel told her, leaving it there.

"No."

"No?"

"We're not going anywhere until our search and rescue operation inside what's left of the visitor center is complete."

Now it was the colonel who stepped forward. "Ma'am, you have your orders and—"

"Last time I checked," she interrupted, "the National Guard offers support personnel and assistance to on-site jurisdictional command." Delgado flashed her phone. "How about I get the director of the FBI on the line and you can sort that out with him? Short of that, your men can secure the area, while SAC Jarvis's team completes its sweep inside the Arch."

The colonel's expression remained flat. "Your team has thirty minutes to complete its sweep. Then I want all of you to vacate these premises. We'll pick up things from there. That's an order . . . ASAC Delgado."

Michael could see Delgado fuming, as she swallowed whatever she was about to say back down.

"Ma'am." The colonel nodded with a slight tip of his black beret, then turned and walked off in the shadow of his men.

"What the hell was that?" Jarvis asked.

"I have no idea," Delgado told him, following the colonel with her gaze.

CHAPTER 47

‣•‣•⬦•‣•‣

WEST VIRGINIA

The newest national park, New River Gorge, is located
in West Virginia about two hundred miles from
Charleston.

Lantry knew something was wrong as soon as he lost the picture on the cell-phone-sized device connected to the drone. It happened from time to time, but this occasion seemed different, a feeling borne out when the picture didn't return.

He was trailing the convoy on his motorcycle, a restored ancient Triumph, staying a half mile back on rural Route 28 through West Virginia. He'd already used his cell phone to get the next drone prepped and ready fifty miles ahead, giving its operator plenty of time to work his way into position. The convoy was heading south, where he guessed they would jump onto Route 39 in Huntersville to head west.

All the convoys they were aware of so far had headed west, but the group Lantry was a part of had yet to determine where the cargo those convoys were hauling was ending up. That group, Fallen Timbers, had assumed the mantle of the Native American mission from generations past as guardians of the land, committed to exposing the companies responsible for ravaging the environment. Whenever possible, they fought their battles with lawyers to tie those companies up in court for as long as possible, indefinitely in many cases. When the courtroom failed to produce the results they wanted, though, they resorted to more traditional means of battle to achieve their ends.

Gray Rock Trucking, the company responsible for hauling all the loads, was based in Washington State but operated depots across the entire United States. It ranked among the country's largest long-haul trucking companies. Lantry knew no more than this, because that was all he needed to know to prove himself to his people at long last. He embraced the opportunity to do that by being part of the team that would ultimately uncover the terminus where Gray Rock Trucking had been off-loading its deadly cargo for months now.

With the drone disabled, he had no choice but to follow the convoy on his Triumph to its next fuel stop. The problem was that if they had disabled one drone, they'd do the same with the next one, and the one after. That made continuing with the current plan a fool's errand.

Lantry had never been much of a hunter, fighter, or warrior, but was a wiz when it came to electronics. He'd been flying drones since they'd first come out and thought the call from Fallen Timbers to enlist his services had been a prank. He wasn't involved at all in intelligence gathering and had no idea how the group had pinpointed that former West Virginia trucking depot as the primary demarcation point. His job was to acquire the drones, rig them, and train members of Fallen Timbers to use them to uncover where the convoys were ending up once and for all.

The leaders of the group presented him with a warrior talisman necklace each member wore on his neck. It was comprised of three different pendants representing compassion, wisdom, and strength. Lantry believed he had an ample amount of the first two, but far less of the third. The boy had never been in charge of anyone before, but the Fallen Timbers warriors assigned to him had their marching orders and were receptive to all his lessons on operating drones. The challenge lay in the logistics of all the coordination, since drones had a limited flying range before their batteries wore down. Lantry had modified the surveillance models they were utilizing to stay up for a hundred miles or so, depending on wind currents, and that meant lots of communication to make sure the handoffs from one drone to the next went smoothly to follow the convoy all the way to its ultimate destination.

And now that one of those drones had been shot down or otherwise disabled, all bets were off. Lantry needed to develop a whole new strategy, given the likelihood that any further drones they launched would suffer the same fate as his. He used the satellite phone to call in an update to Fallen Timbers and then returned to the Triumph to shrink the gap between him and the convoy.

He closed to within visual range and then drifted back to between an eighth and a quarter of a mile. He still didn't have a firm plan when the convoy finally made its first refueling stop. Lantry pulled into the parking lot and brought his Triumph to a halt at a pump to refuel himself. He filled his small tank slowly, eyeing the heavily armed guards protectively enclosing the convoy.

What would my uncle do, what would the real warriors of Fallen Timbers do?

Channeling the legend with whom he shared a last name, the man who'd stepped in to raise him after his father had died, Lantry was struck by an outlandish idea more in keeping with men of action he'd never be among. Dangerous and risky for sure, but he had learned from his uncle that a man, or a boy, should trust his first instinct.

He always carried matches with him so he'd be able to light a fire if circumstances forced him to spend the night outside. Lantry eased the gas spigot out of the Triumph's tank and let up pressure on the handle enough to create a pool of gasoline under and around the bike. Then he lit the entire matchbook and placed in on the asphalt within easy range of the spreading pool.

He pretended to head toward the diner and convenience store located at the head of the truck stop. Halfway there, he heard the explosion and swung to see shards of his trusty Triumph still raining downward. Just as he'd hoped, the convoy's security detail moved out from their positions, alerted by the blast and watching to make sure the fire spread no further. Lantry looped around to their rear, none of them looking toward the eighteen-wheeler in the convoy's center when he grabbed hold of the ladder on the far side and hoisted himself upward onto its roof.

So long as he found sufficient handholds, he'd able to remain with the convoy as literally a part of it. He was lifting his satellite phone from his pocket to report the new plan to Fallen Timbers when the engine roared and the big truck lurched forward, separating the phone from his grasp. He scrambled to retrieve it, but it rattled over the side of the truck's roof before he could snare it.

Lantry watched the phone bounce when it hit the ground, scattering shards of metal and plastic as the convoy tore off with him clinging tightly to the roof and the flames he had unleashed shrinking in the distance.

‖•◦•◦•◦•‖

CHAPTER 48

SEATTLE, WASHINGTON

The Space Needle was once the tallest structure west of
the Mississippi River, standing at 605 feet.

"We don't know who they are, sir," Rathman reported.

Jeremiah turned from the view of Seattle he had memorized atop the
Space Needle as a young boy and enlarged the footage of the soldiers
who had shown up at the Gateway Arch as much as he could on his
phone's screen. "But you don't believe they were National Guardsmen, as
reported."

"Not at all, sir."

"Then what do you believe? What does the general say?"

"You'd need to ask him that, sir."

"I haven't been able to reach him. So I'm asking you."

The Space Needle was Jeremiah's favorite place in the city of Seattle,
in large part because his family had been involved in its construction. It
had been built to serve as a centerpiece of the Seattle World's Fair in 1962.
A year before that, though, it consisted of nothing more than architec-
tural plans for a structure that had no site and was about to be abandoned.
Then, at the proverbial last minute, an empty lot within the fairgrounds
that contained switching equipment for the fire and police alarm systems
was uncovered. Work had to begin almost immediately to assure completion prior to the start of the fair, also known as the Century 21 Exposition,
in April of 1962.

The company that had financed and built the Needle had retained a
company originally started by Jeremiah's great-grandfather Silas Hobbs to
handle all excavation and concrete work. That company, Gray Rock Construction and Excavation, had been the forerunner of his own Gray Rock
Trucking. Jeremiah still owned Gray Rock C and E, as well as Gray Rock

Trucking, but had taken little interest in its day-to-day operations since his priorities had abruptly changed three years before.

Jeremiah had been born on April 21, 1962, the day the Century 21 Exposition had officially opened. Thus, he had no recollection of the event itself, but did recall his initial visits to the Needle in the years that followed. They said it was impossible to have memories prior to turning four or so, but he was convinced he recalled the first time he had taken in the view of Seattle from the top, shortly after turning three. To commemorate that, he'd taken his own children here on their third birthdays, but the experience had been forgotten by the time they turned four.

The first time he'd visited the observation deck, people were everywhere, towering over him. Today, he was alone. The Space Needle wouldn't officially open for another hour, Jeremiah's presence owed to a trusted associate with a key and the proper security codes.

"Based on what I've observed from the footage, sir, I believe they were Special Forces," Rathman reported.

"Cause for concern, then."

"Yes, sir. Active-duty military can't operate on U.S. soil. That's why they came in the guise of National Guardsmen. They could be nothing more than a rapid-deployment force responding to a national emergency."

"But you don't think so."

"No, I don't. A force like that couldn't have been cobbled together in the wake of Liberty Island. I've been part of enough of them to know. This force was already assembled to await insertion."

"But it wasn't one of them who got the better of one of your men in that hospital, though, was it?"

"No, sir."

"So who rescued the boy, Rathman?"

"By all indications, it was the same park ranger responsible for thwarting the attack on Independence Hall. He was also identified at the Gateway Arch. His name is Michael Walker, sir. I've just texted you his picture."

Jeremiah's phone beeped, and he opened the text Rathman had just sent. The picture was actually a reprint of an announcement that had run in some Park Service periodical, celebrating the return of law enforcement ranger Michael Walker in his new capacity as a special agent of the Investigative Services Branch, now fitted with a prosthetic after having lost a foot in a tragic incident.

A tragic incident on Mount Rainier.

The world seemed to darken before Jeremiah and then compress. It was as if he were briefly suspended in some kind of void, before the light returned. A verse from the book of Jeremiah 15:15 filled his mind:

You understand, O Lord; remember me and attend to me. Avenge me against my persecutors.

"Where do we stand with the next attack?" he asked, changing the subject.

"Right on schedule, with a stroke of good fortune added to the mix, sir."

Jeremiah didn't bother to ask what that good fortune was. "In that case, there's something else that requires your attention, Rathman," he said instead. "Stand by."

Jeremiah ended the call and immediately called Archibald Terrell again.

"Sorry I've been indisposed, Ferris," he greeted.

"I need something from you, General," Jeremiah told him. "I need you to make a phone call to our associate in Washington."

PART FOUR

—◆—

Most of the people who visit the parks, whether
they realize it or not or whether they put it into
words, are impelled to visit them because of
the quest for a supreme experience.

—Newton B. Drury,
fourth director of the National Park Service

—◆—

CHAPTER 49

GATEWAY ARCH NATIONAL PARK, ST. LOUIS

Jefferson National Expansion Memorial became
Gateway Arch National Park in 2018.

"I need to get back to New York," Delgado said to Michael, easing her phone back into her pocket. "Jarvis is JTTF, too, so he can take over the scene from here."

"I'll wave to you from the Gates of the Arctic." He watched Will Jarvis conferring with the colonel who'd pronounced himself in charge of the scene. "They're definitely not National Guard."

"I think we've established that much."

"So who are they, ASAC Delgado?"

"I don't know and neither does my boss. That was him I was just talking to and he has no clue. But Jarvis said the order for us to stand down came from FBI headquarters."

"And who confiscated the phones belonging to the surviving park rangers?" Michael asked. "Better yet, who gave the order? Tell me you don't see a connection to our uninvited guests over there, Gina." Michael looked toward the recently arrived squad of soldiers before returning his gaze to Delgado.

Meanwhile, the slow but steady evacuation of those trapped on the viewing platform continued, and would continue well into the night. There was no way at this point to determine the structural integrity of that space, or the extent of the damage done by the blast to the supporting infrastructure. That made an already deliberate process all the more unnerving, not to mention the fact that if the viewing platform began to fail no means existed to speed up the evacuation.

"Our mystery battalion leader only gave you thirty minutes to clear out," he said to Delgado.

"Doesn't matter," she said, aiming her gaze toward the Arch. "We're going to be here for as long as it takes."

‡‡‡

It was nearly two hours later, the sun burning lower in the late-afternoon sky, before Delgado and Jarvis were comfortable turning the scene over to the mysterious army unit, though Jarvis would remain on-site in his capacity as Joint Terrorism Task Force lead for St. Louis. In that time, over twenty survivors had been freed from the visitor center, and the bodies of the four park rangers who'd stayed behind to supervise the evacuation had been hauled out, along with three civilians.

"Come on," Delgado said to Michael, angling for the SUV that had brought them there, "I'll give you a ride to the airport."

"Why do I think my time flying in private government jets is over?"

She paused dramatically. "Wow, you can see the future. Care to peer a bit deeper into your crystal ball?"

"Already have, Delgado, and I don't like what was there."

CHAPTER 50

ST. LOUIS, MISSOURI

Named for a French king born in 1214,
and founded in 1764.

Gina had hoped to grab some sleep on the plane, but then heavy thunderstorms in and around St. Louis, typical for summer, grounded all flights, leaving her on the FBI's private jet with only her thoughts.

She'd lost all track of time. All she knew was that she didn't feel tired at all. Her boss and mentor Rod Rust liked to call this "revving in the red" for so long a stretch that you could no longer slow your thinking down. Her mind just kept fixating on the events of the past day and a half, conjuring up images out of context and order, and wouldn't stop until she found something else to occupy it.

In search of a distraction, Gina focused on her promise to follow up on the murder of Michael's wife on Mount Rainier nearly three and a half years ago.

"Still have the pictures?"

She recalled the offer she'd made to give the shots taken of the figure in the hunter's blind back on Mount Rainier National Park a closer look.

"Text me everything you've got, including those shots your wife texted you lifted from the security-cam footage of that white SUV. Let me take a run at this."

Gina checked her long scroll of text messages and, sure enough, there were several from Michael containing the photos she requested, along with others associated with the investigation into poaching on park grounds. With the delay, the timing seemed perfect for her to take that run she'd promised Michael.

Instead of opening the files on her phone, Gina emailed them to herself and fired up her laptop on the fold-down table before her. She opened the file and clicked on a series of photos that were the last ones Michael's wife had taken, all more or less the same. In all, the face of the hunter suspected of poaching was obscured by both the brush and the blind's cover. The few that captured larger portions of his face were similarly obscured by the fact that he was wearing tactical goggles. It turned out she was familiar with them from her work with the FBI's Hostage Rescue Team: Xaegistac Airsoft goggles that were very popular with the military and law enforcement, but not all that common for hunters. The man had chosen the green variety to mesh with his camouflage garb, the lenses smoke-colored instead of yellow or clear.

Gina concluded that he'd donned the goggles more to further conceal his features than for safety. She knew it was a long shot, but she screen-shotted his face, used the bureau's proprietary software to enhance and extrapolate it, and plugged it into the system for the machine to do its magic. The laptop pinged almost immediately, never a good sign, and sure enough a message had appeared beneath the enhanced picture:

UNRECOGNIZABLE

Meaning there wasn't enough for the software to latch on to even to search for the face in the system.

Gina leaned back and considered that tragic day on Mount Rainier from a different angle. The plan had been to lure Michael and Allie into a trap and then to kill them. She'd heard that a surprisingly large number of tourists went missing in national parks every year, and, under that scenario, Michael and Allie might have ended up among them.

That led Gina to turn her efforts to the Web. The bureau didn't maintain detailed records of such disappearances, but the National Park Service did. The first set of numbers referred to SARs—search and rescue operations. The vast majority of missing individuals were found or returned on their own, but every year over a hundred people disappeared in the country's national parks and were never seen again. According to the data from two years ago, there were 3,453 reported search and rescue missions and 182 deaths in the parks. Those were both staggering numbers in Gina's mind, but it was hard for her to pin down those who had vanished for good, found neither alive nor dead. Strangely and inexplicably, the Park Service did not make a comprehensive list of missing persons available for public, or even professional, dissemination.

With that information not at Gina's disposal, she pulled up the daily and local papers and scanned through headlines revealed when she searched **MOUNT RAINIER DISAPPEARANCES**. As near as she could figure, six people had vanished on park grounds in the past three years and never been found. Probing further, she learned that four of those who'd vanished were made up of two couples, the fifth being a hiker and the sixth a marathon runner who'd been training in Rainier. The two couples were of special interest to her.

Because Michael and Allie had been a couple.

All of Gina's training had taught her to rely on patterns when it came to crime, particularly violent crime. So she turned her focus on the disappearance of those two couples, digging deeper.

Six months prior to the attack Michael had survived but Allie hadn't, a married couple who were experienced hikers went out on an overnight hike along the Mother Mountain Loop trail near Mowich Lake. They were serious lovers of the outdoors who had hiked and camped all over the world, and on this excursion were well stocked with camping equipment and provisions. But they never returned to their campsite, and a comprehensive search carried out by the National Park Service and local law enforcement came up empty. Other hikers who had seen the couple along the route reported that they'd seemed normal and did not appear to be in any distress.

To keep her emotional distance and not be tempted to look into their backgrounds, Gina came to think of them as Couple Number 1. She decided to start there and logged into a database called NLETS (National Law Enforcement Telecommunications System), a secure information-sharing system that local, state, and federal law enforcement agencies used to communicate and share data. NLETS linked together every law enforcement, justice, and public safety agency, including the Park Service, for sharing and exchanging criminal justice information.

All the files pertaining to the disappearance of Couple Number 1, compiled by the investigative bodies involved in the search, were readily available via the NLETS. Gina initially avoided the written reports to focus on the array of video files instead. She wasn't sure exactly what she was looking for until she found it six files in.

Unfortunately, there was no surveillance footage of the area around and leading to Mount Rainier's Mother Mountain Loop trail, which meant there was nothing for her to study in the hours preceding Couple Number

1's disappearance. The nearest parking lot seemed the best place to start, and she was ninety minutes into reviewing the footage when she spotted the figure of a man wearing hunter's camo late in the afternoon, just hours before Couple Number 1 went missing. Since hunting was prohibited in all areas of the park, she found the use of such gear strange, but not unprecedented given that camouflage garb made it easier to remain concealed from the bears and mountain lions that roamed Rainier.

Then she spotted something else that stood out even more. The man was holding a backpack in one hand and something else in the other. The footage showed him tucking that object into the backpack. Gina froze the shot there and zoomed in, recognizing the object the man was holding immediately: the same green Xaegistac Airsoft goggles worn by the hunter perched in the blind the day Michael's wife had been killed in a gunfight that had cost him his foot.

Gina felt a tremor of excitement. She proceeded to review all the parking lot footage that had been pulled, finding that original shot to be the only one that revealed the potential suspect in any capacity, nothing connecting him to any of the vehicles stacked up behind him. The pictures Allie had shot of the hunter in the blind provided no indication of his height or weight, nothing beyond the goggles and camo gear to form a connection. Nebulous at best, and certainly not enough to hold up in court, but that wasn't her concern right now.

She made a note on a memo pad of the timeline, then opened the file on Couple Number 2, who'd gone missing in the Paradise section of the park. Unfortunately, there were very few video files available on NLETS, and none showed any man decked out in camouflage hunting gear or meeting the general description of the figure from the parking lot, no matter how many times she watched the scant footage available.

Couple Number 1 had disappeared six months before the attack on Allie and Michael. Couple Number 2 had vanished around six months before that.

A pattern was emerging, and as near as she could tell, no couples had gone missing in the three and a half years since Allison had died on the mountain. Gina went back to that one decent still shot of the man in camo gear carrying a backpack she'd managed to grab off the video surveillance footage associated with Couple Number 1. She had nothing to lose by plugging it into the system, expecting nothing, and that's exactly what she got again:

UNRECOGNIZABLE

Gina checked her watch. She'd been at this for nearly two hours straight and felt recharged by the conviction that she'd found a clue the original investigation into Allison's murder had missed. The bodies of the young couple Michael and Allie had killed in self-defense had never been found. Someone had gone to great pains to remove them. There had been a slight blood trail and the footprints of a single man who wore size 12 outdoor boots identified to be among the most popular brands. Another dead end.

Gina stretched and yawned, feeling tired at last. She'd gone as far as she could with this, both in terms of time and her limited level of technical experience. If she was going to take this any further, she needed an expert to do the heavy lifting. She grabbed her cell phone and hit the contact for Special Agent John Milton.

"I've got something I'd like you to look into outside our current concerns, if you've got the time," she said after catching him up on the Gateway Arch.

"I'd love the distraction," Paradise said. "What have you got?"

"I'm not sure," Gina told him. "That's why I called you."

‡‡‡

She'd just finished laying out for Paradise what she needed and had emailed him her findings so far, along with all the pictures Michael had forwarded her, when the cockpit door opened and the pilot leaned out.

"Sorry for the delay, Chief Delgado. We just got clearance to take off. We'll have you on the ground in New York in two hours."

She felt the jet lurch ahead into its taxi, her eyes feeling heavy, and was asleep before it lifted into the air.

CHAPTER 51

ST. LOUIS, MISSOURI

The Eads Bridge, built in 1874 across the Mississippi River, was the first large-scale use of steel for structural purposes.

Delgado had just dropped Michael off at the airport when he received a text from Angela Pierce.

Change in plans. You're headed to Zion National Park instead of Alaska. Congratulations.

Let there be light, Michael texted Angela back. **Thanks.**

Wasn't me. Turlidge made the call. You must have gotten through to him.

Fat chance.

Michael counted his blessings, not really caring what had led Turlidge to change his mind. He was going to Zion, which had become his favorite park after he committed himself not to return to the Park Service until he could manage the climb up the challenging and precarious Angels Landing trail all the way to the summit. Then, after he'd achieved that goal, he shaved five minutes off his mark the second time he climbed it and another two minutes the third time.

There were no direct flights that evening out of St. Louis bound for Harry Reid International Airport in Las Vegas, the closest airport to the part of Utah where Zion was located, which would still require a more than three-hour drive.

Michael knew chartered helicopter flights were behind him as well. The flight he'd booked to O'Hare wasn't scheduled to leave for another two hours, and after the connecting flight to Harry Reid he had a long drive in a rental car to look forward to. He thought about staying over in Las Vegas and then driving the 170 miles to Zion tomorrow morning.

"Hey, boss," he said to Angela Pierce, after she answered his call.

He'd intended to discuss the change of plans with her, but Angela beat him to the punch once he'd explained the delay.

"Whenever you get into Vegas, I'll have a car waiting for you at the airport to take you the rest of the way."

"Hopefully, Secretary Turlidge won't notice that line item in the expense report."

"How much sleep you get last night, Michael?"

"I'm too tired to remember."

"And that's why I don't give a shit about what Turlidge thinks. There's a ranger at Zion who's about your size. I'll have him leave a uniform at your hotel. What about your prosthetic?"

"It's weathered the last couple days well. I think there may be a crack in the plastic of the housing," he told her, thinking of all the exertion the device had undergone. "But I'd know if it was anything more than minor."

He was more concerned about his stump at the lower ankle. All the activity was likely to result in blisters, and he could only hope the irritation didn't extend beyond that. Sitting in the airport terminal, he could feel a dull ache that had already subsided once he'd propped his leg up on an adjoining seat for a stretch before the terminal grew too crowded to spare the space.

Michael had almost never felt the phantom pain many amputees associated with their lost limbs and counted himself fortunate that his prosthetic fit and wore as well as it did.

"What about shoes?" Angela asked him. "Do you need a fresh pair?"

"Not without inspecting the heel height. Because of my prosthetic, my shoes have to be custom-fitted. I can make do with the ones I'm wearing."

"How well do you know Zion?"

"Well enough to know it doesn't offer nearly as appealing a target as the sites that have been attacked so far."

"Then I'll rely on you to keep it that way, Michael."

CHAPTER 52

BROOKFIELD, OHIO

Brookfield Air Force Station was constructed as part of
the Air Defense Command permanent network
and opened in April 1952.

Lantry couldn't believe what he saw illuminated by the big construction lights that turned the area inside the fence the convoy had just passed through almost daylight bright. The lights cut through the mist and fog to reveal what looked to be an old, decaying military base. Beyond those lights, there was nothing to see at all, as if this base had been dropped into the middle of nowhere. That made it the perfect place for the convoy to make a pit stop.

Prior to the convoy's arrival here, Lantry had been dozing, falling into a strange rhythm while clinging to the top of the eighteen-wheeler that rode the center of the convoy. Nightfall had brought with it a sense of security, given that it greatly reduced the odds of him being spotted up here.

He tried to think beyond that, given the stakes involved, how far the forces behind this convoy would go to keep their secrets. It was one thing for Lantry to have committed his technological expertise to the project for Fallen Timbers, quite another to have become the kind of operative he lacked the training and experience to be.

A warrior.

He hadn't been thinking when he concocted the plan of climbing atop the eighteen-wheeler. He'd acted out of instinct, out of duty to his mission, out of a desire not to be disregarded by his peers and the people of his tribe. He'd never be like his legendary uncle, but that didn't mean he couldn't be more than he currently was.

Lantry had been fortunate in the sense that he'd found exactly what he'd hoped for on the truck's roof: a pair of thick rubber hoses running side by side, one red and one blue. The red hose was the emergency line that provided a constant air supply to the brake system and would engage in the event of a detachment. The blue line supplied the air required to apply the brakes.

Lantry had curled his left arm around the red hose and his right around the blue, able to hold his position through every jolt, thud, and sharp curve that pinwheeled his legs in the opposite direction. According to his watch, they had been driving for eight straight hours along rural West Virginia roads when he spotted a sign on the highway that read WELCOME TO OHIO.

That had been barely a half hour ago. Lantry's knowledge of shuttered military bases was negligible, but that was clearly what he was gazing at from the top of the truck. The convoy's stopping here left him vulnerable in the open, so his immediate task was to slip down off the roof and find cover. Fortunately, the convoy had parked in the darkest reaches of the sprawling space, well removed from the spill of the construction lights that might well have given him away.

He slid down the truck's trailer the moment it squealed and hissed to a complete stop, then took initial refuge beneath the chassis, feeling the cool of the pavement in stark contrast to the works and gears above, super-heated from the rigors of driving continuously here from the truck stop. He had spotted no drones providing overhead surveillance, so his warning to Fallen Timbers before he'd lost his satellite phone must have been heeded.

What he was able to glimpse from beneath the truck, though, made Lantry wonder if the group truly grasped whatever it was dealing with. A bevy of men wearing military uniforms had spilled out of buildings that appeared ill-equipped to house them. The site looked to be abandoned, with all structures in varying states of decay. The building and barracks roofs that hadn't collapsed were caving in, and the concrete of the road-ways crisscrossing the complex was warped and pockmarked with cracks as well as gaping holes.

Yet the men who'd appeared from both the buildings and areas of dark-ness numbered in the hundreds, continuing to grow before Lantry's eyes. He could make no sense of what he was seeing. This was no storage facility or demarcation point where the deadly contents the convoy was hauling would be off-loaded. From beneath the truck's chassis he could see training grounds and, farther off, an airstrip with big planes he thought might be C-130 transports stacked up off to the side. What exactly, though, would they be transporting and to where?

When Fallen Timbers had approached him, they'd insisted they needed his help to expose a massive government scandal, while preventing a potential environmental disaster of epic proportions. Seen through the spray of those construction lights, though, what Lantry was viewing portended something else entirely, something infinitely more ominous and terrifying, especially when considering the contents of the steel drums and casks this and other convoys like it had been hauling. This might not have been the final destination of the convoy's cargo, but it certainly suggested something previously unknown about the greater purpose of whoever was now in possession of this cargo and all the others.

Lantry knew he had to find more suitable cover, knew he had to find a way to call the number Fallen Timbers would still be monitoring.

It's not what we thought, he began to compose in his mind, as more troops continued to emerge from the darkness, *it's much, much worse.*

CHAPTER 53

WASHINGTON, D.C.

The location for the new nation's capital,
which was founded on July 16, 1790,
was selected by George Washington.

Gina didn't awaken until the jet's wheels thudded down against the runway, jarring her slightly. She snapped off her seat belt, stretched her arms, and opened the shade to gaze out the window into the darkness.

This wasn't New York.

Gina checked the view from the other side of the plane and found it similarly confounding.

What am I doing at Joint Base Andrews?

She had her phone out and was calling Rod Rust before completing that thought. The phone rang several times before going to voicemail. Gina was about to leave a message when the cabin door was yanked open from the outside and three marines entered, the one in the lead a captain with a wide spectrum of awards pinned to his chest.

"I'm sorry for the subterfuge, ASAC Delgado," he greeted. "You'll understand why it was necessary in short order." The captain extended an open palm toward the door. "If you'll be kind enough to accompany us, ma'am . . ."

Gina started toward him. "Where are we going?"

The captain didn't respond, and she saw yet another black SUV waiting for them just beyond the steps leading downward. Its engine was running, its lights burning through the last of the night. Gina spotted the first break of dawn on the horizon, grateful and longing for the sun, as if it might shed some light on what was going on here.

"I'm going to need your cell phone, ASAC Delgado," the captain said, extending his hand when she reached him.

‡‡‡

The captain climbed into the front and the other two marines into the third seat, leaving her with the middle row to herself. Her mouth was dry. Her life and career were all about making sense of the unknown, but not when it pertained to herself.

They hadn't asked for her weapon, only her phone.

She didn't know what to make of that. Gina looked up and saw two bottles of water stashed in the cupholders centered before the middle seat. She took one and guzzled half of it down.

With her marine guards offering no further information, Gina let her thoughts roam with her eyes as the Washington, D.C., skyline drew closer. Traffic was thin this time of the morning, even on a Monday, and she began to wonder if their ultimate destination might turn out to be the J. Edgar Hoover Building, in which case such subterfuge seemed unnecessary. But that thought was extinguished as soon as the black SUV cruised past FBI headquarters, angling for Pennsylvania Avenue.

It pulled into the loading dock of a government office building she didn't recognize four blocks from both the White House and the Treasury Building. The SUV continued straight into what looked like a garage bay off to the side. Before she could pose another futile question to the marine captain, the platform began to descend like an elevator, and it was fifty feet down when it reached a long, dimly lit tunnel that looked to be one of those built for the planned Washington underground trolley system, prior to construction of the Metro superseding it.

Instead of two sets of tracks, what ran through the tunnel was a single long, shiny road that cut beneath Washington, D.C.'s halls of power. Gina saw no indentations in the sides of the tunnel to indicate any entryways to the myriad of buildings on Pennsylvania Avenue above, and the tunnel ended at what seemed to be a solid wall, nowhere else to proceed—until that wall slid open in the center to reveal a similarly dimly lit parking facility. A fleet made up of additional black SUVs, together with shiny new Humvees, was squeezed off to the side. Hers was the only other vehicle inside at present.

I know where I must be, Gina thought.

Shortly after the Japanese attack on Pearl Harbor, in December 1941, construction had begun on a hardened bunker to the east of the White

House grounds that would provide a secure refuge for the president in the event of an air raid against the city. To hide construction of the facility from the public, the East Wing was built on top of the bunker. This facility would later become the Presidential Emergency Operations Center. As a stopgap measure, the fortified vaults in the basement of the United States Treasury Building were converted into living quarters for the president and his family, to be used in the event that an attack came prior to the bunker's completion.

Unlike the White House, a fragile structure with what was then a shallow basement, the Treasury Building boasted a deep basement built into a foundation of granite, and its vaults were nestled in stone. The ten-room presidential suite sat two floors below the cash room behind a steel bank vault door and was described as every bit as nice as a luxury hotel suite. The tunnel, connecting the White House to the open areaway of the Treasury Building, was excavated to allow the evacuation of the president from one building to the other without the need to venture outside.

None of that was news. What was news was the fact that the old Treasury vaults in question must have been converted into something else entirely.

"Are we going to the White House, Captain?" Gina asked, after the officer opened the door for her to climb out.

"No, ma'am," he told her, adding almost immediately, "somewhere more important."

CHAPTER 54

ZION NATIONAL PARK, UTAH

In 1909, Mukuntuweap National Monument was
designated by President William Howard Taft.

Michael slept so soundly on the brief flight to Chicago from St. Louis that
he almost missed his connecting flight to Las Vegas. Much to his surprise,
he'd slipped off again before that flight had even finished its taxi to the runway, awaking surprisingly refreshed when the plane landed at Harry Reid
International Airport in the early hours of the morning. The car Angela
Pierce had ordered had taken things from there, Michael falling asleep a
third time through the duration of the ride to Utah.

The Investigative Services Branch had a room reserved for him at the
Best Western Plus Zion Canyon Inn & Suites in Springdale this time, just
outside Zion National Park. Dawn was breaking as he got there, though,
and he was rested enough to forgo trying out the bed, opting for a shower
instead. Fortunately, his stump was unmarred by cuts or abrasions, showing some irritation he treated with the bathroom moisturizer squeezed out
of a tiny bottle.

The fresh uniform Angela had promised was hanging in the closet
when he arrived and, though he'd forgotten to mention socks and under-
wear, an ample supply of both had been placed inside one of the bureau
drawers.

He was able to grab the first shuttle to Zion, arriving before the park
officially opened. The majesty of Zion never ceased to amaze Michael; it
was not just one of the most picturesque national parks, but also one of
the most beautiful places in the world. Everything about the space, from
the quiet to the clean scents of nature to the postcardlike scenery, made
for an incredible contrast with the ugliness that had dominated the last
two days.

A ranger drove him to Zion Lodge at the beginning of the Emerald Pools trails, so he could clear his head and start fresh amid the beauty of Zion.

The Lower Emerald Pool Trail followed the sloped design of the main canyon. The trail wound through pinyon-juniper trees and past waterfalls Michael stopped to stare at and listen to. Being alone amplified the majesty of the scene and the sense of contentment that suddenly filled him.

That thought made him think of Danny Logan, who'd be growing up alone now. He had promised to check in on him, but the chaotic whirlwind of the past forty-eight hours had kept him from doing so. Gina Delgado had provided him with the direct number to the FBI detail now guarding the boy in an undisclosed location that was likely another Manhattan hospital, one deemed easier to secure.

He got the head of Danny's detail on the line and asked to be connected to the boy.

"Hey," Danny greeted a minute or so later.

"Hey back."

"Where'd you go, Mike?"

"A whole bunch of places."

"I've got a TV, but I'm not allowed to watch any news. That would probably have given me an idea where you've been, right?"

"Yes," Michael said, without elaborating further.

"And I haven't gotten my new phone yet."

"I'm on it."

"You guys kept mine, so you owe me one."

"You'll have it today, tomorrow at the latest."

Dead air filled the line for a few moments—so long Michael thought the call had been dropped. Then the boy resumed.

"My aunt and uncle are here."

"That's good. You told me you liked them."

"They've got a dog, a German shepherd. We couldn't get a dog, because my sister's allergic. I'm going to train him to attack in case the bad guys come back." Michael could hear the boy take a deep breath on the other end of the line. "I'm going to live in Florida."

"There are some great national parks in Florida."

"Like what?"

"Everglades National Park."

"Yeah, they've got a lot of snakes there, big ones. They're eating every-thing, screwing up the ecosystem."

"That's because pythons lay fifty to a hundred eggs a year. And they can grow to over thirty feet and two hundred pounds."

"Wow, that's why they can eat alligators and deer, pretty much any-thing. Swallow them whole. Maybe I can train a couple of them, too."

Not a bad idea, Michael thought.

CHAPTER 55

WASHINGTON, D.C.

During the last days of the Reagan presidency,
the tunnel was allegedly used to allow Richard Nixon
discreet access to the Oval Office for at least
one consultation with Ronald Reagan.

The marine captain accompanied Gina from the garage, escorting her through a heavy steel door that slid open after he entered the proper combination of numbers into an adjacent keypad. Gina would have expected something more high tech, like a retinal or fingerprint scan, but keypads must have been state-of-the-art when this facility had last been upgraded.

A matching door lay at the end of a fifty-foot hallway, guarded by two marines wearing body armor and wielding M4 assault rifles. Gina didn't detect any cameras, but knew they must be there, following every step she took.

At the end of the hall, the marine captain presented his ID to be scanned. Then both officers inserted their keys into matching stations on either side of the shiny steel slab door. They looked at each other, nodded, and turned the keys in the same instant, the way she had seen done in movies by officers manning nuclear-missile silos.

The steel door slid open without making a sound, as if it were floating. The marine captain gestured for Gina to enter.

"You're not coming along?"

He handed her back her phone. "Don't bother turning it back on. All signals are blocked down here."

Gina nodded and stepped through into some kind of antechamber set before yet another matching steel door. The door behind her whisked closed, again without making a sound. Then the door before her slid open in identical fashion.

To reveal Rod Rust, her mentor and superior at the New York field office.

‡‡‡

"The others will be along shortly," Rod Rust continued. "I wanted to get here first to fill you in before they arrive."

"The Vault," Gina said, gazing about. "I didn't think this place existed anymore."

"We've been using it because no one can know we're here. No one can know we've been meeting. They can't know that we're on to them," Rust added after a pause.

Gina didn't question him on who the group that met in the Vault was on to. Rust was tall and gaunt, with thinning gray hair. His head came to a peak on the top and the knobs of his bony shoulders were visible through his suit jacket. From the first time they'd met, when she was a teenager, Gina had never seen him without a tie and had seldom seen him without a suit jacket. Today was no exception.

"Your back seems fine," she said, stopping just short of a wink.

Rust cracked a thin smile. "I had to come up with a cover story to explain my absence, especially after the Statue of Liberty got hit."

Gina gazed about the sparsely furnished room. No effort had been made to disguise the Vault's steel walls, likely left over from the time it had served as just what its name indicated before being turned into a safe house for the president in the wake of Pearl Harbor. It looked to be about thirty feet square, with a low ceiling and recirculated air that made her feel as if she were in an airplane. The conference table, whiteboards, standing screens, and rolling chairs—with a laptop placed before each chair—made the room functional, though whoever else was part of this task force in addition to Rust would count themselves fortunate for the high-level security it offered.

"You were expecting an attack like that, I assume."

"We didn't know what to expect, Gina. We only knew that this country was facing the greatest threat in its history."

‡‡‡

Rust continued after they'd sat down opposite each other at the table. "We think it goes back as much as three years."

"Think? A task force of this level isn't sure?"

"This is different, Gina. The bad guys have learned from the last time they tried, in January of 2021. Nobody's talking. We don't know shit."

Gina leaned forward. "Well, I know a dozen special-ops soldiers out of what was then Fort Bragg who died in a helicopter crash are about as far from dead as it gets. The crash happened two years ago."

Rust nodded. "I read your report. That's why you're here. You figured it out."

"I'm guessing your task force beat me to it."

Rust nodded again, just once this time. "When a military aircraft crashes, there's always at least one accident investigation; if it resulted in death or injury, there is generally more than one investigation, each conducted by the military. At times, a third may be conducted by the NTSB or the FAA, sometimes both. In this case it was an FAA investigator who turned up some anomalies in the crash."

"Like there was no pilot on board?"

"His findings dealt more with inconsistencies in the mechanics. He was able to determine, and prove, that the craft flew straight into the side of a mountain. That it wasn't spinning or out of control prior to impact. He also determined it was picking up speed just prior to the crash." Rust's stare hardened a bit. "I could go on about his findings, Gina, but the bottom line is you uncovered the very same thing."

"What exactly did I uncover, boss?"

Rust sucked a breath deep enough for Gina to see his ribs expand through his white dress shirt. "I mentioned that the bad guys learned from the chaotic mess they made the last time. You know what they learned?"

"No."

"That they could win, if they had more men and firepower, along with better leadership and weaponry."

"And that's what this is about," Gina surmised.

"That's what it's always been about. The names of the bad guys kept changing, and the methods, but the one thing they all had in common was a lack of coordination. Random acts by crazy people with loose associations to white men whose membership in militias was no different to them than the Lions Club or Rotary, Timothy McVeigh being a prime example. As devastatingly tragic as Oklahoma City was, it was a one-off by a crackpot who got caught by a traffic cop."

Gina shifted uneasily.

"What is it, Gina?"

"I don't know. Traffic cop," she repeated, still trying to discern what that image had triggered in her mind. "You made me think of something I already lost track of. My thoughts are all jumbled. I have to keep reminding myself which city I'm in."

"It's been a tough couple of days, but it's about to get worse, a lot worse, believe me. Let me give you the short version, Gina. All those disparate groups are now united. And they're going to play a major role in whatever this country is about to face. Whack Jobs Anonymous isn't so anonymous anymore." Rust's Apple watch beeped. "The others are on their way, including a special guest."

"Besides me, you mean."

"The president."

CHAPTER 56

BROOKFIELD AIR STATION; BROOKFIELD, OHIO

Brookfield Air Force Station was closed in 1959.
The property was sold to a private entity in September
of 2012. More than 350 installations have been
closed in five rounds initiated by the Base Realignment
and Closure Act of 1990.

Lantry waited until the group around the parked convoy dispersed before easing out from beneath the chassis of the eighteen-wheeler. The smattering of guards left to watch over the vehicles all had their vision trained on the activity at the center of the base, so he skirted around in a wide loop to the darkest reaches of the grounds behind the cover of dilapidated storage units.

He squeezed between two of the rusted husks, which gave him a clear view of the activity transpiring inside the area under the LED spray of the construction lights. He focused not so much on the troops as on the base itself. In addition to C-130s parked along an active runway, there were training grounds and a firing range, along with a series of recently completed bare wood structures. Lantry's first thought was that they must have been hastily erected barracks for the multitude of troops housed here. Then, though, he glimpsed a small group of soldiers in black tactical gear emerge from one and a second group storm another in assault-team fashion. Their entry was followed by the dull clack of assault-rifle fire, accompanied by slight flashes through the empty holes where windows should have been. There were three structures in total, all of them different in size, shape, and configuration.

Lantry concluded that the structures might well be mock-ups to allow the assault teams to practice their incursions in a real-world environment.

Exactly what, though, were they rehearsing to assault? And why do that in a base that hadn't been active in much longer than Lantry had been alive?

He felt safe now, and his eyes had adjusted to the conditions enough to take in the scope of the base, which seemed to stretch to the west as far as he could see through the darkness. There looked to be other structures set along the very rear of the base, including a neat row of what looked like airplane hangars, their aluminum structures catching enough of the moonlight and spray from the construction kliegs for him to count five of them. There looked to be another two wooden structures at the farthest reaches of the base, larger in scope. Lantry would have to get closer to glean anything beyond that.

He studied the thick, overgrown brush that hugged the fence line. To approach the other end of the base, as much as a quarter mile away, all he needed to do was tuck himself within that brush and cling to the cover it provided. So Lantry pressed himself as close to the fence itself as he could and clung to the small gap between it and the start of the thick brush, enough to secure passage free from sight. He covered most of the ground in a crouch, knees bent low to keep him beneath the height of the brush, flattening himself out onto his stomach whenever he neared a guard patrolling the perimeter.

Even with the presence of those guards, Lantry was able to fall into a strange rhythm, until about the halfway point, when the brush grew right up against the fencing. The branches were thick, knobby, and difficult to part with his hands without making a rustling sound that might alert the nearest guard. That left him crawling on his stomach, feeling the brush scratching against his flesh through his clothes. Again, he found a rhythm to the movement, stopping and hugging the ground tighter whenever he heard the shuffle of a guard's footsteps. It made him think of his legendary uncle's exploits in Vietnam.

Lantry's path along the fence line took him behind the row of those airplane-like hangars, and he continued toward those larger wooden structures, which appeared to be much more elaborate in design. He saw a rope line enclosing the entire perimeter of the first of the two, as if to simulate fencing or something to that effect.

Lantry spotted no guards on patrol in the immediate area, so he shimmied on his stomach beneath the brush until only a thin sliver of it was left to provide cover. That gave him a clear line of sight to the first of the large wooden structures, which didn't look right to him, for reasons that immediately revealed themselves. What he was looking at wasn't a structure at all.

It was a façade.

A façade of a building Lantry recognized through the bare wood framing.

The White House.

‡‡‡

Lantry held a hand against his heart, as if that would help quiet its pounding. He considered the assault maneuvers he'd witnessed on the mock-ups of buildings he'd glimpsed earlier. Those structures must have represented the interiors of buildings, which meant the troops he'd witnessed were practicing assaults on a specific target or targets. In that scenario, the façade of the White House would allow the same troops to rehearse their approach and breach of the building itself.

What was happening?

He'd been enlisted by Fallen Timbers in a mission to protect the environment from the contents of those steel drums and casks—to prove toxic contamination by whoever was behind the shipments. This might not have been what he signed up for or had been expecting, but it was the place in which Lantry now found himself.

He heard a sporadic burst of gunfire, followed by a long series, then a virtual nonstop flurry coming from behind a second recently erected wooden structure just beyond the mock-up of the White House grounds. Lantry shimmied his way through the brush for another hundred yards or so before he was close enough to recognize that second structure. This one came complete with a steep series of wooden steps. The classic shape and dome of the actual structure the façade represented were missing, but it was still clear what he was looking at:

The U.S. Capitol.

Dozens of heavily armed troops were rehearsing assault-style maneuvers, clearly aimed at seizing control of the building. Based on the size and scope of the base, Lantry figured there were probably around a thousand soldiers training here. That brought his thoughts back to the corrugated-steel storage hangars he'd slid behind to get this far.

As the gunfire ratcheted up again, he retraced his path along the fence line and stopped at the first hangar he came to. The rear wasn't guarded, and he could see a crack between the door and the seam. Approaching it meant a dash through the open for a fifty-foot stretch, but none of the patrolling soldiers were about in the area, so Lantry steadied himself with a deep breath and bolted into the open.

For generations, legends had been passed down among his people about warriors of old who could render themselves invisible. He'd asked his uncle once about those legends and got only a cryptic answer in return. He chose not to believe in such things himself, but on this night could only wish he was capable of just that feat.

He made it to the back door of the storage hangar without incident. The door looked warped or bent along the seam, explaining why it hadn't closed all the way. Lantry squeezed his fingers through the resulting crack and released the catch, allowing him to open the door enough to squeeze through and then close it behind him.

A sliver of light slipped through the crack between the door and the jamb, more than enough for Lantry to identify what stood before him:

Twin rows of tanks, dozens and dozens of them.

‡‡‡

Lantry retraced his path out of the hangar, careful to reseal the door behind him just as he'd found it. He knew the remaining storage hangars would be similarly filled, if not with tanks, then with other weapons that were about to be unleashed by what looked to be a private army. Except, by all indications, this was the *real* army. As soon as he cleared the reach of the remaining hangars, his thoughts turned back to finding a way to contact Fallen Timbers.

I need to find a phone, somehow I've got to get hold of a phone.

That was Lantry's last thought before he felt something cold and hard press against the back of his neck.

"Move and I'll blow your head off," a voice said from behind him.

CHAPTER 57

ZION NATIONAL PARK, UTAH

> "On January 22, 1937, President Roosevelt
> established a second Zion National Monument,
> preserving over 36,000 acres (Proc. No. 2221).
> The second Zion National Monument, which is now
> referred to as Kolob Canyons, was incorporated with
> Zion National Park in 1956."

"We've got enough problems already without this," Zion National Park superintendent Bud Ricketts said, after Michael had climbed into his standard-issue Chevy Tahoe, white with green markings. It smelled like coffee, making Michael long for a cup.

Ricketts was a rawboned man who looked born for the outdoors. He had Popeye-like forearms attached to the pair of meat-slab hands gripping the Tahoe's steering wheel. His face and neck shined with sunscreen to keep them from getting as red and blistered as the back of his neck. Michael caught the slight scent of coconut oil mixing with that of the coffee from the thermos squeezed into one of the vehicle's cupholders.

Ricketts gnashed his teeth as if he were chewing a nonexistent piece of gum. "You hear about the runoff?" he asked Michael, referring to the huge volumes of snowmelt that normally washed down the canyons into the rivers that cut a spiderweb pattern through the park.

"What about it?"

"There wasn't enough, thanks to an unusually cold spring. So now we're going to have snowmelt and lots of it in peak season for the first time since I came here fifteen years ago. Frigging climate change," he added, shaking his head.

"Sure to add to the flash-flood problem," Michael said, referring to the all-too-regular flooding that sprang up with little or no notice when the nearby Virgin River was overrun with either stormwater or runoff and poured into the slot canyons that crisscrossed the park.

"For sure. And now I've got climatologists crawling up my ass, warning me about this and that. I know they work for the Park Service, but still."

Ricketts was a lifer in the National Park Service, having begun his career as a glorified tour guide before climbing the ranks. He'd worked in a host of different parks in any number of capacities, including law enforcement ranger for a stretch. Park superintendents were chosen for the myriad of skills they'd honed, foremost among those being able to serve in a supervisory capacity in an emergency. Each national park came with its own set of unique challenges in that regard, from the collapsing roadbeds in Yellowstone to giant pythons in the Everglades to the infamous flash floods here in Zion. But Michael figured nothing in Ricketts's experience could have prepared him, or anyone else, for the threat the parks were facing now.

The Tahoe continued along, slipping past one of the park's tandem shuttle buses, which were the only means this time of year by which the public could travel along Zion Canyon Scenic Drive. The route covered the park's primary attractions, making seven stops, which included Court of the Patriarchs; the Human History Museum, where park headquarters was located; the Lodge, boasting the Lower Emerald Pool Trail; Big Bend; and the Temple of Sinawava that encompassed the Virgin River Narrows and Riverside Walk. Park patrons were free to disembark at any stop and board another shuttle bus going in either direction at their leisure. Other, more outlying roads that cut through Zion were open to public vehicles, but the vast bulk of those coming to the park started at the visitor center, where the shuttle buses were based and which also housed a giant parking lot.

"So what would these sons of bitches target here?" Ricketts asked him.

Before Michael could answer, a beep sounded and a message flashed across the Tahoe's dashboard screen:

BIG STORM IN THE FORECAST FOR TOMORROW, CHIEF

"Who calls you 'Chief'?" Michael asked him.

Bud Ricketts squeezed the steering wheel tighter as they continued their drive along the paved, clay-colored, two-lane road that weaved its way through Zion like a snake, climbing at some points only to drop in others.

"The climatologist currently on-site. If it was up to him we'd shut down every time the wind blew."

"Let's head back to the visitor center . . . Chief."

"Very funny," Ricketts snickered. "Why?"

"Because if Zion's the next target," Michael told him, "that's what they'll hit."

CHAPTER 58

⊢•⊙•⊣

YAKIMA, WASHINGTON

The city is named after the
Yakama Nation tribe.

Jeremiah arrived purposely late to the meeting being held in an abandoned warehouse on the outskirts of Yakima that had been empty for so long that the metal FOR SALE signs were faded and warped. He took his place among the others standing in the back, the rows of chairs set up hastily and the dim lighting courtesy of a propane-fired generator. General Archibald Terrell, decked out in army combat fatigues, acknowledged him with a slight nod.

"As I was saying," Terrell resumed into a microphone, picking up on whatever thought Jeremiah had interrupted, "the last time I wore this uniform I was serving my country in combat, commanding men in battle. I donned it again tonight because I'm fighting a different war to preserve the country I served until my plain speaking got me fired."

Around him, Jeremiah heard hoots of agreement and saw heads in ball or trucker caps nodding. Those present had been alerted to park a few blocks away on the dark side streets populated by closed businesses and others hanging on by a thread. The old building's windows no longer opened, and the poor ventilation had turned it into a Petri dish of stale sweat, hair oil, and rank work clothes or army fatigues donned by the various militia leadership groups from the Pacific Northwest. Jeremiah looked out over the crowd as they cheered Terrell and saw a smattering of sheriff's uniforms mixed among the crowd. The real law of this country, elected by their fellows to serve communities instead of being appointed by politicians. Men with badges pinned to their chests who knew how their neighbors thought and considered protecting them against the intrusion of that which they neither wanted nor needed in their lives to be paramount in their job description. They reminded him of the local sheriff of Pierce County who'd refused to comply with a federal writ to evict the Hobbs family from their farm, forcing the federal marshals who'd murdered his father to do the deed themselves.

"This country is sick," Terrell continued. "This country is hurting. We've got ourselves two choices in that regard. One is to watch it die. The other is to give it the CPR it so desperately needs."

The hooting and nods of assent became more feverish, the assembled crowd stopping short of cheers to avoid attracting any attention to what was transpiring beyond the building's grime-encrusted windows.

"We can all be saviors, we can all be heroes, because this country needs its share of both. Plenty of good people who don't know what's coming are sure to jump to our side when we make our move. We've tried prayer, haven't we? But it hasn't worked and we let ourselves believe that God wasn't listening. So we wallowed in our failure and our pity, not realizing He was waiting, waiting for us to act. He's done listening because He's as frustrated as we are about how things have gone so wrong in this great nation. The blessing being that it's not too late, that we still have time to set things right, to get America back on the tracks it had been riding until a whole bunch of folks hijacked the train and drove it off the rails."

A smattering of applause rippled through the crowd, quickly fading out.

"We are about to wage a holy war for the soul of America, my brothers. That's right, this is a holy war for certain and I need you standing by my side when the dying starts and the chaos begins. I need you holding your spot on the wall to defend what used to be the country nobody remembers anymore. Those others like us need to be shown the way and, when the time is right, I need you to take them by the hand and lead them. I need you to stand ready because that day is about to dawn. And when it does you know where you need to be and what you need to do. You have your instructions, you have your assignments, and when the time comes, I know you won't fail me or our once-great country that's going to be great again.

"We can be mice or we can be men. And we've been mice for too long. Give us our six-packs and our sitcoms and our sick leave and they thought that would be enough to keep us happy, keep us numbed to the pain everywhere. We made that pain a part of ourselves and you know where it hurt the most?"

Jeremiah watched Terrell tap his chest.

"Right here. They thought they'd broken our hearts, broken us. But we fooled them, didn't we? And now we're gonna make them eat their words and their deeds. Before long, they'll be begging us to step in 'cause they won't have anywhere else to turn. The wall they've built to keep us out is high and thick. I say it's time to blow straight through that wall, friends. And I promise you this, as I stand here tonight. I promise that you're gonna love the sight you see on the other side of that wall. I know you've heard this kind of thing before, but you haven't heard it from me. Because a lot of people are about to die, a whole lot, and we're going to be the ones digging their graves."

‡‡‡

Ironically, Jeremiah had first met Archibald Terrell in downtown Yakima three years ago when the general was speaking at the historic courthouse on South Third Street that had been turned into a theater. He'd struck a more moderate tone back then, and there'd been no need to come and go in secret, but his message was pretty much the same.

Jeremiah was waiting on the steps when Terrell emerged after signing a spate of autographs for his adoring faithful.

"Did you mean it?"

"Mean what, sir?" Terrell had asked.

"What you said about taking our country back."

Terrell regarded him curiously, like a dog trying to decide whether to lick or bite a man's extended hand. "I never say anything I don't mean and never have. You got a problem with that, sir?"

"Not at all. It's why I'm here. I'm of the same mind, and I thought I might be able to help."

Jeremiah had told him about Gray Rock Trucking, the biggest long-haul transport company in the country, which his father had built from a trio of rebuilt eighteen-wheelers with leaky trailers.

"Must be a hell of a man," Terrell had said, "I'd love to meet him."

"You can't, because he's dead. Gunned down by the government you served."

"If you were listening in there, sir, you must have gotten the notion that I don't serve it anymore."

"No, you want to remake it in your own vision, take it down first if that's what it takes. And I bring a couple things to the table in that regard. First, I can get pretty much anything from point A to point B."

"And what's the second?"

"Motivation. I understand what it's like to lose something you can't get back. I know what it's like to feel all this hatred bottled up inside and that the only way to relieve it is to move to action."

Terrell had nodded, all lick now and no bite. "Tell you what, why don't you give me your number so we can discuss this further at a more opportune time?"

The call Jeremiah had been waiting for came six months later. General Archibald Terrell laid it all out for him, what needed to be transported and to where, a haul more dangerous than any hazardous or radioactive waste Gray Rock had ever moved.

"So what do you say, *Jeremiah*? You the kind of man who puts his money where his mouth is?"

"When do we get started?"

‡‡‡

The men who'd filled the floor left as soon as Terrell finished laying out what was expected of them, not wanting to linger in a way that might have invited attention from anyone passing by. Jeremiah watched them filter out, aware that the future of America would soon rest in the collective hands of men like these, already in place in strategic locations all across the country, awaiting the general's orders.

The general waited until they were the last two men present to approach Jeremiah in the back of the dusty warehouse floor that had once held all manner of home appliances.

"The uniform suits you well, General."

Terrell pulled at one of the sleeves. "It does, doesn't it? The latest convoy is holding at our base in Ohio," he reported, "and there's no further intelligence on who's behind that drone one of my men shot down."

"So we still have no idea who's flying them."

"An environmental group would be my best guess, given the cargo we've been transporting."

"You should look at those Natives I warned you about," Jeremiah said, feeling heat building beneath the surface of his skin. "They've been protesting at my depots for years because Gray Rock's the biggest long-hauler still willing to transport toxic and hazardous waste."

"Fallen Timbers," Terrell said, nodding. "I sent a team to check out their base of operations. Looks like they're in the wind."

"An indication in its own right, isn't it?"

"That's not the biggest threat facing us, my friend."

"What is?"

"The footage shot by that boy on Liberty Island has rendered us, and the entire operation, vulnerable."

Jeremiah had to fight to keep his breathing and his tone steady. "You mean the boy one of your men failed to take off the map?"

"My man being bested by a park ranger was a fluke and he's paid the price for his failure," Terrell said, leaving things there. His phone rang, and he squinted to better make out the caller ID. "I need to take this."

Jeremiah watched him move aside and keep his words hushed through a brief conversation, then watched the general pocket his phone.

"New developments," Terrell said simply.

"In Washington?"

"No, Ohio."

CHAPTER 59

ZION NATIONAL PARK, UTAH

The shuttles used to transport people from Springdale
and around the park had 6.8 million riders in 2019.

"Hit the visitor center?" Ricketts said, either not believing it or not wanting to.

"An especially congested area at Zion because of the reliance on shuttle buses."

"That was the first thing we considered when the alert came in hours after the Statue of Liberty fell. You saw the magnetometers we added to check all tourists for firearms. We're also checking every car that enters the park for explosives."

"What if they'd already been set, Bud?"

"Then the dogs the Utah Highway Patrol brought in would have found them."

"Dogs didn't find all the explosives in the Assembly Room at Independence Hall or at the Gateway Arch. There are limits to their effectiveness, especially in a place like this."

Bud Ricketts aimed his gaze downward at Michael, as he steered their Tahoe along Zion Canyon Scenic Drive back toward the visitor center. "So what's it like?"

"What's what like?"

"You know, getting around on a prosthetic foot."

"You want to know if I fall out of bed every morning?"

"That's not what—"

"The answer is I did at first," Michael told him. "You get used to it, just like you can get used to anything."

"All the same, losing a foot couldn't have been easy to deal with."

"Losing my wife was harder."

Ricketts looked uncomfortable. "Why'd you want to come back?"

"I didn't. I used to be a law enforcement ranger. Now I'm ISB."

"Less traipsing around, right?"

"Not lately," Michael said.

"You like catching bad guys?"

"I like preventing further crime. I like keeping the parks safe. Ordinary rangers are the ones doing the real heavy lifting. I still wear the uniform, but they're the ones with their noses in everything day in, day out."

"Like your wife."

"Like my wife."

"I tried to get her to transfer to Zion a couple times."

"Don't take it personal, Bud. She loved Rainier."

"Sure, but this place grows on you. We've had record attendance the last four years running."

"Speaking of which," Michael said, glad for the opportunity to digress, "how many of those tandem buses are you using to move tourists through the park?"

"An even dozen in a constant loop along the drive, making the usual stops at the places we just passed ourselves, so the tourists can get out and enjoy whatever they want to explore. We're expecting six hundred thousand visitors to the park this month alone, twenty thousand per day. I know that's about the same as Liberty Island, but here they're spread over almost two hundred and fifty square miles compared to twelve acres. And, even at peak afternoon time, we're not expecting more than twelve thousand in the park at any one given time. That's still a lot, but for what it's worth, I think being assigned here is a waste of your time."

"I hope so, Bud, I really do."

‡‡‡

The visitor center looked small when measured against the rock formations towering over it. It was rustic in design, with natural wood inlays amid brick the same color as the reddish rock face that looked down upon the one-story structure. There were several matching overhangs where visitors to the park could wait under cover for the next bus to arrive. Michael spotted four buses with engines buzzing taking on passengers, who lined up and filed on neatly. True to Bud Ricketts's word about the buses running in a constant loop, two of the buses departed, then the third and fourth, and were replaced by two incoming buses. The first shuttles of the day departed the visitor center at 6:00 A.M. and the last at 5:00 P.M. In all, it took forty-five minutes to cover the entire loop, which meant a ninety-minute round trip.

The visitor center and its adjacent grounds were set near the Watchman trailhead. The front and back of the building were dominated by walls of windows that looked out over the figurative beginning of the park. Inside, tourists milled about atop wood floors fashioned from trees plucked from the surrounding woods to avoid overgrowth. Michael exchanged smiles with several, as he and Bud Ricketts walked past the various displays and wall hangings that depicted Zion's colorful history. He could see Ricketts's point about a park this big and sprawling making for a poor target to attack, except for the fact of the beauty that encompassed it. Whoever was behind the bombings might see that as cause to make this the most likely of targets by upending that beauty, dirtying the pristine landscape with the ugliness of blast residue, char, and the blood of the lives lost.

The thought made Michael's stomach flutter.

He moved about the visitor center alongside Ricketts. Security here at the most congested area of the park had been increased significantly, including law enforcement rangers at every entrance and exit, in addition to being dispersed through the crowd in plainclothes. They still stood out to Michael, in large part because he knew most of them.

"We brought dogs in to sweep it this morning," Ricketts reiterated. "You'll notice one over there, patrolling the center with its handler. They tell me the dogs can only stay alert for a few hours at a time, so we're rotating them."

Michael nodded. He felt everything to secure the visitor center had been done. He considered the possibility that the plotters might have rigged the clay-colored rock face that towered over the scene behind the building with explosives, but the jagged natural structure was set too far back for the rubble and debris to create a catastrophe on the order of the ones at Liberty Island and the Gateway Arch, or Independence Hall if things had turned out differently there.

Michael cast his gaze out the array of floor-to-ceiling windows at the steady comings and goings of the tandem tour buses, leaving off one load of passengers to pick up another. What was it Bud Ricketts had said?

"An even dozen in a constant loop along the drive, making the usual stops at the places we just passed ourselves, so the tourists can get out and enjoy whatever they want to explore."

"Oh my God," Michael said out loud, realizing.

CHAPTER 60

WASHINGTON, D.C.

America's Front Yard encompasses over one thousand
acres, which the National Park Service maintains.

"How long before they arrive?" Gina asked Rod Rust.

"Twenty minutes."

"Enough time for you to tell me what I'm doing here, what you need
me for."

"I read your reports, Gina. You already know more than you think. I
told them they had to bring you in, before you figured it all out on your
own and became a problem for us."

"A problem?"

"Go back to your initial sit reports from the Statue of Liberty, what you
uncovered thanks to that video footage the kid shot with his phone."

"Dead Special Forces operatives who aren't dead at all," Gina told him.

Rust let her remark hang in the air between them.

"There are more troops like that, aren't there?" Gina picked up.

"Not exactly like that. But it's where all this started from our end a little
over a year ago. The FBI was put in charge of an undercover operation to
look into right-wing nationalist infiltration into all branches of the military, especially the army, active and retired. We initially thought it was for
recruiting purposes, and, in part, it was. But, primarily, it was for tactical
training to help destabilize the country they'd sworn to protect."

Gina fingered her chin dramatically. "A year ago was when you started
having back trouble. . . ."

Rust nodded slowly, the motion making him look like the Ichabod Crane
character from "The Legend of Sleepy Hollow." "Because of my work with
New York City's Joint Terrorism Task Force, I was put in charge. The agents
I was able to put in place didn't yield much right away, but six months ago

we started getting a notion of how saturated the military has become with fanatics. The first thing our investigation uncovered was that the infiltration has been going on for fifteen years."

"That would date back to 2009, when Barack Obama was elected president."

Rust nodded. "The election of the nation's first Black president was just what the doctor ordered for these nationalist groups who are convinced the true Americans, as they call themselves, are being marginalized, that they have to save the country from itself to preserve their way of life. To enough of them, this is a holy war. We should have seen the writing on the wall when the Capitol was overrun in 2021. Call that a dress rehearsal."

"Lots of ex-military among those we arrested, boss."

"And that's the real rub, Gina. The number of military veterans joining up or even establishing these extremist groups is staggering. We always knew there was more of that going on than we cared to admit. What we didn't know was the level to which the command structure was compromised.

"I lost four of the men we'd placed inside in a single week," he resumed. "The last bit of intelligence all of them furnished was names of career officers they suspected were compromised. Then they just dropped off the face of the earth. I pulled the others out because I knew my operation had been made. The officers in question all took early retirement and dropped off the face of the earth, too. You can see what I'm getting at here."

"I can see we've got one hell of a problem on our hands."

"There's more. We've been following the movements of members of militia groups on their cell phones. Nothing we could ever use in an evidentiary capacity," Rust continued, before Gina could state the obvious, "but arresting these bozos isn't what we're after. And I can tell you that, after these groups went uncharacteristically dark for the past six months or so, they've started to concentrate numbers in large patches across the entire country where they've also managed to infiltrate the law enforcement community. The best advantage we had going for us for years was that they were too disparate to work with each other. That went out the window on January 6, 2021, and now it's blown straight through the door."

"You're suggesting that someone has brought them together."

Rust nodded, his expression so tight that it looked as if the slight motion pained him. "We have strong evidence that a former army general is the wizard behind the curtain on all this, pulling the strings. More on him at the briefing. The real wild card here is someone we haven't been able to identify yet. All we know is that he's based in the Pacific Northwest and calls himself Jeremiah."

"How?" Gina wondered.

"A single intercepted communiqué. Totally random, the one bit of luck we received when the frequencies got crossed and a Washington state trooper, who happened to be an ex–Green Beret, heard enough to call in the cavalry. Jeremiah's appearance on the scene led to an escalation in activity going back around eighteen months. He's become the real game changer in all this, but no one seems to know who he really is."

"Except for this ex-general."

"The planning for the attack we're facing started escalating three years ago and has been increasing ever since, during which that ex-general and his cadre have managed to bring all the elements of the white nationalistic movement together. These people want chaos, they thrive on chaos. We think Jeremiah, whoever he is, was brought in to help unleash it."

Rust rose, wincing as he stretched his arms.

"Your back?" Gina prodded.

He winced again. "It got bad, after I used it as an excuse." His eyes fastened on hers. "Right around the time our intelligence indicated the enemy had infiltrated all levels of government, too, up to the highest doors of power. That's why we're meeting here, in a place everyone forgot existed. Outside of this room, we don't know who we can trust."

"A terrifying proposition, boss."

"We have no idea how deep their penetration goes."

Gina stood up and paced to the wall. "So the attacks on national landmarks are, what, a precursor?"

"I think they're sending a message about bringing this country to its knees. Take out the symbols that define us the most, our very history."

"So they can write a new one."

Rust nodded again. "Wipe the slate clean and start from scratch." He held Gina in a long gaze. "We were looking for those missing soldiers a long time before you caught on. Fortunately, we've established our own counterinsurgency force."

"You mean the National Guard out of Fort Liberty?"

"Was it that obvious?"

"It was to me. So the order to confiscate the park rangers' cell phones . . ."

"That was us," Rust confirmed, "to make sure nothing got out from on-site until we had a rapid-insertion force in place."

"How many of these rapid-insertion forces do you have in operation?"

"Not enough," he said evasively.

Rust's phone beeped and he lifted it from the table. Concern flashed across his face, seeming to tighten the skin stretched over his gaunt features.

"The meeting's been postponed until tomorrow, Gina."

"What's going on?"

"I have no idea," Rust said, pocketing his phone. "But it can't be good."

CHAPTER 61

⊱•◦◦•⊰

ZION NATIONAL PARK, UTAH

The Olympic torch made its way through Zion National
Park before the 2002 Winter Games in Salt Lake City.

Michael's gaze locked on the scene beyond the window glass. "Bud?" he
called, repeating it when he saw that Ricketts had drifted away from him.
"Bud!"

Ricketts stopped and turned at Michael's approach.

"The buses have been checked, too, right, all of them?"

Ricketts nodded. "Up, down, and sideways."

"Tires included?"

"Tires?"

Michael directed his attention to a tandem bus that had just pulled up at
one of the pickup stations. "See the waves of heat emanating from them?"

Ricketts looked baffled. "I didn't know you could see heat."

"You see it more than you think, usually because of the contrast, in this
case those big tires superheating from all the stops and starts against the
cooler pavement. It's a kind of refraction, when the light changes speed
when it encounters the temperature variation."

"I didn't know light changed speeds."

"It does," Michael said.

He jerked his phone from his pocket to call Gina Delgado, but it rang
unanswered. He kept the phone in his grasp, on the chance she called back.

It rang seconds later.

"Where are you, Gina?"

"I . . . can't say. What's up? How's Zion?"

"That's why I'm calling. Could you rig the tires of a bus to blow up at a
high temperature?"

"You're talking about a flash point, Walker."

"So it's possible."

"Not just possible, it happens more often than anyone realizes, usually by accident."

"How so?"

"Remember that ship that blew up in a Beirut port and practically shut down the city?"

"Vaguely. I heard it was sabotage, but no one was ever caught or charged."

"That's because it wasn't sabotage. The ship had several metric tons of chemicals stored in its hull and a few were leaking combustible vapors into the air. When the unventilated cargo hold reached a certain temperature, the flash point, those vapors exploded. Technically, it's called a thermal-kinetic explosion."

"Tires aren't ventilated either, Gina," Michael said, eyes still focused out the window, now fastened on the tires of the buses as they came and went. "If you pumped them full of an explosive vapor . . ."

"Tire temperatures can reach over a hundred and fifty degrees, even more if conditions are right. It can cause something called tread separation, like the Firestone fiasco about twenty years ago. How hot is it out there in Zion today?"

"Over ninety, making up for the cold spring they had here."

"Not good, Michael. Those Firestone tires blew with nothing inside them except hot air. Pump an explosive vapor in through the air valves . . ."

"I get the idea. What would you pump in?"

"There are a bunch of choices, but I'd go with azidoazide azide. It's part of a class of chemicals known as high-nitrogen energetic materials. Michael, you need to—"

"I know, Gina."

Michael ended the call and looked from the windows toward Ricketts. "Shut the buses down, Bud, shut them down now!"

CHAPTER 62

WASHINGTON, D.C.

The Residence Act was signed into law on July 16, 1790,
creating the site of Washington, D.C.

Gina returned the phone to her pocket, regretting that she hadn't told
Michael to keep the line open to enable her to follow what happened next
in Zion. He was clearly a quick study when it came to dealing with high
explosives. She'd met experts who never would have considered bus tires.

Virtually everything, though, posed an explosive threat, given the in-
stability of so many chemicals at high temperatures. All she could do now
was wait for Walker to call her back.

Rod Rust told Gina a room had been reserved for her at the Mayflower
Hotel under an assumed name. She had provided that name upon checking
in and was not asked to provide an ID or means of payment. A change of
clothes in her precise size and some additional toiletry supplies from her
favorite brands were waiting for her in the sixth-floor room. Gina could
only assume Rust had arranged all this at the same time he arranged for
her to be flown to Washington. With the circle that met in the Vault kept
to a minimum, he wouldn't have trusted anyone else to handle the task or,
perhaps, didn't have a subordinate available to trust.

She'd been going non-stop for three days and was now running on fumes.
Gina felt a deep throb in the back of her head, born of all the stress and
fatigue. If not for the sleep she'd been able to grab on board the FBI jet, she
probably would have slipped off at the conference table while seated across
from Rust. It was still early enough in the day, though, to grab double-digit
hours of slumber to be ready and refreshed once she got the call from Rust
about tomorrow's meeting in the Vault.

She guzzled a bottle of room-temperature water, took a long, hot shower,
climbed into one of the Mayflower's famed bathrobes, and lay down atop

the bedcovers. She was thinking of reaching for the remote to switch on the television just to have some soft noise in the background, but drifted off before she could even manage the task. She thought she heard the phone ring, but passed it off as the product of a dream, only to be awoken a few minutes later by it ringing again atop the night table.

"Boss?" she rasped, not bothering to check the caller ID.

"Sorry to disappoint you, Chief."

Gina checked the phone display and saw it was John Milton calling. She sat up on the edge of the bed and cleared her throat, as Paradise continued.

"Where are you? I thought you were headed back to the site."

"I got rerouted," she said, leaving it there.

"You sound tired."

"Exhausted."

"I think I've got something that might just wake you up," he told her. "It's about those incidents in Mount Rainier National Park, Chief."

For a brief instant, Gina didn't know what he was referring to. "Tell me more," she said, remembering the video and JPEG files she'd sent him of the man she suspected had been the hunter in the blind the day Michael was shot and his wife Allie was killed.

"You were right about the picture of the suspect. Not nearly enough discernible features to make an identification. But you were also right about those green Xaegistac Airsoft goggles."

"How so?"

"Well, they're common—not exactly a dime a dozen, but too many in circulation to find your guy by back-checking sales."

"Tell me something I don't know."

"There was a scratch on one of the lenses of his pair, pretty deep."

Gina felt herself growing alert and sat up straighter, waiting for Paradise to continue.

"Okay, so we've got those three separate incidents, each approximately six months apart. In the first two, both couples vanished. I don't have to tell you about the third, other than the fact that the bodies of those twins Walker and his wife killed had been removed by the time park rangers got to the spot. There was some blood, but it was too degraded by the freezing temperatures and contamination to get a DNA match from. The samples were even mixed up with Walker's and his wife's, further complicating things."

"Okay," Gina said, prodding him to go on.

"So I went back and rescanned all the security footage from the hours preceding and following all three attacks. I don't have to tell you that national parks are pretty much a wasteland when it comes to security cameras."

"Except for the entrance and parking area at Rainier, anyway."

"If there was something on those, you would have found it and both of us know it."

"So you're calling to tell me *what* exactly?"

"There was a traffic camera up the road a bit, couple miles back at the last traffic light. As near as I can tell from the police reports, nobody ever checked it."

Gina felt her heart skip a beat. She could feel that Paradise was getting to whatever he had called her about.

"I just sent you a text."

Her phone beeped as it came in. Gina clicked on it, putting Paradise on speaker as she regarded the photo he'd just texted and worked her fingers on the screen to make it as big as she could. Enlarging it reduced the resolution and she was left with little more than a blur.

"What am I looking at, Paradise?"

"You'll see it much clearer when you view this and the other still shots I pulled off the video. Nothing of the driver or license plate, but enough to identify the vehicle as a white SUV, a GM model that could be either Buick or Chevrolet. But the picture I sent you is of something the camera caught sitting on the dashboard: a pair of green Xaegistac Airsoft goggles with a scratch on the same lens as our suspect's pair."

‡‡‡

Gina took a deep breath, hoping it would steady her. It didn't, because she could tell Paradise wasn't finished yet.

"So we've got the goggles and a white SUV," she said, prodding him.

"That's not all we've got, Chief. We've also got the murder of that park ranger in Rainier."

Gina went numb, recalling part of her conversation with Rod Rust back in the Vault.

"What is it, Gina?"

"I don't know. Traffic cop. You made me think of something I already lost track of."

But it had been that park ranger she'd been thinking of, shot twice in the chest in the midst of a traffic stop.

"When did this happen?"

"Right around six months before Walker's wife was killed, Chief."

"How close to the disappearance of that second couple?"

"They were reported missing the following day."

"And no one picked up on this before?"

"There wasn't a lot to pick up on. The only thing two of the three tourists in the general area of the traffic stop at the time recalled seeing was—"

"A white SUV," Gina completed for him.

She felt her mind racing, picturing that unsuspecting park ranger making a simple traffic stop on park grounds. Maybe for speeding, or poaching, or drinking from an open container. He pulled over a white SUV being driven by a man who'd likely just claimed the lives of the second couple. Then she went numb, recalling an exchange that Michael related to her between him and Allie on the day she was murdered.

"*You check the picture I texted you?*"

"*What picture?*"

"*The SUV with the covered animal in the back.*"

"Oh my God," she heard herself say. "There was a picture Michael Walker had that his wife pulled off social media of a white SUV in the background with what she thought was a covered animal carcass in the back. It was taken in the area of the traffic stop either right before or right after the park ranger was murdered."

"You included it in that batch of photos you sent me, and I'm looking at it right now, Chief. It was posted on Facebook twenty-four hours before the second couple was reported missing, which means the day they disappeared."

The timeline, Gina reasoned, made perfect sense. It would explain the motive behind the hunter murdering a ranger. Maybe he'd spotted the bodies of the murdered couple covered by a tarpaulin in the back. Maybe he'd only been looking that way.

"The slugs they pulled out of the ranger didn't come from the same gun that killed Walker's wife," Paradise resumed, anticipating her next question. "Local sheriff's department might have checked that much, but there's nothing mentioned about it in their report. And they never found the slugs that shattered Walker's foot, although the bullets were identified as coming from a .357 Magnum, same caliber that killed the park ranger."

Gina tried picturing how Michael would respond to the news that, at long last, there were strong leads about the man who'd likely orchestrated everything that day, just as he'd orchestrated the disappearances, and likely murders, of two other couples in the year prior. Then, too, he had probably utilized the same young man and woman as bait in some fashion, just as he had to dupe Michael and Allie.

"Anything else, Paradise?"

"You bet." Gina could almost picture him smiling on the other end of the line. "I ran the shot pulled off social media through our system that searches grids for vehicles with comparable specifications, and I got a hit on a traffic camera twenty miles from Mount Rainier the day the park ranger was killed, farther out than anyone had checked before. As soon as I'm able to isolate the license plate, I'll text it to you, Chief. Then you'll have your man."

CHAPTER 63

ZION NATIONAL PARK, UTAH

The hike to Angels Landing, named because it is so
high only an angel could land on it, is considered one
of the most dangerous in the world.

Park ranger headquarters at Zion was contained in a section of the Zion
Human History Museum, about a two-minute drive from the visitor center.
Michael and Ricketts headed straight there, while Ricketts barked orders to
the dispatcher over his walkie-talkie to shut the buses down immediately,
evacuate them, and get the tourists as far away as possible.

Clambering down the stairs, Michael was left to picture what it would
be like if the warning came too late for a few of the buses. All those explosive vapors of whatever Delgado had called it wouldn't just shred the
tires if they blew, they'd eviscerate the entire bus, potentially vaporizing or
melting parts of it.

When they reached headquarters it was already humming with activity.
Since there were no security cameras along Zion Canyon Drive, which
cut through the various slot canyons that comprised the park, there were
no exterior shots of the buses. But all of them were outfitted with internal
cams that allowed those rangers monitoring the park to view the buses being emptied of passengers in orderly fashion. Michael watched six security
monitors that were switching between the various buses. He was able to
identify the location of each by the views captured beyond the windows.

Meanwhile, the two tandem buses that were currently parked in front
of the visitor center to load or off-load passengers had been shut off and
locked. As an added precaution, because of the potential damage to the
visitor center if one of them exploded, it was in the process of being evacuated. All patrons who'd been inside were asked to leave Zion if they had
come by car. Those who had reached the park via public shuttles from

Springdale were moved far, far back from the building to wait there for the tour buses that had been summoned back to pick them up ahead of schedule.

"What now?" Bud Ricketts asked Michael.

"How close are you to the local sheriff's department or highway patrol?"

"It's the sheriff's department and close enough."

"Alert them to what's going on and ask them to send some cruisers to back up our efforts to clear the park. Tell them the FBI is arranging for the dispatch of a bomb-disposal unit that's already en route. Nobody approaches any of the parked buses until they're on-site."

"You sure about all this, Michael?" Ricketts asked him.

Michael looked again toward the screens now showing empty buses, glimpses caught of those who'd just been on board walking away to put as much distance between them and the vehicles as possible.

"As sure as I can be without checking what's inside those tires myself," he replied.

‡‡‡

The nearest bomb-disposal unit capable of handling a situation this big was located in Las Vegas. Michael received a call from the squad's commander that they were coming via helicopter. They ordinarily never landed in the park, but there was ample open space set not far from the visitor center to create a makeshift landing pad. The unit's ETA was sixty-two minutes, with anticipated headwinds whipped up by the approaching storm front that had put drenching rain in the forecast for tomorrow. Meanwhile, the local sheriff's department assisted Zion's hefty complement of rangers in managing an orderly evacuation of the park, no easy task given its vast sprawl and the fact that cell phone coverage was spotty or nonexistent in several sectors.

The Las Vegas Metropolitan Police Department's bomb-disposal unit arrived on-site with a rough plan already in mind, based on the mapped-out locations of the shut-down tandem buses along Scenic Drive. The first suggestion had been hauling the buses out of Zion with extended tow trucks capable of handling the load. That idea was quickly dismissed, given the notion of having tires potentially filled with devastatingly powerful explosives thumping and bumping down roads that cut through pockets of civilization, not to mention routes traveled by other vehicles.

Instead, upon arrival the squad commander showcased a tool normally utilized by EPA hazmat teams devoted to removing toxic gases from confined spaces. He demonstrated how the tool would be fit, via a jerry-rigged adapter, into each pressure valve in order to drain the contents of the tire, including the temperature-rigged explosive gases, into specially designed and insulated canisters that resembled big oxygen tanks.

First on the agenda, though, was to test the tires of one of the buses parked far enough away from the visitor center to assure no collateral damage in the event something went wrong. Michael and Ricketts viewed the process from what was deemed a safe distance, which meant they could discern very little at all, beyond a bomb tech in full padded gear taking samples from each tire and then bringing them to squad commander Newbury to be tested. Newbury explained that they'd be using a gas detector known as a catalytic bead sensor to handle that task.

"Has one of these machines ever let you down?" Michael had asked Newbury.

"I wouldn't still be here if it had," he'd told them.

Now Michael and Ricketts watched him raise his blast visor and ease off his helmet as he approached them, remaining silent when he drew even and regarded them both.

"Zion gets to live another day, gentlemen," he pronounced. "The only thing in those tires was air."

‡‡‡

"I'm sorry," Michael said, as they rode the Tahoe back to the visitor center, after the Las Vegas bomb disposal unit checked the tires on all the other buses in an abundance of caution.

"Nothing to be sorry for," Ricketts told him from behind the wheel. "You were doing your job, playing it safe. And I'm the one who gave the evacuation order."

"You shouldn't have to clean up my mess, Bud."

"It's not like you cried wolf, Michael."

"But I was wrong."

"And what if you'd been right? Look, we both know why you're here. Ethan Turlidge is no friend of mine, or the national parks, either. He wants you out of circulation, so you know what? Screw the bastard and just enjoy the scenery. You just made Zion safer by exposing our biggest vulnerability.

I'm going to put guards on the buses overnight to make sure nobody can get anywhere close to them. Then tomorrow it's business as usual."

"Except for the weather," Michael reminded him.

"We've been lucky with no flash floods so far this season."

"That might not be the only storm that's coming, Bud."

CHAPTER 64

># BROOKFIELD AIR FORCE STATION, BROOKFIELD, OHIO

A controversial UFO incident occurred here on
December 14, 1994.

A sound Lantry recognized as an approaching helicopter jolted him alert in the chair to which he was tied. Through the window he spotted the black helicopter lowering toward a makeshift landing pad in an area of the base cordoned off into a circle by cinder blocks, beyond which a half dozen men wearing officers' bars stood at near attention.

The rotor slowed, and before the helicopter came to a complete stop its cabin door slid open and a man in a general's uniform dropped out, crouching to remain below the spin of the blade. He reached back inside to assist a second emerging figure, manually easing that figure's head down to avoid the rotor as well. Shadows seemed to cling to the general, but the second figure emerged into some stray light cast from the construction lights attached to overhead poles. He was wearing a Carhartt jacket and had the leathery look of a man used to working outdoors. The man was sinewy and lean and looked to be about the same age as the general, maybe sixty or so.

Lantry watched as the officers stepped over the cinder blocks and approached the two men, saluting both when they reached them. The general looked comfortable with the gesture, while the other figure looked awkward when he returned it.

A few minutes later he heard a key turn and the door to the office open. The man in the Carhartt jacket entered and closed the door behind him. There was no sign of the general who had accompanied him in the helicopter.

The man approached the chair to which Lantry had been secured.

"I'm Jeremiah," he greeted, standing over Lantry now. "You want to tell me your name?"

The boy remained silent, looking up from the chair his arms and legs were fastened to with plastic flex-cuffs. He willed himself to be brave, just the way his legendary uncle would have been, as the sinewy man loomed over him.

The skin on his face and arms was leathery, patchy with what looked like lumps of dry, flaky skin on both cheeks. He looked like he had a sunburn. They were alone in a room that had been an office before the base was shuttered, but had been cleared out except for the chair.

"That's okay," the man resumed, in a voice so calm it was unnerving, "we can put that off until later. Why don't we start with how you got here, son? You can tell me that much, can't you?"

Lantry swallowed hard, figured he could. "I rode atop one of the eighteen-wheelers."

Jeremiah grinned. "No shit? Now, that's impressive. You're a Native, aren't you?"

Lantry nodded. "Lakota Sioux."

"Your people have a great history. I respect that. Just like you should respect that your people belong by my side, after all the injustice they've faced. That's what I'm all about, son, injustice. This country is rank with it. America's rotting at the head, just like a fish, and the rot is spreading. Natives like yourself were among the first to be victims of that rot, which is to say you were given a royal screwing when what passed for a country stole your land right out from under you. I can relate to that. You folks got a bone to pick with this country and so do I. You ever lose somebody close to you?"

Lantry nodded. His mother had died giving birth to him, and a liver rotted by alcohol had claimed his father just short of Lantry's twelfth birthday. He'd been raised by extended family members, especially his uncle, along with the tribe itself when his uncle disappeared for long stretches, without explanation at times, to this day.

"Me, too, son," Jeremiah continued, looking at him differently. "The hurt never goes away, does it? You can either let it eat you alive or let it push you in the direction you need to go.

"You know the best way to relieve your pain? By making others feel it, too. People go about their daily lives like they own the world, in a fog, not even seeing what's right in front of them. Those barrels and casks we've been hauling? They were delivered onto me for a reason, because now I can make people open their eyes and know what pain really feels like. I want them to hurt the way I've been hurting, to know what it's like to lose everything. I want them to go to bed not knowing what the world will look like when they wake up. So many people out there hate the world, just like I do, and you know what? The world hates us back. That's all going to change now, thanks to the contents of those barrels Gray Rock Trucking has been hauling. The country's going to get a do-over, son, another chance to get things right."

A satellite phone flashed in Jeremiah's hand, as he knelt in front of Lantry so they were eye-to-eye.

"I know you want to be brave, son, but that's just being stubborn since both of us know I could get you to recite the alphabet backward, if I let a couple of the boys here have their way with you. So let's try something else, son."

With that, the man who called himself Jeremiah removed a six-inch buck knife from a sheath clipped to his belt and angled it toward Lantry. It glinted in the sunlight, and the boy felt his bowels loosen. Then Jeremiah cut off the flex-cuffs fastening his wrists to the arms of the old desk chair, and repeated the process with his ankles and the chair legs.

"That's better, isn't it? Go ahead, stretch yourself out. Get the blood flowing again."

Lantry did, watching Jeremiah stand back up and return the knife to its sheath. The boy reached up for his warrior talisman necklace, as if to make sure it was still there, pulling his hand away quickly so Jeremiah wouldn't notice.

"We're on equal ground now, son. You got a best shot, now's the time to take it, but I don't figure you for much of a fighter. How old are you?"

"Eighteen."

"I had you pegged for a couple years younger. That drone we shot down, I'm guessing you were the pilot."

Lantry nodded. The long hair that had fallen into his face when he stretched was embedded with the smell of oil, hot steel, and the road he'd spent all those hours feeling from the top of the truck.

"You ground the others after we got wise to what you were up to?"

Lantry nodded again. He knew the man wanted him to lunge and take that best shot. He could see it in Jeremiah's eyes, almost like he was pleading with him to do it. But the boy held firm to the arms of his chair.

"This is all about the environment, isn't it? You Natives got a thing for preserving nature. Me, I got a thing for taking back whatever I can from the natural world, whatever serves my interests. You hooked on to us at the depot in West Virginia where we took in our load, right?"

Another nod.

"You got any idea what we're hauling?"

This time, Lantry shook his head.

"You're lying. How long your people been ghosting my trucks?"

"First time for me," Lantry said, finding his voice.

"But not for whoever put you up to this, right?"

Lantry remained silent and motionless.

"Don't make me ask you again, son."

"Yes."

"And the people who put you up to this, they think this is about polluting the land?"

Lantry nodded.

"They got a name?" Jeremiah asked.

"No."

Jeremiah grinned. "You're lying but I don't much care. I heard your people got a group called Fallen Timbers that's staged protests a couple times at my depots and pick-up points, but that doesn't matter." He eased forward the satellite phone he'd been holding. "We found the remains of yours all busted up back at that truck stop, so I got you a replacement. That way you can call your people and tell them we're still headed west and you'll call again as soon as you get the opportunity. You got that?"

Lantry just looked at him.

"I'm going to ask you again, son. You got that?"

Lantry looked away. Then he watched Jeremiah move to the door and open it to reveal a pair of uniformed soldiers standing there.

"You got a choice to make," he said. "You either make that first call now or I leave you alone with these boys long enough for them to change your mind. So what'll it be, son?"

Lantry extended his hand.

CHAPTER 65

WASHINGTON, D.C.

Though few buildings were completed, the government
moved from Philadelphia to D.C. in 1800.

The first thing Gina did upon waking the following morning was check her phone, but no text from Paradise had arrived, nor had she received a single phone call, both of which struck her as odd. It also wasn't like Agent Milton to overpromise, so she pressed his number to get an update. Knowing how badly Michael could use some good news, especially after the false alarm he had triggered at Zion yesterday, Gina wanted to share that the FBI was now closing in on the man complicit in his wife's death.

At first, she thought her call to Paradise hadn't gone through, because it didn't ring. Gina was about to redial when she heard a droll, recorded male voice over the line:

"This line is being monitored for reasons of national security. No outside contact is permitted at this time."

That would explain why there were no voicemail or text messages on her phone when she awoke. Gina had barely had time to consider the ramifications of that when she received a text in all caps without an originating number, as if somehow the sender knew she had opened her phone and was holding it.

**A CAR WILL BE DOWNSTAIRS TO PICK YOU UP IN
TWENTY MINUTES**

‡‡‡

Gina rushed to get ready in time, showering and dressing in the clothes hanging in the closet in her exact sizes. She made coffee in the room's single-serving maker while she dressed, and sipped it as she walked to the elevator.

A black SUV that might have been the same one that picked her up yesterday was waiting outside, this time with a plainclothes driver.

"Good morning, ma'am," he greeted, and then pulled back out into morning traffic.

No further words were exchanged between them before he pulled into the same parking garage and onto the same warehouse platform that descended into the underground parking lot. A pair of marines were waiting for her arrival. One opened the door for Gina to climb out, and then they positioned themselves on either side of her for the walk toward to the steel door that accessed the Vault. One of the marines worked the keypad, and the door slid open.

Her marine escorts accompanied her to the matching door at the end of a fifty-foot hallway, guarded by the same two marines as yesterday, wearing body armor and wielding M4 assault rifles. Her escorts presented their IDs to be scanned. Then both officers again inserted their keys into matching stations on either side of the shiny steel slab door. They looked at each other, nodded, and turned the keys in the same instant, and Gina watched the door slide open soundlessly, revealing the cramped antechamber. The door accessing the Vault itself opened only after the one behind her had sealed.

Rod Rust was already seated inside, and rose when he saw her. She recognized a figure seated near the head of the table as the secretary of state, with the secretary of defense seated next to him, and the director of the CIA on his other side. She also recognized the chairman of the Joint Chiefs of Staff, the president's chief of staff, and the chair of the National Governors Association, a close ally of the president who was rumored to be her chosen successor. That might have explained the absence of the vice president, although Gina believed it was more likely due to the imminent threat that had activated the Vault, thus necessitating that the president and vice president not be in the same room together. Congress was not represented at all—with good reason, Gina surmised, given that body's propensity for leaking. The president had yet to arrive, and Gina waited for Rod Rust to gesture to the seat next to him before moving to take it.

Gina had barely sat down when the sliding, elevator-like door on the opposite wall from the one she'd entered through opened and the president entered, trailed protectively by a trio of soldiers in black fatigues associated with special operations. She recognized the lead soldier as the colonel she'd encountered in St. Louis, head of the platoon pretending to be National Guardsmen. He nodded her way, making it clear he recognized her as well, then claimed a post against the wall behind the president's perch at the head of the table, while the other two soldiers stood vigil before both of the two sliding doors. That made Gina wonder why the president had come here under the protection of what, by all accounts, was a secret army unit instead of the Secret Service. She could only conclude that the Secret Service was feared to be compromised.

The president boasted a lithe, athletic figure. When she was still known only as Jillian Cantwell, she'd been part of a national championship crew team at the University of California, Berkeley, where she'd also played soccer. She'd never served in the military, but her husband had been killed while fighting in Afghanistan in the wake of 9/11. That had left her a widow with three small children, who were now all in their twenties. Gina had seen recent side-by-side photos of the president pictured with her girl and two boys, one from the present day and one from more than twenty years ago at her husband's funeral. The latter shot resembled the famous photo of three-year-old John F. Kennedy, Jr., saluting at his father's grave. Incredibly, the president looked as if she hadn't aged a day.

"Sorry I'm late," she greeted, as the others at the table waited for her to sit down before retaking their chairs. "It couldn't be helped, because we've just acquired some new information."

CHAPTER 66

ZION NATIONAL PARK, UTAH

The first known paintings of Zion National Park,
by Frederick Dellenbaugh, were displayed at
the St. Louis World's Fair in 1904.

"You get the word yet?" Bud Ricketts asked Michael, after he'd climbed into the Chevy Tahoe outside the Best Western early Tuesday morning.

Michael watched the windshield wipers slapping away the rain that had been falling steadily since last night. "What word?"

"Oh," Ricketts said, turning away without pulling away from the entrance of the Best Western. "I guess not."

Michael didn't respond, just waited for Ricketts to proceed, which he did after a long sigh.

"The false alarm you triggered yesterday rang all the way to Washington. You've been suspended on an order direct from the—"

"Secretary of the interior," Michael completed for him, reaching back for the door handle.

"But you haven't been advised of that yet . . . at least officially, if you know what I mean," Ricketts said, stopping just short of a wink. "And with flash floods likely in the park today, I can't spare anybody. How about I assign you to the Narrows?" he suggested, referring to a slot canyon at the northern outskirts of Zion. "Where there's no cell phone coverage."

"So no one can reach me."

"Except by walkie-talkie, which means me. I should be able to buy you the time you need to plan out your next step, like appeal. Or buy a broom to stick up your former father-in-law's ass."

"Thanks, Bud."

"Don't thank me, Agent. Like I said, it's all hands on deck today."

‡‡‡

The Narrows, appropriately enough, was the narrowest section of Zion Canyon. The gorge in question featured walls a thousand feet tall rising over the Virgin River, which was already swollen with water from the mounting storm. Michael could see that Ricketts wasn't exaggerating when he warned of flash flooding today. The park had remained open, though attendance was expected to be light for summer due to the inclement weather.

Hiking the Narrows required wading into the river itself, since there was no trail. That made it an especially precarious part of the park when flash floods struck, because there were few areas to seek refuge in. Flash floods in Zion were difficult to predict, but impossible to overestimate given their ability to wreak destruction. Michael remembered reading that last summer a flash flood had decimated the main parking lot, laying waste to a multitude of vehicles. The floods could spring out of nowhere and sweep away an able-bodied man standing in only a foot of water. During storms, runoff was funneled rapidly into the canyon, making the waters rise without a moment's notice. Hikers in Zion had been stranded, injured, and even killed, with no canyon spared the onslaught, the Narrows being the most precarious.

Once at the park, Michael checked out a matching Tahoe and drove to the Temple of Sinawava, where the parking area nearest to the Narrows was located. He found he still had cell service and remained in the vehicle as the rain pounded it.

He needed to make a phone call. Before Michael could place it, though, his phone rang. **ANGELA PIERCE**, his caller ID read.

‡‡○‡‡

CHAPTER 67

WASHINGTON, D.C.

The administration of the parks in the area
was transferred to the Park Service in 1933.

"Colonel Beeman," the president continued, turning toward the officer Gina had recognized from the Gateway Arch, "you have the floor."

Gina watched the officer who'd mysteriously taken charge of the scene at the Gateway Arch two days before step up to the head of the table, standing even with the president in a protective posture.

"Ladies and gentlemen," Beeman began, "I'm a soldier, so please excuse me if I speak bluntly without sugarcoating what we've learned, specifically the chatter we've picked up of a coming attack of epic proportions on the country."

"Where did this chatter originate, Colonel?" the secretary of defense asked him.

Beeman looked toward the president, who nodded. "We've had ears on several members of the military, high-ranking I might add, who we suspected of being duplicitous."

"In other words," started the secretary of state, "a part of the insurrection we are currently facing."

"That's correct, ma'am. Instead of me reciting that chatter, let me play you some of what we were able to capture."

Colonel Beeman laid his cell phone atop the conference table, jogged it to an app, and touched the screen. Instantly, those gathered in the Vault heard the first of several scratchy male voices. The recording was imperfect, not all the words intelligible, but enough came through to terrify Gina to her very core.

"*There's got . . . be sacrifices. That . . . mark . . . beginning.*"

"*How many we . . . about?*"

"*Ten million, give or . . . a few. That's the word from on high, from Jeremiah and the general himself.*"

The recording ended with one of the men on it laughing. In the pause that followed, Gina watched anxious glances being exchanged throughout the room. For her part, she kept her eyes glued to Beeman, who caught her gaze and nodded respectfully, just as he'd done upon entering the chamber.

Then another recording started up, clearer than the first.

"*Where you headed?*"

"*Atlanta.*"

"*I drew Memphis.*"

"*Gonna be messing with people's shit wherever we go.*"

"*Blowing up people's shit be more like it.*"

Gina watched Beeman hit stop. "The first recording was of two active-duty military personnel. The second was of two individuals who are ex-military currently associated with a known militia group."

"The phrase 'ten million' along with mention of sacrifices," Rod Rust started. "I assume we're talking about American lives here."

"We believe that will mark the beginning of the attempted takeover of the United States government," Beeman responded. "And we believe we know how."

ı-ı-◦-ı-ı

ZION NATIONAL PARK, UTAH

In ancient Hebrew, "Zion" means "refuge"
or "sanctuary."

"Boss?" Michael said.

"I'm not your boss anymore, Michael. That's why I'm calling. I wanted you to hear it from me."

"What happened?" he managed, through the fog slowly clearing from his mind.

"I've been replaced as special agent in charge of the office. First move by the new head of the Park Service."

"*What?* Who?"

"A former congressman named Frank Von Hool. Sound familiar?"

"Sure. Von Hool's the one who cut our funding and introduced a bill to privatize the entire system when—" Michael stopped abruptly, his thoughts sharpening. "Don't tell me: Ethan Turlidge was behind this."

"Call it the Monday-night massacre. Turlidge is putting his sycophants in charge of the National Park Service so he can finally realize his dream of sucking out everything the land has to give, before opening the parks to developers to build condos and golf courses."

Michael was struck by a realization. "You getting fired—that was be-cause of me, wasn't it? The false alarm I triggered yesterday."

"It was inevitable. Graves told me to fire you and I told him to shove it."

"I'm still fired—well, suspended for now."

"Not by me, though. There are lines I won't cross, Michael, but unfortu-nately the same can't be said for Ethan Turlidge."

‡‡‡

"Agent Walker," Bud Ricketts's voice squawked over his walkie-talkie, as soon as Michael's call with Angela had ended.

"Read you, Bud," Michael said, holding the walkie at his ear.

"Flash-flood warning was just upped to extreme and we've got a wedding anniversary party taking place on Riverside Walk where it intersects with the Narrows."

"Who celebrates a wedding anniversary in a storm like this?"

"A couple who got married here thirty years ago and wanted to renew their vows."

"What do you need?"

"For you to get them out of harm's way fast."

"Any word from Ethan Turlidge's office?" Michael asked Ricketts.

"Who?"

CHAPTER 69

WASHINGTON, D.C.

Federally owned parks in the area date back to 1790.

"We know a vast amount of chemical munitions reserves that have been stored in secret for decades have gone missing," Colonel Beeman resumed, picking up just where he'd left off.

"I ordered them to be destroyed, as soon as I learned of their existence," the president interjected. "I asked for a complete report on the means and manner by which that would take place, and set up a task force to oversee everything as quietly as possible," she continued, guilt ringing in her voice.

"We're not talking about the actual chemical weapons, the last of which were recently destroyed in accordance with several disarmament treaties," Beeman picked up. "We're talking about the individual ingredients that, for some reason, were never destroyed. We've been storing them in unfinished underground sections at the Greenbrier facility in West Virginia."

Gina knew instantly that he was referring to an emergency Cold War fallout shelter carved deep into a West Virginia mountainside. Once a top-secret U.S. government relocation facility for Congress, it was now open to tours for a public that reveled in entering a living part of history. Clearly, though, there was much more to Greenbrier than had ever been revealed, and giving public tours of a facility so close to vast stores of deadly chemicals, while dangerous, made for the perfect camouflage.

"So these barrels are missing," she heard the secretary of state say, "that's what you're telling us, isn't it, Colonel?"

"No, sir. The barrels are still there, but they're empty. Someone removed and replaced them. This all transpired while President Cantwell was waiting for the task force to complete its report, a report that's been rendered moot."

"What kind of chemicals are we talking about?" asked the secretary of state.

"Primarily, benzene, phosgene, chlorine, arsenic trioxide, dimethylcadmium, and fluoroantimonic acid."

"And who would have known about the existence of this stockpile?" asked the president's chief of staff.

"It's a short list, sir," Beeman said, "focused on the members of that task force, but I can tell you that we have investigated them exhaustively and found nothing actionable at all."

"With all due respect," Gina interjected, unable to contain herself, "based on everything I've heard in this room so far, how can you be sure the investigators, at least the leads, can be trusted? Who was in charge?"

"That would be me," Rust said, from alongside her.

Gina didn't bother to hide her embarrassment. "How about I take a look?"

She wondered how Rust would react to her inadvertently degrading him. "Moving forward, I see no harm in the redundancy. I think a fresh set of eyes on the task force members might be just what we need here." He turned to Gina, who was already breathing easier at his response to her jumping into the conversation the way she had. "I'll get you the files my investigation compiled, ASAC Delgado. Time was our first priority, so I might have missed something in the rush to find whoever was responsible."

"Speaking of responsible," Colonel Beeman said, retaking the floor, "I'd like to introduce you to the man we have strong reason to believe is the primary force behind this plot."

Beeman pressed an unseen button beneath the sill of the desk, and a screen built into the room's front wall filled with an army officer in full dress uniform.

"You're looking at disgraced General Archibald Terrell, a.k.a. General Terror. For those who don't know the story, Terrell should be spending the rest of his life at Leavenworth for war crimes. A real shame, given that at one point he was one of the finest commanders the Joint Special Operations Command ever had."

Gina realized that the twelve special operators in the staged helicopter crash, along with who knew how many others, must have served under Terrell and remained loyal to him. The man must have spent decades in a command position, the ideal place from which to build his own private army.

"That is," Beeman was saying, "until he began freelancing on missions, disregarding orders he didn't agree with in favor of his own. Terrell doesn't believe there's such a thing as a civilian in a theater of war, and should have paid the price for it. But politics intervened and he got himself a pardon from a previous president."

Gina glimpsed the chairman of the Joint Chiefs recoil at that, unable to disguise his revulsion.

"That allowed him to make a graceful exit from the military via early retirement instead of the court martial and life sentence he deserved. General Terror has made no secret of the fact that he wants to lead a second civil war to overthrow the government. He'd been advocating for that publicly for years, before he dropped off the map once his plan became operational. His name has come up in some of the chatter we've collected and we believe he's in regular, direct contact with the man who goes by Jeremiah."

"Wait," said the secretary of defense, leaning as far forward as the table would allow, "are you saying this madman might well have, likely has, a stockpile of the deadliest chemicals ever known to man in his possession?"

"Regrettably, by all accounts that is the case, sir, yes," Beeman confirmed.

"And that's all we know about Terrell's involvement at this point?" said the head of the National Governors Association.

"Not anymore. Terrell has slipped every tail we've tried to put on him and lives like a Luddite to avoid electronic surveillance. He's always been a paranoid son of a bitch, which helped make him a combat legend for a time before he became a pariah. But we've been able to confirm some of his movements as of late have been centered in the Pacific Northwest, specifically Washington State. That, of course, is where we have every reason to believe Jeremiah is based. Toward that end," Beeman continued, "we've poured assets into the general area in the hope of sniffing the former General Terrell out. So far, he hasn't popped up to even take a leak or a breath. The man has run black-flag mission ops for much of his career. Now that he's on the other side of one, he's putting that experience to good use."

"Secretary of Defense McAfee," the president said, once Beeman had yielded the floor, "that brings us to you. The floor is yours."

Gina watched Colonel Beeman recede back to the Vault's front, while McAfee rose.

"We have now confirmed the amount of military ordnance in the form of heavy weaponry and equipment that has gone missing," McAfee reported. "We're talking about tanks, attack helicopters, transports, missile launchers . . . I have compiled a complete inventory I didn't want to circulate, even to this group, in writing for obvious reasons."

"How could that kind of equipment simply go missing?" the secretary of state wondered.

"Ma'am," Colonel Beeman replied, when Secretary of Defense McAfee hesitated, "we don't advertise the amount of equipment we leave behind in war zones because of the excessive cost and labor it would take to bring it home. It's also routine in due course for a tank, chopper, or C-130's cycle to be phased out and replaced by the next generation of weaponry. The previous generation is then mothballed and stored in vast depots. The fact of the matter is that the United States has a massive weapons surplus, and now we have a notion as to where some of that surplus has ended up. We've already discussed the fact that a large number of former military personnel has been enlisted in what we're facing. We believe they have either constructed training grounds or are using one or more shuttered military installations to base their operations."

"I should expect," started the director of the CIA, "that at least checking out these shuttered installations would be eminently doable."

"Doable," said Secretary of Defense McAfee, "yes, but eminently? I'm afraid not. More than three hundred and fifty bases were closed as part of the Base Realignment and Closure Act in five rounds through 2005. Add to that hundreds more that were closed between World War II and 1988 and the number is closer to a thousand. Many of these have been repurposed by local communities. But many more have not. Most are scattered across the countryside, others tucked away on the outskirts of large cities."

"We're attempting to recon all of these bases," said Beeman, "but we have strong reason to believe our efforts leaked, leading the enemy we're facing to take countermeasures like painting buildings and equipment to blend in with the surrounding scenery, vastly diminishing reconnaissance efforts by air or satellite. We're working our way to inspect all of these facilities with boots on the ground. Based on the chatter I just shared, though, we believe that we're running out of time."

"At the potential cost of ten million American lives," noted the secretary of state caustically, "once these chemicals are deployed."

That's when Gina felt a buzzing in both ears, as if she had detected a sound no one else in the Vault could hear. Call it experience, or even pre-cognition, but from the time she'd rigged her first explosion, she had de-veloped a kind of advance warning system that alerted her to when a blast was coming a few long seconds before it ignited. She knew enough to be sure that's what she was feeling now, as everything seized up inside her in the last moment before the explosion sounded.

CHAPTER 70

ZION NATIONAL PARK, UTAH

Isaac Behunin, who helped construct the Erie Canal,
built a log cabin in 1861 near the site of what is now
the Zion Lodge.

Since the area around Temple of Sinawava was as close as a vehicle could get to the Narrows, Michael headed on foot to where Riverside Walk rose over the gorge. He had drawn close enough to see the happy couple and their family celebrating their anniversary by renewing their wedding vows when he heard the rumble.

His first thought was that it must be thunder kicked up by the pounding storm that had pushed raging waters into the canyon below in the kind of flash flood Zion National Park was infamous for. He could see the family members determined to celebrate the milestone, regardless of the elements, and watched them popping champagne corks atop the platform that hung out over the waters cascading below. A smattering of umbrellas was all they brought with them to ward off the storm. Michael heard another rumble and then a third, as he drew closer to the viewing platform on which the anniversary party was perched.

It's not thunder. . . .

Michael had felt those rumbles in the pit of his stomach, the feeling akin to experiencing an earthquake on its periphery. He turned his gaze upward and, through the storm, saw three huge dark clouds funneling upward and outward.

Explosions. . . .

As he formed that thought, Michael gaped at the sight of massive bursts of white intermixed with the black-brownish color of rubble from the mountaintops pouring downward in a trio of landslides that joined up into a single massive one as much as a hundred yards across. Dragging all that snow and ice that hadn't yet melted, thanks to the unusually cold spring, in a churning blanket.

He picked up his pace as much as he could along the path, glimpsing the terrified expressions of the men and women who only moments before had popped celebratory bottles of champagne turning their gaze toward the loudening sound that shook the platform beneath their feet. Michael was still forty feet short of that platform when he felt the cold blast shed by the vast tonnage of ice and snow barreling downward. He ducked into a crevice barely wide and deep enough to accommodate his bulk and involuntarily held his breath as the white blanket, broken by chunks of brown rock, barreled past him.

It continued long enough to force Michael to breathe in what felt like snow, which made him realize his clothes were now dotted with flecks of ice crystals. The sound of ice, snow, and rocks slamming into the already raging waters of the Narrows canyon below was deafening, kicking up a vast wall of water that stretched toward the crevice in which he'd tucked himself, chilling Michael to the bone. He had never been to Niagara Falls, but had seen videos where the sound, with the volume cranked up, was eerily akin to the noise that had just made his ears feel as if they were fluttering. He was conscious of the screams and cries coming from the nearby platform.

"Walker to Base, Walker to Base!" he yelled into his walkie-talkie.

"This is Base."

"I'm at the Narrows. We've got explosions! Repeat, a trio of explosions have shook loose the runoff! The platform has collapsed! Repeat, the platform has collapsed and we've got people in the water here! Do you copy?"

"We copy, Walker."

"Need help here! Repeat, people in the water! People in the water! There's been an explosion! Repeat, there's been an explosion! Expect a huge flood surge coming your way!"

"Roger that. Rescue is en route."

But Michael knew rescue wouldn't be able to get here while it still mattered. The avalanche's spill from the peaks above was merging with the floodwaters in the canyon below. The landslide had sheared a large portion of the platform off and broken it apart. He could see that some of the party had made it off onto the path, while others had been washed away and were clinging to whatever desperate handholds they'd managed to find:

exposed brush, roots, rocks—anything to avoid being swept away by the waters that had risen with the force of what looked more like a tidal wave, fed by months of stalled runoff unleashed by the landslide.

Michael squeezed out of the crevice and quickly reached those who'd made it off the platform, directing them back in the direction from which he'd come along the same path, now riddled with debris in the form of ice, rocks, stone, and gravel.

"Move!" he said firmly. "Watch your step, but don't stop! Don't stop and don't look back!"

"What about, what about," a dazed woman, barely recognizable behind the muck soaking her, kept repeating.

Michael turned his gaze toward the jagged remnants of the platform.

"I'll get them," he promised. "Just keep moving!"

CHAPTER 71

WASHINGTON, D.C.

U.S. Park Police stables are located west of the D.C. War
Memorial and across Independence Avenue from the
Martin Luther King, Jr. Memorial.

The Vault shook, literally shook with the vibrations culled from the blast
that had ignited directly above the reinforced structure. The lights flick-
ered and died, emergency bulbs snapping on in their stead.

Gina had watched Colonel Beeman instinctively dive atop the president
and take her out of her chair and beneath the cover of the conference table
to protect her from falling debris shed by the blast. The iron ceiling ruptured, caving downward in jagged sections that crushed the secretaries of
defense and state, along with the chairman of the Joint Chiefs of Staff. It
would have crushed Rod Rust, too, had Gina not yanked him away from
the debris field and back against a wall outside the primary blast pocket.

He was mumbling something and gasping at the same time. Gina
caught the smell of char and burned concrete, different from what had
been hanging in the air on Liberty Island. This scent must have been shed
by cinder-block construction reinforcing the steel shell of the Vault. She
knew some kind of shaped charges must have been employed, designed to
focus all the power of the blast downward, widening into a cone-shaped
funnel as the explosion fed off the oxygen to feed itself further.

The emergency lights barely made a dent in the cloud kicked up by
the debris pushing in from beyond the walls and ceiling. They seemed to
flicker as thicker concentrations settled before them.

Gina sank to the floor with Rod Rust, settling down next to him as both
coughed the superheated embers and microscopic metallic fragments
from their mouths and lungs.

"The president," he rasped, shaking all over, blood sliding down his face from lacerations in his scalp.

"I'll find her," Gina managed, before a coughing spasm overcame her.

She felt Rust grab her arm in a trembling hand. "Now, Gina, now! They can't win! Don't let them win!"

Gina nodded, even though she wasn't sure Rust could see her through the debris cloud. Clearly, the existence of both the Vault and this ad hoc task force had been compromised. Maybe the enemy had known about both for months but had chosen this moment to strike, now that their plan was coming to fruition. And what better way to begin their civil war than executing those few government officials with close knowledge of what the country was facing and who were committed to stopping it?

Gina dropped down on all fours and pulled a penlight from a holstered slot clipped to her belt. The air was less gritty at floor level, allowing the beam to pierce enough of the debris cloud for her to spot Colonel Beeman still holding the president in a protective grasp beneath the conference table. Gina shimmied under the remains, pulling herself closer to them.

Beeman's face was bleeding, and one of his legs was covered in debris.

"Take her!" he ordered, between labored breaths. "Take her and find a way out of here, Delgado!"

Gina saw that the president was conscious, caked in debris dust but otherwise unharmed, save for a few lacerations on her face and tears in her clothes. Beeman eased the president toward her as best he could with his leg pinned. The president was in too much shock to lend much to the effort, so Gina grabbed firm hold of Jillian Cantwell and pulled, retracing her path backward out from beneath the ruptured table with the president in tow.

"You have your phone?" Beeman managed.

She nodded. "Yes, but it's blocked."

"I'll unblock it as soon as I'm clear. When I call, you'll see all zeroes in the caller ID. Don't answer it for anyone else. Understood?"

Gina succeeded in extracting the president all the way out from beneath the table.

"Wait," Beeman called to her in a raspy voice.

He extended the pistol that had been holstered on his hip toward her, and Gina took it. "I've got my Glock."

Beeman gritted his teeth, then eyed the president, whose gaze was empty and glazed. "You may need both. Now get her the hell out of here!"

CHAPTER 72

ZION NATIONAL PARK, UTAH

Kolob Arch, deep in the backcountry of Zion,
is second only to Landscape Arch in
Arches National Park in terms of size, at 287 feet long.

Michael shimmied sideways across the last of Riverside Walk, only ten feet above the raging waters that had been over forty feet beneath before the explosions. Two-thirds of the platform had been sheared off. The deafening roar of the avalanche had meshed with the waters raging below, a torrent released exponentially greater than the one that flooded the visitor center parking lot last summer.

As he worked his way toward the high-pitched screams and cries for help, Michael maintained the presence of mind to picture all of Zion's slot canyons that crisscrossed the park filling with floodwaters of unprecedented power and ferocity, fed by the avalanche of runoff. Anything that wasn't bolted down would be washed away. He could only hope the flood indicators had provided enough advance warning for Bud Ricketts and the rest of the rangers to evacuate the visitor center, for the second time in less than a day, before the waters converged upon it.

His walkie-talkie squawked as he closed on the jagged remnants of the platform.

"Michael, this is Ricketts. What's your status?"

"What's the status of my backup?"

"The road's washed out. They had to turn back."

Michael felt his stomach flutter.

"I've got choppers incoming. Twenty minutes out."

"Too late to help me. I'm going to save as many as I can. Looks like a few may have been washed away. Walker out," Michael finished, and clipped the walkie back on his belt.

He picked up his pace across the path and reached the jagged remnants of the platform to find two sets of hands clinging to it and an older man who'd managed to drag his upper body back up over the edge but looked to be on the verge of slipping off. Michael wondered if he was part of the couple that had come here to celebrate their anniversary by renewing their vows.

Sure enough, he slid backward, his eyes starting to fade as they met Michael's. Michael felt the rickety remnants of the platform creak and crack under his weight as he padded toward the man and grabbed both of his hands to drag him back up all the way.

"Thank you, thank you," the man managed dazedly, his consciousness ebbing.

Then a woman's wails reached his ears, and Michael eased himself to the edge of what was left of the platform, the front section having broken off and plunged into the waters cascading through the gorge below.

He had to lie on his stomach to reach down for the woman, whose second hand had slipped off and was slapping at the soaked wood to regain purchase. Michael grabbed hold of that hand first, then stretched his head and free hand over the edge, dangling his fingers toward the woman kicking at the air with her feet.

"Grab my other hand!" he yelled to her. "Grab it!"

She tried, but her hand flailed at the empty air, flopping back down.

Michael stretched himself farther over the edge, hearing a louder series of cracks as the sodden wood of the platform threatened to break away altogether. "Again! Reach up to me again!"

This time, there was less distance between the woman's flailing hand and Michael's outstretched one. She still couldn't clasp it, so he jerked his upper body farther forward and grabbed hold, both hands grasping hers now with a firm enough grip to hold fast as he pushed himself backward, yanking the woman with him.

"Get off the platform!" he ordered both her and the man he'd saved earlier. "Start down the path and don't stop for anything!"

Then he dropped down again and moved to a younger man with his arms wrapped around an exposed L-shaped support that fastened the platform to a base of wood drilled into the rock face over the gorge. But there was no way Michael could reach the man without the man's weight sending both of them into the brown foam lifting off the rising waters below. The man was young and looked to be in shape, giving Michael an idea.

He grabbed a heavy board that had splintered and extended it toward the man.

"Grab hold! Quick, before the platform gives way!"

The younger man started to reach out, then pulled his hand back, cowering.

"Come on, you can do it!"

A look of grim determination crossed the man's features and he reached out again, this time grabbing the board.

"Now, the other one!"

The man looked at Michael in disbelief, as the platform shifted and shook.

"Now!" Michael implored.

The man sucked in a breath and held it as he stretched his hand out at the same time he pushed off on the support. His second hand grabbed hold of the board halfway up, and Michael jerked him back atop the platform before he could release his grip and fall. Michael pointed to the platform and then looked down. He had no idea how many people had accompanied the older couple, though clearly a number of them had been swept away. He saw four who'd fallen or slipped off the broken platform pressed against the canyon walls, having been lucky enough to have found footholds or handholds before reaching the water. Another guest who'd been enjoying the celebration was somehow holding on to a thick nest of brush and branch growing out of the gorge face against the torrent of water determined to tear his grip away. The final guest who hadn't been swept away by the flood, or fled down the path, looked to be only semiconscious, half in and half out of the water with her jacket snared on a thick knobby branch.

Giving his prosthetic foot all it could take, Michael lowered himself onto a ridge that extended precariously beneath the platform. He nearly lost his balance, but recovered it in time to turn and slide down the slippery rock face to the woman.

"Ma'am, ma'am!"

He tried to rouse her gently, and when that failed he shook her harder, but not so hard as to strip her jacket free of the branch, which was all that was keeping her from being whisked away by the waters that continued to rise. Her eyes fluttered, then sharpened, and Michael helped her position herself so she could grab the branch with both hands.

"I'll be back for you!" Michael promised, moving on to the man whose face had just disappeared under the water.

He reached him the very instant the man's grip on the brush gave way. The pounding waters showered Michael with a stream thick and powerful enough to make him feel as if he were underwater. The rampaging flood that had kicked up that stream was so powerful that Michael couldn't hoist the man back to a position where he could gain a firmer handhold. So, holding on to the same brush himself, Michael dropped into the swirling waters next to him. He stretched his free hand outward and just managed to latch on to the man dangling below the surface. The man grew more alert, coming to life as Michael brought his second hand to join his first, gaining purchase.

"That's it," Michael coaxed, "that's it. . . ."

But the man tired quickly. Michael could feel him go slack and shifted positions to angle himself to prevent the man from being washed away. The new angle allowed Michael to add more of his own heft to the effort, feeling the man's frame rise and watching him raise his second hand to grab hold of the thick brush alongside the first.

"Now, hold on! You hear me? Don't let go! Help's coming," Michael added, clinging to the hope that it was.

He retraced the precarious stretch back to the woman who was clinging to a branch that extended from a ridge just beneath the remnants of the viewing platform. The floodwaters had already climbed higher, swallowing all of her lower body and forcing Michael to take a more circuitous route along the rock face to reach her. His first thought was to find enough purchase to help hoist her all the way back onto the platform. But his angle, and the higher level of water, made that impossible. All the sheer canyon wall had to offer was the branch she was already barely holding on to and a ledge wide enough to accommodate both their seated frames ten feet to the right.

"Okay," Michael said, angling himself alongside the woman, "I'm going to take hold of you. When I tell you, I want you to let go of the branch and we're going to slide sideways together. I'll be holding on to you the whole time."

The woman's eyes widened in fear, looking at Michael like he was crazy.

"No," she managed. "I . . . can't."

"You can."

"I can't let go."

Michael risked his already precarious footing against the rock face, up to his waist in the climbing floodwaters, to move closer to the woman so she could feel his grasp upon her. She looked to be in her midforties and not in the greatest of shape.

"You feel me holding you?"

The woman nodded.

"Now lower your right hand from the branch."

Michael watched her tighten her grip instead. His footing had started to slip under the increasing force of the water.

"Start with your left," he instructed instead.

Even though that hand was farther away, the woman was able to curl her fingers and then ease it from the branch. Michael tightened his grip on her, about to tell her to follow with her right hand, when she slipped off altogether. All her bulk piled onto Michael, stripping away his boots' meager hold on the rocks beneath the racing water.

They both fell backward into the currents, which swept them away as if they were weightless. Michael maintained the presence of mind to position the woman over him, holding her the way a lifeguard would when rescuing a swimmer, as they were swept downstream. He felt her thrashing about atop him, pushing him under, and tightened his grip to gain better control.

All manner of debris in the form of brush, branches, logs, and rocks churned through the water. They were impossible to avoid, and the best he could do was try warding the debris off with what little reach his hands had left or trying to twist his frame from its path. It was like riding a crazed amusement park attraction, as the surging floodwaters swept through the slot canyons, picking up more speed and debris along the way.

Michael angled his gaze so he could see ahead of them and glimpsed a thick patch of gravel climbing up a bank resting between two of the canyons. He pulled his feet to the right to act as a rudder, steering him and the woman he was holding toward the bank.

"We're almost there!" he said, hoping she could hear him through the deafening sounds of the raging waters. "Just hold on!"

He could feel the woman stop flailing and bring her arms in. Michael started pushing her off him as they neared the bank, intending to ease her onto it before following himself. Though still panicked, she let him turn her enough to facilitate his plan, and he shoved hard against her when the bank of gravel drew close.

The woman lifted out of his grasp, half in the air and half in the water, when Michael gave a final, hefty thrust that pushed her entire frame up onto the gravel. The water propelled him past her, but there was still plenty of bank left for the woman to find respite. Michael's hand scraped through the gravel, seeking something to grab hold of, and closed on what felt like the dead root system of a tree claimed by these waters long before. That was enough to hold him in position against the force of the water.

Michael pulled hard with his left hand and was stretching his right upward to join it when a tree trunk came barreling toward him. He redoubled his efforts to hoist himself onto the bank, but the trunk slammed into him and swept him away into the raging waters.

CHAPTER 73

WASHINGTON, D.C.

**The Treasury Building was designated a
National Historic Landmark in 1972.**

Gina pulled President Cantwell forward, the leader of the free world's words garbled and muffled. The LED penlight was all she had to cut through the darkness and debris clouds that riddled the entire underground facility. The Vault itself was now behind her. The sliding, elevator-like doors through which she'd passed had collapsed downward, their hefty weight sinking into whatever subsurface or base layer had been constructed beneath the secret facility during World War II.

Gina dragged the president over the collapsed steel doors and into a jagged tunnel carved out of the fifty-foot hallway that connected the Vault to the garage. Their trek quickly became serpentine in nature, like negotiating a labyrinth, which meant, Gina knew, that they could hit a dead end formed by impenetrable rubble at any moment.

"Can we stop?" the president asked suddenly, as if suddenly roused from her daze. "I need to catch my breath."

"No, ma'am. This isn't stable. We can't risk it collapsing."

"Call me Jillian, please. And you're Delgado, right? I've heard a lot about you."

In spite of everything else, Gina felt a hefty measure of pride at that, wondering how her *abuela* might have thought of such a thing, the president saying she'd heard a lot about her *nieta*.

"I am, Madam President, and excuse me for being more comfortable calling you that."

"How about we make a deal? If we get out of this, you call me Jillian."

Gina managed a smile. "Deal."

She knew escape was only the first challenge before them. If the man known as Jeremiah and General Terrell, a.k.a. General Terror, suspected that their efforts had failed to kill the chief executive, there was no telling what resources they'd bring to bear to finish the job. They might even have forces lying in wait, on the chance that someone from the Vault managed to spirit the chief executive to safety through the collected rubble fifty feet below ground level. Certainly, rescue efforts might already be underway. That said, the utter secrecy maintained by this task force made Gina wonder who in the White House or the government had even been aware of the president's true whereabouts. None of that mattered, though, if Gina was unable to get Jillian Cantwell back above ground to safety.

Think!

A blast triggered by the kind of shaped charges she suspected had been employed focused the vast bulk of its explosive force downward, with that force dissipating significantly the farther out in the blast cone from the original source she drew. That meant the sledding should grow easier and the rubble thinner the farther they got from the Vault. Based on the length of the hallway, Gina estimated that the parking garage would still be reasonably intact, its structural integrity barely compromised by the explosion.

If they could reach it. Because a wall of debris rose up before them, cutting off their path. Gina looked toward the president and saw the fear swimming in her eyes. Their options were limited, virtually nonexistent. Going back wasn't an option and the way forward was blocked. She swept her penlight about, searching for an alternative to the choices that weren't choices at all.

But her penlight illuminated a break in the debris piled before them. Gina rose as much as the confines allowed, hunched at the knees when she shined her penlight through the gap. It looked like the ceiling had collapsed on an angle, creating an air pocket that stretched as far as her penlight reached. Gina rose further, testing the gap to see if it might be wide and long enough to accommodate her bulk. She shimmied upward, not unlike entering the chimney in the Assembly Room two days before. The width of her shoulders stopped the process in its tracks, but Gina felt she could force her way through. But she couldn't go first, out of fear she might get wedged in the gap, trapping both her and the president down here until help came or the tonnage of debris collapsed altogether.

"Help *me* up?" Cantwell asked in disbelief, once Gina had told her the plan. "What about *you*?"

"I'll be right behind you," Gina told her, though unsure she'd be able to manage that task. "No time for discussion. We need to move, ma'am."

She positioned the president before her and guided her toward the air gap. Jillian Cantwell was the same height as she was, but lighter, with narrower shoulders and hips that were hopefully narrow enough to squeeze through the opening in the wall of debris. The president was through all the way to the waist, when more rumbling shook the world around them and Gina was filled with fear that the opening was going to close up and impale the leader of the free world. But that couldn't happen. Gina couldn't fail; if she did, the forces behind this would find their path to power.

So she shoved harder, then harder still.

"That's it," Gina mumbled through the penlight held between her lips, pushing up the president's legs now. "Feel around for something to grab onto to help pull yourself up."

"Ouch!"

"What happened?"

"I cut my hand on something sharp."

"Keep feeling around."

"I found something that feels like a hose. It's within reach. I can grab it."

"Electrical cable," Gina realized.

"Is it safe to grab?"

"If it wasn't, you'd already know."

"Got it," the president said, after a pause.

Her progress sped up from there, Cantwell pulling and Gina pushing. Finally, the president was gone, all of her having disappeared through the gap.

"Okay," she said, breathing rapidly from the exertion. "What about you, Delgado?"

"I'm going to hand you the penlight, ma'am."

"That doesn't answer my question. And I'm not leaving you here. We're going to do this together."

Gina knew she had a point. With no one to protect her, the president might walk straight into a strike team who'd come to finish the job the bomb had started. Getting Cantwell safely through the maze of debris was only part of Gina's job, and to do the rest of it she had to force her way through that opening, too.

"That's an order, Delgado," the president added.

Gina extended the penlight up and watched her take it. "Push backwards a bit, ma'am. See if you can shine the light straight and down."

That created a thin shaft of light that Gina pushed herself toward, squeezing through the opening again. Only this time, she didn't stop. Just kept working her way forward, even as she felt a stinging pain from the jagged edge of ruptured steel shredding her clothes and tearing into her skin.

"Are you okay?" the president asked, after seeing her wince through the narrow spray of the penlight. "You're almost there. Keep pushing!"

Gina pushed harder, the pain growing worse with each small measure of progress that was enough to keep her pushing. She held her breath and gritted her teeth, as her torso finally came free and she dropped into the narrow gap between the collapsed ceiling and the rest of the debris the blast had shed.

Gina took the penlight back from the president and slipped past her to lead the way on toward the garage.

"You're bleeding," the president said.

"I'll live."

The dark tunnel in which they found themselves narrowed and shrank the farther they pulled themselves through it. Gina began to fear it would close up altogether before they reached the garage area, forcing them to double back and start over. Fortunately, though, the gap between the debris pile and the collapsed ceiling shrank no further. The gap actually enlarged the closer they drew to the garage, and she counted her blessings they had reached the edge of the blast cone. She knew they were almost there when she smelled gasoline from vehicles that must have been damaged by rubble collapsed by the powerful blast. Along the final fifteen feet or so, they were almost able to stand fully upright, reaching what Gina recognized as the sliding door that accessed the connecting tunnel that led to the Vault. Concussion from the blast could have bent the steel and made passage through it impossible. Instead, she saw that the door's workings must have been short-circuited by the blast and it was frozen in a partially open position, leaving enough room for them to slip through.

Gina emerged through the opening into the garage and then reached back to help the president mount the debris that had collected in the space between the jamb and the door. All but one of the parked vehicles had been entombed by rubble. The elevator platform was encased in it as well, rendering it a nonstarter as an escape route.

"What now?" the president asked her.

"I was just about to ask you that, Madam President."

"Me?"

"A facility like this would have a backup escape route in the event of an emergency. It's got to be somewhere around here."

Cantwell swung her eyes about. "News to me. I've never seen it."

Gina focused her attention on the far wall, which was dotted with a mere smattering of rubble as collateral damage.

"This way," Gina signaled.

They reached the rear wall of the structure, and Gina started feeling about for a protruding ridge or a telltale discoloring of the concrete to indicate where the door to the emergency exit must have been concealed.

"What are we looking for exactly?" the president said, mimicking Gina's actions in feeling about the wall.

"Something we can grab hold of to access the emergency exit."

"You mean like this?" she said, after Gina had finished.

Cantwell had found just the ridge Gina was hoping for, raised enough to indicate a seam. The wall gave inward with a shove of her shoulder, opening to the left, the emergency lighting revealing a set of winding stairs that might have climbed all the way to heaven.

"You can call me Jillian now," the president said, as they started up them.

CHAPTER 74

BROOKFIELD AIR FORCE STATION; BROOKFIELD, OHIO

Established in 1951, and became operational
in April 1952.

"We did it!" General Archibald Terrell proclaimed, after taking a call on his satellite phone. "The Vault's history. Everyone inside must be dead, including the president."

As if on cue, one of the monitors inside the base command center, which was located in one of the original buildings that had weathered the years, ran a **BREAKING NEWS** banner with reports of an explosion detected at the Treasury Department. Details were scant, other than the fact that smoke was reported in the hallways and an evacuation of the structure was underway.

"You know what this means, Ferris: We've won!"

"The fight hasn't even begun yet, General."

"Read Sun Tzu, my friend. The outcome of all battles is determined before the first shot is fired. By the time the country learns their president is out of the picture, we'll be painting a new one. And it's all thanks to you, my friend. You're a hero. You made all of this possible. You answered the call. I'll have the jet take you back to Seattle, where you'll be safe and sound when the bodies start dropping."

Jeremiah shook his head. "I think I'll ride the rest of the way with the convoy to its final destination. See this thing through to the end firsthand."

Terrell smiled in smug satisfaction. "History will remember that day, Ferris, because it's when the fire begins to burn." He seemed to think of something else, expression changing. "What about our prisoner?"

"Oh, I've got plans for him, General. Rest assured."

PART FIVE

—⊰⊱—

At Grand Teton National Park, we stood on the
shores of Jenny Lake. . . . I could imagine—I could
feel—my daughter holding the small hand of
one of her children some day at that same, still
unchanged place, feeling the same thing. And
I thought, this is as close to an encounter with
eternity as I will ever get in this life.

—Dayton Duncan

—⊰⊱—

CHAPTER 75

ZION NATIONAL PARK, UTAH

Zion was the second-most-visited national park
in 2021, with over five million visitors.

Michael reminded himself to breathe every time he was able to claw his
way to the surface of the floodwaters carrying him. He'd lost all sense of
direction, feeling weightless and utterly at the whim of the raging currents.
He could only hope that Bud Ricketts had managed to evacuate the visitor
center and clear the park for the second time in less than twenty-four hours.

Only this was no false alarm.

Michael had been in Zion twice when there was flash flooding, and the
flood level today had climbed beyond six feet up the canyon walls, making
this likely the highest ever recorded. With each additional foot, the force
of the water rose in kind, all manner of debris riding the brown foamy
currents with him.

The floodwaters were life-threatening on their own, even before all the
branches, brush, logs, and refuse entered the mix. Michael's soaked uniform had been torn by encounters with jagged rocks that had been washed
upstream as well. As he was whipped around a bend, one of those rocks
smacked him in the forehead, leaving a nasty cut that oozed warm blood to
mix with the chilled water. He was only vaguely aware of the blood seeping
from the wound, since the waters kept wiping it away. The impact, though,
left him dazed, and Michael felt his hold on consciousness ebbing.

Pass out and he'd drown, so he clung desperately to consciousness even
as the world seemed to turn upside down, leaving him looking downward
at the patchwork sky revealed above the canyon walls, instead of upward.
The illusion passed quickly, but he still felt like he was fading, his eyes
closing for blips at a time like those of an exhausted driver nodding out for
brief spurts behind the wheel.

Michael felt a deep sense of ease, akin to slipping off to sleep, before he came awake retching, coughing plumes of water from his mouth only to have more take its place. He felt himself gasping for breath, no idea where in the park he was or in which direction the floodwaters were whisking him. He finally found the presence of mind to swing round, so that he was facing the direction in which he was being carried to better keep clear of another brush with debris that could steal his consciousness for good.

He fell into a twisted rhythm, flowing in tune with the waters that sped him into a narrow slot canyon he didn't recognize. He had a vague sense from the angle of the sun that the Virgin River was carrying him north of the West Rim Trail in the western part of Zion. These slot canyons criss-crossed the park in the pattern of a spiderweb, and waters of this height and force would have pushed their way into all of them, covering the roads to take out the shuttles and cascading past the Zion Lodge all the way to the visitor center.

Michael tried to clear the water from his face, finding there was none there. His vision had blurred, which made him wonder if he'd suffered a concussion even after it crystallized again. He maintained the presence of mind to suck in deep breaths every time the opportunity presented itself, so he could briefly survive in the event he was pulled under.

When opportunity allowed, he scanned ahead to search for something to grab on to close to the rocky shoreline. Michael felt himself being whipped around to the left, then the right, as the shape of the canyons turned S-like. Reaching a point where a slot canyon with a larger mouth joined this one shoved him under with a force that felt like someone was pushing down on his chest. He couldn't find the surface, the world above a dark, murky patch broken by an occasional sliver where the light managed to push through.

Michael saw the light brightening and thought he was being lifted back to the surface, but then he felt his prosthetic snare in what felt like mud. He tightened his shoulders and forced his neck upward, his face rising just enough out of the water's cascade for him to suck in some breath. But those waters were continuing to climb, leaving Michael to jostle his prosthetic in the hope of freeing it from the cluster of debris that had collected against the side of the canyon wall like the beginning of a beaver's dam.

No matter how much he shifted, pulled, and jerked, his foot wouldn't give and only seemed to wedge in tighter, as if the reeds and vines were of a mind to hold him in place. Even if Michael had a knife, there was no way he could cut himself free without drowning first. And the swirling and steadily rising waters left him with one chance and one chance only.

Michael sucked in as much breath as the waters would allow and dropped below the surface, canting his body and bending upward at the waist in order to reach the housing that held his prosthetic foot in place. He needed to repeat his nighttime ritual of easing the device from the stump it had been custom-fitted to, but he could barely reach it and lacked the purchase he needed to unstrap the prosthetic, which had wedged into the muck even tighter.

Michael didn't dare chance another rise above the surface, fearing the floodwaters would steal all his breath away. So, as his lungs began to burn and his head began to fill with pressure, he twisted onto his side. The new angle allowed his right hand to first scrape against the prosthetic's housing beneath his shredded pant leg, and then find the catch to loosen the fitting that held it in place.

In the last moment before he had no breath left to hold, fighting against panic, Michael finally got the strap undone. Then he pushed off the debris clump, jiggling the rest of his leg in a desperate attempt to separate it from the prosthetic still wedged in the debris. His efforts yielded no progress, and he had no choice but to push himself up over the surface to breathe, jolted by a fierce surge of water that spun him around like a top.

Only then did Michael realize he was free, the waters speeding him away with his foot left behind.

CHAPTER 76

WASHINGTON, D.C.

D.C. averages five inches more rain per year than
Seattle, Washington.

Still holding the gun Colonel Beeman had given her, Gina moved ahead of President Cantwell as they neared the top of the emergency stairs that spiraled upward from the garage back to the surface. Gesturing for Cantwell to hold her position, Gina thrust her shoulder into the single, heavy exit door at the same time she pressed down on the push bar.

The door opened into a pounding summer rainstorm. Gina kept the president protectively behind her as she peered out, recognizing her surroundings immediately. They were at the intersection of F Street Northwest and Fourteenth Street Northwest. She could see that the exit door from the emergency stairs was disguised as a shuttered entrance to the Washington Metro, unlikely to attract any attention.

"What now?" the president said, drawing closer.

"Please stay back, ma'am."

"Jillian, remember?"

Gina was having trouble addressing the president of the United States by her first name. "The rain's a blessing, like a built-in disguise," she said.

She realized she'd lost her own pistol somewhere along the way and lowered Colonel Beeman's gun to her hip, but only after emerging far enough to identify her surroundings from beneath a slight overhang. In addition to the weather, the best thing Gina had going for her was that the perpetrators had no way of knowing the president had survived and escaped.

So now what?

Even if Gina had wanted to, she couldn't simply "return" Jillian Cantwell to the White House. The leak of her whereabouts had more likely than not originated in that very building. Gina's job now, above everything else, was to keep the president safe and secure. Beeman, though pinned by debris, had survived the blast and had told her to wait for his call on a phone she couldn't currently use.

She felt Cantwell draw even closer to her. "Where to now?"

Gina shrugged. "Not the White House."

"I figured that out for myself. How about a Starbucks? Know any vacant Airbnbs in the area?"

"No," Gina said, a realization striking her like a lightning bolt, "someplace better."

‡‡‡

The steady rain was a blessing not only for lowering foot traffic and keeping people's vision veiled by umbrellas or hoods, but also for bringing out the usual army of sidewalk pitchmen hawking cheap umbrellas and even cheaper ponchos. Gina still had her wallet, enough cash inside it to buy two of each for twenty dollars total.

The ponchos were black, little more than Hefty bags with sleeves and a hood. Gina pulled hers over her head, then helped fit the president's in place, yanking its hood as far down Cantwell's forehead as it would go to obscure her features, which would be further cloaked by the umbrella.

"I want you to stay behind me, Madam—"

"Jillian. . . ."

"—and keep your face angled downward. If someone recognizes you and calls out, keep walking and don't acknowledge them."

Gina held the gun in one hand beneath her poncho, umbrella in the other. She didn't like not having a free hand available at all times, but needed to keep Beeman's pistol at the ready. It was a half-mile walk from their current position to the Mayflower Hotel on Connecticut Avenue. As far as Gina knew, the room she'd stayed in the night before was still being held. The front desk didn't need to know the identity of the woman accompanying her.

Gina took solace in the fact that the president, with rain-sodden hair, the cheap black poncho over wet clothes, and the umbrella, was completely unrecognizable. It also aided their plight that she was wearing slip-on shoes with rubber soles that would facilitate any quick motions they needed to execute. She tried not to linger too long on the thought that she was spiriting the leader of the free world along a busy sidewalk, clinging to the hope that no one would notice.

Incredibly, they reached the Mayflower without incident, though Gina could feel her head pounding with tension over the longest half-mile walk of her life. She ushered the president in through the entrance ahead of her, lowering her umbrella and shaking the water from it.

"Stay behind me," she whispered to Cantwell, heading toward the reception desk.

The same clerk who'd checked her in yesterday was manning it. He took one look at her garbed in what looked like a trash bag, and handed Gina a key card without being prompted. A second glance led him to duck down behind the counter, popping up with a plastic first-aid kit in his grasp. She nodded at him gratefully once he'd handed it over, noticing that the man never seemed to regard the figure shaded behind her.

Gina was breathing easily again as she and the president rode the elevator alone to the sixth floor. She had Beeman's gun palmed again as she peered out from the cab to make sure the scene was clear and only then gestured for the president to follow her into the hallway. Gun poised and ready, Gina was cognizant of every alcove and wall break wide enough to conceal a person's frame. The hallway lighting was too dim to give up any shadows, but they reached her room without incident. Gina found it exactly as she had left it, imagining that maid service was not included for these types of "visits."

She'd been too exhausted to give the space a thorough look when she first arrived and too keyed up and rushed to do so that morning. The deluxe Mayflower room was spacious, with an alcove where the desk and an armchair were placed just short of the bathroom. A couch she hadn't even noticed before was pushed up against the foot of the bed, a flat-screen television mounted on the wall before it. The matching night tables looked modern compared to the rest of the room's more rustic furnishings, and Gina noticed that the room faced out to the rear of the hotel, where there was nothing to see but other buildings. It was conceivable that someone from a window of one of the nearest buildings would be able to see inside, so Gina pulled the shades closed.

"I need to call the White House," President Cantwell said, her eyes falling on the room's speakerphone.

"I'd advise against that, ma'am, er, Jillian," Gina said, quickly correcting herself. "At least until we hear from Colonel Beeman."

"Is that the plan?"

"What passes for one at this point."

"Sit and wait?"

Gina nodded. "For now. You're safe, and we need to keep you that way."

"'We' meaning you," the president said, stating the obvious.

"Consider me your security detail for the time being."

"A bit smaller than what I'm used to."

"Not for long, hopefully."

Gina switched on CNN to find a **BREAKING NEWS** banner stretched across the screen. Her heart rate picked up when she saw the exterior of the Treasury Building above the words **EXPLOSION REPORTED AT TREASURY**. As near as she could tell, there were reports of casualties inside the building but no mention of either the president being among them or anything about the Vault itself.

Gina turned down the volume, but left the picture on. The report was a positive, given that no one was intimating yet that the president was missing and unaccounted for. That would have set an all-out panic through Washington. Bad enough that the ad hoc team assembled to battle the greatest threat the country had ever faced had been taken out; it would be even worse if the country learned Cantwell had been among them and came to fear the worst.

While waiting for Beeman to call, Gina cleaned and bandaged both the president's wounds and the ones she'd suffered back in the Vault and while leading Cantwell through the rubble. They had both managed to avoid serious injury, a miracle in its own right coming when they needed it the most.

"What now?" the president wondered, gaze still lingering on the television screen.

"I thought you might want to take a shower. I've got an extra change of clothes you can use."

"Do you have an extra gun?"

Before Gina could consider whether the president was serious or not, her phone rang, all zeroes in the caller ID.

"Colonel?" she greeted.

"Don't tell me where you are, soldier. I already know. And I'm going to assume the package is safe."

"The package is safe, sir."

"I'm sending a team over to retrieve it."

"Negative on that, sir."

"Excuse me?"

"Unless you're a part of that team, I'm not answering the door," Gina said, leaving it there.

"You're as good as advertised, soldier," Beeman responded after a pause. "I'll lead the team myself."

"And bring me the names of the task force members charged with figuring out how to dispose of those missing chemicals," Gina told him, thankfully back in investigative mode after the last few agonizing hours.

"I take it back, soldier—you're better than advertised."

Gina felt safe trusting Beeman. He never would have facilitated their escape from the Vault if he'd been in on the plot. She was about to respond when a slew of messages appeared on her screen, collected over the course of the hours her phone had been deactivated and topped by the text message she'd been expecting from Paradise with the identity of the poacher she believed was behind the death of Michael Walker's wife and the two couples that had gone missing in Rainier.

"You there, soldier?" she heard Beeman ask.

She couldn't resist opening the text, noticing that there was a graphic attached in the form of the license plate Paradise had used to identify the suspect in the murder of a Mount Rainier park ranger as a man named Ferris Hobbs. She glanced at the license plate above Paradise's message and felt a chill.

"Oh my God . . ."

"Delgado," she heard Beeman call out, "what's wrong? Talk to me, soldier!"

Gina couldn't take her eyes off the license plate.

"I think I know who Jeremiah is, Colonel," she told Beeman.

CHAPTER 77

ZION NATIONAL PARK, UTAH

Toxic cyanobacteria blooms occur frequently in Zion
water streams, so bring drinking water when visiting.

Michael came to, coughing water laced with gravel from his mouth. He couldn't catch his breath at first, and once he did, he couldn't stop taking breath after breath. He sat up all the way on a rocky shoreline he'd somehow washed up atop and coughed out yet more of the water he'd swallowed while being swept away by the floodwaters.

Michael gazed about and saw Angels Landing towering over him, its majestic beauty making for a stark contrast with the muck-strewn, brown ribbon of water slicing through the Narrows. That meant that the Zion Canyon Scenic Drive, the park's main road, was somewhere around a half mile to the east, though he'd have to find a way to somehow cross the Virgin River to get there, the very waters he'd narrowly escaped.

It would be hard enough to manage that with two feet, never mind one, and Michael looked down at his shredded pant leg on the left side, flattening out below his ankle. Fortunately, the floodwaters had washed all manner of debris atop the rocky shoreline, including tree branches thick enough to serve as a makeshift crutch. He wouldn't be able to move fast, but he would be able to move. His watch had broken somewhere, but reading the sun told him it was midafternoon, somewhere around three o'clock. That meant he must have washed up hours ago and had lain here unconscious ever since.

Next, Michael checked himself for other wounds, starting with his head. He found some bumps on his scalp, along with cuts and abrasions on his face and arms, the worst being the gash he'd suffered on his forehead, which had already clotted up. He was scraped up pretty much everywhere, the pain starting to register either as dull throbs or stinging sensations.

Nothing that would hold him up, though, and he did not appear to be suffering any concussion symptoms that would have complicated his plight even more.

Michael had no doubt that search and rescue teams were being dispatched all over the park. But the immense size of Zion, coupled with the fact that the floodwaters were still surging, made it unlikely that one of those teams would venture this far afield from the primary park area. That meant he was on his own, to either make his way closer to where he might be found, or head toward civilization.

Of course, heading anywhere right now presented a serious challenge, given that he'd have to do it on one foot. Unless he intended to crawl his way out of here, that made the first order of business finding a tree branch he could use as a crutch, something thick and sturdy enough to handle his weight.

Shuffling backward in that direction allowed him to propel himself with his arms and single foot, only the leg on his left side dragging. A combination of the slick surface and his wet clothes made sliding himself along, even slightly uphill, an easy task. He scraped his palms a few times on jagged shards of rock protruding from the shoreline, but that was the only impediment to reaching the thicket of debris the floodwaters had deposited here.

Things got harder from there. First, it took far more exertion than he'd anticipated to free an individual branch from the pile in which it was snared. There were several thick enough to serve as a makeshift crutch, but most were too short and a few were too long.

After further exhausting himself by yanking, pulling, and twisting, he finally found what looked more like a long log than a branch. Lying on his back and positioning it under his arm revealed it was only a few inches too long, likely the closest in size to what he needed that he would be able to find.

Sure enough, when he used the narrow trunk to help boost him upright, he found it fit snugly in his left armpit. It wouldn't be a comfortable process, or fast or smooth either, but Michael was convinced he could cover maybe a mile per hour or so, meaning he'd be able to move several miles in either direction before night fell. Hopefully, enough time to find help.

His best, perhaps only, hope at this point was to make his way to the Zion Canyon Scenic Drive. It had been constructed to maximize drainage, which made it his best, and closest, opportunity.

The rocky grade of the land, coupled with slippery conditions that tested every knob of his single remaining ranger-issue boot, made heading east toward the road slower than he'd anticipated. Worse, he was at the mercy of how that rocky land bent with the contours of the surrounding canyon walls. His progress was slowed a few times by Great Basin rattlesnakes crawling out from crevices amid the rocks where they'd sought protection from the flooding. They were the only venomous snake in Zion, well adapted to both the elements and the park contours. Their light brown coloring, with darker brown blotches down the middle of their backs, made them difficult to spot amid the rocks, but the ones Michael passed paid him no heed whatsoever.

The rocky land leveled off for a time, allowing him to fall into a steadier rhythm while manipulating his makeshift crutch over the hard surface, trying not to put all his weight on his right foot. The bottom of the birch tree trunk slipped a few times, and once when Michael put too much of his weight on it to avoid falling he heard a crack and feared he might have snapped it, with no replacement visible anywhere in his line of sight.

The crack must not have extended all the way through the trunk's lower base, because it continued to support his weight, although his remaining foot started cramping, forcing him to stop and rest it. After a few moments, Michael set off again and, almost immediately, detected sounds of rushing water and reached the top of a small hill formed of uneven rock to find the Virgin River directly before him. Michael chose his footing carefully in a descent that proved steeper than it had looked originally.

But the height of the river had lowered considerably, and so had the force of the floodwaters that had nearly killed him, to the point where he thought he could cross to the other side, if the bottom didn't betray him. Normally, it would have been a foot or so in height with a soft, rolling flow of current. Today it was somewhere between three and four feet, the currents dramatically slower than the ones that had swept him away, but still challenging.

Michael knew he had no choice. He waded in tentatively, the water quickly climbing up to his waist, higher than he'd anticipated. The force of currents against him felt like ocean undertow, slowing but not stopping his progress across.

He had just crossed the halfway point when his makeshift crutch sank between some rocks and stuck in the bottom. Michael fought against panic and worked it free, only to have it sink in again. He couldn't risk the birch trunk snaring any tighter or snapping off when he tried to free it, so Michael dropped down onto his stomach, head peaked above the water as he tried to swim the remaining stretch to the opposite rocky shoreline. No easy task while clinging to his crutch and trying to find a rhythm with only a single leg and arm to push and steer him.

He managed to toss his crutch onto the rocky shore on the other side and then pull the rest of himself up, hands clawing at the rocks until he found the purchase he needed. He sucked in a deep breath, let it out slowly, and then sucked in another, needing to fully catch his breath before setting off again. He felt invigorated, the most precarious part of his trek now behind him and the Zion Canyon Scenic Drive somewhere between a quarter and an eighth of a mile away.

Michael saw a broad shadow fall over him and turned onto his side. Gazing up into the last of the afternoon sun, he saw a massive shape standing there. He was relieved for a brief moment, before the pistol the man was holding glistened in the sunlight.

"All that for nothing," said Abel Rathman.

CHAPTER 78

꠵꠵◦◦꠵꠵

WASHINGTON, D.C.

Residents consume more wine per person on average
than anywhere else in the United States.

Gina was studying the picture Paradise had sent her of the license plate yet
again when a one-word text message in all caps flashed on her screen: HERE.

She took one last look at the Washington State license plate of a vehicle
identified as a white GMC Acadia registered to Ferris Hobbs, the man she
suspected was behind the murder of Michael's wife. Red letters framed the
white plate featuring Mount Rainier embossed beneath the random letters
and numbers, centered top and bottom:

PREDESTINED FOR A PURPOSE
JEREMIAH 29:11

A single knock fell on the door when Gina was already moving toward
it. She checked the peephole to find Beeman, one bandage on his forehead
and butterfly stitches on both cheeks, standing there rigid as ever.

Gina opened the door to also find a dozen soldiers wearing black tactical uniforms fanned out strategically along much of the hall.

"I shut the floor down," Beeman said, entering and then closing the
door behind him. "I've also got troops in every elevator and all emergency
stairwells accessing this floor." He finally acknowledged the president, currently garbed in a Mayflower bathrobe, with a nod and a simple greeting.
"Madam President."

Gina wondered if Cantwell was going to tell the colonel to call her
Jillian.

"What's the plan?" she asked instead.

"Once my team establishes that the site is secure enough to move you,
we get you out of here."

"Back to the White House?"

Beeman didn't hesitate. "Undetermined at this point, ma'am." He looked back toward Gina. "In the meantime, tell me how you figured out who Jeremiah really is."

‡‡‡

Gina started by showing him the license plate and then backtracking to the secondary investigation she'd been conducting into the killing of Michael Walker's wife, how that had resulted in her identifying a suspect named Ferris Hobbs.

Jeremiah.

"Walker," Beeman repeated. "I met him at the Arch."

"You did."

"Good man. He's come a long way for a man with a prosthetic foot."

"You get that from his file?"

"No, soldier. I got it from these," Beeman said, pointing at his eyes. "Seen far too many amputees in my time." He held her gaze as he paused. "But I did get plenty from your file."

"Which one?"

"The one with nothing left out, including your detachment to an Army Special Forces A-team in Iraq. Pretty damn impressive. And demolitions to boot."

Gina let his words hover in the air, feeling the president's eyes rooted upon her.

"Holding out on me, Gina?"

"We haven't had a lot of time for conversation . . . Jillian."

Beeman's expression tightened quizzically.

"I told her to call me that, Colonel," Cantwell told him. "You can, too, if you like."

"I'll stick to 'ma'am,' if you don't mind . . . ma'am."

"Can I give you an order, Colonel?"

"You're the commander in chief, ma'am. I'd be disappointed if you didn't."

"I need your phone. I've got a country to run and for now that's the way I'm going to run it."

Beeman didn't argue, just handed the president a phone extracted from his pocket. Gina spotted a matching one clipped to his belt, meaning he'd come prepared.

"Tell me about the casualties, Colonel."

"The rescue team got your chief of staff out, along with Rod Rust," he said, leaving it there. "Your chief of staff is already back on station—his words. The governor's at the hospital. Everyone else . . ."

The president nodded stiffly. "I'm going to get dressed."

She headed into the bathroom, closing the door behind her.

Beeman looked toward Gina. "So your working theory is that Ferris Hobbs, a.k.a. Jeremiah, was behind the disappearances of these two couples in Mount Rainier National Park."

"It is, yes."

"And, by connection, since you were able to identify Hobbs in the park the day of this shoot-out that claimed the life of Walker's wife, the two of them were supposed to be his next victims."

Gina nodded. "That was the plan, yes. What I haven't figured out yet is where the young man and woman Walker and his wife killed fit into all this."

"I have, soldier. I did some background on Hobbs on my way over here." Beeman hesitated, seeming to hold his breath. "They were his children, both twenty-six. Twins."

✝✝✝

"And there's more," Beeman continued, after a pause. "Hobbs's family lost their land in Washington State to Mount Rainier National Park in 1988 via a form of eminent domain called the Washington Park Wilderness Act."

"So, you figure the murder of those two couples, and Michael Walker's wife, were about revenge? Justice?"

"All I can figure is that Hobbs, Jeremiah now, is batshit crazy. But, yes, I think him murdering victims in Rainier is about getting even for his land being taken. And how can we be sure those two couples were his only victims?"

Beeman was right; there was no way they could be. Conceivably, the man who now called himself Jeremiah could have been behind any number of the other disappearances in the park over who knew how many years, visitors who'd vanished without a trace.

"What about the connection between Hobbs and Terrell?" Gina asked the colonel.

"Our best guess is that they met for the first time around six months after his kids got killed at a speech Terrell was giving in Yakima, Washington. We had eyes on General Terror at the time."

"You knew he was dangerous even then and this is where we're at now?"

"We had plenty of reason to keep watch on him, but none to take action. We've got this thing in the U.S. called laws, like them or not. By the time we had intelligence Terrell had turned his intentions operational, he'd slipped off the map. Which brings me to another tidbit about Ferris Hobbs. He owns a company called Gray Rock Trucking, one of the few long-haulers willing and able to transport hazardous materials for the right price."

Gina thought of the missing chemicals. "You think that—"

"For sure," Beeman interrupted. "And the timeline fits like a glove. Hobbs must have shown up at Terrell's speech to offer his services, the death of his kids having pushed him all the way off the edge he was already teetering on."

Gina assembled all the pieces she had in her mind. There was still a lot they didn't know, the circumstances involving the theft of those chemical reserves being foremost among them, but the picture was growing clearer. She visualized Hobbs three and a half years ago trudging along the same path his twins had taken in Rainier, coming upon their dead bodies. Those bodies had never been recovered, meaning he'd somehow lugged both of them all the way back to wherever his car was parked, at least a mile by her calculation. A truly Herculean task. The next image Gina conjured was of him driving out of the park with the bodies of his kids covered in the rear of the GMC Acadia, instead of Michael's and Allie's.

"Please tell me you've got eyes on Hobbs, Colonel."

"Wish I could. He's in the wind, but every security camera in this country is waiting for him to come into view. He pops up, we'll know it."

"Those chemicals are still the key, Colonel. We find them, maybe we end this before it starts."

"Tall order, soldier."

"Maybe not. You bring me that list of task force members charged with disposing of the reserves?" Gina asked him. "Because one of them must be the one who made it possible for Terrell to take possession of those chemicals in the first place and for Hobbs to transport them."

She watched him unclip the phone from his belt and saw the screen change as he jogged it to something before handing it to her. The task force members were in alphabetical order, and Gina's gaze froze on the final name listed, not believing her eyes.

"I think I found our man," she told Beeman, pointing to one of the names.

CHAPTER 79

ZION NATIONAL PARK, UTAH

The Temple of Sinawava is named
after the Paiute wolf god.

The still shot Gina Delgado had isolated from security-camera footage of a work crew on the ferry didn't do Abel Rathman's size justice.

"Stand up," Rathman ordered, stepping back.

"I can't," Michael tried. "You'll have to help me."

"Stand up," Rathman repeated, holding the gun a bit higher.

This time, Michael complied, crimping his body forward and rising on his good leg while pushing off with the birch trunk he then positioned back under his armpit. The thought to sweep it outward into the big man flashed through his mind, vanquished when Michael realized he wouldn't be able to generate nearly enough force to do him any good against someone of this size and strength.

"How'd you find me?"

"Easy," the big man said. "Your picture's been all over television, listed as missing in the park. Since this is where the last few bodies washed up in flash floods, I figured I'd find you dead, too."

"Sorry to disappoint you," Michael told him, stalling. "You must know Zion."

The big man regarded him with a flat, emotionless stare. "I've done some training in the park. It simulates conditions in a few places I've been deployed on missions."

"What do you call the mission you're on now?"

"Patriotism. And don't even think about it."

"What?"

"Using that branch as a weapon. Try it and I'll break your arm."

"Be hard for me to keep moving if you did that."

"That's your problem." Rathman gestured straight ahead. "Walk on, straight down that path."

"That where you left your car?"

Rathman gestured again, this time with the gun. "That's where we're going."

Michael moved ahead of him down the jagged, sloped, wide passage amid the towering rock faces that were farther away than they looked. He was no longer paying enough attention to the sun to guess what time it was, too busy contemplating his next move. Abel Rathman wasn't going to kill him; he would have done so already if that had been the plan.

"Who are you working for?" Michael asked, tilting his gaze backward. "Who's behind all this?"

"Walk."

Michael thought Rathman had finished, but then he resumed.

"He wants to deal with you himself. Says the two of you have a history."

"With me?" Michael was genuinely baffled, no idea what Rathman could have been talking about. "Who?"

"Walk," came Rathman's command again, instead of an answer.

Michael knew that once they got to the big man's vehicle, it was over. Even if Rathman was working alone, Michael stood no chance against him at all with a single foot. Out here, in the park, at least he had the advantage of knowing the terrain. Once confined, he'd be out of options.

Even here his choices were limited, nonexistent really. Whatever Michael did to gain a momentary advantage would be squandered by his hobbled state. Rathman was a trained killer who had forty or fifty pounds on him, all of it muscle. Even with his prosthetic intact, he wouldn't have stood a chance.

Maybe waiting to reach the vehicle presented a better option. Then he heard the whir of an approaching helicopter, feeling hopeful for a moment until Rathman raised a walkie-talkie to his lips.

"Heading to the coordinates now. Prepare for evac."

It made perfect sense that Rathman had reached Zion via helicopter, changing the scenario entirely. Michael's thoughts halted when he spotted a brown shape camouflaged on a small shelf in the rock face. Startled, the Great Basin rattlesnake slithered into a gap in the slippery rock surface, only its tail protruding. There had been no telltale rattling sound because this snake's rattle had broken off at the end of its tail. Common here, thanks to Zion's unforgiving landscape. Together with the snakes' being colored to match the terrain, that had led to so many park patrons getting bitten that all rangers now carried emergency syringes filled with antivenom with them at all times.

Michael realized he had his chance, the best and only one he was going to get.

In the next instant, before he could think further, he faked slipping on the sheer surface where the grade suddenly bent upward. He didn't fake the fall that followed, going down hard and hitting his head, though not hard enough to cause the unconsciousness he was now feigning.

Michael felt Rathman jostling his shoulder. "Walker."

A harder jostle.

"Get up, Walker. I know you can hear me."

Michael didn't move.

"Jesus Christ," he heard Rathman mutter.

Then a pair of hands grabbed hold of him from the rear, lifting upward. He felt weightless, a rag doll when measured against Rathman's size and strength. He kept his legs limp, hands crimped close to his waist so the big man wouldn't see what he was holding.

Rattlers weren't easy to neutralize, but holding them just behind the base of the head made it impossible for them to bite. Rathman didn't even see the snake until Michael twisted as the big man tried to shake him alert again. He turned into the motion, bringing his right hand holding the snake up toward Rathman's face.

His intention was to use the snake as a distraction to gain the advantage he needed. When he saw Rathman's mouth drop for a scream at the sight of the rattler, though, Michael altered his strategy, pushing the snake's head straight into the dark maw.

Rathman's cheeks expanded. He began shaking and writhing, his massive hands closing around the snake's slithering frame and trying to yank it from his mouth. But his efforts succeeded only in forcing the rattler down deeper. Rathman's eyes bulged in shock and pain; his face was darkening, his breath shut off to boot.

Finally, Rathman's arms flapped uselessly to his sides and he dropped to his knees, clawing at the hand Michael still had latched to the rattler, the big man's throat bulging from the snake's shape lodged there. Michael dropped with him and didn't let go until Rathman's eyes glazed and then froze. The big man fell over forward, the rocky ground seeming to shake on impact.

Michael watched the rattler emerge from beneath him and slither away. Then he retrieved his makeshift crutch, located Rathman's fallen pistol, and stuck it in the pocket of his torn-up green ranger jacket.

He started on again, the adrenaline rush fueling his efforts. He heard the ratcheting whine of the helicopter drawing closer to whatever rendezvous point had been arranged. Michael looked around and saw that the sun was lower in the sky, the afternoon having appreciably darkened. He'd lost track of all time and space, and was beginning to fear that banging his head had done more damage than he'd thought. It felt like he was asleep on his feet, his eyes open but his mind only processing what lay before him in fits and starts. The adrenaline rush gave way to mental numbness. Michael's motions slowed, becoming almost dreamlike. Instinct pushed him on, directing him straight for the single road that cut through the park.

The next time Michael's senses sharpened, he found himself in ankle-deep water collected atop what could only be Zion Canyon Scenic Drive. Looking up, he could see dusk fast approaching. He was moving in a daze, barely conscious of the makeshift crutch supporting him.

Then it finally snapped, and Michael went down hard in the muck-strewn water. He ended up on his back, propping himself up on his elbows amid the silence and growing darkness around him. Then the silence was broken by the roar of an approaching vehicle that screeched to a halt. Michael felt for the pistol tucked in his pocket, figuring it could only be a backup team there to finish the job Rathman had started.

CHAPTER 80

WASHINGTON, D.C.

The Department of the Interior was created
on March 3, 1849.

Gina entered Secretary of the Interior Ethan Turlidge's office without being announced, ID badge in hand.

"Excuse me," he said, rising and reaching for his phone.

"FBI, Secretary Turlidge. Please sit down."

Turlidge clung tight to the receiver, his other hand suspended in the air.

"Now, Mr. Secretary."

Turlidge replaced the receiver and obliged. His deep-set, hooded eyes narrowed on Gina, looking more fearful than annoyed. She noticed the dark heavy bags beneath them. He had a high forehead and a receding hairline. His eyes looked bigger behind his horn-rimmed glasses, too small for a face dominated by flabby jowls that appeared ready to slide off both jawlines.

Gina had showered and changed clothes after Beeman had left with the president in tow, leaving behind a pair of his men to accompany her here. It had been the most welcome shower of her life. The downpour might have washed most of the filth from her clothes, but she'd led the president through so much debris laced with gravel and grime that it had left a coating on her skin the rain hadn't reached. On the one hand, she was reinvigorated by the sense that things were coming together. They had Jeremiah's identity, and once he and General Archibald Terrell were out of the picture, it would be game over. That sense of optimism, on the other hand, was counterbalanced by Michael Walker having gone missing in Zion. Gina had heard of the flash flooding that plagued the park, but could never have conceived an explosion triggering an avalanche of runoff to turn a more or less regular occurrence into a not-so-natural disaster.

"Whether you leave your office, and this building, in these is up to you, sir," Gina said, flashing a pair of old-fashioned handcuffs, an unplanned gesture she'd opted for after noting the fear in Turlidge's eyes. "You know what a cooperating witness is?"

"Witness to what, Agent . . ."

"Delgado, Mr. Secretary. And it's not Agent, it's Chief. I'm the assistant special agent in charge of the New York field office. You already know that, because I was working with Michael Walker until you arranged to have him pulled off the investigation. I'm sure you understand what a conspiracy is, that all participants in a conspiracy can be charged with any crimes associated with it. Do you know how many people died on Saturday on Liberty Island?"

"Why are you asking me that?"

"I'll take that as a no. The answer is over seven hundred and climbing. That means you could be charged with a like number of murders."

Turlidge started to stand up again. "I have no idea what you're—"

"Sit down, please, Mr. Secretary." Gina cocked her gaze toward the door she'd closed behind her. "I've got two soldiers posted outside your office."

"Soldiers? What in God's name for?"

"Depending on how the next few minutes go, they have a plane standing by at Joint Base Andrews to take you to Guantánamo." Judging by Turlidge's expression, her threat had achieved its desired effect. "I'm going to ask you some questions, Mr. Secretary, and you're going to answer each of them truthfully."

"I want a lawyer," Turlidge said, his voice suddenly cracking.

"No, you don't."

"I said, I want a—"

"I know what you said, and they might let you talk to one at Guantánamo. I don't know how jurisprudence works down there, so I'm not sure. What I do know is that right now you've got two choices: Either answer my questions truthfully or board that flight out of Andrews. Do you understand?"

Turlidge nodded.

"Tell me about the chemicals, Mr. Secretary."

"Chemicals?"

"You were appointed to a presidential task force spearheaded by the Department of Energy's Office of Environmental Management. Your seat at the table came courtesy of the fact that Interior coordinates with the EPA and the task force's job was to determine a means by which dangerous and deadly chemical reserves could be safely disposed of. But you had other ideas, didn't you? You saw an opportunity and that opportunity led to the vast bulk of those reserves disappearing, to be replaced by empty barrels and casks. Am I right?"

Turlidge didn't respond.

"Am I right?" Gina repeated, raising her voice.

"I, I, I . . ."

"Answer the question, please."

"What's, what's going to happen to me?"

"That depends entirely on how cooperative you are, starting with answering the question I just asked you."

This time, Turlidge's nod preceded him saying, "Yes, I am aware of the chemical stockpile, those barrels and casks."

"Because you were involved in stealing them."

It wasn't a question, but Turlidge nodded anyway, just once.

"Are you familiar with General Archibald Terrell?"

"I, er, I, I . . ."

"You may know him as General Terror, but he was just a colonel when you first met him. You were in the National Guard, Mr. Secretary. You served in Kuwait under Terrell during the Gulf War in 1990 when he was still a colonel who'd been removed from a special-ops command position in Iraq because he ordered his snipers to kill civilians, but that never came up in the background check that was run on you as a task force member, because anything pertaining to Terrell had been scrubbed by the Defense Intelligence Agency once the army cut ties with him."

Turlidge was just staring at her, and Gina paused to let everything she said so far sink in.

"Once you learned about the chemicals, you contacted your old friend Archibald Terrell first, didn't you? Because you knew he'd have the kind of contacts who'd be interested in acquiring that stockpile, and you were also aware he was capable of transporting and securing those chemicals. Because this wasn't the first time you worked with General Terror, was it?"

Turlidge looked at her quizzically.

"You also arranged for the transport of large portions of nickel, lithium, and cobalt that had been stolen from the Strategic National Stockpile. The bureau's New York field office was in charge of the investigation and I was running point. But Terrell and his well-placed friends in the government got the investigation squashed, because you were already moving stockpiles of the deadliest chemicals on the planet for them."

Turlidge looked utterly befuddled, his eyes wide with uncertainty now, as well as fear. Gina knew it wasn't an act this time; he must have had no idea of the extent of what he had become involved in.

"You thought General Terror was going to broker the deal with some rogue state or terrorist group. But that was never his intention. His plan all along was to position the chemical stockpile so it could be used right here at home to destabilize the country and set the stage for the government to be overthrown."

Turlidge swallowed hard enough to make his Adam's apple look like it was going to burst out of his throat. "I don't know anything about any of this."

"Here's something else you don't know," she picked up. "A few hours ago, an attempt was made on the life of the president."

Turlidge's hooded eyes widened.

"You might not be aware of that, but I'm sure you're aware of the explosion at the Treasury Department. She was there at the time and barely escaped. The conspiracy you're a part of extends to that, another charge added to the list. You're looking at spending the rest of your life in jail, starting at Guantánamo, unless you get smart and cooperate. No lawyers and no deals. You're in no position to bargain. So I'm going to ask you again, where are the chemicals?"

"I don't know," Turlidge said, barely above a mutter.

"Well, I know you changed Michael Walker's assignment to Zion National Park on Terrell's instructions. But he didn't tell you why, did he?"

Turlidge remained silent.

"Allow me to fill in the blanks. Terrell has a coconspirator named Ferris Hobbs who's been moving the chemicals you stole across the country. His kids were the ones whose bodies went missing on Rainier. You're working with the man who killed your daughter, Mr. Secretary."

Turlidge's mouth dropped.

"Hobbs arranged for Michael's transfer to Zion, so he could have him killed. If he succeeds, that would also make you an accessory to murder."

Gina hesitated to let her point sink in. "You've got one chance and one chance only to avoid Guantánamo, Mr. Secretary: Tell me how we can reach your old friend General Terror."

She watched Turlidge grab a notepad and jot down a phone number.

†††

Gina moved to the back of the office, never taking her eyes off Turlidge as she called Colonel Beeman.

"Get me Turlidge's phone number," Beeman said, after she laid out what she'd just learned. "Then wait for my callback to give you the go-ahead to have him call Archibald Terrell. We're going to ping the line to isolate wherever Terrell is talking from. It's time we nailed this son of a bitch once and for all."

CHAPTER 81

ZION NATIONAL PARK, UTAH

**Zion resides in part of three counties in Utah:
Washington, Kane, and Iron.**

Michael felt hands probing, lifting, carrying . . .

He felt like he was floating, just a few feet off the ground but so much closer to the sky than he'd just been. He wondered if he had died and this was the route to heaven, though he doubted anyone got to heaven in a black extended-cab pickup truck. He recognized it as a Ford F-150 Raptor, designed to be driven off-road, including through water up to two feet, with tires over three feet in height.

He heard, but couldn't process, what a pair of people were saying. Michael wondered if he had really killed Abel Rathman by shoving a rattlesnake down his throat or just dreamed it. If he'd dreamed it, maybe this was an extension of the same dream.

"Who are you?" he heard himself ask.

He closed his eyes without waiting for a response, and when he opened them he was lying across the rear seat of the pickup. It smelled of fresh leather, showroom new. A pair of figures climbed into the front seat, the truck lowering slightly as their weight settled. Michael couldn't make out much of their features, but he saw enough to know he'd never seen them before.

And they were both Native American, the one in the passenger seat sporting a coal-black ponytail.

The nearest tribe to Zion was the Kaibab Band of Paiute, their reservation located about an hour away in northern Arizona where it met the Utah border.

"Who are you?" Michael heard himself say again.

"Rest," a voice said from the front.

"Where are we going?"

"Rest," the voice repeated, coming from the passenger seat.

Michael closed his eyes again and didn't open them until he was being eased from the truck by hands that smelled the same as the ones that had originally placed him there. He felt calluses and the rough skin of some-one who worked with their hands. He glimpsed a gurney a moment before he was lowered onto it and wheeled away.

Around him, children were kicking a soccer ball about. Native women sat on the front porches of small homes all of generally identical design. The houses ran in twin rows directly across from each other, with a road formed by chipped, patched pavement running between them.

Suddenly, a shadow blocked the sun, the shape of the man with the ponytail hovering over him.

"How badly is he hurt?" a woman's voice wondered.

"We can't tell."

"He lost his prosthetic. We'll have to do something about that."

"Any word from the others?"

"Not yet. I'll advise them we've found Walker."

They know who I am, Michael thought. How? Why? And what had brought them to Zion?

"Let's get you fixed up first," the woman said.

Michael hadn't realized he'd asked a semblance of those questions out loud.

"Are you in any pain?" the woman asked him.

"My . . . head."

"Understandable. Anything else?"

"My foot."

"It hurts?"

"It's gone. I mean the prosthetic one."

"More of a challenge, but we'll come up with something."

Michael realized that the man who'd driven the Ford Raptor here from Zion was angling the gurney toward a building that matched the others on both sides of the street. His vision sharpened, his mind clearing, absorbing the dry, dusty surroundings from the gurney. "Who are you people?"

"Fallen Timbers," said the man with the ponytail, walking alongside the gurney.

CHAPTER 82

OFF I-90 WEST, SOUTH OF CHICAGO

Interstate 90 runs from Seattle, Washington,
to Boston, Massachusetts.

Lantry gulped down the water the man who called himself Jeremiah had handed him in the back of the eighteen-wheeler. He had been placed there with his hands and feet both bound. He'd lost track of time, other than the levels of light on those occasions the door had been unlocked and lifted open: five times so far on what felt like roughly two-hour intervals. Each time, Jeremiah had unbound him, handed him the same satellite phone, and had Lantry call in his status and report the location from a fake map that had the convoy heading southwest.

"The latest X is the location you are to report," Jeremiah told him.

He felt like a coward doing so to the voice on the other end of the line. He wished Fallen Timbers had provided some code word or phrase to use if he was in trouble, wished he could have come up with another means on his own to alert the group that something was wrong. They had dispatched him and the team he had trained to track polluters of the environment when, clearly, something with far greater stakes was in the offing. Whatever chemicals the convoy was hauling were not destined to be illegally dumped, but weaponized. But how? And where exactly was the convoy really headed?

"You're doing God's work, son," Jeremiah told him, "filling a vital role for a noble cause. You may even come around to seeing things our way before this is over."

"I don't think so," Lantry said, his mouth still dry.

Jeremiah shook his head. "Tell me what I'm missing here. Your people, all Natives, set the bar in this country for being mistreated, taken advantage of, hung out to dry. I know the hurt in that because I felt the same pain myself when the government stole my family's land out from under us and made it part of Mount Rainier National Park. You know what I did about that? I claimed the whole park for myself, deeded in blood, just like they spilled my father's because he stood up to them. I watched him die and every time I took a life inside that park it was for him. But it wasn't enough, it was never enough. You know what is enough? What I'm doing now, aiming at the whole government, and when I pull the trigger it's going to fall."

Lantry watched Jeremiah shake his head.

"If anyone belonged on our side, I'd think it would be Natives. If your people were of a mind to do that, I'd give them their choice of land. Get off those reservations the government stuffed you in. That's what this is all about, son, righting a whole bunch of wrongs and us setting this country straight in the process."

"Who's 'us'?" Lantry asked.

"Patriots, son, citizens who aren't going to let this country continue spinning off the rails. We intend to make things right, including the direction America is headed."

Jeremiah smiled placidly. The trailer had a high enough ceiling for him to stand fully upright, and beyond him, Lantry could see that the convoy had stopped this time on the side of the road itself, as opposed to a refueling station. This was the second stop they'd made since night fell. Once again, the convoy had clung to sparsely traveled roads, keeping its speed slow. Lantry felt every bump and every pothole. To pass the time, he'd close his eyes and try to picture where they were and how far had they come. His uncle could do things like that, had tried to teach him how to empty his mind and become one with the world, but Lantry had never managed to pull it off.

In a few moments he'd be handcuffed again amid the steel drums filled with who knew what. Lantry had never seen anything like them. They had temperature gauges and other LED readouts monitoring levels that would serve as an early-warning system if the barrel was damaged or leaking.

"There's going to come a time not long from now," Jeremiah resumed, "that folks who didn't join us are going to wish they had." His expression sombered. "I had kids not much older than you, same age I was when the government stole my family's land. Know what happened to them? They got killed, just like my father. Now that they're dead, I've got nothing to lose but plenty to fight for. Their deaths left me empty, left me broken. The work I'm doing today made me feel worth something again, gave me purpose, something to believe in." He pointed toward Lantry's necklace, the talisman Fallen Timbers had given him. "Like you believe in whatever that is, a god or something."

Lantry fingered the three components of his talisman. "It's just a symbol."

"Like I said, something to believe in. Everybody needs that to keep them going. I realized I didn't believe in this country anymore. But now I do again, more than ever. Because I've got a part in changing it, righting the ship. When we get where we're going, son, you're going to have a front-row seat for all the festivities."

CHAPTER 83

WASHINGTON, D.C.

The Mayflower Hotel opened in 1925.

"Nice work, soldier," Colonel Beeman said to Gina. "The way you put this whole thing together gives us a genuine shot to find these bastards before it's too late."

She had responded to a knock on the door to her hotel room, where she had returned on Beeman's orders after her interview with Ethan Turlidge had ended with him placing a call to Archibald Terrell so the colonel could isolate his location.

Beeman entered the room and closed the door behind him. As near as Gina could tell, he was alone, but had a tote bag slung over his shoulder.

"Got some news I wanted to share with you. General Terror spoke to Turlidge from a spot in southeastern Ohio, the same area where there happens to be a mothballed air force base. We've got ourselves a target, soldier."

"You could have delivered that news over the phone, Colonel."

"But it's harder to say no in person."

"No to what, sir?"

"We need to hit that base in Ohio, but I'm short men and can't call up the cavalry when trust is at such a premium." Beeman eased the tote bag from his shoulder, grimacing from the pain left from one of the injuries he'd suffered in the blast that morning. "I need somebody who can blow shit up, so I took the liberty of bringing your gear with me." He extended the tote bag toward her. "So what do you say, soldier?"

CHAPTER 84

KAIBAB INDIAN RESERVATION, ARIZONA

NPS oversees Pipe Spring National Monument,
which lies on Kaibab land.

Michael awoke again, this time atop a cot squeezed with three others into a room that smelled of alcohol. He remembered the black pickup truck, remembered being eased out of the back of it and placed on a gurney.

The pungent smell of alcohol told him this must be the reservation's clinic or infirmary, comprised of a small reception area and two or three examination rooms. He got a good look into the other exam room, but not through the doors of either of the others at the end of the small hallway. Night had fallen beyond the windows; beyond that, he had lost all track of time.

"You're awake," he heard a female voice pronounce.

Michael hadn't been aware of the woman's presence in the room. She wore a white lab coat and glasses, a member of the tribe almost for sure. He recognized her voice as that of the woman who'd accompanied him here after he'd been lifted out of the pickup truck.

"I'm Dr. Yolanda Rivers," she said. "And it's closing in on midnight."

"I didn't ask you what time it was."

"You didn't have to," Rivers told him. "And you can thank me later."

"What's wrong with now?"

"You haven't looked down yet."

Michael saw he was lying atop the bedcovers instead of beneath them. His clothes had been swapped for a pair of medical scrubs, top and bottom, and something was protruding where his prosthetic would normally be.

"What," he started, maneuvering himself to look closer.

"I come from a long generation of healers, Agent Walker. My forebears have been dealing with amputees for centuries. It might well be that our tribe was the first to use prosthetics—crude but effective."

She pulled the left leg of the hospital scrubs he was wearing up over his knee, and Michael saw that what looked to be a wooden prosthetic was affixed to his stump via an assortment of straps and buckles. It finished in a foot carved out of wood the same size as the real one on his right side. The foot was affixed to the ankle portion of the prosthetic by some kind of ball joint, allowing for limited rotation.

"You did this?"

Rivers nodded. "Like I said, my family's been doing it for centuries. That's the late-nineteenth-century model. Not quite what you're used to, but it should get the job done."

Michael had a host of questions for Rivers, but before he could pose any, a man wearing a black leather blazer and matching black hat appeared in the door. Michael recognized him as the man in the passenger seat from his coal-black ponytail.

"I see our patient is awake," the man said, leaning against the doorjamb.

"I owe you some thanks, too," Michael greeted. "A lot of thanks."

The man entered and approached the bed. "The name's Ty Segundo and no thanks are necessary. We're fighting the same war. You just don't know it yet."

"I know I'm trying to stop the group behind attacks on national parks and monuments."

Segundo nodded, his ponytail flopping slightly. "They want to break it all down so they can build it back up again. Strike at the nation's heart by destroying its most iconic symbols and places." Segundo narrowed his gaze on Michael, his eyes as black as a crow's. "I'm going to assume that you have no idea about the chemicals."

"What chemicals?"

"Guess I'm right. Suffice it to say, Agent Walker, that everything you've seen over these past four days is just the preliminary round to set the stage. Over six hundred thousand people died in the first civil war. That's not even a drop in the bucket compared to how many are going to perish in the second."

Michael felt a chill up his spine. "You saved my life."

"Maybe. You're tougher than you think."

Michael wondered how much Segundo knew about him, but the fact that he'd been in Zion at all was far more perplexing.

"You came to Zion to rescue me."

Segundo nodded. "As soon as word of the blast reached us, quickly followed by a report you were among the missing in the flooding."

Michael just looked at him, his mind still too foggy to connect all the dots here. "But how did you know I was there, that I was a part of this?"

"We've been following your movements since Liberty Island. One of our members serves as a park policeman there. We also had someone watching Zion and they spotted you there yesterday."

"Fallen Timbers," Michael said, recalling what the man had told him earlier.

Segundo nodded. "You haven't heard about the attack in Washington yet, have you?"

Michael felt another chill. "Where this time?"

"A secret facility beneath the Treasury Building. The president was nearly killed. The FBI agent you've been working with got her to safety and handed her over to a man we've been working with, a man I served with. He was a captain then and I was a sergeant. He's a colonel now, one of the finest officers the army's got."

Michael remembered the colonel who'd taken over the scene at the Gateway Arch, the pieces falling together.

"And he's on the front line of the second civil war that's coming," Segundo resumed, "along with me and you. Fallen Timbers has been fighting for our environment for as long as there's been one. That's what we thought we were doing here."

"Those chemicals you mentioned . . ."

"But they're not going to be dumped illegally. They're going to be used to kill millions of Americans. Call it this war's shell fired over Fort Sumter. The beginning."

Michael tried to make sense of everything Segundo was saying, but his mind wasn't moving fast enough. Then he couldn't find the words to form his next thought.

Segundo jumped back in. "We believe we know where those chemicals are headed. We'll have people on the ground there soon." He took a step closer to Michael's bedside. "That includes *you*, Agent Walker. Oh, almost forgot . . ."

With that, Segundo extracted Michael's ID wallet, complete with badge, from his pocket. It still looked sodden and was discolored in patches from getting soaked in his ride through the canyons of Zion.

"We leave for the airstrip in twenty minutes," Segundo said, handing the wallet back to Michael. He turned his gaze on Michael's left leg and smiled. "That will give you some time to get used to your new foot."

⊢┄┄◦┄┄⊣

CHAPTER 85

JOINT BASE ANDREWS, MARYLAND

After World War II, Andrews served as headquarters
for Continental Air Command, Strategic Air
Command, the Military Air Transport Service,
and Air Force Systems Command.

"You were born to wear that uniform, soldier," Beeman said, when Gina emerged from an SUV driven by one of his men on the tarmac of Joint Base Andrews just short of midnight.

President Jillian Cantwell was safe and secure in a so-called undisclosed location, the White House no longer considered to be either. That drove home the point of how close the entire country was to falling off the edge of the cliff on which it was currently teetering.

The troops gathered on the tarmac before her numbered somewhere around a hundred. They stood over or sat upon their duffel bags in the darkness broken only by the base's floodlights, an added bonus of which would be to keep their presence here secret. The scene brought back memories of her deployment to Iraq, originally as part of the Army Corps of Engineers. The biggest difference was in the character and composition of troops standing over their gear stowed in matching duffel bags; serving under Beeman, they were clearly the best of the best, now waiting to board the C-130 transport plane. Its engines were already warming, and she glimpsed the pilot and copilot through the big plane's cockpit windows. Gina had no such gear with her, but figured what she needed would be provided when the time was right.

"I need somebody who can blow shit up."

Gina took it as a good sign that Beeman's troops were about to head to the mothballed military base in Ohio where Archibald Terrell had taken that call from Ethan Turlidge. She figured these troops must be Special Forces, as Rathman and the others who'd "died" in that helicopter crash had been. They were clearly men Beeman knew he could trust and had likely deployed with, on multiple occasions in all likelihood, all of them going under the radar. She'd never asked him what specific unit he was part of and doubted he would have told her if she had.

"I checked on Special Agent Walker's status," Beeman told her. "Search and rescue teams haven't located him. They're still scouring Zion for him and others the floodwaters washed away."

Gina had figured as much when Michael hadn't tried to contact her or answered her calls, in the wake of Terrell and Jeremiah's forces having made Zion their latest target. She feared the worst, but anyone who'd survived what he had three and a half years ago could survive a flood.

"The best thing you can do now, soldier," Beeman resumed, "is help me get the people who did a number on that park, too. Thanks to that phone call you arranged Turlidge to place, aerial reconnaissance via high-altitude drones has confirmed General Terror is based out of what used to be Brookfield Air Force Station. That's our target."

"What's mine?"

Beeman smiled tightly. "I'll explain that when we get to our staging area."

CHAPTER 86

>-+-0-+-<

COLORADO CITY MUNICIPAL AIRPORT, ARIZONA

The airport boasts two runways,
but services no commercial airlines.

"Where we headed?" Michael asked, sitting in the same black pickup truck that had brought him to the Kaibab Indian Reservation, its headlights slicing through the night.

Michael rode in the backseat next to Ty Segundo. Theirs was the lead vehicle in a convoy of four, a dozen men and women riding inside them by Michael's count, including Dr. Yolanda Rivers. He'd used the half hour or so before they'd set out to do some mobility training with the makeshift, jerry-rigged prosthetic she had fashioned for him, now contained inside a boot that was a close facsimile of the one he wore on his right foot. It worked remarkably well, given the limitations of its components and the haste with which it had been assembled. Held in place by an assortment of straps and buckles, it wasn't a perfect fit by any stretch of the imagination, but felt firm and secure enough for him to handle everyday tasks like walking with only a slight limp. Neither too loose to risk coming free nor too tight to shut off the circulation to his ankle. He could feel far more friction with the stump of bone that had been molded to the fittings for his state-of-the art model, but this jerry-rigged version seemed to wear better the more he practiced. He couldn't twist or pivot quickly, but hopefully wouldn't have to wherever they were going.

Segundo drew his phone from his pocket as soon as the convoy drove through the gates at the entrance to the Kaibab Indian Reservation. It made Michael realize he still hadn't contacted Gina Delgado to let her know he was safe.

"You have one of those for me, Ty?" he asked, watching Segundo scroll through page after page of text messages.

"Sorry," Segundo said, not looking up from the text message he was typing, "we're radio silent right now. Internal communication only."

"I get that," Michael told him, "but we're going to need more good guys to win this fight."

"And we've got them," Segundo assured him, and went back to typing.

‡‡‡

Michael saw a Gulfstream G650 waiting for them on the tarmac when the convoy pulled through the gates of Colorado City Municipal Airport. The U.S. Bureau of Land Management had recently transferred land to Colorado City that had nearly doubled the size of the airport property, allowing for significantly lengthening the runway. The airport had been built in the 1960s with dirt runways that weren't even paved until 1991. Doubling the size of the small, recreational airport in a community of only ten thousand had made no sense to him at the time, and now he suspected that the presence of the Gulfstream might be somehow involved.

"Looks like we're traveling in style," Michael noted, as they neared the jet.

"Our cause has a patron, Agent Walker, someone who furnishes us with whatever we need to support our efforts."

"Whatever?" Michael repeated.

"He has immeasurable resources and contacts available to back our cause."

"But this is a different cause, isn't it? I've heard of Fallen Timbers; everyone in the Park Service has. Since when does your group, and this patron of yours, take on domestic terrorists?"

"Since they targeted the environment. That's how we first learned of their existence. At first, we thought they were dumping toxic chemicals. It was months before we began to realize what we were truly dealing with."

"Cause for concern for your patron, I'm guessing," Michael said.

"And we have every reason to believe his nephew has been captured."

Michael considered the flatness of Segundo's tone. "Why do I think that doesn't surprise you?"

"It was an eventuality we considered and prepared for, yes."

"You always this cryptic, Ty?"

"Only when the fate of the country is at stake."

"Tell me more about this patron of yours," Michael said.

The convoy came to a stop on the tarmac close enough to the Gulf-stream to hear the whirring hum emanating from its warming engines. Segundo threw open his door.

"Our flight is waiting, Agent Walker."

⊢•◦•◦•⊣

CHAPTER 87

GREELEY, COLORADO

**The town was named after Horace Greeley, who paid
the community one visit in 1870 and never returned.**

Lantry had no idea where they were when the trailer door was hoisted up the next time to reveal the night sky beyond. Jeremiah had only come himself the last time they'd stopped, leaving that task to others the rest of the way. This time, Lantry could see they had made a refueling stop. The man clad in black tactical gear handed him the same satellite phone after dialing the number the boy had provided.

While providing the false location the man had marked on a map he held up before him, indicating that the convoy was headed south instead of west, Lantry focused his attention on determining where they were. His line of sight offered no signage or any parked vehicles nearby with license plates to read. There was only darkness broken by a smattering of light emanating from what must have been a small outbuilding where a clerk could watch over the fueling stations while dispensing sundries and snacks.

After the phone call was concluded, Lantry drank his water slowly to buy himself more time to figure out his location through the open trailer door. He focused on the night sky off in the distance, saw the outline of what could only be the Rocky Mountains. He felt a breeze, cool for summer, and a rancid stench invaded his nostrils, reminding him of how his uncle had tried to teach him how to better use his sense of smell on numerous occasions. The lessons had never stuck, but Lantry nonetheless tried to put them to use here.

The smell was something like manure, only more astringent and sharp, more like the smell of death in the form of roadkill left steaming on the side of a freeway.

A slaughterhouse. . . .

The realization that they must be in the vicinity of a rendering plant struck him hard and fast. And if they'd driven west out of Ohio nearly to the Rocky Mountains they must be in . . .

Colorado! Lantry realized.

There was an infamous rendering plant north of Denver in the town of Greeley. His uncle had always counseled him to rely on instinct, and instinct told him that that was where the convoy loaded with barrels and casks of deadly chemicals was at present. Still steaming west, Utah being the next state they would cross into.

"Finish," the man before him ordered, extending his hand.

Lantry drained the rest of the water and extended the empty bottle back to him in a trembling hand, then clutched the talisman dangling from his neck.

Because he realized where the convoy was headed.

CHAPTER 88

HUBBARD, OHIO

The village was named for Nehemiah Hubbard, Jr.,
a founder of the Connecticut Land Company.

The C-130 carrying Gina and Colonel Beeman's team of ninety special operators landed at Youngstown-Warren Regional Airport, because it was the closest to the former Brookfield Air Force Station, where General Archibald Terrell's troops were headquartered.

"How many do you think we're going up against?" Gina had asked Beeman, while waiting for the big plane to complete its taxi.

"Hard to say. Based on the activity we've been able to confirm via that drone, best guess is somewhere around a thousand."

She'd been expecting a number like that. "So we're going to be outnumbered ten to one, pretty close anyway."

"I'd put my one against their ten any day of the week. But that's not the point, soldier, and it's not the mission either. Our mission is to keep them, and whatever ordnance they've managed to stockpile, right where they are. That aerial reconnaissance has confirmed sixteen to eighteen transport planes parked on the tarmac for the base's landing strip. Those planes aren't there only to carry men, they're there to carry heavy weapons. We keep them grounded and maybe we keep the shit from hitting the fan."

"We still need to find that chemical stockpile," Gina said. "That's the tipping point. What exactly are Ferris Hobbs and General Terror planning to do with them, how are they going to be deployed? You don't go through all the trouble of stealing and storing those reserves, if you don't have a plan to use them."

"I've got my people looking for Ferris Hobbs under every rock he may have crawled under. He crawls out, we'll know it. So let's go, soldier," Beeman had said to her, once the C-130 had come to a halt. "We've got a war to win."

‡‡‡

Beeman had ordered buses to pick them up at the airport, because that would attract the least attention while traversing the city under cover of darkness to the staging area, which turned out to be a Best Western hotel.

When they pulled up before the entrance, Gina noted a sign reading CLOSED UNTIL FURTHER NOTICE. It was obviously Beeman's work, assuring that they had the facility to themselves. While military flights into this area were hardly unusual, close to a hundred special-operations troops prepping for battle most certainly would be. A large nesting of tables located off the lobby, in an area reserved for the establishment's free breakfast service, had already been retasked as a briefing room, where the former air force base's layout could be displayed in order to review the plan to neutralize General Terrell's troops currently stationed there.

On the surface, the gathering had an almost academic feel, or at least look, with the tightly clustered group, uniformly garbed in black tactical gear, sitting attentively in complete silence. But Gina knew that beneath the surface these were the best troops the United States had to offer, no doubt chosen specifically for this unit not only for their prowess but for their proven loyalty. If any were troubled by the fact that they were about to wage an attack on a force ten times their number, they didn't show it.

After providing introductory remarks to his seated special operators, Beeman turned things over to a captain to give the briefing on the mothballed base's logistics. Gina noticed the trio of big flat-screen televisions, mounted on posts outfitted to accommodate them, placed strategically about. The screens came to life as the captain began speaking, not introducing himself since he was already well known to the soldiers with whom he served. Gina figured a portion of these troops had been the ones who accompanied Beeman to the Gateway Arch, further driving home how few people were now entrusted to keep millions of Americans from dying.

Gina's thoughts again turned toward Michael. None of her calls to him had been returned, and the fact that they were going straight to voicemail could very well mean the phone had been damaged or destroyed. Of course, he could still call her, and she clung to the belief, the veritable certainty, that he would. She'd put her phone on silent, but left a hand in her pocket so she could feel it vibrate if a call came in.

Exhaustion made it hard for her to focus on what the captain was saying, doing her best to commit the schematics of Brookfield Air Force Station, culled from overhead reconnaissance photos displayed on the flat screens, to memory. She felt as if she were back in Iraq after being assigned to that Special Forces A-team, sleep as much a premium now as it had been then. The size of the base would serve them well, since there was so much real estate to defend. But their attack would be coming in daylight, which pretty much eliminated the element of surprise. The captain addressing the soldiers was just getting to the plan itself when Gina felt the phone vibrate inside her pocket.

She jerked it out and saw **BLOCKED** lit up on the screen, but answered anyway.

"Hello?"

"It's me, Gina," greeted Michael.

CHAPTER 89

RAPID CITY, SOUTH DAKOTA

Rapid City, named for the limestone spring stream that
passes through the city, was founded in 1876 by a group
of disheartened prospectors that had come to the
Black Hills in search of gold.

Michael had moved up the aisle toward Ty Segundo as soon as the Gulf-stream landed at Rapid City Regional Airport.

"It's Wind Cave, isn't it?" Michael had asked him, referring to the national park. "That's where they're hiding the chemicals."

"'Stockpiling' would be a better word, Agent Walker."

"If you already knew that, why are we doing this alone?"

"First off, we didn't know it."

"Then how . . ."

"You remember that I told you the nephew of our patron had been captured?"

"Yes."

"We planted a tracking device in his ceremonial necklace, the group's talisman. Fallen Timbers has been following his every move since he left West Virginia. The convoy carrying the chemicals is approaching Wind Cave now."

"I need to borrow your phone, Ty," Michael had said, leaving no room for argument this time. "I need to borrow it now."

‡‡‡

"You're alive!" he heard after greeting Gina.

"Apparently."

"Where are you?"

"South Dakota, soon to be heading for Wind Cave National Park."

"Wind Cave? How did you get there? What happened in Zi—Never mind that," Gina said, cutting herself off.

"You're with Colonel Beeman," Michael said, before she could resume.

"How could you know that?"

"Because I'm with a group called Fallen Timbers that's been working with him. They have every reason to believe that the missing chemicals are being stored in Wind Cave National Park. Whoever's behind this is going to blow them up, aren't they? They're going to turn the deadliest chemicals known to man into some kind of toxic cloud capable of killing millions."

"Ten million, Michael," Gina told him. "And there's something else you need to know. . . ."

‡‡‡

Michael felt numb. He'd heard what Delgado said, but it didn't seem real, more like the residue of a waking nightmare.

The twins he and Allie had killed in the incident that had claimed Allie's life were Roman and Rebecca Hobbs, age twenty-six. Their father was Ferris Hobbs, owner of one of the largest long-haul trucking companies in the country known for its willingness to carry hazardous waste. And now millions of American lives hung in the balance, thanks to Hobbs's trucking company being retained to move thousands of barrels and casks in which the deadliest chemicals known to man were stored.

Retained by Ethan Turlidge.

"I only wish you could have been there to see the look on his face," Delgado said, after laying it all out for him.

Michael's head was pounding, so much coming at him at once.

"You and Fallen Timbers need to stop them, Michael. You've got to secure that chemical stockpile."

"What about you, Gina?"

"I've got my own mission."

‡‡‡

"We can't do this alone, Ty," Michael said, gingerly descending the Gulfstream's stairs right behind Segundo.

"I've already told you, we're not alone."

As Segundo said that, five vehicles, a mix of pickup trucks and SUVs, streamed onto the tarmac.

"The land where Wind Cave sits," he resumed, "was stolen from the Lakota tribe that currently resides on the Pine Ridge Indian Reservation. The site is vital to their culture and their history. This is their chance to defend land they still consider to be rightfully theirs."

At the bottom of the stairs, Segundo was met by a man several inches taller whom Segundo addressed as Crow. Crow's single eye matched his coal-black hair, the other covered by a patch. He glanced at Michael, but otherwise paid him no regard, conversing briefly with Segundo.

When the bigger man took his leave, Michael joined Segundo at the foot of the stairs. "Does he have any idea where the convoy is now?"

Segundo nodded. "According to the tracking device I told you about, it's almost to Wind Cave, just ten or so miles away. The problem is the park stretches for fifty square miles, and we have no idea where they've been off-loading and storing the chemicals."

"I think I do," Michael told him.

CHAPTER 90

WIND CAVE NATIONAL PARK, SOUTH DAKOTA

Established as a national park on January 3, 1903.

"End of the road, son," Jeremiah said, after hoisting up the trailer's cargo door.

The early-morning sun blinded Lantry and he reflexively tried to raise a hand to shield his eyes, only to remember they were bound together. The last stretch of the trip, the final few miles, had been made over what felt like a gravel or dirt road, jarring him at times as the truck bounced on its springs. If he was right about Wind Cave being the convoy's ultimate destination, they could have been riding along the little-traveled NPS 5 or NPS 6 backcountry roads that covered the wilderness areas in the northeastern section of the park.

"Know where we are?"

Lantry waited for his eyes to adjust to the sudden wash of light enough to recognize the general area and see that his initial instinct had been correct. "Wind Cave National Park."

"You're smarter than you look. And you're tougher than you look, too."

I wish you could meet my uncle, Lantry thought. *He could stop you in your tracks all by himself.*

"What else you got figured out?" Jeremiah asked him.

"This is where you're storing all the chemicals you've been stealing."

"How much you know about Wind Cave?" Jeremiah asked him.

"I know it's got around a hundred fifty miles of caves and plenty more that have never been explored."

Jeremiah nodded. "We're sitting atop one of the biggest now. A cavern maybe the size of three football fields. That's where all of this ends with a big bang that's going to create what I like to call an acid cloud. It's a lot more complicated than that, but that's the gist of it. And it's going to get bigger as it moves east across the country. Hell, the cloud could be the size of a small town by the time it reaches the East Coast. No escaping it for people who live in all those cities there. Estimates of the death toll run around ten million, but that's just for starters."

Lantry felt a chill. "There's no aboveground entrance to this cavern you've been storing the chemicals in," he managed.

Jeremiah grinned. "That's where you're wrong, son. Dead wrong."

CHAPTER 91

—▸◂—◦—▸◂—

HUBBARD, OHIO

Considered "the Whiskey Capital of the Nation"
in the 1880s.

"It's Wind Cave," Gina told Colonel Beeman as soon as the briefing ended and the troops dispersed to gear up.

"I know."

"You know?"

"Just got the word from that friend I told you about. He's on the ground in South Dakota."

Gina thought of Michael telling her that's where he'd just landed.

"That call you just took," Beeman continued. "Walker?"

Gina nodded. "He must be with your friend there. Why do I think your captain's briefing left something out?"

"We still got some tricks up our sleeve, soldier, along with a secret weapon."

"What's that?"

"You."

✝✝✝

Beeman led Gina to a storage room outside the eating area and just down the hall. Inside, the shelves of tablecloths, flatware, plates, utensils, napkins, and drink dispensers had been shoved aside to make room for a trio of metal folding tables.

"Just what the doctor ordered, right?" he asked her.

Gina had explained that cratering asphalt was a lot more like what she did for the Army Corps of Engineers than like her demolitions work for the Special Forces. She needed to do the kind of damage that would render the airstrip inoperative for days, if not weeks. She'd laid out what she needed to get the job done, having worked with it in Iraq and seen its potency up close on Liberty Island:

Astrolite X.

Each of the three tables held the same objects, primarily a trio of what looked like housings for retractable garden hoses.

"Lightweight, retractable garden hoses," Gina noted, inspecting them closer.

"Already filled with that liquid explosive in the precise concentrations you requested. Pretty potent shit. Hope you're right about it being stable until it's time to go boom."

"I am," Gina assured him. "You didn't bring me into this to get it wrong."

Upon detonation, the Astrolite would render the airstrip incapable of supporting a C-130's massive weight without being totally reconstructed, not just patched. The width of the runway at the former Brookfield Air Force Station was right around 150 feet. The lengths of currently coiled hosing measured an even hundred, more than enough to effectively do the job.

Gina inspected the capacitor that would serve as detonator and the wires that would carry the electric charge, then tested the heft of one of the coils of hose.

"Fifty pounds," Beeman told her. "I've got three men assigned to you to carry each one."

"Can you spare three men?"

"Not really, but cratering that runway is priority number one."

That made priority number two securing the hangars to prevent Terrell's troops from moving any of the heavy equipment Beeman believed was stored inside. Based on the briefing that had just concluded, that potential equipment ran the gamut from tanks to armored personnel carriers and Humvees to rockets and heavy machine guns.

Even that, though, told only a part of the story.

"The briefing left out Wind Cave, Colonel."

"Second front in the same war, soldier. I imagine you've got some thoughts on that subject."

"By the time it reaches the East Coast," Gina told him, "the cloud could be the size of New York City, even bigger potentially."

"I was hoping those chemicals might dissipate."

"Possible, but not likely. The blast will be rigged in a way to blow the chemicals upward. And it'll be powerful enough to crash straight through all that rock, shale, and dirt. Microscopic portions of the debris, inundated with those chemicals from the stockpile, will become the basis of the toxic cloud. Light enough to travel with normal air currents while heavy enough to maintain the cloud's integrity."

"How toxic are we talking, soldier?"

"The only fair equivalent we can use are the nuclear blasts in Hiroshima and Nagasaki. The worst of the radiation that ultimately took the most lives through exposure wasn't in the air so much as soaked into the debris. Like the chemicals, the radioactive materials were bonded into that debris. In those cases, the victims needed to deal with both radioactive clouds and standing debris that had been irradiated. Here the only real danger is posed by the cloud that could conceivably break off into several smaller ones, all headed east on the jet stream. Dipping south before heading up the East Coast. You won't be able to hide from it, outrun it, shut it out from behind closed doors and windows. Highways will become parking lots of death. Imagine breathing in acid, Colonel. The lucky ones exposed first will die fast."

Beeman weighed her words briefly. "Then we'd better prevail on the second front of this war, too."

"Something else, Colonel, that the briefing didn't cover. How are we going to approach that base without being spotted?"

Beeman stopped just short of a smile. "Glad you asked, soldier, glad you asked. . . ."

CHAPTER 92

PINE RIDGE INDIAN RESERVATION, SOUTH DAKOTA

The Wounded Knee Massacre occurred on
December 29, 1890.

Michael rode with Ty Segundo in the rearmost seat of an SUV, laying it all out for him on the way to the Pine Ridge Indian Reservation, thirty miles from Wind Cave.

"Greenbrier wasn't the only nuclear bunker constructed during the Eisenhower administration at the height of the Cold War. There were three others scattered across the country, none of which were ever finished."

"Don't tell me," Segundo said. "One of them was Wind Cave."

Michael nodded. "Way up in the northeast corner of the park, an area almost nobody ever visits."

"And you know this because . . ."

"Two years ago, I was investigating a disappearance on park grounds there that led to me being informed about the bunker's existence. The government made use of a massive cavern that's been kept off every map of the park ever since. While the bunker was never completed, an entryway was dug and a hydraulic lift installed to handle the heavy equipment and supplies."

"Why not just build some kind of tunnel?"

"The contours of the land would have required too much blasting, attracting the kind of attention the government wanted to avoid at all costs. Why bother building a bunker if you're going to advertise its existence to Soviet spy planes?"

"Then how did Jeremiah's people find out about it?"

"General Terror, almost for sure. I noticed a military presence around the bunker when I was handling that case at Wind Cave. They must have been Terrell's men, either securing the bunker or prepping it."

Michael watched Segundo stiffen. "So our only way in is the one Jeremiah is going to beat us to."

"Not exactly, Ty," Michael told him.

‡‡‡

They drove through the fence line rimming the entrance to the Pine Ridge Indian Reservation, a little over an hour from Wind Cave National Park. Even in the depths of night, Michael was struck immediately by the abject poverty of the tribe, which left a lump rising in his throat. The government had stolen the rich and vital lands in and around Wind Cave from the Oglala Lakota tribe and, in exchange, left them with land where virtually nothing could grow. Pine Ridge was one of the largest reservations in the country, and one of the poorest as well. It pained him to see the depths of the squalor in which these Native Americans lived, filling him with guilt and sorrow over how the tribe had been treated. How could more not have been done about their plight? Perhaps because so few were aware of the nature of the problem.

They drove on atop a two-lane flattened gravel road through parched, dying land, among the two million generally worthless acres deeded to the tribe in the original agreement that had formed the reservation. Drought conditions had killed most of the trees and turned the grass a dried brown color, obvious even in the moonlight.

I'm going to do something about this, he thought, then added in his mind, *if I survive.*

The vehicles drove on for several miles to an encampment of tents, where two dozen more men, intermixed with a few women, were gearing up for battle with all manner of weapons, both modern and primitive, under the spill of flaming torches mounted on wooden poles. They made for a ragtag bunch in the spill of the headlights, some dressed in the army uniforms they must have worn while defending the United States, perhaps in Iraq or Afghanistan. Others wore tactical gear, and still more were garbed in the tribe's traditional attire, including war paint made from a combination of berries, clay, and tree bark striped across their faces.

"Welcome to the temporary command post of Fallen Timbers, Agent

Walker," Segundo said, as the vehicles came to a halt. "We knew you were delivered unto us for a reason."

Segundo introduced him to the other leaders of Fallen Timbers, as well as the tribe that would be joining their efforts. Then Michael watched as the makeshift force gathered around him to be briefed on what he had just shared with Ty. Michael asked for something to draw on and was led to a small patch of cleared land the size of a sandbox and handed a stick shaved to a point at one end.

With flashlights shining downward, he started by using the stick to draw a facsimile of Wind Cave in what felt more like clay than dirt. That part wasn't hard, given that the park was generally rectangular in design. Michael started with that rectangle and added more of the park's general contours, while highlighting the approximate locations of the visitor center, primary cave entrance, and other landmarks he recalled from his investigation there. He saved the location of the unfinished bunker in the northeast section of the park for last, adding more detail, including the primary entrance.

The second entrance to the bunker was actually an emergency exit camouflaged from sight by the rolling hills rich with prairie grasses and lines of ponderosa pine trees. Michael drew all that into the ground with his stick, approximating distance and cover as best he could. He could only hope that the tree line was as thick as he recalled and that the rolling hills were as high to disguise their presence.

"We'd stand a better chance if we hold off on the attack until night," the head of Fallen Timbers, the one-eyed man named Crow, suggested. "Darkness is our friend. The more, the better."

"We can't risk the explosion being triggered while we're waiting for the sun to set," Segundo told him. "Besides, we'll be fighting inside a cave, where it's always night."

Crow shook his head. "There'll be lights powered by generators. It might as well be daylight."

Then Michael remembered something else he'd learned about the bunker during his investigation.

"In that case," he said, "I know a way to turn day to night."

CHAPTER 93

WIND CAVE NATIONAL PARK, SOUTH DAKOTA

Modern Lakota refer to Wind Cave as Maka Oniye, or "breathing earth."

"You're going to have a front-row seat," Jeremiah had said.

And, true to his word, Lantry had been tied to a fifty-five-gallon drum that smelled like old paint. The yellow barrel shined under the soft spill of lights fueled by massive generators he could hear humming but couldn't see. The barrel was one of an incalculable number of virtually identical drums, all affixed with the same high-tech LED screen measuring temperature and pressure.

Lantry's front-row seat allowed him to witness the latest shipment of barrels being lowered by hydraulic lift into the massive cavern and added to the long rows. Back on the surface, it had taken a while for Jeremiah's forces to locate the cavern entrance, poking at the ground with spear-like objects the size of shovels until Jeremiah himself jabbed against something hard. No digging was required, because the covering was actually an elaborately fashioned patch of artificial grass. Lantry watched Jeremiah's men find one of the seams, peel back the edges of the large strip, and then roll it up the way they might a tarpaulin in a baseball stadium.

Lantry's legs were free, but his arms had been bound to the drum with tight cord, his shoulders extended as far back as they could possibly go. Even jostling his arms slightly sent jolts of pain through his shoulders and upper back, making escape seem impossible.

What would my uncle do?

Lantry swung his gaze about the vast cavern, as if channeling the great man, trying to see it as he would. The walls and ceiling were dominated by boxwork, a mineral structure formed of thin blades of calcite into a honeycomb pattern. To Lantry, it felt like he was inside some kind of hive, imagining that the rows and rows of barrels were really eggs laid by some unseen monster. He also noticed that dozens of the larger storage casks had been placed in rows nearest the hydraulic lift, to eliminate the need to move their vast weight elsewhere in the chamber.

As barrels continued to be lowered and laid in place by Jeremiah's men to further lengthen the rows, Lantry again tried to channel his uncle. He'd been taken prisoner twice in Vietnam but had somehow escaped both times. Those exploits had become part and parcel of his uncle's legend, but he had never shared the means of escape with anyone as far as Lantry knew. Had the Vietcong bound his uncle to something just as he was now bound to this drum? He pictured his uncle doing whatever he needed to do to cut through that rope.

With that in mind, Lantry considered the design of the barrels. They had no seams or edges, nothing potentially sharp protruding to cut the cord binding him. His only chance was to work the cord up over the top of the heavy steel drum, thereby freeing himself. But his hands were bound behind him three-quarters of the way down, a vast length to cover given that his early attempts to even budge the cord had failed at every turn and left him with bolts of agony shooting through his shoulders.

But Lantry had no choice. He needed not only to free himself, but also to find a way to neutralize Jeremiah's forces. It wasn't about trying so much as succeeding. Failure meant he'd be disgracing the proud name he carried but didn't really deserve. That could change today. The alternative, beyond his own death, was too awful to contemplate.

Lantry tried to find an angle that would allow him to shift the cord upward without tearing his shoulders apart, but everything he tried failed to work and resulted in only more stabbing pain. Then he saw a number of Jeremiah's men step off the hydraulic lift, lugging heavy green crates that reminded him of old-fashioned footlockers, no doubt containing explosives. He watched the men position the crates along the rows at strategic intervals, starting at the front and working their way backward toward where he had been bound.

The hydraulic lift lowered again, carting yet more of the green, explosive-laden footlockers. Lantry lost count of how many there were, couldn't even imagine the force of the blast when they blew and tried not to picture the contents of the barrels and casks being blown up with them. The lift was raised, then came back down, over and over again, more explosives being set into place even as still more were hauled off the platform.

Seeing them being set along his row filled Lantry with fresh resolve, his presence ignored as if he weren't even there. That triggered a memory of the one thing his uncle had told him as a young boy about being taken prisoner by the Vietcong.

"How did you escape, Uncle?"

"I went somewhere else."

"I mean before you got away."

"So do I, Nephew."

And now, after so many years, Lantry finally understood the meaning of those words.

I went somewhere else.

They had made no sense then, but they made plenty now, and Lantry realized he needed to go somewhere else, too, when the lighting in the underground chamber died all at once.

CHAPTER 94

BROOKFIELD AIR FORCE STATION, OHIO

The property was purchased by an anonymous buyer in 2012.

"How are we going to approach that base without being spotted?"

Gina found the answer to her question as soon as she followed Beeman's now fully geared-up troops through the lobby. Waiting outside the shuttered hotel's entrance were a pair of tour buses marked VALLEY TOURS. She could hear their engines grinding and smell their exhaust as soon as the first men exited through the automatic doors into the morning sun.

Gina was virtually positive there was yet more to the plan the final briefing hadn't covered. Or maybe it had been covered after Beeman led her into the storage room that held the explosives now being carried by three special operators walking behind her. Their sole job once they reached the Brookfield Air Force Station would be to spirit her safely across a fire zone to the base's single airstrip while carrying the fifty-pound coils a.k.a. lawn hoses, filled with Astrolite X.

"You're going to be riding up front with me in the lead bus, soldier," Beeman told her, suddenly by her side when she emerged from the lobby into the heat and light. He handed her a paper bag. "There's civilian clothes inside. Put them on before we leave."

Gina didn't bother to ask why. She was back in the mode she recalled all too well from her service in the army: Listen, don't speak, and do whatever you're told.

She rode in the lead bus, the front seat all to herself right next to Beeman, who spent the drive to the outskirts of the base performing a check on a variety of weapons pulled from a utility bag on the seat next to him.

The last stretch to the former air force base was made over a ruddy, pockmarked road that had deteriorated badly over the years. No effort had been made to repair it, even though the property had supposedly been purchased several years back by a private entity who'd been notoriously diligent about keeping trespassers away, according to Beeman. That made perfect sense now, and Gina had no doubt who was behind that private entity.

The perimeter of the base came into view just over thirty minutes into the ride, the fence obscured to a great extent by untended, overgrown vegetation. Gina was able to catch slivers through the gaps in the foliage, enough to tell her that the security fence was topped with barbed wire and electrified. The front gate came into view at the head of the private road marked AUTHORIZED PERSONNEL ONLY on a rusted metallic sign. The aerial photos displayed back at the hotel had covered the vastness of the base, its sprawl encompassing hundreds of acres on which decrepit outbuildings were barely recognizable amid the overgrowth. A trio of airplane hangars aligned in a row near the back of the base had either been reconstructed or replaced. The same held for buildings that must have served as a de facto headquarters and barracks for all the troops stationed here, along with scale mock-ups of the buildings the enemy had targeted.

It was the airstrip itself, though, that had commanded the bulk of Gina's attention. Her designated target looked freshly paved in the close-ups, even though the concrete had been tinted a faded gray in color to make it appear old and decaying. Up close in the aerial photos, she'd also noted that the patches of blight and deterioration were actually the result of clever discoloration that created the illusion of decay. The latest aerial photography captured by a drone revealed that a total of sixteen similarly repainted C-130s sat parked with their noses angled toward the runway— aircraft she had to prevent from taking off at all costs.

Before her, the main entrance was sharpening in view. It had been to- tally reconstructed as well, although a guard shack just inside what looked to be a sliding gate appeared as dilapidated as the base's outbuildings.

Gina felt the bus hiss to a stop, only Beeman rising from his seat as it came to a halt thirty feet from the gate.

"We're on, soldier."

Gina complied, rising, too. The soldier dressed as a bus driver opened the doors as a trio of armed guards in nonmilitary tactical gear emerged from the guard shack. Beeman looked like a tourist in his Hawaiian-style shirt, sandals, and sunglasses. He'd added what looked to be a hearing aid to the disguise. But Gina noticed a .45-caliber pistol wedged into the back of his belt, exposed to facilitate a quick reach with a round already chambered and the hammer cocked back.

She walked in step with Beeman, just slightly behind him, realizing that she was just window dressing. A man and woman approaching would not raise nearly as much scrutiny as a man alone.

"Say," Beeman said to the three guards who stood rigidly inside the fence line, "is the base open for tours?"

"Stay back," the one who must have been in charge said, leaving no room for doubt in his voice. "This is private property."

Beeman turned his head to display his fake hearing aid. "Come again? I don't think I got that."

The man in charge took a step closer to the fence. Before he could speak again, Beeman yanked the .45 from his belt and shot him point-blank in the forehead. Gina's ears were ringing as she watched him turn the pistol on the man in the middle, then the last one in the row, dropping them all before they could go for their guns.

"Showtime, soldier!" he told Gina, finger on the fake hearing aid that must have doubled as a communications system. "Move, move, move, move!"

Beeman yanked Gina aside as the second bus, which had stopped a modest distance back from the first, tore around it, crashing straight through the sliding gate and rolling over a pair of corpses as it surged onto the grounds. The lead bus followed in its wake, the soldiers riding the trailing one already spilling out by the time it screeched to a halt.

An alarm went off somewhere inside the base. Men armed to the teeth began pouring from structures a few hundred yards before them. A teetering guard tower that looked ready to topple over any moment sprang to life with heavy machine-gun fire trained their way. This time it was Gina who yanked Beeman out of harm's way, behind the cover of one of the buses as bullets tore through glass and steel.

She cast her gaze across the base grounds toward the airstrip, eyes widening not at what she saw but at what was missing.

"The C-130s are gone."

"No surprise," Beeman said calmly. "Something must've spooked them, so they parked them somewhere else for safekeeping, somewhere close enough to bring them back when it's time to deploy."

"I hope you've got some more tricks up your sleeve, Colonel," Gina said, over the steady ratcheting of gunfire.

"As a matter of fact, I do," he said.

Gina heard the rumble an instant before the quartet of UH-60 Black Hawks soared onto the scene.

CHAPTER 95

WIND CAVE NATIONAL PARK, SOUTH DAKOTA

Lakota believe that the caves link to their spirit world.

Michael moved at the front of the pack with Ty Segundo and Crow across the tall grass rising from the hills that dominated this little-traveled area of Wind Cave.

He glimpsed a few mule deer grazing about, not spooked by the approach of the Fallen Timbers warriors at all. He even caught sight of some of the elk and bison that had been reintroduced into the park more than a century before and were now flourishing. The nearest elk raised its head and sniffed at the air, then returned to munching on brush. Hawks soared overhead as if to follow the congestion of men making their way across the land.

Michael would have preferred to be at the rear of the group, so as not to slow them down with the limitations imposed by his jerry-rigged prosthetic foot. But Dr. Yolanda Rivers had fashioned a surprisingly effective device. He couldn't run or perform any motion that required a lot of torque. But he could walk and even trot effectively enough, while dragging the new prosthetic slightly behind him. And he needed to be near the front, because he alone could find the location of the emergency exit that would allow the group to access the bunker originally envisioned as a near twin of the one constructed in Greenbrier, West Virginia.

Rivers, meanwhile, had insisted on accompanying the group in order to tend to any of those wounded immediately, often the difference between life and death. She moved at the back of the pack and would not be entering the cavern with the Fallen Timbers fighters; Ty Segundo had been very clear about that, not mincing words.

A scout Segundo and Crow had sent ahead had already reported that the area in the general vicinity of the emergency exit was clear and unguarded.

Hardly a surprise, given that it was exceedingly unlikely that Terrell's force was even aware of its existence.

Because the investigation he'd conducted on park grounds required him to be aware of its unique topography, Michael had been briefed on the existence of the emergency exit leading out of the bunker. But he'd never actually seen it himself and possessed only a vague recall of where it was situated.

It all made sense. Investigating that hiker's disappearance two years ago, Michael had started here after it was determined the last post the missing man made on social media had been a picture of a bison most common in this area. Because of the possibility that the hiker had somehow ended up in the unfinished bunker, Michael had been allowed to venture inside with the only Park Service official aware of the bunker's existence, the park superintendent, via the main entrance. He'd learned quite a bit about the unfinished facility, but the hiker had never been found and now he understood why.

Now Michael figured that man must have stumbled upon Terrell's men laying the groundwork for storing the stolen chemical stockpile inside the would-be bunker. Under that scenario, the man would have been killed on the spot, his body buried either somewhere nearby on park grounds or perhaps within the underground bunker itself.

Michael was at a loss for how to pinpoint the emergency exit's location, until he spotted a patch of sagebrush that was quite common in the park, but not in this area, and the only such patch for as far as he could see. Michael limped toward it, the uneven terrain testing the limits of his makeshift prosthetic with every step. He scraped across the bed of sagebrush and found it to be uncommonly stiff and coarse.

Because it was artificial.

While the others looked on, he quickly located the position of a steel hatch built into the ground and used a knife to cut away strips of more faux growth. Then he fit his fingers into beveled handgrips in the steel and lifted the hatch upward.

"After you, Agent Walker," Segundo said to him.

‡‡‡

Ty and Crow trailed him down the steep steel stairs. Michael had to descend gingerly, because Dr. Rivers's work was tested every step of the way, and he clung to the rails the whole time in case the prosthetic gave. It felt a bit looser at the bottom, but had remained intact.

Crow signaled the others to hold their position while he scouted the area, disappearing around a corner and then returning quickly.

"They're rigging explosives, dozens and dozens of trunk-sized containers," he whispered. "Enough to blow a hole in the world."

"Get the rest of your people down here," Michael said. "I know how to turn off the lights."

CHAPTER 96

BROOKFIELD AIR FORCE STATION, OHIO

For almost twenty years it was the site of a nursing home facility.

These weren't ordinary Black Hawks, Gina quickly realized. They had been outfitted with heavy armaments, making gunships out of the U.S. Army's primary medium-lift utility transports. Sixteen Hellfire missiles, eight on each side, were loaded in launchers affixed to a truss extension that included .50-caliber forward-firing heavy machine guns on each side, turning the choppers into formidable attack machines.

As they soared overhead, Gina also noted the side mounting locations that allowed for .50-caliber GAU-19/A machine guns, or General Electric M134 7.62×51mm six-barrel miniguns, the two platforms equally effective and fearsome. Almost instantly, the four Black Hawks opened up with both the .50-caliber machine guns and the Hellfire missiles to thwart the advance of the occupying force that greatly outnumbered Beeman's forces.

All of Beeman's troops had spilled out of the buses when shoulder-fired missiles blew both of the vehicles into the air. They thudded back to the ground aflame on blown tires, smoking fiery carcasses missing all of their windows.

The three men holding the tightly wrapped lawn-hose coils containing the Astrolite X joined Gina and Beeman behind one of the scorched husks, now taking heavy fire from the guard tower.

"It's all about you now, soldier," the colonel told her. "We'll hold them off as long as we can. Just blow that airstrip to hell."

✝✝✝

Archibald Terrell was overseeing the prepping of the M1A1 tanks for loading. Once he brought the C-130s back from the airfields where they'd been stashed, the planes would be loaded with a combination of those tanks, fully armored Humvees, missile canisters, heavy machine guns, and the troops required to prep them for the coming invasion of cities to take over municipal centers of government. These were the tools needed to assure his movement's rise to power amid the chaos sure to follow the initial chemical attack. His people already had the infrastructure in place to fill the resulting void of a detached federal government. And out of the refuse of the former United States would rise a new vision for a country run by those committed to order and imposing their will on a weak and ineffectual public.

He was waiting for another update from Ferris Hobbs at Wind Cave when he heard the initial flurry of gunshots that swiftly gave way to incessant fire. The base was under attack. Terrell grabbed an M4 assault rifle from an open crate and crashed through the storage hangar's front door.

He emerged into a maelstrom of gunfire, the blown-out carcasses of what looked like buses explaining how the invading force had breached the base. He watched a Black Hawk equipped with a full ordnance package take out the guard tower with a pair of Hellfire missiles. A second fired a burst from a .50-caliber machine gun that cut down the troops on either side of him, the fire coming close enough for Terrell to feel the heat of the bullets as they sizzled past him.

Though vastly outnumbered, the attacking force had made great use of the element of surprise, and now they had the advantage of close air support to enable their charge forward in what had become a vicious firefight staged behind the cover of debris from collapsed structures as well as those buildings that remained standing. His troops were firing from inside any number of those, after the first lines to advance had been cut down by the Black Hawks' missiles and machine guns.

The attacking force's maneuvers and positioning were clearly meant to clear a passage to disable the airfield, preventing any of the big transport planes from landing or taking off. And, sure enough, through the smoke clouds he glimpsed four figures carving a desperate path through the carnage, lugging what could only be high explosives.

"Team B," Terrell said into his wrist-mounted communicator, "fall back to the airstrip. Repeat, fall back to the airstrip."

‡‡‡

For Gina, it all unfolded in a surreal blur. Enclosed by the three soldiers assigned to her, she dashed along the outer perimeter of the firefight. She'd already prepped laying out the three rolls of Astrolite X in her mind, reviewed the process over and over again in the hope it would be second nature by the time she reached the airstrip. Combat, though, has a way of obscuring all thoughts other than survival. She carried the latest version of the M4 assault rifle and started to wish she'd declined use of the heavy flak jacket that made her feel as if she were slogging through mud.

That is, until a round hit her dead center in the chest. Impact took her feet out, and there was so much pain that Gina thought the round must have penetrated the Kevlar. But there was no blood and she quickly recovered her breath, regaining her feet with the help of one of the soldiers.

His face seemed to explode, spraying her with blood and bone. She dropped back down to unsling the pack holding the explosive coil he was toting, and held it in both arms as she resumed running, with the two remaining soldiers flanking her on either side. They were halfway to the airstrip now, more gunfire tracing them across the overgrown grass.

One of the Black Hawks came in fast, nose angled downward as a trio of Hellfire missiles burst from their pods, obliterating a pair of crumbling outbuildings where enemy riflemen had claimed the roof. She watched the Black Hawk turn in the air, its minigun unleashing a torrent of fire before a pair of Stinger missiles blew it out of the sky in a fiery blast.

Gina and the two remaining soldiers seized on the curtain of smoke and flame as camouflage, their dash toward the airstrip obscured enough to make them elusive targets. Each soldier unleashed his M4 on the converging troops with one arm, while the other held his explosive-laden coil. Attempting to shield her, one was pulverized by rounds fired by four of Terrell's men, who'd stopped their charge into the open long enough to steady their aim.

Her final escort shoved Gina to the ground and dropped to take the pack containing the dead man's explosive coil in his grasp. But the fire she avoided thanks to his efforts stood him back up. It almost looked like he was performing an odd dance before he crumpled, the pack he'd been holding landing at Gina's feet.

More of the enemy had begun to advance, nothing between them and her, until another of the Black Hawk gunners opened up on them with a relentless fusillade that dropped General Terrell's men amid a shower of ground debris the heavy machine-gun fire had kicked up. The Black Hawk shadowed her as she scooped up the coil the last dead soldier had shed and slung it over her free shoulder. Gina felt her knees buckle from the weight. No way she could handle a third one; she left it behind and lit off on a final dash to the airstrip, two of the explosive coils held against her chest in either arm.

CHAPTER 97

WIND CAVE NATIONAL PARK, SOUTH DAKOTA

All visitors are now required to walk across a
decontamination mat when exiting the cave,
due to a bat disease called white-nose syndrome.

The emergency exit stairs had ended well short of the actual cavern, and
Michael recalled that the controls for the diesel-powered generators lay
down an adjacent natural passage that would bring them closer to the
main chamber. He quickly located the gray metal junction boxes, which
were warm to the touch as he opened them in search of the primary switch
that powered up the facility.

He found it inside the third gray metal box, a lever ten inches in size
with an extended handle to grab hold of.

"Get ready, Ty," Michael said, watching Segundo hold the walkie-talkie
at his mouth.

Michael grabbed the handle and jerked the lever downward. Instantly,
a soft whine that had sounded like background noise died along with the
light shed by the many wall-mounted lanterns.

"Go," he heard Segundo say.

‡‡‡

Lantry heard the muted sounds of gunfire erupt from the surface above
him in line with the hydraulic platform, evidence that Jeremiah's forces up
there had come under attack. The shooting had just intensified when dim
emergency lighting snapped on throughout the cavern, casting thin slivers
of light about the scene.

Then fresh rounds of fire clamored closer, muzzle flashes bursting
through the semidarkness. The men who'd been setting Jeremiah's explo-

sives in row after row dropped one after the other. The members of
the invading force weren't dressed alike and, as near as Lantry could tell,
the force was comprised of both men and women. He glimpsed enough
of their movements to realize he was looking at his own people, the forces
of Fallen Timbers having somehow homed in on Wind Cave.

Stray bullets pinged off the drums around him, and Lantry began to fear
that one or more would puncture and shower him with the deadly contents inside. He also glimpsed the dark-clad shapes of the enemy falling to
more primitive weapons like ball bearings hurled by slingshot, tomahawks
whizzing about, and arrows sizzling through the air in a blur, making it
hard to tell whether Jeremiah's men were falling to bullets or something
else. The presence of his own people led him to redouble his efforts to
work the cord binding him to the drum up and over it, while the opposing
forces continued to exchange fire with him planted squarely in the middle.

The boy felt his mind drift, seeming to separate from his body, just like
his uncle had tried to teach him. Then he felt the cord moving, shifting
in rhythm with his upper body's efforts to raise it. He felt no pain, where
there had been agony just moments before. His shoulders stretched to the
limit, his arms upraised behind him, as the cord continued to rise, soon to
clear the drum altogether.

‡‡‡

Jeremiah had taken cover when the shooting started at the entrance to the
bunker. He caught enough sight of the attacking ragtag force to identify
them as Natives, no doubt the ones behind the boy who'd been operating
the drone. They must have tracked the kid here somehow, but their presence was about far more than just a rescue. They must have located another way into the unfinished bunker where the chemical storage drums
had been tucked away. His men down there, which included Special Forces
troops provided by Terrell, had had plenty of time to rig the explosives before the fire commenced, meaning the plan, and his ultimate fate, could
still be salvaged, if he could trigger the blast himself.

He could do it right here, right now. For all intents and purposes, he
had died that day in 1988 with his father. Nothing he had done could make
up for that day. All the lives he had taken, the land he had soaked in blood,
how he had made his own children a party to the justice he sought—that
should have been his legacy.

Until his children had died for his cause.

So he turned his focus toward a greater justice, biblical in its scope, a true Apocalypse that would leave only the righteous standing. Jeremiah didn't need to be there to stand among them, secure in the knowledge he had sowed the seeds that sprouted a future of his own making. He didn't need to see the dawning of the new America; he just wanted all of those whose lives would be ended or destroyed to know the pain he had felt watching his father die. The millions of victims he was about to claim would be no different from those he'd claimed on Mount Rainier, and claiming them would be no different from hunting game. Watching them squirm, feeling them die. Just as his father had and then his twins. The country needed to pay for its crimes, its sins, and pressing a single button could set all that in motion. Just as his life had never been the same from that awful day in 1988, the lives of everyone in this country would never be the same again once Wind Cave blew.

A pair of the huge storage casks sat atop the hydraulic lift, ready to be lowered. Jeremiah opened up with his assault rifle toward the heaviest congestion of the gunfire, clearing a path for him to dive behind the casks for cover. He had just freed the detonator from his pocket when an arrow hissed through the gap between the two casks. It grazed the right side of his face, leading to a burst of hot, stabbing pain accompanied by the sense of warm blood dripping down his cheek. He lost his grasp on the detonator, snatched at it in the air, and ended up knocking the device into the darkness below.

Jeremiah thrust himself into the open, tempting more arrows and gunfire as he reached for the exposed control button that would send the platform downward. He felt it begin its descent, as more bullets clanged off the storage casks and arrows whisked past him overhead.

‡‡‡

Not comfortable wielding an assault rifle, Michael had opted to carry only a nine-millimeter pistol that felt comfortable in his grasp. In the murky light before him, he could see det cord wrapped around row after row of the steel drums filled with deadly chemicals. So long as it was in place, a single electronic signal would be all it took to blow all of the green explosive containers that had been rigged.

Michael had lost track of Ty Segundo but knew what he had to do. He lifted the utility knife from the sheath clipped to his belt and moved as fast as his jerry-rigged prosthetic foot would allow toward the nearest row of drums, crouching as low as he could to avoid the crossfire he was now trapped within.

He still managed to hear the thud of the hydraulic lift dropping into place, a figure emerging from behind a trio of storage casks ten times the size of a single barrel. Even through the semidarkness, Michael recognized the figure from the picture Gina had texted him:

Ferris Hobbs, the man who now called himself Jeremiah!

He had just stooped to retrieve something when Michael fired at him with his pistol as fast as he could pull the trigger. From this distance, two hundred feet or so, the shots had virtually no chance of landing. But they startled Hobbs enough to distract him. He abandoned whatever he was reaching for and unslung an assault rifle.

Michael didn't realize he was rushing at Hobbs until his makeshift prosthetic nearly buckled amid Hobbs's bullets pouring his way. Even then he kept going, plowing ahead between the barrels amid the firefight still raging. Hobbs kept firing until the gun clicked empty. Then he dropped down again, feeling about the floor, his hand closing on something in the murky emergency lighting that could only be a detonator.

‡‡‡

Lantry felt his arms come free. Still, there was no pain. The world around him was quiet and still, in spite of the shooting. He felt detached, everything moving in slow motion around him, except for the figure surging past him, dragging his left foot.

He followed the man's path, his gaze capturing a figure he recognized as Jeremiah lifting an object from the floor that looked like a cell phone and steadying it in his grasp. Lantry threw all of his weight into the steel drum before him. He didn't think he was strong enough to even budge it, but the drum teetered and then tipped over. It banged into the next barrel in line in the next row, toppling it, too. Then he watched as the rest of the drums in the same line followed, falling like dominoes straight for Jeremiah.

CHAPTER 98

⊢·+·○·+·⊣

BROOKFIELD AIR FORCE STATION, OHIO

It was a working air force base for only seven years.

Gina could hear the deafening sounds of the Black Hawk hovering overhead to provide cover, close enough to feel the chopper's powerful rotor wash nearly sweep her off her feet. She managed to stay upright and reached the airstrip as the side gunner continued to strafe the area with the minigun he was wielding. The fourth Black Hawk, meanwhile, had just taken a position to cut off the farther reaches of the base when a pair of shoulder-fired missiles hit it simultaneously.

The explosion split Gina's eardrums, the flash as bright as the sun. That left only the Black Hawk positioned to cover her advance, the other three reduced to flaming piles of wreckage. She unslung both packs containing the explosive coil from her shoulders. With only two to rig, she'd need to adjust the spacing, but she was still confident she could render the airstrip inoperable.

Gina glimpsed Beeman's troops somehow winning the day, steadily advancing on the enemy's superior numbers, which the Black Hawks had substantially reduced. Then small-arms fire punctured the final Black Hawk's windshield. She could see the blood splatter even with the pilot's seat, the copilot struggling to regain control as the helicopter spiraled downward.

‡‡‡

Wind Cave National Park, South Dakota

Jeremiah used the handheld control box to stop the lift before it had lowered all the way, giving him a better view of the unfinished bunker before him. His finger found the detonator's button, flashing red to indicate that the signal was active and connected to the capacitors that would ignite the explosives layered around the long rows of barrels before him. He wondered what he would feel, what he would see as the world came apart before him.

A metallic rattle jarred him from his near trance. Jeremiah looked up to see a line of barrels toppling over, rolling his way. He twisted to the side to avoid them, straight into the path of a man he recognized as Michael Walker.

‡‡‡

Brookfield Air Force Station, Ohio

Miraculously, the copilot was able to set the Black Hawk down to a jarring halt without doing any further damage. And it had landed on an angle that placed the side gunner manning the still-functional minigun directly before the enemy forces still surging forward.

Feeling as safe as she could reasonably hope for, Gina rolled out the first explosive coil across the width of the airfield. She decided to do the same with the second before rigging the high-potency liquid explosives inside.

Gina was out of breath by the time she finished taping down the second explosive coil. Next up, she needed to slide blasting wire through a depression in the head of each hose and then connect those wires to the capacitor with enough voltage to trigger the twin explosions.

Getting the wires into place made for the most precarious part of the process, because the slightest spark could set off the blast prematurely, taking her with it. Gina took a deep breath as she began to thread the wire through the slight depression with a predrilled pinhole in the center. It had been filled with a light epoxy that was easily punctured. Once that task was complete, she fit the first wire into a slot tailored for it in the housing of the capacitor acting as a detonator and followed the same process with the second wire.

All that remained now was to get to a safe distance and trigger the blast. Then a flash of motion made her swing to her right, where General Archibald Terrell stood twenty feet away, assault rifle trained on her.

‡‡‡

Wind Cave National Park, South Dakota

Michael crashed into Ferris Hobbs with all the force he could muster. Impact rattled the man, but failed to dislodge the detonator he'd been holding. To stop him from finding the button, Michael clamped one hand over it, then raked at Hobbs's eyes with his other. He bent Hobbs backward over the hydraulic platform, still unable to pry the detonator free, but managing to get his free hand clamped on the man's throat.

Michael thought of Allie as he squeezed, of her dying in his arms on Rainier, his foot held in place by mere sinews of cartilage and tendons. He squeezed harder, the man's face purpling as his eyes bulged to the point where Michael thought they might pop out of his head. Hobbs's feet were kicking madly—spasming, Michael thought, until one of the kicks slammed into his makeshift prosthetic, tearing it partially from its housing as a big pistol flashed in Hobbs's hand.

‡‡‡

Brookfield Air Force Station, Ohio

Gina's eyes met Terrell's. She thought she detected a smile, Terrell enjoying himself as he trained his assault rifle on her. Then she heard a burst of automatic fire, but his M4 remained still and puffy mists of red burst outward from the bullets that had pulverized his upper body.

She swung to the left to find Colonel Beeman snapping a fresh magazine home.

"Let's blow this shit, soldier," Gina heard him say, as Terrell's corpse dropped to the ground.

Gina eased the second wire into the slot tailored for it in the capacitor's housing. A counter starting at 30 appeared, the numerals for the countdown beginning to tick down.

"We need to be somewhere else, Colonel," she said, lowering the detonator to the ground and backing away.

"We do indeed, soldier," he said, taking off in a sprint with Gina alongside him. "I'm thinking Hawaii." He pulled at the shirt beneath his flak jacket. "I've already got the wardrobe."

The dual explosions blew simultaneously, kicking up a huge plume of fractured concrete along with gravel and stone from the layers beneath it.

Even from more than a hundred feet away, Gina felt her skin pricked by a few of the smallest pieces. The debris cloud seemed to expand, spreading its dark curtain outward, making her think of what would be spreading across the country if Michael Walker failed.

‡‡‡

Wind Cave National Park, South Dakota

Michael felt the makeshift prosthetic give, unable to support any weight. His momentum carried both men off the lift to the bunker's floor. Michael kept the detonator pinned between his and Hobbs's hands and clamped his other hand on the wrist holding the .45-caliber pistol. Denied the leverage he needed with only a single foot to support all his weight, though, there was no way Michael would be able to wrest control of the pistol from Hobbs. And if his left leg collapsed, it would be over for far more than just him.

He spotted a rectangular object resting atop the platform in line with Hobbs's head. Since Hobbs was holding firm to the detonator, the object could only be . . .

Finishing the thought fueled a move born of desperation. Michael pulled his hand from Hobbs's pistol and lurched for what could only be the hydraulic control; in the same motion he shoved the man's head into the gap between the platform and the floor. The pistol steadied on him when he hit the control button, and the platform jerked downward over Hobbs's face. A muzzle flash erupted and a roar split Michael's eardrums, something that felt like static filling his head.

Am I shot? Am I dead?

His ears were still ringing when he realized that Hobbs's feet were thrashing and spasming, whatever was left of his face flattened under the weight of the hydraulic platform. He fell backward, feeling the warm soak of blood from the side of his scalp, where the bullet had grazed him.

"That was for Allie," he said, barely able to hear his own words.

Michael heard steps approaching and turned to find himself looking into the eyes of a Native American boy with long, black hair and hands laced together by some kind of cord.

"Can I borrow your knife?" the boy asked him.

THE WHITE HOUSE

The Oval Office construction was overseen by President
William Howard Taft.

Michael and Gina were ushered through a side entrance into the White
House and brought straight to President Jillian Cantwell's private office in
the residence upstairs. They took the stairs instead of the elevator, the new
prosthetic Michael had been fitted with an upgrade from the old one.

They hadn't expected Colonel Beeman to be there, but weren't surprised by his presence either.

"I know you have a lot of questions," the president said, ushering them
to a sitting area with only Beeman remaining standing. "Let me try to answer them straightaway."

Nearly two months had passed since the country had narrowly averted
disaster. Michael had been on leave since then and had been advised to have
no contact with Gina. They'd both been heavily debriefed, and some of the
information had been released to the public and still more had leaked out.
The nation, though, remained utterly in the dark about how close it had
come to dissolving into a chaos from which it might never have recovered.

"First and foremost," Cantwell continued, "the chemical stockpile has
been removed from Wind Cave and is now in what I'd like to think is a
secure location under heavy guard while we dispose of it." She looked toward Beeman on that note, before resuming to Michael and Gina. "Thanks
to your efforts, General Terrell and the man known as Jeremiah no longer pose a problem. But they leave thousands of supporters in their wake,
many of whom were willing to take up arms against their own country. We
can't detain or arrest them all, but we are in the process of identifying the
leaders of these groups and dealing with those at the very least."

Michael had expected the president to elaborate on that further. He took the fact that she didn't as a significant message in itself, especially in view of the government's commitment to keep the entire truth from ever getting out.

"Michael," the president said, turning toward him, "as you already know, Angela Pierce has been reinstated to the Park Service, but her former posting won't hold for long because I'm going to nominate her to replace Ethan Turlidge as secretary of the interior. And I've already fired Frank Von Hool as head of the Park Service. How'd you like your boss's old job?"

Michael hedged. "Thank you, ma'am, but I didn't join the Park Service to sit behind a desk. I think I'm needed more where I am now."

The president nodded, then smiled. "I'm not surprised." She turned to Gina. "Gina, your boss and mentor, Rod Rust, will be retiring from the bureau with full benefits. He suggested you as his replacement to run the New York field office. I told him I had bigger plans for you."

Michael watched Gina regard Jillian Cantwell quizzically.

"I'd like you to consider becoming a senior special agent without portfolio."

"There's no such position, Madam President."

Cantwell smiled. "Jillian, remember? And, no, there isn't. I made it up, because I want you to be free to operate without the limits of geography. I want to be able to send you anywhere at any time, without raising any jurisdictional issues."

"Count me in," Gina said.

Cantwell nodded in satisfaction. "Some of those assignments may come directly from this office. We've faced down one threat, but others are surely looming out there. Not necessarily political in nature, but potentially just as dangerous. In other words, I need someone I can trust—the *country* can trust—to handle the great unknown."

"Whatever I can do to help . . . Jillian."

The president smiled and sat back, this portion of her presentation complete. "Now, I'm sure you have questions."

"I have one," Michael chimed in immediately. "If not for a group of brave Native Americans, a number of whom gave their lives at Wind Cave, we'd be looking at an entirely different result." He leaned forward on the couch he shared with Gina. "What's going to be done for them?"

"What would you suggest?"

"That the country give them back the land it stole. But since that's not going to happen, how about a multibillion-dollar commitment to change the face of the Pine Ridge Reservation? I'm talking about installing irrigation systems to make the land suitable for farming, new schools, increased pay for teachers, radically improved medical services, guaranteed job placement and income. For starters," he added.

"Can I get back to you with a number?"

Michael was surprised that the president had accepted his request without any equivocation. "So long as it's big enough."

"It will be, I assure you. The United States can't atone for all the mistakes we've made, but that doesn't mean we shouldn't try."

‡‡‡

After the meeting ended, Colonel Beeman pulled Michael aside, while Gina chatted with the president as if they were old friends.

"I need you to come with me, Agent Walker."

"Should I ask where?"

"Don't bother."

‡‡‡

Undisclosed location

Michael was blindfolded in the back of a big black SUV by one of Beeman's men, after he climbed into the backseat. He felt Beeman settle in next to him for the drive, which lasted about twenty minutes.

Upon arrival at their destination, a still-blindfolded Michael was led through a door and into an elevator, which descended several levels. He was escorted along a hallway, and then the blindfold was removed to reveal only Beeman alongside him and Ethan Turlidge seated in a high-tech jail cell directly before them. Set before the bars that were much thinner than the traditional variety sat a steel table, several matching chairs, a television, and a galley kitchen.

"Mr. Turlidge says he has something to share with you and no one else, Agent Walker. I gave him my word whatever he says won't be recorded or videoed." He backed up for the door. "I'll leave the two of you alone."

After Beeman left the room, Turlidge rose and gripped the bars of his cell.

"I know you hate me."

"It's the country that hates you, Ethan."

"The country doesn't even know what I've done and they never will."

"Too bad."

"I'm not going to say I'm sorry, Michael."

"It wouldn't matter if you did."

Turlidge squeezed the bars tighter. "There's something else I need to tell you. I know I'm never getting out of here or some other place just like it, even though I had no idea about the part I was playing in the plot. I was used, duped."

"Save it for someone who doesn't know you. You've never cared about anyone other than yourself, and that includes Allie. You hated me because I finally took her away from you, opened her eyes to your bullshit. You duped yourself. But, yes, Archibald Terrell and Ferris Hobbs used you because the dollar signs flashing in front of your eyes kept you from seeing the damage your actions were going to cause."

"That's why we're talking, Michael, so I can make amends."

"No such thing."

Turlidge's expression remained flat, empty, resigned. "You may want to reserve judgment on that, because the country could be about to face something even worse than what you helped stop. Want to hear more?"

‡‡‡

Crazy Horse Memorial, Black Hills of South Dakota

A pair of Lakota Sioux manually lowered Lantry on a scaffolding from the staging platform constructed atop the face of Crazy Horse. The boy knew that work on the monument atop Crazy Horse Mountain had begun in 1948 and, after more than seventy-five years, was nowhere near completion. He knew this and much more because his uncle had joined the crew committed to its completion, in between the unexplained disappearances that sprang up regularly from time to time.

Lantry's platform snailed past the monument's forehead, eyes, and nose, coming to a rest next to the mouth on which his uncle was working with old-fashioned tools. His uncle didn't look away from using his hammer and chisel to etch lines on the right side of the likeness to match the ones he had already etched on the left. The lines were so small they would likely never be noticed, something Lantry had always wondered about since his uncle had dedicated so much of his time, his life, to something that would be forever unseen. Lantry unhooked the carabiner that had fastened him to the scaffolding's housing, and looped it through a safety hook before joining his uncle on a platform he worked from with no such belay.

"Uncle Johnny?"

Johnny Wareagle finally turned his nephew's way. Lantry remembered when his uncle's ponytail was coal black. Now it was mostly silver, with dark streaks sprinkled in. But he still stood seven feet tall and looked no less capable of the acts that had made him a legend. It struck Lantry as ironic that one legend had dedicated the rest of his life to completing a monument to another.

"Neither of us will ever live to see this finished, will we, Uncle?" the boy asked him, awed by the awesome nature of what had been completed so far.

"A task is defined not by its completion, Nephew, so much as a commitment to the process itself. One generation, then the next, can only take things so far. But that commitment will leave the task of competition to other generations. You have a question for me?"

Lantry swallowed hard, kept his eyes fixed on his uncle to avoid looking down. "Why devote so much attention to features no one will bother noticing?"

"Because it is not for them to notice; it is for us to know we have portrayed the greatest legend of our people here exactly as he was in life, down to the smallest detail. To compromise on that would be to deny this monument its true heritage. Honor can never be compromised, Nephew, not in a monument carved from stone or in a man who is only flesh and blood." Johnny Wareagle regarded his nephew closer. "We fail too often to honor our legends in life, which places a greater burden upon us in death. I say this to you, because your actions have honored our people today, just as Crazy Horse's honored our people in his time."

Lantry managed a smile. "I don't think anyone will ever be building a monument to me, Uncle."

Wareagle lowered his hammer and chisel, and swiped the granite dust from his face with a sleeve of his shift. "That makes what you did no less worthy of one. You saw a vital task to its end, to its completion. How does that make you feel, Nephew?"

"Proud," Lantry said.

"Good."

"I did things I never thought I could do. All the wisdom you've tried to give me . . . I didn't understand it until faced with such challenges."

His uncle smiled. "You weren't supposed to. I gave you wisdom I hoped you'd never have to use, but knew the day would come when you'd have to. I also know you've always wanted to be a better man, a more capable man."

Lantry Wareagle almost corrected his uncle, by reminding him he was still a boy, but realized that was his uncle's point.

"I never wanted you to be like me, Nephew, even though you wanted it for yourself. I never wished that fate upon you, but when it came you embraced it."

"Not like you."

"*Exactly* like me. The greatest weapon is not a bow or a gun, it's the mind," his uncle said, tapping his head with a hand the color of the mountain's granite face. "The mind tells you what you can do, and what you can't. It's all about limits. You exceeded yours. That's why today you stand next to me before the greatest hero of our people."

Lantry swallowed hard. "Like you?"

"And what is a hero?"

"I . . . don't know."

"And you shouldn't, because there's no such thing. There are only those who do what they must and those who don't. You are one of the former."

"Like you, Uncle," Lantry said proudly.

He watched Johnny Wareagle smile. "Someday, I'll introduce you to a man who defines what it is to do what must be done. In the meantime," his uncle continued, pulling a spare hammer and chisel from his tool belt and extending them toward him, "why don't you join me?"

‡‡‡

Liberty Island, one month later

"Ladies and gentlemen, the president of the United States!"

Raucous cheers and applause accompanied Jillian Cantwell's appearance on the temporary staging set on the east side of Liberty Island, erected before the jagged remnants of the pedestal on which the Statue of Liberty had stood since its dedication in October of 1886. Both lingered for several moments, as she took her place behind a podium affixed with the presidential seal. A trio of heavy utility cranes towered over the scene.

Cables strung from those cranes were latched to a truss erected around the Statue of Liberty in its toppled state. A temporary pedestal, meanwhile, had been erected over the course of the last three months, once the remains of the original one had been hauled away and the land cleared. Today's ceremony was by invitation only. A large portion of the five thousand standing before and around the temporary staging were members of the public selected on a lottery basis, though the space closest to the temporary stage was reserved for those who'd survived the attack.

Michael stood next to Gina in the front row—a good thing, since his hearing was still not all the way back from the damage done by the percussion and the bullet that had grazed his scalp. They watched the president take the stage with the toppled statue as a fitting backdrop. She didn't try to forestall the crowd's celebratory cheers, because she knew those cheers were for the country, and not herself. Michael watched Danny Logan take his place at the president's side atop the staging. The boy looked down at him and smiled. Michael gazed to his left at the aunt and uncle who were on the verge of formally adopting Danny clapping louder than anyone.

"My fellow Americans," Cantwell started, once they'd finally died down, "we have endured a great and grave crisis and emerged from it stronger as a nation than ever." She paused until a fresh round of cheers and applause abated. "We found the fortitude to withstand a threat from the deepest and darkest part of our national consciousness. And while that darkness has not been vanquished, it has been subdued, thanks to the heroism of ordinary Americans like this boy standing by my side, who lost his parents and sister on these grounds but stands with me today as a testament to the enduring power of the American spirit."

With that, the president lifted a medal from the podium and moved behind Danny Logan, looping the ribbon around his neck.

"Daniel Logan, it's my pride and pleasure to present to you this Presidential Medal of Freedom for your unwavering heroism and sacrifice that exemplifies the tenacity that beat back the greatest threat this country has ever faced."

Michael clapped and didn't stop until all the other applause had abated.

"So," the president resumed, "to those who would subvert the values and freedom the Statue of Liberty has always stood, and always will stand, for, I have a warning: We will forever accept dissent and disagreement, but we will never accept any American taking up arms against another."

The loudest cheers and applause yet rocked Michael's and Gina's ears as they joined in.

"There will always be arguments. There will always be protests. There will always be battles of will. For any among us who would choose a different battle, those who would shed blood in pursuit of their ideology, know that the true America's tolerance only goes so far, and that when you knock us to the ground, we will rise stronger and taller to face you down."

There were screams and cries this time, the crowd well aware of what was coming next.

"To illustrate that, let the greatest symbol of our freedom and heritage rise to see the light of day again. Let Lady Liberty return to her eternal post to remind this nation of everything we stand for."

And with that, to a deafening crescendo, the trio of cranes began raising the statue slowly upward until, guided by a mass of workers atop the temporary pedestal, Lady Liberty regained her perch. A bit wobbly, and worse for wear, but intact and upright once more.

Again, Jillian Cantwell waited for the celebration to fade before resuming.

"As Emma Lazarus wrote in 1883, 'Give me your tired, your poor, Your huddled masses yearning to breathe free, The wretched refuse of your teeming shore. Send these, the homeless, tempest-tost to me, I lift my lamp beside the golden door!'"

The sun burned high in a cloudless sky, the statue seeming to shine under the unbroken rays cast upon lips that, from Michael and Gina's view, made it appear Lady Liberty was smiling, as the president concluded her remarks.

"And now that lamp shines brightly again."

ACKNOWLEDGMENTS

Thank you to the fantastic people who helped shape *Leave No Trace* from an idea into a novel.

Commander Rick Mossman, director of the Park Ranger and Basic Law Enforcement Reserve Academies at Skagit Valley College, for details into the world of being a ranger on the enforcement side.

Mount Rainier National Park East District Ranger Geoff Walker (now retired and no relation) and Mount Rainier Trails Supervisor James Montgomery for providing insight into the world of being a Park Ranger.

Special Agent in Charge of Operations, NPS Investigative Services Branch Christopher Smith, and Special Agent Investigative Services Branch-Pacific Field Office "Sanny" Lustig for assisting with the ISB's operations in the National Park Service.

Literary Agent John Talbot for his career guidance and friendship.

The talented team at Minotaur includes vice president, associate publisher, and editorial director Kelley Ragland, executive editor Keith Kahla, editorial assistant Grace Gay, copyeditor Terry McGarry, and publicity manager Hector DeJean.

Doctor Jill Behm for all things medical and her assistance with prosthetics.

Retired Special Agent Jerri Williams for her help in all things FBI.

Senior Director, Communications & Engagement at the National Parks Conservation Association Zach Ragbourn for helping make our vision a reality.

Kristoffer Polaha, for helping Michael Walker find his voice.

Patrick Yearout for his knowledge of the National Parks and terrific photography of those locations.

Terry, Greg, and Samantha for making every day memorable and putting up with the nuttiness.

The International Thriller Writers for support, encouragement, and education. There are too many of you to name, but you know who you are.

K.J. Howe, for your trust, reflection, and advice.

And, finally, to the tens of millions who visit America's national parks every year, honoring our country's heritage as reflected in the beauty and majesty that endures now and forever.